The Forbidden Passions of
Dark Shadows

"You must not tempt me, Barnabas," Angelique said. "I must never fall in love."

"Why do you say that?"

She struggled to speak, but her words were only enigmas. "Everything . . . in the world has its shadow. Grief . . . is love's reflection. Love is not for me, Barnabas. I learned that a long time ago."

"But you are so beautiful. You were made for love."

At that instant, she heard a familiar laugh and turned to see Josette moving toward the balcony, two young men bending over her, whispering.

"It's too late," Angelique cried desperately. "You must leave me alone. It's too late!" And she turned and ran down the stair and away from him, into the night.

Angelique's Descent

Lara Parker

HarperEntertainment
A Division of HarperCollinsPublishers

HarperEntertainment
A Division of HarperCollins*Publishers*
10 East 53rd Street, New York, N.Y. 10022-5299

This is a work of fiction. The characters, incidents, and dialogues are products of the author's imagination and are not to be construed as real. Any resemblance to actual events or persons, living or dead, is entirely coincidental.

ISBN 0-06-105751-7

Cover photographs © 1998 by Dan Curtis Productions, Inc.

First printing: December 1998

Printed in the United States of America

Visit HarperEntertainment on the World Wide Web at
http://www.harpercollins.com

❖ 10 9 8 7 6 5 4 3 2 1

To my mother and father,
with love

I wish to acknowledge with great appreciation some of those whose help made this book possible:

First of all, Jim Pierson, *Dark Shadows'* champion and custodian who initiated this *Dark Shadows* novels series. He has produced the *Dark Shadows* videos and promoted the annual *Dark Shadows* Festival, in an ongoing effort to keep the show out of the shadows.

I am grateful to all of the *Dark Shadows* fans who have given me their love and support, especially Marcy Robin and Kathleen Resch, editors of SHADOWGRAM, who generously shared their research on 1795, and their own novel on Angelique, *Beginnings: The Island of Ghosts.*

I would like thank from my heart:

My writer friends, Trudy Hale, Celeste Fremon, and Carolyn Lowery who graciously read portions of this book, made suggestions, and were willing to talk for hours when I was bewildered or lost. They were like wandering birds who left eggs in my nest which hatched into amazing ideas.

Warmest gratitude goes to my patient, intelligent editor, Caitlin Blasdell, whose nurturing guidance gave me courage to write this book, and for her gentle suggestion that "metaphors are like jewelry; one necklace is enough."

The writers of this period of the television show *Dark Shadows*: Sam Hall, Ron Sproat, and Gorden Russell, have been a continuing inspiration, as has Kathryn Leigh Scott, who first published my writing in *The Dark Shadows Companion*. I constantly referred to the many books she has published based on the show to jiggle my memory and always found myself drawn into that magical world once again.

I am deeply grateful to my husband Jim Hawkins and my daughter Caitlin for their constant enthusiasm and love.

And I am forever indebted to Dan Curtis, whose inspired vision was *Dark Shadows*, who gave the world these immortal characters that never cease to exasperate us and enchant us, and who gave me the role of Angelique.

My lady abandoned heaven, abandoned earth,
To the nether world she descended,
Inanna abandoned heaven, abandoned earth,
To the nether world she descended,
Abandoned lordship, abandoned ladyship,
To the nether world she descended.

—SUMERIAN MYTH, 2000 B.C.E.

chapter

1

Barnabas woke trembling, his heart pounding, his breath coming in gasps. An enormous weight seemed to be pushing down on his body, and his limbs felt sluggish and bound. He dug his fingers into the pillow smothering his face, and clawed his way out of the dream. For a long moment he lay panting in the darkness, floating out of the nightmare, feeling himself drift as the harrowing visions faded and spiraled down into a dark, deepening vortex.

He rolled over with a sigh and forced open his eyes. Reaching for the sheets, he nervously stroked their cool surfaces with his fingertips; then he twisted toward the window, where the sky brightened with false dawn and pale curtains glowed, ghostly white.

Aberrant thoughts ran through his skull as he struggled for release from the panic that gripped him. He wondered whether he should wake Julia and ask for another injection. She kept the vial on her dresser and would be pleased if he woke her, glad to be of assistance.

His eyes darted around his bedroom, craving some reassurance. Dim streaks of light wavered on the familiar bedpost, the deep carving of the dresser, the gleam of the huge mirror. Outside his window, the heavy branches of the oak tree slashed the moon with thick, black shadows.

He sat up heavily, swinging his feet off the bed onto the prickly texture of the carpet. As he stared into the dark, the tendrils of the nightmare wound their way back into his mind. The woman in his dream had been eager, moaning to meet his embrace, lifting her mouth to his, her warm body pressing against him. Her hair was fragrant and her skin smelled of musk, and he could recall the pity for her that formed itself into a smoky cloud around the hunger flooding through his empty veins. He barely knew her, a downtrodden girl from River Street; and he had found her as he had found all the others, in nightly foraging through the gloomy bars huddled down by the docks. How trusting she was as she bent to him. His hand had moved beneath her heavy cape, up the small of her back, where he could feel the seams of her dress stitched at her slender waist. He ached with a helpless, limb-weakening need, and his mouth soured at the thought of his contemptible obsession.

"I can't breathe . . ." she whispered as he crushed her to him.

He meant then, before it was too late, to let her go. But she touched the back of his neck lightly with her fingertips, and he shuddered. He could read her thoughts, even as her movements betrayed her motives: her heady incredulity at his advances, her fantasies tumbling together in a jumble of possibilities. "Collinwood—lady of the estate—the envy of her friends—position and ease . . ." Her provincial mind could hardly conceive of the wealth! Was it possible that he could love her? Make her his wife? She was desperately, recklessly willing.

She slipped the tie of her cape, revealing the sheen of her breast, and he caressed her silky skin. She gave him a quick, wanton glance, and grasping his huge hand in both her pretty ones, she covered it with feverish kisses. Then, with a musical sigh, she melted in his embrace.

He gathered the fall of her perfumed hair and slid it back gently. It was not her breast he sought. His lips grazed the collar of her dress and brushed against the curve of her neck. Her pulse was drumming there. . . .

NO! No more! With an effort Barnabas wrenched himself back into consciousness. Breathing raggedly, he rose, walked to the window, and looked out. The moon was full and lay cradled in the branches of the great oak tree behind Collinwood. It shone on the silvered slates of the round tower roof, and across the gray stone walls, thickly veined with vines. It floated on the flagged portico with its carved balustrade and on tall leaded windows, flush on the first floor, arched above, wherein slept the family he called his own.

As always, the moonlight seduced him, and he ached to walk there, liquid silver in his veins rather than blood. But he was calmed by the newest thought he had now upon waking, and he could still hear Julia's incredulous voice in his mind. "Barnabas! We have done it! You are cured!" The realization that he was no longer a creature of the night, and that at last he could with a clear conscience return to his bed and rise with the sun—that simple acceptance of a gift so profoundly longed for, yet so unappreciated by ordinary men, flooded his mind with desperate joy.

From where he stood at the window, he could just make out, far off, beyond the woods, the Old House nestled in a glade, gleaming with the mysterious ghostliness of a Grecian temple. He felt a throb of nostalgia and, at the same time, malevolent fascination. The house was a graceful neoclassic beauty misplaced among New England maples and hemlocks, and he envisioned, as he had so often in the past, a home more destined for music and laughter: lovely balls with candlelit chandeliers and swirling couples, charming girls in flowing skirts, dashing young gentlemen. The many rooms would have been maintained by good-natured slaves who roasted venison with spices, ironed linen and polished silver, and did all things necessary, that the fortunate gentry might pursue their lives in pleasure and comfort.

But this had not been the fate of that doomed mansion, hidden away in a cold New England town, though magnolias hung their ivory blossoms over the lawn. Instead the moon cast an icy sheen on the pale edifice, effacing any ambience of warmth or gaiety. Now abandoned, it was not a temple, but a tomb, its empty rooms still echoing with generations of the

Collins family, where he himself had lived, hidden, sleeping in a basement room, leaving, only to return again to Collinwood in yet another disguise, as a cousin or distant relation.

Recalling these memories now was like tasting the most foul and rotten fruit. "So like Barnabas," they always said. "Why, you could be his twin!" And, as before, he was welcomed into the incestuous fold, embraced by the secrets and unspoken guilt that isolated and distanced the family from the outside world. "It is amazing. He is so like the portrait," they would murmur to themselves.

And he, enduring shame and unspoken horrors, had remained among them for seven generations, feigning a semblance of normalcy, dead, but not dead, his grisly hungers rising and abating with the years of feeble experimentation. His hope would brim into vague promise, only to crash again and again in utter despair as the inexorable grasp of the curse, like iron manacles, twisted once again around his soul.

Until now.

Now, finally, unbelievably, inconceivably—he was free. "Barnabas! We have done it! You are no longer"—he grimaced at even the memory of the word—"a vampire. . . ." The realization that he was cured was still difficult for him to accept. He had lived so long as a prisoner of his abominable hungers.

He threw open the casement and breathed in the cool night air. He could smell the sea, damp and pungent, and the soft mist as it rose from the wide lawns of the estate, sweet with the perfumes of gardenia and narcissus in bloom. An owl hooted two quavering notes, and far off another answered. The lure of the moonlight was strong as it revealed the world below in stark and glittering detail. Everything was as clear as in the day, but devoid of color. The shades of gray were infinitely various, and the whole was textured in a divine chiaroscuro that sculpted every object. He could still see the dew on the grass, the curve of the thick leaves of the magnolias, the fleshy perfection of the flowers.

Barnabas felt his composure returning as his breathing quieted, and his beating heart regained its normal pattern. He was free. Cured at last. Human. Why then was he haunted by these dreams? Almost nightly he woke in a fevered rush of shameful memories. If those ghastly years, those centuries of anguish, were truly behind him now, if his life was finally to be easy and normal, unfolding in the most ordinary fashion as he aged, grew old, and died—like any other man—why, then, was he still tormented by these visions of the life he had lived before? Surely they would soon fade and disappear forever.

A dog howled, long and mournfully, and another answered, plaintive, lonely, night-bound, and Barnabas grimly recognized a kindred soul. He, too, had roamed the moonlit stretches of that lawn, which hugged the stone stairway and the flagged walk, when his only social interaction had been after the sun had set and the fireplaces were lit in the great parlor. Only then could he enjoy human companionship, grow to know—perhaps even to love—the many Collinses who called this house their home. This was where it had all begun.

This was where he had welcomed his bride from Martinique, the dark-eyed girl with alabaster skin and radiant smile, his beloved Josette. This was also where her maidservant had traveled with her, the green-eyed vixen who had haunted and destroyed his life, the mysterious and beautiful Angelique.

Barnabas shivered, thinking to close the window, but he felt captured by the moonlight falling on the far-off mansion, and by the melancholy within his breast. For this was, of all nights, the very last night the house would stand.

He and Julia had agreed, after much discussion, even argument, with the rest of the family, that it was to be razed and destroyed. The wrecking crew was coming in the morning. Perhaps that accounted for the intensity of the dream, and he hoped that with the destruction of the house would go the anguished memories. Julia was right. It was ridiculous to keep the Old House standing when for two centuries the family had lived in the elegant new estate, the Great House at Collinwood, where he now slept, and rose, and walked in the sun. The Old House was rotting, falling to ruin. Only the moonlight gave it solidity. Its rooms were empty and abandoned. Too long it had been a residence of ghosts.

Barnabas shivered truly now from the cold. The howling dogs wailed again, as if mourning for some lost cave of comfort, and he reached to close the window against the night air. Just then the wind gusted and caught the trees, tossing their black branches, and the moon reeled. He looked across the gables of the roof and down to the wide lawn, and started suddenly, his breath catching in his throat. For he saw, or thought he saw, the figure of a woman standing in the shadows of the trees.

It was only her silhouette he saw, but she was slender, dressed all in white, and her skirts skimmed the grass. She was wearing a cape that covered her hair and shadowed her face; but from the angle of her head she seemed to be looking up to the window where he stood, and he caught the gleam of her eye.

Was this some vision conjured up from his ruminations? Had he let dreams and reflections bring forth ghosts? No, this was no phantom. She stood clearly outlined against the long windows of the front parlor. Then she turned and began to walk away, disappearing into the dark trees.

Who could this woman be? he wondered. Perhaps her car had broken down on the road, and she had ventured up the long driveway where, intimidated by the dark windows, she was afraid to come to the door. Now she was lost, unable to find her way back to the road. Curiosity fluttered at the window of reason, for his guilty recollections were as active as ever. Some victim, he found himself surmising, perhaps the lady in his dream, some haunted soul seeking recompense, craving solace, still wandering in the world of the undead. Reaching for his robe and slippers, he smiled bitterly at the caprices of his imagination. There were no ghosts at large this night. Still, who was she? If she was in distress, he should come to her aid.

Moving across the room, he caught a glimpse of his reflection in the massive gilt mirror above the dresser. He remembered when he had been unable to see his image in the glass, and it distracted him. There, in the moonlight, stood an elegant gentleman with dark hair softly curled and only slightly graying at the temples. He was a man of sophisticated, even noble, lineage, possessing an aristocratic visage: wide cheekbones; an aquiline nose; coal black eyes set deep beneath heavy brows; a delicate, sensuous mouth; lips that curved into a charming, secretive smile with only the slightest lift of the corners. It was a face of exquisite sensitivity, the face of a poet. But, smoldering in the hollows of the eyes, there was a glance so intense as to be fiercely hypnotic.

Making his way down the long hallway to the stairs, Barnabas passed the door to Julia's room. Momentarily, he hesitated, wondering whether he should wake her and send her to investigate in his place.

He had made her a solemn promise to cease all visits to the Old House. It had been a condition of his cure and the long weeks of convalescence. He thought of her patience and her professionalism, her tireless experimenting, never giving in to despair, a scientist at work, searching, testing, hypothesizing, always with such optimism. Dear Julia. He knew her motive was love; she was more devoted than any woman he had ever known. Her strength was in her knowledge. She had saved him, and it was only right that he make her his wife. She had spoken so seriously, her eyes bright above high cheekbones, "You are like an alcoholic, Barnabas, who must never again take even a sip of wine, you understand? Promise me never to return to that place!"

This was the reason he hesitated, but deciding that he would only look over the lawn, he moved resolutely forward down the grand stairway and into the foyer.

The moonlight glazed the hallway with an icy sheen. As he made his way toward the door, he glanced—as he had done thousands of times before—at his portrait hanging on the wall, thought by everyone to be the portrait of his ancestor, Barnabas Collins. There he was, dressed in the costume of an eighteenth-century gentleman, imperiously grasping a cane, the silver handle shaped in the head of a wolf. Shaking his head ruefully, he opened the door and entered the world of the night.

Barnabas moved across the damp grass toward the woods. The wind tumbled the branches of the trees, and a scattering of leaves fell about his feet. The dew was heavy on the grass, and the aroma of cherry and plum trees in spring bloom perfumed the air. The mournful owl uttered its oboe notes again, and Barnabas looked up to see the great bird swoop with amazing silence over his head, its wide wings drawing a swift curtain across the moon and leaving a following shadow on the grass. Barnabas felt almost giddy as he saw that he, too, cast a long silhouette across the lawn.

But he was the sole human wanderer in the landscape, and the old bitter loneliness ached in his heart. The woman was nowhere to be seen. She had vanished, and he wondered if he had imagined her.

Still, something tugged at him, drew him farther. He reached the edge of the trees. As if in a dream, he trudged through the woods, searching for the fleeing phantom and still seeing nothing. Only the dark trunks stared out at him, until he noticed the unmistakable shape of the bird once again, this time on the reaching branch of one great oak. As he drew nearer, the owl cocked its rounded head in his direction, looking down at him curiously. Then it lifted, like a sail catching the wind, its wings silvering as it floated across the tops of the trees.

Barnabas considered turning back. Some vague foreboding hung in his chest, but he kept on, crossing one more clearing and then another.

Mysteriously, his thoughts turned to Angelique and their last encounter. At that time, her death had moved him to compassion. After inflicting lifetimes of suffering, she had been grievously contrite, and she had tried once more to lift the curse. "Is it possible for you to forgive me?" she had whispered. "All I did was for love of you."

He had been drawn into those azure eyes once again, brimming with tears, and he had faltered. His lips close to her cheek, he murmured, "Yes, I forgive you. I love you. I have always loved you." Before she had died in his arms, he had said those words!

What covenant had he made through eternity

that would never release him from its grasp? And yet he had been amazed at her beauty, even in death. He had marveled at the shape of her arm and the curve of her shoulder as she fell against him.

Over a century ago he had wavered in his responsibility to himself and to his family and risked everything: love, youth, and life itself, to be with her. Why? She was everything he despised; she was of questionable parentage, traitorous, violent, devoid of virtue. But she had kindled a fire in him; even now he remembered the pure agony of wanting her.

That first night, after he had told her to leave, Angelique had walked to the door, her skirts flowing like molten gold over the carpet. Then she had turned to look at him with a gaze so unwavering, so filled with the promise of abandon, her opal eyes dark and luminous, a glistening drop on her lip, a gaze so knowing and so locked into his that he fell into the sea of it. She was liquid silk when he reached for her, with an odor all her own, like grasses near the sea, and her kiss was as he had remembered it, so full and moist, that he had imagined, as his body throbbed to her, that he could live on her mouth. Then he had lost all memory of himself as he plunged into the fierceness of her embrace, and she sucked the marrow from his bones and filled them with her own fire.

Barnabas shuddered to think of her again. Surely she had been the pursuer, and he had been hypnotized by her power. How many thousands of times had he turned the facts over in his mind, arranging and rearranging them to leave himself feeling guiltless, without blame. He had lost his soul to Angelique. For a time that was true. He was sure of it. She had been ecstasy greater than any man should know.

In that moment before her death, he had faltered in the strength of his resolution and spoken to her the words she longed to hear. Once again he wondered how he could have been faithless to his tender Josette?

Josette! Her unblemished mind, her radiant sweetness, were as real to him now as they had been the day he met her. She was gently bred, full of kindness, delightful in manner and in conversation. Suddenly he had an overwhelming desire to see Josette's grave, to stand at the place where the family had buried her after her desperate flight from the horror he had become.

He was tired, exhausted even, from his futile search through the woods, but he decided to make his way to the graveyard. He felt certain that standing at Josette's grave would relieve this sick sensation in his stomach.

It was some time before he was moving along the cliff at Widows' Hill. He was breathing hard from the effort, such exercise being rare since his cure. He resigned himself to the fact that he did not have the strength he had become accustomed to as a vampire, when these stretches of cliff and meadow were but a moment's flight on the wings of the wind. When he stood at the spot where Josette had flung herself to her death, he could smell the salt air and hear the waves crashing far below. He looked out at the dark sea. The moon hung at the edge of the horizon, its dappled moonstream flowing across the water. He turned and started for the graveyard.

At last he arrived at the entrance to the burial place of the Collins family. Jasmine twined profusely through the iron enclosure, sweetly perfuming the air, and there was another aroma, of gardenias, tropical and heavy in the mist, blooming waxen on black bushes by the gate. From where he stood he could see the mausoleum and the carved gargoyles of the vault, where his years of daylight had been spent, hidden behind a stone door, sleeping in a casket. His heart lightened in anticipation as he walked toward the place where he knew Josette was buried, remembering how often in the distant past he had come and stayed for hours, praying for her soul.

But somehow he became confused; Josette's grave was not where he remembered it. There were only flattened markers and toppled headstones, carved heads, and once elegant Victorian statuary now ruined by time. There were sepulchers enclosing the remains of the deceased, and here and there a stone sarcophagus stretched as a tomb. He began to wander, searching among the gravestones, disoriented and angry with himself. Had his mind as well as his body lost its strength with his transformation? He became impatient with his inability to recall Josette's resting place, as if he could have possibly forgotten a thing so important to him, and he began retracing his steps, stopping by gravestones, brushing off leaves and dirt with his hand, attempting to read the names obscured in the shadowy dark.

Thoroughly frustrated, he found himself standing beneath a large marble angel, deeply weathered and softened by moss. Barnabas had no recollection of having seen the monument before. The angel hovered above its guarded grave like a medieval figure from a Gothic cathedral, dark wings lifted against the sky. The deceitful moonlight played upon the rain-streaked features as if the tracks of tears were traced there. The marble drapery of the robes seemed to fold softly and float away from the body. For a long moment he stood mesmerized by the heavenly vision, and he reached out to touch the form of the leg beneath the garment, musing on the dissembling capacity of marble to appear pliable as flesh or as supple as fabric, when it was in actuality nothing more than cold, hard stone.

Then his eye fell to the inscription, which was quite clear in the moonlight, and his blood froze! "ANGELIQUE BOUCHARD, 1774—1796," and beneath it: "LOVE SLEEPS IN DEATH'S EMBRACE." He was appalled. It was the grave of Angelique! Who had placed such a memorial there? An angel! Good God! Surely this was an absurd representation, he thought, superficially based, perhaps, on her name, but so incongruous with the woman it represented. He shivered unconsciously to think of her again—Angelique—his lover and nemesis, now gone, while he, having vanquished her forever, still breathed on this earth.

The angel was abruptly transformed in his mind. No longer endowed with a gentle holiness, it appeared macabre and threatening. Barnabas backed away, more disturbed than curious, and the search for Josette's grave ceased to be important. He had started toward the gate, intending to return to Collinwood, when he glimpsed the woman he had seen earlier— behind the far gravestones. It was she!

She was moving quickly, her smoky shape wavering among the tombs. His throat tightened, and a new energy pulsed through his limbs. This time he determined to stop her, and he rushed toward her as though she were his release from darkness.

He was surprised, some moments later, to find himself on the grounds of the Old House. The mansion seemed to float in the moonlight, like a ghostly palace. He reached the brick steps, and his hand rested against one great alabaster pillar. He was out of breath. The portico was now deserted, and only the wind whistled through the columns, tossing frosted leaves along the long corridor of the porch. The woman was nowhere to be seen, and he was intensely disappointed and furious with himself for having lost her. He felt a vague premonition of danger, which he shook off impatiently, even angrily, as he climbed the steps.

There, suddenly, in the shadow of the porch, he saw her again. Something about her posture seemed to indicate that she had been waiting for him. There was a quickness to her movement as she turned toward the door. Now curiosity was burning in his gut. He was certain she was a ghost, leading him into the house.

Once again he hesitated. Was it foolish to risk

entrance there? It had been over a month since his cure, and the pain of his transformation had subsided to various annoying discomforts, with every sign pointing to the success of the medication and the permanence of the change. Still, it had been many years since he had felt the need for what one would call courage. He had been rash and arrogant as a youth, before the curse, possessing a willful craving for adventure. Now, once again life would be a challenge. He felt eager to risk, to pit himself against the perils of the world, to rejoin truly the land of the living. And the house held so many memories! He felt a sharp pang of regret that it was to be torn down. He suddenly had an overwhelming desire to walk through the rooms and hallways one last time. He pushed open the heavy door and jerked back inadvertently when the hinge whined like a wild animal caught in a trap, and the bolt fell with a clang.

Barnabas was met by a silence so deep it seemed the house was wrapped in a velvet cloak. Odors, both dank and familiar assailed his nostrils: the mildew of the carpets and drapes, the dust thick on the furniture, cold damp ashes in the fireplace, and the stale smell of things long abandoned, flattened and faded by a veil of cobwebs. There was another odor, less suffocating, but vile nevertheless—the putrid reek of decay and death. It hung in the air like wisps of smoke, and seemed to come from beneath the floor, as though the rats that lived in the basement of the doomed house had starved and perished.

He walked across the parlor, his footsteps a hollow tapping, and looked out through the tall windows of leaded glass. He thought he heard a rustling sound, and he turned and gazed about the room. It was empty save for the shadows. Then he heard the sound again and glanced at the massive fireplace. He saw that a box of long wooden matches had been spilled and left there on the brick hearth, but the grave of the chimney was cold and dark. He steadied his nerves, closed his eyes, and listened. He fancied the air was fluttering with vague whispers and murmurings, but he waited, until he was certain he heard nothing except the dull pounding of his own heart.

He moved with determination across the entrance hall and up the wide stair with a heavy banister to the rooms above, where Joshua, Naomi, Jeremiah, Sarah, and so many others once had slept. A ghost among ghosts, he wandered through each chamber, his gaze lingering on some remembered texture or pattern of rug or spread. All of the paintings and valuables had been long since taken away. But there were still papers and photographs, odd pieces of clothing, trinkets and toiletries—the undesirable debris of lifetimes—piled on chairs or floor.

With inescapable sadness, he looked into Josette's room. Memories flashed upon his inward eye and caressed his senses as he relived the freshness and sweetness of her face. He remembered with a hollow ache the delicacy of the hand she lifted to be kissed, the modesty of her glance when they had first been introduced, and her gentle voice. "Monsieur Collins. My father has told me you come from America and that you are a gentleman of enviable reputation and charm. It is a pleasure to meet you."

Drawn down the back hall to the servants' quarters, he now stood opposite Angelique's doorway, which was closed. His heart skipped a beat as he imagined that once again he heard the soft rustling sound and something like a sigh. He paused, then, brushing aside the silly apprehension, turned the doorknob.

The room was quite chilly, for the window had been left open. Barnabas remembered the few times he had entered this room in the past. It was much like the others, though smaller and less refined, and he realized with some distaste that his dealings with Angelique had usually been in his own bedroom, in the parlor, or elsewhere on the estate. He had always resisted coming here, and when he did it was for the purpose of making amends.

With a sharp pang he recalled the night he had asked her forgiveness, hoping they could be friends, saying he would always think of her with affection, and she had, in her fiendish seductiveness, enticed him, melted his resolve, and lured him to her bed. "Lie to me," she had whispered. "If all your pretty words were lies, then lie to me again."

With a shudder, he glanced at the small cot with its satin pillows, the small vanity, perfume dried to an amber stain in a crystal bottle. A faded green gown, which he recognized, with raveled lace at the collar, hung in the wardrobe. A single wrinkled glove and a bonnet with a limp ostrich plume lay on the shelf, grimy with dust.

He was about to turn and leave when the fragile organdy at the window fluttered, and its ragged edge lifted a little and fell. He thought this must be the source of the sound he had heard earlier, for, even though the night was still, a breath of air rustled the curtain. As he watched, the breeze grew stronger and shuffled the pages of a small book lying in the dust on a table by the window, almost as though an unseen hand were flicking through them.

Barnabas crossed to close the window, realizing the absurdity of the gesture, since the house was to be razed in the morning, and he began to feel somewhat ashamed, invading, after all these years, this private place that had belonged to someone he had known for so long. Better to have let everything be demolished with its secrets, buried away beneath the earth. This little room, he thought, betrayed Angelique's provincial roots. She was, after all, born to be a servant, despite her pretensions to wealth and gentility. Nothing about her chamber spoke of an aristocratic nature.

And yet she had been determined to be his wife, even force him into marriage. She had returned again and again, in every lifetime, to taunt and plague him with her insatiable desires.

There were times when his hatred of her was so intense that he plotted her death, and other times, fierce and unfathomable, when he had longed for her with unabated lust. There were times when he knew in his deepest heart that only she understood him in his torment, she being the cause of it, and only she shared with him his desperate secrets and his profound knowledge of evil. At those times he had allowed himself a sense of oneness with her, and even something close to—dare he to think such a thing—something close to love. If love is hatred's twin, the only other emotion as all-consuming, then it was true that he had felt toward her a bitter and remorseless love.

He reached for the casement. Angelique's room was on the side of the house facing the sea, and far off the moonstream still glowed upon the water. Barnabas began to tremble, for the house was thick with fearful memories. He no longer possessed the strength of twenty, or the indomitable power of the Devil's apostle. He was as vulnerable as any ordinary man, not only to physical danger, but also to the plagues of terror. It had been a mistake to come here. He stood at the window paralyzed, fearing to move and yet aching to flee.

Once again a cold breeze swept into the room. The pages of the book ruffled as before and, undeniably, he heard a sigh, then a low moan—like the moan of pleasure in love—then another long sigh. The hair on the back of his neck rose, and he was suddenly certain that she was there.

He turned and saw her, and his blood turned to ice in his veins. She was lying on the bed, which before had been empty, her filmy garment spread around her like the tissue of moonlight. Beneath its smoky mist he could see her breathing body and the graceful curve of her thigh. She held out her ivory arms, and he glimpsed the soft gleam of her eye and the invitation in her smile. With a savage effort, he backed away, wheeled, and lunged for the door.

He ran like a madman, stumbling down the dark hallway, not stopping until he was in the dim parlor. He lurched for the fireplace, his hands jerking awkwardly at the scattered matches, grasping, breaking, cursing, striking, until at last he had a tiny flame. He cupped a quivering palm around it and, dropping to one knee, held it to the edge of the nearest drapery.

The threadbare velvet caught and rippled as a stream of fire ran up the edge of the fabric and hovered a moment beneath the golden fringe before it exploded in flame. The fire hissed across the top of the window, drenched the room in a golden aura, and hummed with the sound of burning. He wrenched the curtain loose, and a blazing part of it fell to the floor, where he dragged it to another tapestry and set that aflame as well. Now the room shone with the fires of Hell and was filled with a roaring sound, deafening and implacable. Then, buried deep within that tone—reverberating, pulsing, taunting him—he heard the echo of Angelique's chilling laughter.

Barnabas bolted, ran out into the night, and did not stop until he was in his own room at Collinwood again. There, from the safety of his window, he could see the glow on the edge of the night as the Old House burned like the torch of a distant volcano against the dark sky.

chapter

2

Sunshine streamed through the tall leaded windows into the elegant dining room where silver and china sparkled on the white damask cloth. Collinwood matriarch Elizabeth Collins Stoddard, her brother Roger, her daughter Carolyn, and Julia were already at breakfast, speaking in hushed tones, and Barnabas was aware of an abrupt pause in the conversation when he appeared.

"Beautiful morning!" he said cheerily, ignoring the grim atmosphere as he seated himself, reached for a linen napkin, and unfolded it upon his impeccably pressed trousers. He forced himself to concentrate on the bouquet of jonquils and anemones at the center of the table, their joyous creams and scarlets floating like impressionist watercolors against the parchment of the tablecloth. His sleepless night had left him exhausted; a hot cramp knotted his shoulders in a spasm, and his eyes burned as if particles of sand were trapped beneath the lids. But he was determined to remain composed, and he murmured a polite "thank-you" to Mrs. Johnson as she poured fragrant coffee into his cup. It was his aunt Elizabeth who broke the oppressive silence.

"Barnabas, we have dreadful news."

He looked up, showing a quizzical mask. Elizabeth was still a beauty. This morning her lustrous black hair was pulled away from her face, and she wore the pearl necklace of which he was so fond. Her voice was husky with privilege, her speech rolling and long-voweled, with the slightly nasal intonation of upper-class Americans.

"What is it?" Barnabas asked ingenuously.

"You will be devastated, I'm afraid," she said. She still resembled the debutante who at seventeen had graced her father's arm at the ball. Her skin was, he thought to himself, very much like the cup he held in his hand, the purest Irish porcelain, snow-white, tissue-thin, and translucent. At this moment heavy lashes shadowed her ebony eyes, and a small wrinkle of concern centered itself on her brow.

"Why, whatever has happened? Tell me, Elizabeth, please."

"Last night . . . the Old House caught fire and burned to the ground."

"You're not serious!" Barnabas lifted his napkin to his mouth. He could feel a blood vessel throbbing in his temple.

"I'm surprised you weren't awakened."

"Why, no. I heard nothing. Nothing at all. How distressing!" His lips touched the smooth surface of the linen, and he was struck by his immediate tendency toward mendacity. Lies came easily, as though they were the very substance of his thoughts.

"Willie saw it first," Elizabeth continued. "He was up before dawn, saw the smoke, and roused Mrs. Johnson, who came to me with the news. We called the fire brigade, but by the time they arrived, the house was very nearly gone."

"Was . . . anything saved?" Barnabas asked.

"The skeleton, the columns. But the interior is gutted I'm afraid. Oh, Barnabas, I am so very sorry."

"Shocking . . . really . . ."

"My God! What's all the fuss?" came a contemptuous voice from the end of the table. "We're well rid of that old cadaver." Roger—the patriarch of the family, silver-blond and aristocratic—spoke with the glacial disdain and the cultivated speech patterns of a Shakespearean actor. His heavy blond brows curved in the center to hold a permanent frown in place, the only disturbing feature of a perfectly chiseled face. "I thought you said, my dear man, that it was to be demolished today?"

"Yes. It was," answered Barnabas. "The crew is scheduled to arrive sometime this morning. This only makes it easier for them, I suppose." He was amazed at the congeniality of his tone. It was as though someone else were speaking. "Now they can push it all away with a bulldozer."

"Perfectly serendipitous then," Roger observed.

At that moment, a young boy of about fifteen years of age, sandy-haired and robust, bounded into the dining room and slipped into his seat.

"I want to go to the Old House! When can I go and see it, Aunt Elizabeth?" he cried, reaching for the sugared cinnamon rolls.

"Not until we are certain the fire is all out, David," said Elizabeth.

"But I want to look through the ashes for souvenirs!"

"And I insist that you first study your lessons," she said sternly, and David groaned, slumping in his chair.

Elizabeth turned to Barnabas. "How do you think the fire could have started? There was no lightning last night. The moon was full, and the sky clear."

"Maybe the Old House chose its own way to go," mused Carolyn. She was a restless girl and often bored, spoiled by privilege and wanting more of life. What set her apart from other girls—other than pale blue eyes and a sharp tongue—and gave her an aching prettiness, was her hair, long and golden, cascading like a shimmering waterfall below her shoulders.

"The sooner we sell the property, the better," Roger continued, "to some upwardly mobile young couple, I suppose, who will build a modern monstrosity dedicated to conspicuous consumption and give exquisitely boring parties." The frown on his forehead deepened and his ice-blue eyes narrowed. "It goes without saying that we will all be invited, and they will feel the necessity of playing that atrocious music. I can't for the life of me imagine what people appreciate in that toneless drivel."

"Well, Uncle Roger, you won't have to go," Carolyn said. Nothing would have suited her more than a party with atrocious music. She turned to Barnabas. "So, Cousin Barnabas, how do you think it happened?"

"I beg your pardon?"

"What started the fire?"

"Why, I have no idea." His starched collar had begun to bind, and he regretted his morning attempts at sartorial splendor.

"Are you sure you didn't sneak down there and do the dirty deed yourself, just to save the price of the demolition?"

Barnabas was startled at how close she came to the truth. He could see the humor glinting in her eyes and the sly smile on her face. He hesitated. Perhaps the truth was better. What did it matter? But he could not make himself be honest.

"I think the wrecking crew will be needed nevertheless, to carry the carcass away," he found himself saying.

"Do they have one of those cool cranes with a huge, swinging ball?" asked David. Elizabeth frowned at him for interrupting.

"You must go over there immediately, Barnabas, and ascertain the cause of the fire," Roger said.

Julia looked up at him in alarm. "Why does Barnabas need to go?"

"Why? Because the last thing we want are rumors of an arsonist at large, sheriff involved, that sort of thing."

"But Willie has already told Elizabeth, there's

hardly anything left. Surely he doesn't need to bother . . ."

"It's clearly Barnabas's responsibility to take an interest in estate matters. We have had several inquiries since the property went on the market. Anything which would affect the selling price should be of concern to you as well, Julia, if"—Roger spoke dryly, with irritation—"you are indeed to become a member of the family." He had been waiting with ill-disguised impatience for Barnabas to become involved in the business, ever since his appearance—a long-lost cousin from England, with some claim to the family fortune. And now, the proposed marriage gave Roger even greater cause for concern.

Barnabas felt uncomfortable under Roger's keen focus. His throat tightened, and his collar constrained his breathing as though it were a noose. The necessities of his cure had entailed constant excuses and compromises and, naturally, absence during the entire day, which had only served to annoy Roger and cause him to question both Barnabas's integrity and his sense of purpose.

"I must insist that you investigate, then bring yourself into town this afternoon. We'll have a meeting in my office. There are many things we need to discuss, not merely the fire at the Old House, but other matters more pressing."

"But Roger, Barnabas has been very ill," Elizabeth said softly to her brother. "He needs time to recuperate. Isn't that true, Julia?"

"Yes. Yes that's entirely right," agreed Julia,

attempting to keep her voice calm and professional. "The last thing we want is a relapse. Time. And rest. And the love and support of his family." She glanced at Roger and smiled genuinely in response to his irritable glare. But Roger ignored her, threw down his napkin, and rose from the table. He turned to Barnabas.

"You arranged for the demolition, against my better judgment, if you recall. I thought the Old House was better sold as an historical monument. Now it has become an eyesore. I assume the trucks are still coming. At the very least, I would be grateful to you if you would deal with these difficulties today. Providing it's not too much of a strain." He turned and left the room.

A nervous Julia drove Barnabas around by the road, and they turned in at the long colonnade of plane trees, newly leafed in green, their painted trunks lifted in strong and graceful arches over the avenue. He dreaded what was to come, and he tried to clear his mind of all thought until they at last reached the smoking hulk.

They parked the Bentley and got out. It was a warm spring morning, and the air was sweet with the fragrance of bloom. Throughout the grounds, thousands of jonquils nodded in clumps of butter yellow; dogwood floated like filmy clouds, so delicate his heart ached. Barnabas longed to enjoy the daylight, with all its joyous gifts, but he could not escape the melancholy that seemed to reside within him. He sighed, and Julia took his hand.

"So you heard nothing? You slept soundly?" she said.

"Of course, I always sleep soundly," he said indifferently.

She knew the reverse was true, and he could sense her concern. As they drew nearer, Barnabas could feel the ache in his shoulders tighten and his head begin to throb.

Smoke was rising from the charred remains, but there were still pieces of iron balustrade lacing the roof, and he could see the massive columns yet standing, their fleshy trunks and classic crowns, like a long line of sentinels, circling the house—forty, perhaps forty-five, graceful pillars, lifting the yawning roof out over the porticos.

"Barnabas, you must try not to let it upset you."

"But, Julia, I am not in the least disturbed," he said, still remaining dispassionate, though his chest felt in the grip of a vise and the air seemed too scorched to breathe. The coolness of his demeanor was amazing even to him; the memory of the night, its visions and demons, was becoming a dimly remembered dream.

A bird sang in a tree beside the lawn, a fluting sound, followed by a trill and a quick rattle. It could have been three different birds, but Barnabas remembered the song.

"Listen," he said, "a mockingbird, practicing his repertoire." Julia smiled at him and took his arm as they approached the house. Embers still smoked, and a sickly odor rose from the ashes. Barnabas stepped gingerly through the debris, recognizing an odd piece of furniture, but he was relieved to see that almost everything was destroyed. It was difficult to find traces of the walls, and the huge brick fireplace was a blackened pile. All the while, the mockingbird whistled and chucked. Barnabas caught sight of him sitting on the highest point of the ruined chimney, flicking his tail.

A quarter hour's search revealed nothing significant, and their hands were grimy with ash and soot, when Barnabas finally said to Julia, "As you heard at breakfast, I'm bound to stop in at Roger's office this afternoon. Is there anything you might do in town? If so, you could accompany me."

"Nothing pressing, but I'll be happy to go with you," she called, wandering a little away. "What about the crew?"

"They don't seem to be coming, do they? Let's be off." Thinking that perhaps he need never return to this site, he started for the car.

That was when Julia called out and stooped over something on the ground. Reluctantly, Barnabas came back to her side and looked down at her feet. He was shocked to see a small book, dusted with grime but intact, lying there. He picked it up and turned it over in his hands.

Julia was incredulous. "Impossible for that to survive when so much has burned."

"Still, here it is." He pulled open the burned pages, which crackled in complaint, and began to glance through it. "It's nothing but a lesson book, written by a schoolchild," he said softly.

"Whose was it? Can you tell?" Julia looked over his shoulder. The first few pages were scrawled in an immature script, very much like handwriting exercises. They could barely make out the words.

The sea is endless. Endless is the sea. Islands a long way off. It begins with the tide. Curled inside me, with no rhythm, only a push and a flow. Islands a long way off. Another and another. Some tall with their mountains in the clouds. Some rounded like a woman's body. Some flat with trees all bowed one way, their branches reaching like fingers, stretching away from the wind.

The nuns are teaching us to write, but the lesson must be in English. Sister Lucianna says I am wasting my paper.

The island where I was born is called Madinina. It means Isle of Flowers. But my mother calls it Pays des Revenants. In Creole that means Land of Returnings, or Land of Ghosts.

The French came to this island in 1684. Saint-Pierre was the first town in Martinique. The schooners come for the sugar.

Glory be to God the Father Almighty maker of heaven and earth.

Julia gasped. "Why, I don't believe it! It must have belonged to Angelique!"

"What . . . ?" Barnabas said vaguely. A cold shudder passed through his frame.

"She was born there, in the Caribbean. In Martinique. She was Josette's servant before they came to America."

"But how could a childhood memoir have found its way to the Old House. Even if it was Angelique's?" Barnabas murmured, feigning indifference. "A keepsake," he decided, feeling a numbness in his fingers, as he read a bit more.

I cannot see the wind, but it is there. What plays with the wind? Windmills, kites, parasols, sails, pages in a book, banners, skirts, pareus on the line, hats, flowers, hair, clouds, fog, mist, frigate birds, trees, the branches of trees.

The Lord is my Shepherd. I shall not want. What is a shepherd? A sheep-herd? Here there are only goats and pigs.

"It's a journal," acknowledged Barnabas, thumbing through the parched pages. "Look how thick it is."

"Barnabas, throw it away," said Julia. "I don't think you should read it. The memories are too painful for you. The burning of the Old House is a shock to your constitution, and this is a vulnerable time for you." The mockingbird trilled again, and Barnabas, whose whole being agreed with Julia, found himself arguing with her.

"But, Julia, it's rather remarkable, you have to admit."

"I think it is utterly lonely and sad."

"But impressionable . . . precocious . . . listen." Drawn to the book, he read again, out loud.

The sea has no rhythm. My mother made a sea window, a bucket with a glass bottom, and placed it on the surface of the water. When I looked through it I could see the other world. I could hear the clicking of the coral-eaters, and feel the swaying surge. The wind of the sea is invisible, pulling, jerking, tugging.

"It's extraordinary, isn't it? How could something so lyrical be written by a child?" Barnabas asked.

"Barnabas, throw it back. You really should not read something, anything, written by Angelique, if it is hers. Her presence is too powerful, and—"

"Wait. Listen . . ."

The drums are like the sky sound. They are thunder. The drums speak to one another. They speak of wind and rain. Of the storms of Africa. The rhythm is in the drums. The heartbeat. The Negroes play music from the time of thunder.

"Not like the Angelique we knew, is it?" Barnabas folded the book and placed it in his coat.

"Leave it here."

"I want to keep it," he said, "for a while. I want to look it over more thoroughly. Come. Let's go back. What do you think could have happened to the wreckers?"

"Throw the diary away, Barnabas. Or give it to me!"

"Why, for God's sake?"

"It's . . . I have a feeling that it's dangerous."

"That's absurd. I'm curious, that's all. If it has any effect on me at all, I will. I'll throw it in the trash.

Besides, we are finished with doom and gloom, Julia.
The spells are ended. Now don't argue with me. See . . .
the sun is shining!" And he gave her a gentle hug.

As they drove down the road in the black sedan,
the muscles in his chest and neck began to relax, and
Barnabas lay back against the leather headrest. The
strain of keeping his emotions in check, keeping himself distant from his crime the night before, had left
him drained.

He opened his eyes and looked over at Julia, as if
he were seeing her for the first time, and he allowed
his mind to flood with sincere feelings of affection.
She wore a camel hair suit, the color rather becoming
to her auburn hair. Her face was older, that was true,
but then so was his. The angular line of her cheek and
jaw gave severity to her countenance, but he thought
of the eager sympathy always in her eyes, which
offered him great comfort. Yes, that was what it was:
comfort . . . and ease. She was his old confidant, and
she had never stopped loving him.

His life spilled out before him like a long road,
and he could see all the way to the end: marriage to
Julia, respectability and security, dabbling in the
Collins family business—someone needed to take it in
hand long ago—finding financial success. She would
be an excellent partner; she was so sensible and self-
less. Children were out of the question, but he was
not particularly troubled. David was still young and
needed mentoring if he was to handle the estate when
he came of age. The years would roll by. Julia and he
would grow old together. After suffering the crimes of

pleasure, after tasting immortality, and finding the price too high, Barnabas was satisfied that this kindly, humble existence was all he could desire.

Julia felt his gaze, turned, and smiled at him. He reached for one of her hands—the other still gripping the wheel—and kissed the fingertips. At that moment a cloud passed over the sun, and the treetops, which had been bathed in brightness, fell dark. But it was only a fleeting moment, and in an instant, the day was cheerful once more.

Once alone in his room, Barnabas removed the book from his jacket. He had kept it to burn it, but he was surprised by a strong sense of anticipation when he opened the cover. French was Angelique's mother tongue. He could see that a great many pages were in French, which he read easily. But there were many entries in a hesitant English as well. Perhaps the nuns had taught her in both. He remembered Angelique's accent as a grown woman, rather clipped and British, the result of learning another language.

He sat in the chair by the window and began to read. Was there something he could learn from this child's epistle? Something to reveal the true nature of his tormentor?

I was a mermaid, brown as the sails of a ship, brown as magnolia petals fallen under the leaves, brown as seeds, as gull's wings in the sunset. It was only later that I became white. After they shut me up in the room. Stone against the hurricanes. The wind at my window lifted the brown off me. My skin became the color of rice. That was because they wrapped me, and fed me sweets. My feet became soft. I could no longer walk on the coral.

My mother held my hand in the foam. This is the salty cradle, the invisible under-wind that pulls and tugs, then flows back. I love the world beneath the sea. My mother said, "This time you were born of water."

There are little squid the color of rainbows that swim backwards with their arms folded. I can do that. Today I saw a turtle with a spotted shell walking on the ocean floor. And yesterday I saw a curved wall of tiny silver minnows, like a huge waterspout. When I swam into them, the wall exploded like stars, like rain. And underneath in the gloom, the shark was so still, so still.

My mother sweeps the dust out of the corners of the room. She leaves a bowl of water by the door to trap bad spirits. There are no mirrors. Why did he come for me?

Our little house is painted coral with lavender shutters and a grass roof. All the windows face the sea. People come to see my mother when they are ill and she cures them. She knows how. She has a bag for the magic. I know she thought it was best for me to go with him.

Sister Claire lets me read her book of poems when I have done the lesson. This is the one I love the best by John Milton.

> *"The sea is as deep in a calme, as in a storme."*

chapter

3

Angelique could see her heart when she closed her eyes, small and gray, polished like a stone tumbled in the surf. But today her heart felt like a bird fluttering against the walls of a dark cave. Her mind escaped to the caves by the water's edge, and she wanted to be there, under the tall rocks with the sun streaming in. She dreamed her way back to the turquoise pools, the slapping surf, where the small crabs went scuttling under their red claws, and she swam in the water, floating through the grasses, listening to the fish clicking in the coral.

Today something felt cruel, like a punishment, but she had not needed a scolding. She was a wild child who had never been curbed or threatened. The sea had taught her caution—how to float with the breathing current and stay clear of the fire coral, how to avoid the scorpion fish that could sting with death and skirt the eel's bite.

Her father's hand was rough as barnacles, and his fingernails cut into her palm. His hand was like a giant crab claw crushing her small fingers, pulling her along when she slowed, faster than she could walk on her small legs. She ran along the muddy road at his side, stumbling in the puddles, her satchel of books bumping against her. His fingers pinched her when he lifted her into the cart.

"I want to be proud of you," he whispered, his voice full of warning. "Don't cry." But when he looked at her, she felt he did not see her.

The Negro whipped the pony and the cart lurched forward. She looked down at her white dress as it stuck to her sweaty legs, the dress she had never been permitted to wear, which had always hung in a dark corner of the house. The skirt had red flowers and a hem of lace. She touched the embroidery, the raised welts of the leaves, the satiny curve of the poppies, and she felt a quiver of pride. She had seen the white dresses worn by other girls, but hers was the most delicate.

"But Mama, it's the dress you save for Carnival."

"Careful, it will tear," her mother had said. *"It's made of batiste."*

She looked up at him. Why had he come for her today? What did he want from her, this father she rarely saw? Her mother had told her that he was taking her to Saint-Pierre to raise her as his daughter. Then why had he said so little to her?

"Father? Where are we going?"

She had heard her mother calling her name, the soft tones of her mother's voice floating in through the rocks and flickering in the sun motes. She had run across the sand, eager for some treat, a piece of sweet pineapple.

"Mama! I saw the peacock flounder! With blue-and-silver spots—and two big eyes on top! I swam down and touched it, and it flew through the water!"

But her mother had jerked off her faded pareu, and brushed the sun and the sand from her body. Then she had taken down the festival dress and pulled it on over her head. She had greased her hair, which was too yellow, sun-brightened and tangled like the seaweed where she swam, and darkened it with oils.

"It hurts when you comb my hair!"

Her mother had pulled it tight and tied it with colored ribbons. She looked at her reflection in the window and felt changed into some exotic thing, like a reef fish with transparent fins and red in its gills. "I don't like it. It's too frilly."

Then she turned and saw the bright tears in her mother's eyes.

Her father was a black shadow against the sky, a piece cut out of the blue, like a paper silhouette, his high shoulders looming in his black coat, his nose a heavy beak, his beard like dried eelgrass. But she could see clearly that he was a *blanc*, white-skinned, even with his ebony eyes and coal-black hair. That was why he never came to see her and her mother. Because they were colored, *gens du coulour*, and because her mother had been the daughter of a slave.

Once he had come when she was a baby and held

her on his knee and kissed her, and listened to her laugh. She had played with his beard and touched his high sweaty brow.

"You have the strangest eyes," he said.

"Eyes as changing as the sea," her mother had answered, with some pride. "Transparent as the water in the lagoon. Sometimes they are clear like jellyfish in the sand. Sometimes they are turquoise, or opal. And sometimes they are dark as storms."

Her father made a grumbling sound in his chest. He took her mother's wrist and pulled her sharply to him.

"Where did these eyes come from, Cymbaline?" he hissed. "You said she is mine! Where did she get those sea-green eyes?"

Her mother had looked down at him without fear. She wore her hair tied in a bright scarf that came to a point on her head like a flame.

"Can you not tell? She came from your pride all right. How can you dare to doubt? She has your mark on her."

Her father had pushed her dress up where she sat on his lap, and he had looked at the back of her leg. There was a dark birthmark there—a wine-red blotch in the shape of a coiled snake. He had rubbed it with his thumb and shrugged. Then he had sighed heavily and put her down.

The wind was gusting, and the road was rutted and rough. The palms waved their long leaves like giant knives. Her father was sweating under his heavy coat. She could smell his musty odor, not like the sea air, but something closed up, damp and moldy, like the inside of a stone tower. The shoes her mother had forced onto her feet, black patent leather, had begun to rub. She never wore shoes, and her feet were as tough as tree bark, and the shoes wore against her skin in new places. She stopped thinking her ribbons were beautiful; her hair hurt from being pulled too tight. What had he said to her mother?

"I want her to have the best. She is light-skinned and can pass. But I don't want you to come around and ruin things."

The rain fell in sheets. It was a warm rain, stirred with the odors of the frangipani. All along the road the flowers battered by the gale hung limp, their color drained and bruised. She wondered if it would be a great storm, like the ones which ripped the trees, roots and all, from the earth, and tore the roofs off the houses, sending them flying into the sky like great birds. Those were the storms that left the schooners in splinters, battered against the rocks of the bay, and sent waves as high as houses careening against the cliff.

"Why couldn't my mother come?"

"She . . . decided it was time you came with me."

The falling of the rain was steady, the sky was pale and gray, and the surface of the sea was pitted as though spattered with pebbles. She looked out at the harbor as the cart moved slowly behind the laboring pony along the beach road into Saint-Pierre.

Angelique was anxious to see the ships. Sometimes the bay held as many as fifty, heavy with sail, their high prows trimmed with gold, and their flags bright with color. But today there were only a few, hunched and sodden in the sheltered inlet, some with sails ripped into shreds, others with sheets rolled and folded like the crippled wings of the giant bats that hung in the back of the caves.

She stole a look at her father. He was hunched in the corner of the wagon, his head pulled down into his collar. She gathered her courage, and blurted, "Is it a large house, Father?"

He started at her question, and glanced at her with a frown. When he answered the sound of his voice came from deep within his chest.

"Yes, it's large, I suppose. Large enough."

"Is it made of wood?"

"It's made of stone."

She decided to start searching for the house to calm the sick feeling in her stomach. Perhaps she would know it when she saw it. She wondered if it would be grand, and if her school would be close by. She could feel the sack of books and clothing lying by her feet. She was glad she had brought her journal to show her mother when she came for a visit. Angelique thought again of what he had said.

"I don't want you to come around and ruin things."

The pony pulled the cart onto the new road, which was paved with blue cobblestones. The frame jostled her, but it was better than the jerking of the wheels in the mud and ruts of the dirt path. They passed in front of the warehouses slick with rain, the arched and columned doorways staring bleakly at the empty docks.

Under the awnings she could see, still bound in their chains, a group of newly arrived slaves. Because of their black skin and the dirty rags they wore, they were almost invisible in the shadows, and they huddled together in groups. But she could make out their legs, some muscular, some very small—the legs of children—and there were also the colorful skirts of the women. She had seen slaves sold at auction. Perhaps there would be an auction tomorrow, and she would be allowed to go.

"Do you have any slaves?" she asked. Her father scowled, as though he were preoccupied with other thoughts, but after a moment he grunted.

"Slaves . . . yes, of course."

"How many?"

"Too many. Not enough."

The warehouse guard sat inside a small room that faced the wharf, the oil lamp flickering. Just as their cart rumbled by, the man lurched out into the rain with his whip curled in his hand and shouted cruelly at one of the Negro men. With a harsh cry, he let fly the heavy lash, and the slave shrank into the shadows.

"Oh, that man is whipping them!"

"Without the whip, they are devils."

She felt a sudden pity for the slaves—the bone-breaking work and the humiliation of bondage. Her mother's mother had been freed because she had given birth to a light-skinned daughter. How miserable not to be free! Then she thought of the caves and the reef where she could be a nymph in the sea grass, as free as the tugging surge, where the water was so warm and clear and the colors so bright. She wondered how many days it would be before she was swimming there again.

The cart jostled up the main street of Saint-Pierre. Here and there a shutter was left undone, and banged in the gusts of whistling wind, but most were pulled tight against the possible gale. This must mean a hurricane was on its way, she thought, and she wondered if her mother was safe back inside their tiny shack. She hoped she had remembered to tie down the wooden screens, and to place the pot under the leak in the thatch.

She reached for the charm hanging at her neck and fingered the soft leathery ball. Inside she could feel the snake's tiny skull. She had seen it coiled on the table before her mother had killed it.

"What a pretty snake!" she had cried. "Can I hold it? It's like wriggling grass! Is it a poisonous snake, Mama?"

"A Fer-de-lance came out because of the rain," her mother had muttered. "Poisonous, yes. But a good sign for you, my little one. It will make a powerful *ouanga*."

The green iridescent ribbon had slithered around her mother's wrist as she held it by the neck, opened the snake's mouth with the tip of her finger, and forced its fangs over the edge of a glass. She milked the glands under its jaw until the poison ran down the side in murky tears. Next she had ripped out the flickering tongue and set it beside the glass. It had still quivered and jerked, like a tiny lizard, on the bleached wood. Then she had pulled back the snake's head, exposing the throat, and slit it with her knife. Angelique had not been the least frightened; instead, she had been fascinated. Her mother's powers were the most wonderful thing she knew. Every time she made magic, Angelique watched and remembered.

After she had finished the *ouanga*, she tied it around Angelique's neck. "Here, child, this will keep you safe."

"Why are your hands trembling, Mama? And where are your songs? Are they stuck in your throat?" Then her mother pulled Angelique into her lap. She smoothed her hair and spoke softly.

"This has always been my dream, my darlin'. You'll have a better life than ever I can give you."

"Do I have to go away?"

"Yes . . ."

"But I like it here by the sea, with you."

"A planter's daughter, and darlin', with a velvet coat and a four-poster bed. You'll go to a fine school, not that lonely convent with the old nuns. And you'll have pretty friends, and music and . . . chocolate. . . ." Then she drew her in a desperate embrace and pressed her against her soft breast. A stifled sob bucked out of her.

"What, Mama?" Angelique whispered. "Why are you crying?"

"My precious darling . . . my life . . . my heart . . . if only you were not such an angel . . ."

And then her father had led her away.

*   *   *

They started up the long avenue of overhanging tamarinds, which lifted in a heavy archway. This part of the town was beautiful even in the rain, all stone-built, stone-flagged, with roofs of red tile pierced by peaked windows. They passed the theater with its deep arches and its double stairway. Posters painted on wood signs advertised an opera from Paris with an Oriental ballet. Her heart skipped a beat. Would her father take her? She could not imagine anything more wonderful.

"Can we go to the theater, Father? When I grow up, I want to be a dancer!"

He grunted but did not answer. She thought he must be angry with her, or that he had changed his mind about keeping her. Perhaps he thought she did not want to go with him because she had been so quiet. Her stomach began to flutter like a pool of trapped minnows.

"Saint-Pierre is a pleasing town. It is so many colors, like the coral," she said as brightly as she could. "I'm glad you have brought me here." He did not respond.

"Which house is ours, Father? I want to guess! Tell me when we are close."

The plaster houses of clear yellow, pale orange, or peach held a covert promise of another life, things she imagined only from her mother's stories: treasures from other lands, inlaid furniture, bronze statues, dresses of silk and velvet, music of violins and harpsichords, perfumes and crystals and sweet cakes. Her mother had told her that behind the shutters lay shelves of thick books with leather bindings and gold on the edges of their pages, silver teapots and china cups, and most of all, the private dream-life of the wealthy plantation owners and their families.

Her mother had also told her that there were mulatto women who sometimes lived with the planters and gave them their bastard children in return for a sweeter kind of slavery. Her mother could have done that. She was a vivacious, handsome woman, and many men fell in love with her. But she was too proud. No, that was not the only reason. She had chosen another way, a magical way of healing, and so kept her freedom.

"Is our house on this street, Father?" she asked hopefully. "Will we be there soon?"

The rain drummed on the pavement, and the water ran like a little stream down the gully of the street, purring and splashing between the low walls that divided the road from the buildings. The air was pungent, the streets empty, and still they did not stop. Just when she felt she could bear the wait no longer, the cart pulled into a back street that headed out of the town.

"Isn't the house in Saint-Pierre?" she asked.

He cast a cold eye in her direction. "No. Not Saint-Pierre," he said. Her heart sank in disappointment.

"Then where are we going?"

"Into the hills."

She sat back and tried not to feel too frustrated. She could hear the crunching of the cart wheels, the harsh breathing of the pony, and at times, the low humming song of the Negro slave who drove the cart, his bare back glistening in the rain. She closed her eyes and remembered that when she went into the sea to find a certain fish, a blue angel, or a spotted puffer, they were never where she looked for them. Only when she left off searching and floated in a dream, letting the reef shadow pass beneath her, did she come upon some rare and beautiful creature she had never seen before. She decided to stop asking questions and wait and see what happened. She belonged to her father now. After a while she fell asleep, her head falling trustingly upon his arm.

She woke to hear the sea crashing against the rocks far below the cliff, just as they turned off the road and went down the path toward the end of a peninsula. The rain had stopped, and the sky above the sea was a gleaming silver. The pony stumbled on the loose stones in the path, and she fell forward in the cart. Her father caught her and held her against him. She looked up and was surprised to see that he was frowning at something far down the road. She followed his gaze, and her heart leapt as if a hook had caught it and jerked it in the air.

A massive edifice stood on a rock precipice high above the water. It was built of heavy stone covered with moss, and it was surrounded by a wall. She knew this place. She could remember her mother's stories, at night before she had fallen into dreams. "Once, it was a great house. The stone was shipped over the sea all the way from France, as ballast in the hold of a schooner. And carpenters and artisans came as well. Ah, yes, it was a fine castle made by, oh such a wealthy man, who wanted it for his tender bride. But she died, poor soul, of the vapors on the eve of her wedding night. So it fell to ruin, then became a sugar plantation. That's when the mill tower was built, and the chapel, and the slave quarters. Slaves worked there in the heat until they died. They gave their lives to the sugar."

"What happened to the wealthy man?" she had asked.

"He was killed by his own Negroes. He died for his sins, yes he did. Oh, that house has a long and ugly history."

Angelique became more and more anxious as the cart moved steadily toward the forbidding structure.

"This isn't our home, is it?"

"Yes."

"But it's so dark and gloomy!"

When the slave brought the pony to a halt, her father jumped from the cart and came around to her side. He reached for her and placed her on the ground. His hands were icy cold where they touched her skin.

Then Angelique saw several other little girls her age she knew from school, dressed as she was, in white festival dresses. Why were they here? They all began to walk toward the great house, and she could hear some of the other girls whimpering softly. Her father's hand closed more tightly on hers, and he nearly jerked her off her feet as he strode along. She trotted to keep up.

Many people from the village were there as well, and it was because of them her father had been scowling, but now he ignored them. They were huddled along the path and stood watching the procession. She looked around his dark legs and recognized some of her friends: Celine, Marie-Therese, Sophia—island girls of light color who lived in other little houses along the shore. They proceeded in a long line toward a great iron gate in the wall.

And then she saw the chapel. It was a small building in the courtyard with a cross above the door. Suddenly she thought with a cold flash of fear that this must be the "communion" the sisters had told her about, when girls were taken into the church. "First Communion"—that was it! And at once she was terrified. She was already ten, and she didn't know her catechism. She was supposed to learn it, but she had barely begun to memorize the Twenty-third Psalm. "The Lord is my Shepherd . . ." What was a shepherd? Was the Lord the *Bon Dieu*? Or was he Damballah? She couldn't remember.

And why were the village people so worried? They murmured to one another, their white faces grim and frowning. Some whispered and pointed in her direction. Others shook their heads and made the sign of the cross. Was it because she was so small? She would fail the catechism because she had not learned it in time. She was wicked, and she would disgrace her father.

She looked up toward the castle, at its turrets and rounded walls. Now that the sugar cane was gone, the jungle had reclaimed the peninsula. Vines inched up the balustrades and across the parapets. As she drew closer, Angelique could see where tangled trunks of lianas snaked along the stones, and drooping foliage clung to the walls like moldy seaweed. They passed through the iron gate as tall as a ship, and crossed a bridge over a moat of slimy water. The dark chapel loomed in front of them like a mausoleum.

Suddenly, resolutely, she stopped and pulled back on her father's hand. He frowned and looked down.

"What is it?" he said with feigned gentleness. "What is it, my angel?"

"I don't want to go in there."

She was surprised by the sound of her own voice; it was sharp and clear. Its sound gave her courage, and she began to think of running back through the gate and down the road. Where was he taking her? She belonged with her mother. What right had he to take her anywhere? She had no reason to obey him. She wrenched her hand from his grasp and thrust it behind her back.

"Take me back! I don't like the church!"

Sudden rage darkened her father's visage, and his eyes narrowed. He struggled for composure; the curl of his lip was shiny, and his teeth glistened. He knelt heavily to be on her level and looked in her face.

"Listen to me, Angelique . . ."

"I want to go home!" She felt hysteria welling up, and she thought of how her mother would have challenged him. She would scream, bite, kick, whatever it took. But she would not take another step toward the terrible chapel. She watched her father battle the forces inside him. His eyes were like fiery agates, and his breath came in hot spurts against her cheeks.

Defiantly, she turned on her heel and ran. Immediately she heard his heavy step behind her. Then, suddenly he caught her and pulled her into his arms, smothering her against his rough jacket.

"Listen to me, Angelique!" His whisper was harsh in her ear. "Think back to the day when I came to your mother. When I was so ill. Do you remember? I had the fever, and I was ranting and out of my mind."

It was true; she did remember. He had staggered into their house by the sea, babbling and wild-eyed, his tongue black and thick in his mouth. Her mother had watched impassively as he had heaved himself upon their mat, squirming on the quilt, ripping the worn cotton patches.

"Cymbaline! You must help me. My head is exploding! Please . . . please . . . if you ever cared for me, for . . ." His eyes jerked, and the whites showed at their rims as he caught a glimpse of her. "For the sake of the child, don't let me die!" Her mother had sauntered to his side, placed a hand on his chest, and listened. After that she had gone to her basket and taken a downy gull's feather from a small sack.

Angelique had watched as her mother knelt beside her father and held the feather to his mouth while it quivered with his breath. Then she had closed her eyes and placed two fingers on the side of his neck, muttering to herself. After a moment the woman had risen and looked down at him, her hands on her hips and a wry smile on her face.

"You are not dying, Theodore Bouchard," she said. "And your pain is of your own foolish doing. Some drink, no doubt. Some drug to make you manly and full of your wicked self, no?" Her mother's voice was sweet with contempt. "Some magic potion to make your member hard and huge! No, I will not help you!" She had turned away and gone about her tasks, ignoring him now.

But he groaned even more. "Bitter, jealous woman," he muttered. "Vain vixen!"

"Yes, you are right about that."

"For God's sake, get rid of this . . . agony . . . this devil of a headache. It's gone on for days now. It's no drug. It's . . . it's . . ." his eyes were bulging, "the *fever*! It's one of those wretched Negroes who hates me. My favorite shirt is missing from the wash. I know . . . I'm certain, one of those miserable black demons has taken it and used it as a shroud. Do you hear me, Cymbaline? There is a body . . . a rotting corpse somewhere wrapped in my clothes, and I am dying! Do something, damn you! Take some hair . . . some . . . some blood! Cymbaline! Help me, you filthy wretch!"

Grabbing the kitchen knife, he waved it at her, to bleed him, but her mother turned her back on him and began to sing a soft island song to drown out his complaints. Then, lifting her basket to her head, she took the wash out to hang under the banana trees. Angelique followed her into the garden. Green rows of well-tended peas and yams stretched at her feet. Her mother set the basket down beside a cucumber vine.

"Come take one end, darlin'," her mother said.

She loved to help her mother hang the pareus in the wind. Each one was a faded field of flowers, soft and multihued, like the coral under the sea. She lifted the flapping cloth and let herself be drawn into the colors, touching them with her mind.

Her father lay grunting and moaning on the mat. "Angelique . . ."

He had called her name. She turned, amazed that he would speak to her. Curious, she put down the pins and went in to him, walking slowly to where he lay. She remembered how black he had looked, under his pale skin. She couldn't see the light that pulsed from other people's faces. She wondered where his light had gone and thought it must have been sucked in by his pain. She reached out her small hand to find it, and her fingers had grazed his forehead. He sighed so deeply she snatched her hand away.

"No-o-o-o . . ." he had whispered, "stroke my forehead, my little angel." Hesitant, she touched his head again. "Ah-h-h-h . . . your hand is cool, and your fingers . . . yes, that's it . . . push away the pain." Hesitantly, she pressed on his temples, moving her fingers up his brow, into his hair, then stroking down to his neck, tugging at the soft skin, digging for the lost light. And, to her amazement, with a long guttural sigh, he had fallen asleep.

This all came back to her in a moment as he held her smothered against his chest. His arms squeezed the bones of her back, and her face was pressed against the scratchy fabric of his coat. She breathed in the musty odor of his body. Then he jerked her away from him and stared down into her face. His beard moved as he spoke, and spit flew out of his mouth.

"I knew! That day I knew! You are not like these other girls. They are miserable and weak! You have the power to change what you are about to see. To transform it with your mind." His voice was insistent. "Nothing is real, unless you will it to be!" His fingers clenched her shoulders, digging into her skin. "Make me proud of you . . ." he breathed a moment, then his voice fell to a raspy whisper, "my . . . daughter."

At that moment the stone of her heart opened a little, and it was as if a trickle of water flowed out, like a tear.

"I will try."

He took her by the hand and led her forward. At that moment she would have given her life to please him.

But they did not go in the front of the chapel, and Angelique began to think her fears had been senseless. Instead, the small procession moved into the flagged courtyard and approached the back of the building. There they stopped. Angelique saw the deep-grained wood of a door with heavy iron hinges that yawned open above an underground room.

Once again he whispered to her, his voice hissing in her ear. "No crying out. Do you hear me? What-ever you do, don't blubber or shriek. What you see is not real. It is all a trick!"

The other children, suddenly aware they were to be sent into this room alone, began to moan. They clung desperately to their parents, terrified of being separated. Another sound, a mournful howling deep from within the castle walls, sent a shiver through them all. Angelique felt the fear rising in her stomach.

Her father tugged at the heavy door and pushed her forward, and her head swirled as she felt herself shoved down into the darkness with the others. The door closed on the light, and suddenly she was standing in total blackness on cool earth. The damp wall was behind her, and she placed her palms back upon its stones. She could smell something rank and familiar. Some memory of something she had known before drifted into her mind, then vanished. The reek of dead flesh hung in the air, and again her stomach knotted as she hovered close to the other girls, too frightened to make a sound. They formed a tight cluster like intertwining snakes, their breaths wispy and shivering, all of them trembling, afraid to move. One of the girls began to sob softly.

There was a swishing movement in the blackness, the sound of something exploding, then sconces high on the wall brought the scene to life. As one mass, the girls gasped and shrank back from the sight.

On the floor in the center of the room was the head of a wild boar, ripped from the body. The coarse black fur was spiked with blood. Bone and gristle protruded from the neck, and yellow tusks curved from the gaping mouth. The beady eyes caught the light of the fires and stared out, as if alive, the death terror still shining there.

Children screamed hysterically and threw themselves against the door, scratching and beating it with their fists, sobbing for their fathers. But Angelique pulled away. She thought the other girls were silly, as she did when some girl at school shrieked at the sight of a spider. A vague curiosity filled her mind as she stared at the animal's garish visage. She knew it was real, that it was no trick, and that her father had lied. But she also knew, as ferocious as it looked in the flickering light, there was no way it could harm her. It was dead.

Then she heard a whimpering and a scraping sound, a scuffling, and a mournful chorus of whines that stopped her breath and lifted every hair on her head.

Animals—and these were alive—were scratching at the wood of a separate door in the wall, clawing to be let in. The door sprang back, and six wild dogs sprang forth in a fury of growling and snapping, ravenous, with teeth bared and sides heaving. They leapt upon the head of the boar, and, in their eagerness, clawed at the backs and necks of their own kind, biting in feral savagery with yelps and vicious snarls.

The girls had stopped their crying and were huddled together, breathing one breath, their eyes huge, faces blotched, noses red and watery.

Angelique was silent as she stood apart. She watched, fascinated and confused, as the dogs devoured their bloody meal. She struggled to understand, but her mind was a swirling blur. Her father had come for her. Why had he brought her here? How could he have thrust her into this place?

Anger rose in her chest and roared in her ears like the droning of bees. Suddenly she wanted to punish him, make him regret this cruel abandonment. Her father in name only. Suddenly, she hated everything about him: his hands cumbersome and graceless when he lifted her, his insistent voice: "Make me proud of you!" She felt a weakness in her limbs and ached for the warm safety of her mother in the house by the sea. She sucked in her breath. He had asked her to be brave. She had only to stand and wait.

At that moment her heart jumped; the largest dog turned and looked at her. His eyes were glowing, his muzzle painted with blood, and his lips wrinkled up to his nose, exposing his gleaming fangs. A low rumble quivered in his chest, and he gathered, ready to leap. She knew she was helpless to stop him, but she stood motionless, her mind focused in some dim other place and time. Slowly, she reached for the charm that hung at her neck and pressed it between her fingers. She felt the tiny skull.

The dog growled again and crouched deeper, his eyes like burning coals. Angelique could hear now the keening of the other girls, but she was more hypnotized than afraid. Something was familiar here, some memory or dream, but what it was she could not pull into her conscious mind.

The dog inched toward her. She could feel his hot breath on her ankles and smell the sour blood on his jowls. Wise enough not to move, she stood frozen, searching for a means to save herself. If only she knew more of her mother's magic. Invisible forces were everywhere—winds that tore the trees and currents in the sea too strong to swim against. If only she could become invisible as the wind, fade into the wall, lose herself in the cold stones.

She heard the dog growl again, the warning before the leap. But it was not pain she feared; it was failure—failure to be worthy of her father's faith and her mother's love. She would not cry out. She locked eyes with the dog, willing to be devoured, almost eager to . . . to what? To begin her life again? The dog's gaze was vacant and indifferent. Then some inner demon flickered in his eyes, and they became two flames. His mouth with its cruel, reddened teeth seemed to curve into a fiendish grin.

"I have been waiting for you . . ."

Her skin shrunk with a creeping cold. Did she imagine that he spoke to her? Not in any language or voice, but in a dark thought that floated through her. Or, was it only another growl from deep in his stomach?

For a long moment he stared at her as if to see whether she had heard, or felt, his message, and she stared back, into his flaming eyes. Then he bent his head and sniffed her ankle with the tip of his nose. She froze, waiting for the jaws to open. But instead, he merely licked her foot, his hot tongue leaving a bloody mark. Then, slowly, he turned away from her and bent again to his grisly meal.

chapter

4

The door flew back. Light poured in. The dogs cowered from the whip. The girls collapsed in their guardians' arms, sobbing with relief. Angelique walked into the sunlight. Her father was surrounded by other planters, and he seemed exuberant as they congratulated him, some pressing money into his hand. They all spoke at once.

"Well, you won that bet, Bouchard!"

"Amazing! I'll have to say that. Simply stunning, she was . . . wherever did you find her?"

"Good God! I should never have made that wager with you, Theodore!"

"Just think of it as a cockfight, Luis"—her father laughed—"except that if it had been a cockfight, you would have lost far more."

"So that's what's put you so deeply in debt," said another man.

"It's my cross, Jacob—gambling, wretched gambling. And this"—he lifted his fistful of bills—"pays all my debts. What's more, now they have another little goddess to keep them happy!"

"Just not too happy, let's hope—"

One of the planters, dressed extravagantly in a green riding jacket and tall boots, bent down, glared at Angelique, then straightened and slapped her father on the shoulder.

"Well-done, well-done, my man!" he cried. "A little beauty! Keep your coins on the pile so to speak, eh?" His skin was blotchy from too much drink, and his words were slurred. "S'pose this makes you the master here. At leas' for a while. Very good for the purse, that. Very good indeed."

"Let's hope so, Luis."

Angelique looked up to her father, expecting some praise.

"Was I brave?" she asked. A younger planter stared at her with some interest. He was of stocky build and wore a white shirt open over leather pants; his expression was serious and his demeanor earnest.

"She has huge eyes—of such a flowering blue— why, she can't be more than nine or ten years," he commented.

"Yes, it's a shame that her skin is so light," said her father. "In another time, a better fate might have been waiting for her."

"And you would sacrifice her to your shameless gambling debts?"

"No, no, it's more than that, much more—" Her father moved away. It seemed he did not want her to hear what he had to say. "Nasty business yet to come."

"I can't believe you look forward to that," Luis muttered under his breath.

"Aye, but they want it, don't they?"

"What do they call the sacrifice? 'Debatement'?"

"No, they call it *Manje Lwa* or *mange loa* . . ." and Theodore laughed.

"Oh, yes! The fountain of youth, and all that rubbish!"

"Reminds them all of home. Flesh of a child, time out of mind, and so forth. Listen. They're already drumming."

Angelique walked over impatiently. "Was I?" she insisted.

Her father answered her brusquely. "Very brave indeed. You are chosen. What do you think of that? Go now, and get ready for the ceremony."

"When can I go home to Mama?"

She reached her hand up into his, but he placed his fingers inside his waistcoat and turned away abruptly. He was immediately accosted by a fat priest who wore a long black habit and a wooden cross.

"B-b-b-blasphemy! T-t-t-total blasphemy, Monsieur Bouchard!" the priest intoned. He turned to the ruddy-faced man, his outrage forcing him to stutter. "And d-d-do you support this crime, Monsieur Desalles?"

Luis Desalles glanced at Angelique with a smirk.

"Oh, I'm sure this little goddess is a graven image!" he sneered, then addressed the priest with feigned deference. "But, Father Le Brot, you need not fear, since you have the protection of the church, and the slaves have some esteem for that." His voice was thick with rum. "Oh, no, you need not fear waking up in the night with your house burned to the ground, or your throat cut for that matter. Ha! Ha!" He staggered on his feet, as he chortled, "At least they give lip service to the Mass!"

"Lip s-s-s-service indeed! This is the way to rob them forever of their im-im-immortal souls," responded Father Le Brot huffily. He appeared to think himself superior and was disdainful of the others, almost as though the effort of conversation was a waste of time.

"Rob us all, I should think!" another planter chimed in. He was an older man, with white hair and a brocaded vest. "But what else do they ever do but rob us of our profits and our rum! Sick one day and dead the next!" Long years on the island had given him an air of resignation. "They're always plotting. Plotting. They'll have us in the end."

"Father? Was I brave?"

Her father glanced anxiously about to see if any of the other planters had heard, then quickly turned to the priest.

"Here, *Father*," he said, sarcastically. "She wants to speak to you!"

The priest observed Angelique with some interest. He had noticed her disappointment when, unable to make her father take her hand, she had pulled it back. As he stared down at her, his face brightened.

"I rem-m-m-member this child! She was t-t-taught by the Sisters. A fair student if I'm not mistaken, and a g-g-g-good reader." He smiled at her. "You are the girl who read the entire book of poetry, are you not?"

Angelique was grateful to be spoken to with such regard. She blushed and nodded happily.

"Yes, Father. And . . . and also the Shakespeare!"

"And which was your favorite, my dear?"

"Milton, sir, and Thomas Gray."

"Ah, yes, 'An Elegy Written in a Country Church Yard.' Hm-m-m-m . . ."

The priest turned to Angelique's father and spoke in a low voice. "D-d-d-do you seriously intend to g-g-g-give her up to this atrocious ritual, Theodore? It's brutal, uncivilized. We b-b-brought the Negroes here to work for us, and it's now our job to s-s-save their souls."

"Come now, do you really believe they have souls!" her father said with a mirthless laugh.

"I d-d-do indeed, as all men have s-s-s-souls. They are born with the p-p-purity that enables them to know God."

"If that were true then we would have to do everything in our power to keep them from finding out!" He turned and called out harshly. "See here! Where are the Negresses?"

Two female slaves approached timidly.

"Here, Massa . . ." one mumbled.

"Where the devil have you been, you ignorant sows. Take the child at once and prepare her for the ceremony. For God's sake, bathe her. She's filthy."

They motioned to her, but Angelique would not move. She reached for her father's sleeve and gave it a tug.

"Are you proud of me?" she asked again. "Are you?"

He brushed her aside. "Yes, yes, of course. Now go with these women. They will make you ready."

"Come, child," breathed one of the women softly. Something in the syrupy sound reminded Angelique of her mother. "It will be a big happiness for you. *Trés gentile. Trés bonheur.* A game we play. Come now. Come with us."

Reluctantly, Angelique followed the women. She looked back over her shoulder for one last glimpse of her father. He was talking with the planters. His tall frame in his dark coat beneath his bearded face and hair took on the shape of a burned and blackened tree trunk. His gestures seemed to be the lifting of leafless branches. He had forgotten she was there.

She followed the two slaves across the courtyard and into the small door of a round mill tower. They climbed up a dark winding stairway that turned within the structure like the inside of worm coral. Angelique's eyes were fixed upon the wrapped head and the large-flowered rump of the slave who led the way. The walls were roughly laid and the stone risers triangular and uneven.

Once there was a tiny slit of a window through which she could glimpse a bit of green and the sea, then the coiled path darkened once more. Angelique thought of the caves she had paddled into when the surf was calm, deeper and deeper until she lost the light. It was a game she loved, flirting with the dark-ness, which, like the water and the sand, was simply another friend, never something to fear. She could always turn her canoe and pull for the sun.

But the stairway grew even more dim, and the air in the tower was hot and dank. The only sound was the women's deep breathing and their footsteps clicking on the stone, and Angelique thought again of her father's ragged silhouette against the sky.

At last they came to a narrow landing and a heavy door with an iron bolt. It opened upon a large round room at the top of the tower, which was furnished with a carved bed and dresser. Tapestry curtains hung at tall windows, and muted light flowed across the stone walls. The bed was covered with a red-velvet cloth, and above it hung a sheer lace canopy. Angelique saw in a moment that all the trappings were European, ornate but shabby. She turned to one of the women.

"What did my father mean when he said I was 'chosen'?"

The older, larger woman seemed good-natured, and she had a gentleness about her that Angelique instantly trusted.

"They watches you through a chink in the wall, high up—above where the dogs was," she said, glancing at her companion.

"What did they watch for?"

"Why, to see who be the goddess, chile." Her voice quavered, and Angelique sensed that she was making an effort to be cheerful, for her face sagged, and her limbs hung heavily from her body.

"Now come on over here, honey. We gots to make you pretty and clean. It's a nice bath for you, don't you think?" Gently the older woman led Angelique to a large, round, enamel tub. Her tone was reassuring, but her hand was shaking as she poured oil from a green bottle into the warm water. A ferny fragrance rose in the moist steam. She pulled off Angelique's dress and lifted her into the bath. Angelique had never felt water so warm and smooth, and she let herself sink into its liquid embrace.

But they would not let her enjoy it. Murmuring something in Creole, the younger slave came to join them, and they scrubbed her so hard, she felt her skin would go raw behind her ears, and under her hair. She gave into the scrubbing like a limp doll, concentrating only on the two pairs of brown bare feet on the wet floor beneath flowered skirts, as they moved around her. They muttered to each other in musical words that Angelique recognized but did not understand. It was all so strange and not completely disagreeable, like a dream in which she was tossed about and pummeled and sung to. She felt their strong hands massage her feet and fingers with oil.

They lifted her out of the water, set her upright, and dried her shivering body with a soft cotton robe. They combed her long hair until it was soft and golden, gently untangling the twisted curls. All this she endured in a daze. They pulled a gauzy white gown over her head made of layers of sheer tulle. It was like a wedding dress tied with scarlet tassels, but it was frayed around the hem. Then they draped her with strings of jewels—necklaces, anklets, bracelets of gold and coin, tiny shells and pearls.

They led her to a looking glass in the corner of the room. She barely recognized what she saw there. The convent where she went to school had no mirrors, and she had only seen her reflection in the windows of her house, or in the surface of the lagoon when the water was smooth.

Her skin was whiter than she had imagined, and her golden hair burst like a sunlit aura around her face which was delicate and very pale. The sheer gauze of the dress was bunched at her waist, its many layers caught and pinned with the jewelry, and she suddenly thought of the fat round cocoons she had seen swaying in the manchineel trees, glistening in the sun, each hiding the sleeping worm inside. The older woman brought a pot and brush and began to paint kohl around her eyes. It tickled, and Angelique pushed her hand away.

"Stan' still, ma darlin', and don' blink. There now. Ain't that pretty."

Angelique frowned. "Why are you doing that?"

"Why, so's you be beautiful, ma baby. All the slaves come to see you now."

"To see me? Why? Why to see me?"

"In your robe, an' your fin'ry. 'Cause you sit there, up on the altar."

"What . . . altar?"

"Why you the goddess now, chile. They all come and bow down and worship you, little Virgin Mary."

This description of events seemed like a terrifying prospect to Angelique. Something was happening that frightened her more than the room with the dogs, or her father's coldness. Her thoughts spun crazily, and she looked up at the women.

"I want to go home!" she wailed. "Please, please take me back! My mama is waiting for me!"

"No, no, baby," the large woman muttered soothingly. "You stay here now. You live in the tower. We take care of you, we feed you and dress you, and make you fat and shiny. 'Cause you the new livin' goddess."

Her voice quivered, and Angelique looked into the black woman's eyes for the first time. They were lined with coppery veins, but they were filled with tears, which ran down her cheeks and glistened on her dark skin.

"Why are you crying?" she asked, more confused than ever. "Do you cry for me?" The woman shook her head, but choked as she tried to speak.

Now the younger woman approached, her rusty skirt tight across her thin belly, and gazed sternly down on the weeping one.

"Thais. Stop this! You the fool, all right! What if they hear you?"

Thais looked up at her and said in a pitiful voice, "So, what? We does it again? All again! Look at this little chile! Suzette? So cruel . . . so cruel . . . Is your heart hard as rock?"

"Why, what else can we do?" Suzette retorted grimly. "If we refuse, they kill us. You know that, Thais. You know it as well as the sun go down at the end of the day!" At these bitter words, Thais suddenly collapsed into keening and, holding herself, began to rock back and forth.

"She was ma chile . . . ma precious baby . . ."

"Stop that!" hissed Suzette. "She wasn't your child

at all. She was jus' another poor slave girl like this'n, only this'n look white. Now, is you crazy carryin' on like this? If they catch you, they beat you. Is that what you want? Fifty lashes like fire on your hide? And back into the field for you with your back all in stripes. We is both lucky to be here, workin' in the house, so shut your mouth. You sound like a fool hyena."

The weeping subsided somewhat, and Angelique, growing ever more disturbed, glanced around the room. She could see only the one door, with its metal bolt, and three large windows, leaded and barred, set back in the thick wall. At the same instant, she noticed an enticing odor, spicy and warm, and Suzette approached her with a silver tray, bearing a dish of cakes and sweet pastries. There were sugared fruits and meats wrapped in flaky dough, and there was a goblet of liquid the color of gold.

"For me?" she asked.

"Yes, chile, all for you, an' what you don' eat, that be for us." Suzette's tone held the hint of covetousness. "Go 'head. Take some. You like it fine, honey. "

Angelique felt her stomach tug and she realized how hungry she was; she reached for a pastry. It smelled of lemon and sugar, and there was warm greasy chicken inside. She took a bite. Never had she tasted anything so delicious! She took a dish and Suzette watched with a grim satisfaction as Angelique ate until she was full, licking her fingers, and sipping the sweet juice from the cup.

The whole time Thais stared into space and chewed on her fist, rocking herself as though she were waiting with a smothered dread. Then, abruptly, she raised her head and her eyes flew wide. Angelique heard a far-off sound. Thais rose, sucked in her breath, and let out such an anguished wail, it seemed she had been struck. Suzette, her face contorted, ran to her companion and held her close.

The cry came from the direction of the chapel—a wrenching shriek, not a howl of fear or pain, but a scream of complete and final terror. Angelique rose, her dish clattering to the floor.

"What was that?"

Neither of the women moved, or answered. Thais sank into her chair with helpless resignation. Her face was twisted with grief, and she stared out with unseeing eyes. But Suzette came to Angelique and took her by the hand. She pulled her to her feet.

"Come now," she whispered. "They will be wantin' you. When your time be over, perhaps this will all have ended, and you will go free. You must hope for that and keep your heart away from broodin'."

Angelique had no idea what she meant. She knew only that something terrible had happened, and that she was going down into the church. She whipped her hand away and bolted for the door. The heavy latch was hard to lift, and Suzette had her by the waist, restraining her and crying out. Angelique managed to wrench free by kicking back at her and pushed open the portal with a clang. She slipped through the narrow opening and flew down the dark stairway, feeling that at any moment that she would lose her footing and plunge headfirst into the dizzying spiral. Suzette was close behind her, screaming and clutching for a hold on her dress, but Angelique was quicker than the heavy-footed woman.

When she reached the bottom, she scrambled across the courtyard and threw herself against the gate to the outside. The heavy padlock struck her in the stomach with such a blow that she gasped. Seeing that the chain was tight around the bolt, she looked around helplessly, spied a door in the wall crossing over the moat, and dashed toward it.

Suzette's footsteps echoed behind her, and she shrieked, "Angelique! Stop! They kill us! Come back, please!"

The door gave way with a groan, and she scrambled down another stone staircase and into a corridor that was as black as the grave. She groped along the wall, terrified of falling, as the stones beneath her feet were slimy with moss or scum. Behind her, Suzette's voice was still calling her name, but she half ran, half crawled, on the slippery stones, her breath coming in gasps and her fingers scratching on the rocks. Suddenly the floor beneath her feet disappeared, and she felt herself tumble off some rough edge and splash into cold water up to her knees. She was in an underground moat. She gathered up the gauze of her dress, and sloshed through the pool, which seemed to grow deeper, then more shallow again. She licked her lips, and a taste of the fetid air told her that the water was tidal backwash from the sea.

As her eyes became accustomed to the gloom, she saw the damp stone walls rising around her. There was a far-off drumming sound that she thought must be the surf pounding against the shore, and she rejoiced to think she might escape to the ocean.

It was then she saw a light at the top of another stairway much more narrow than the first, and quite steep, like a ladder rising out of the water. Encouraged, she waded toward it and climbed. The drumming sounded nearer, and there was a shivering moan, like the surf thundering in a deep sea cave.

She came to a wooden door, which she pushed open. She found herself in a small room lined with wooden shelves laden with bottles. At the end of the room there was another, much larger ribbon of glimmering light beneath a heavy curtain, and, thinking this must be her release to the outside world, she scrambled beneath it.

At first Angelique didn't know what she was seeing. It was as though she were poised at the edge of a cavern, and the night sky had fallen and flooded the chamber with its stars. But no, they were tiny flames— sparks of light everywhere! The sputtering embers were actually thousands of candles flickering in the blackness. The humming and murmuring came from the throats of dozens of black men, crowded into the church, each holding a candle, and swaying to the rhythm of drums. She was in the chapel.

Her will collapsed within her, and her limbs ached from exhaustion. She bit her lips and blinked back hot tears. Her desperate race for escape had only led her here. The heavy drums pulsed and their timbre shook the air. She looked in horror upon a swaying mass of sweating bodies. The men were chanting, mesmerized by the drums.

Her eyes darted about, searching for a way through the throng. The food she had eaten was having a stupefying effect on her. Her vision blurred, and her legs became like water. She tried to run, but instead she reeled, collapsing in the arms of Suzette, who had come up behind her. She felt her limp body lifted onto a high wooden platform.

Placed above the men, she could barely discern vials of liquids, fruits and cakes, and slices of raw vegetables through the haze. They were all dusted with a white flour and gave off a rancid odor. There were jars tied with twisted ribbons, concealing small bones and other mysterious floating contents. On a huge porcelain dish she saw pieces of raw meat of some skinned and sacrificed animal, sliced into sections and still oozing. She gagged at the sight and wrenched her eyes away.

Looking up, she saw her father standing at the back of the sanctuary. She felt a flush of hope, but he did not come forward. He was watching her, but his gaze was not one of affection or pride. He seemed both angry and resigned, as though rejecting and accepting a fate greater than he could control. He moved to the center of the dancers and stood holding a long sword above his head, the handle in one hand and the tip in the other, like a bridge over his head. The shaft of the sword glinted in the flames, but it was darkened with a rusty stain.

Then he bent and kissed the blade, placing the

sword on the altar beside Angelique. Next he took up the porcelain dish. He turned to the congregation and moved among them, passing out small morsels of the bloody meat. She saw each dancer take a piece of the offering in his mouth.

The chanting and drumming reached a frantic pitch, and the prancing slaves whirled and rocked. Angelique watched the ceremony through the veil of whatever opiate they had given her. The dancing bodies became apparitions of monsters. There were candles growing from the tops of their heads and from the backs of their hands and feet. The bouncing lights spun and traced arcs of fire in the dark. Several men leapt high in the air and cried out as though struck.

Vaguely she realized that she was at the center of the ceremony. All the eyes of the men were on her; they were bowing to her, circling her. Their teeth gleamed, and their tongues were scarlet.

One man in front of the crowd entered a trance; he uttered a sharp cry, then fell at the foot of the altar, babbling a stream of incomprehensible language. Angelique knew he was possessed. She had seen these things at ceremonies in the village, but her mother had always pulled her away. "*Couchon Gris*," she had whispered. "*Petro!* Don't look. It is evil." The man's eyes were riveted on her until they rolled back into his head, and she could see only the whites. His back arched, and he lunged toward her stomach first as he flailed and jerked.

Her head was thick with smoke, and a swimming miasma flooded her thoughts. She felt as though she were falling from a great height, and she stopped herself with a violent jerk, placing her palms on the platform. Some liquid, wet and warm, was spilled there, and she lifted her hand and recoiled at the sour smell. She looked down. She was sitting in a pool of drying blood that flowed across the altar and dripped off the side of the platform onto the floor, where it collected in a dull, crimson puddle.

She looked at the dark blotch for a long moment, wondering what it could mean, and her gaze traveled to a round mass lying beside it, slick with congealed gore, like a bruised sea anemone, broken loose and washed up on the beach. But the tendrils were more like tangled seaweed, or eelgrass, and beneath what she realized was not seaweed at all, but matted, human hair, glinted the glassy eyes of a dead girl! It was then that she lost consciousness.

chapter

5

When Angelique awoke, she was back in the tower room, alone, lying on the velvet cover of the bed. It was daylight, but the rain was falling again, and she lay listening to the pounding on the roof above her head. Violent bursts of staccato drumming brightened or faded with the whim of the wind, and the continuous rumble of the water spilling down the parapets growled underneath. A creaking and shivering vibrated through the walls. Beneath all these sounds, she heard the noise that she knew had waked her. It was a female slave screaming.

She pulled aside the lace canopy of the bed and looked around. Rough-hewn benches lined the walls, and the white-enamel tub where she had bathed was still filled with oily water. Her satchel of books and clothes lay on the floor of wide, stained planks, and at her feet was a faded carpet.

She heard the voice again, "No, Massa, please don't. I couldn't stop her. Her too fast! Please, Massa, please." Angelique leapt up, ran to the window, and looked down.

The top of the tower was about twenty feet above the earth. The courtyard was empty. Rain silvered the cobblestones, and rivulets of water poured down the gutters to splash into small pools. She could see a stone well, and there were two posts set in the earth, one with three nervous goats tethered to it.

Then her father and another man appeared out from beneath the tower, dragging the slave Suzette. The strange man was dressed in field clothes, but he was strong and a *blanc*. Angelique knew he must be the overseer of the plantation, for he carried a heavy whip and had Suzette by the wrist. Suzette dug in her heels, and with her one free hand clawed at his arm until he caught that wrist as well. He jerked her to the empty post, ripped her ragged scarf from her head, and wrapped it around her wrists, tying her there.

"Oh, please, Massa, don't beat a poor slave. It were not my fault. She run like a rat, and I catch her, you know I did. It never happen again. Never! Never! Oh, please, Massa, no! NO!"

Angelique clung to the bars of the window trembling. The heat rose to her face. She had never seen a slave beaten, and she had never believed such cruelty ever happened.

For a moment the whip writhed on the ground like a snake in hot sand, then it rose, hovered, and sang in the air. Suzette gasped and, when the lash struck, arched and screamed as if her voice had been ripped from her body.

Angelique closed her eyes and turned away. But she could still hear the cracks of the lash and the pitiful wails until the cries became whimpers, then silence, and there was only the hollow hiss and thwack of the whip. When it was finally quiet, Angelique summoned the courage to look out again. She saw the overseer reach for the rag and pull it loose, and Suzette's body slumped to the wet ground.

Angelique's father walked over and stared down at the slave, and then, as if he knew she would be there, he looked up to where Angelique stood at the bars of the tower window.

She realized with a shock that he had wanted her to see everything, and her heart froze. Images flashed in her mind of the night before, moments of what must have been a dream: slaves filing up to the sanctuary in the dark, silently and doggedly, each one stopping a moment at the great front portal. There, a black-cloaked priest, and yes, it had been her father, administered a sacrament, touching each forehead with holy water and placing something in each mouth. Then the door had swung shut, and the long line of men had trudged off into the night.

Angelique waited to see if Suzette would rise, but she lay limp and motionless. Finally, Thais crept out, gathered the slave woman in her arms, and carried her inside. After that the courtyard was empty again except for the three goats who bleated from time to time and jostled one another like fish caught on a line. The dreary rain still pounded upon the earth.

Angelique moved back toward the bed in a daze.

She realized she had bitten into her lip and it was bleeding and swelling. Her body was sticky with sweat, and she was suddenly aware of how hot it was in the tower room, away from the breeze off the sea. She stopped and placed her hand on a post of enormous size that penetrated through the floor.

Looking up, she saw that the post was capped by a spoked wheel that meshed with the huge gears of a horizontal beam protruding through the wall. She realized the windmill was attached to this post, and that the continuous grinding sound was the windmill straining to turn the crushers, which must lie beneath the floor. But the sails were so torn that only the lattice framework offered any resistance to the wind, and the windmill floundered helplessly.

She looked around the room. On the dresser she saw a tray with tempting pieces of pineapple and mango, and pastries with cream and strawberries arranged on a dish with a cup of chocolate. But her stomach felt sour when she thought of eating.

Suddenly, she heard the latch lift at her door, and she turned to see her father. His tall boots were soaked with mud, his black trousers worn, and his coat drenched with rain. He stood staring at her, and under his shapeless hat his face seemed more villainous than ever. He glanced at the tray of food and frowned.

"You haven't eaten your breakfast."

"I don't want it," she said in a voice that was barely a whisper. "I don't want to stay here anymore. Take me back to my mother." She was startled by her own brashness.

She was standing behind a chair, and she closed her hands around the wooden rails and squeezed them tight. She felt prickling in her armpits, and her upper arms stuck to her sides.

Her father shrugged and shook his head as though he didn't understand. "Aren't you tired of living in that shack with your poor mother and never having enough to eat?"

"We are not poor," Angelique said. The garden and the sea provided everything she and her mother needed. She never thought of being hungry.

"Wouldn't you prefer to live here? You can have everything you desire, and the slaves will take good care of you. You will live like a princess."

"And will you beat the slaves that care for me?" she asked, flushed with spite. He hesitated only a moment before he answered.

"Yes. If you try to run away."

She felt a wave of panic. He had tricked her. Her mother's dreams were all her father's lies. She clung to the chair to steady herself as she fought the heat rising in her and the tears. But her father seemed oblivious, and a twisted smile broke through his scowl when he looked at her.

"If only you could have seen yourself last night," he said in a voice that was almost reverent. "They were enthralled. I myself could not believe it. I really think you are a treasure—"

"You promised a school!" she cried. "And that I would have the life of a planter's daughter. You lied!"

Her father sighed deeply again and walked to the

window. "I am . . . a planter," he said, looking out.

"Where are your fields? Where is your fine house?"

He laughed then, a mirthless laugh, more like a cough. "Every morning I myself wake wondering exactly that." He ran his hand across his mouth and rubbed his eyes as if they pained him. "It's a wretched business," he said, as he leaned against the bars. He spoke now in a low voice as though he were talking to himself. "It's been a hard struggle, and several times I thought I was ruined. Last year the hurricane destroyed the crop. Twice the slaves have risen up and staged revolts—futile—but revolts nonetheless. There have been many . . . situations . . . well, let's just say they have their ways with poison. . . . Some kill themselves by eating dirt. Some escape, leap from the point into the sea, to be free. . . ." His voice trailed off as though he thought of something he could not say. Although she did not understand much of what he did say, Angelique felt a surge of pride that he was confiding in her.

"There are things you have no knowledge of," he said, still staring out. "The slaves are savage and bitter. We have tried to convert them to Christianity, but they have ancient practices brought with them from Africa. They worship gods who take on many forms, and are all superstition—by that, I mean they are not real—

"*Loas* are real," whispered Angelique softly.

Her father glanced at her quickly. "What do you know about them?" he said roughly.

"They come into your head."

He frowned, and placed his hand across his chest, staring at her.

"Do you know of a *loa* called . . . Erzulie?"

"The love goddess."

"Ah, so you do. Hm-m-m-m . . . amazing. I can only think your mother . . . well, there is a depraved sort of worship of Erzulie at the plantation. Many slaves there are devoted to her. You—how can I say this—they believe you are her human form—this goddess come to life."

"Me? But she is a woman with ·many husbands. . . ."

"I know—a kind of baby Erzulie—and that you appear by magic, late in the ceremony, and they bring you gifts, and you grant wishes. It's all foolishness, of course, I realize that. But as long as they believe you will appear to them, I think they will be content in their work and remain . . . tractable. . . ."

"Why would they believe such a thing?

"Because I told them it was so."

"But won't they find out?"

"That is the difficulty. In order to perform this ritual, you must remain hidden. If they were to see you, out in the world, or with your mother, they would know they had been tricked. They would be even more inclined to plot against me. And as for you, well, they would probably slit your throat. It's very important for them to believe you are . . . a spirit."

"But it's all lies. I am not a spirit."

He began to pace. He stopped in front of the mirror and glared at his image for a moment, grimacing, his eyes narrowing. He rubbed his hands over his face.

"Come and see yourself," he said, and grabbed her roughly, pulling her to the glass. The touch of his fingers made her shiver. "Is that girl you see there not . . . a goddess?"

Her hair had dried into masses of pale ringlets which even in the muted daylight shone about her face. Her features were delicate but overshadowed by her startling eyes, huge and gray. She felt trickles of sweat running down her body. She reached her hand to her throat and brushed her mother's charm, which still hung beneath her dress, and she trembled, for her father's face hovered behind hers. His eyes glittered as he stared at her.

"What you see," he said, breathing hard, "is a kind of beauty. And beauty is rare, but it is a frivolous talisman. You have a gift that is rarer still. There is something bewitching about you. You are lit by a fire I have never seen, and I need to use it for my own ends. If you refuse, I shall have to find a way to . . . force you."

She felt a wave of helplessness and she could hardly breathe. "But there was blood where I was on that platform. What happened there?"

Her father sighed again, reached into the pocket of his coat, and removed a flask. "It was nothing," he said. "They sacrificed a goat." He took a long swig of rum and sat heavily on the bench nearest the wall. His bones seemed to crumble inside his coat. Angelique felt a stab of pity for him.

"How long would I have to stay?" she asked.

He coughed and took out a large soiled handkerchief and spit into it. The answer was muffled as he wiped his lips. "Not for long," he muttered. "Only a little while." He stuffed the handkerchief in his vest pocket.

Her fingers squeezed the *ouanga* and she had a sudden flash of hope. "Can my mother come and live here, too?" Her father rose and began to pace again, his agitation evident.

"Your mother has her own life."

"Does she know?"

"Yes, of course she knows."

"She wants me to do this?" It was a moment before he answered, and when he did, the words he said turned her heart to stone.

"Your time with your mother has ended, Angelique."

"But why? Why do you say that?" Despair tumbled through her, and suddenly she began to feel stupid, as though the shock of his statement prevented her from comprehending.

"She knows it is your destiny. That she must agree to it."

"That's not true! She would never have sent me away if you had not lied to her! This is not what she wanted for me! This is not what you promised her!"

He leaned forward, grabbed her hair, and jerked her to him. She could feel his hot breath as he bent her face up to his. There was a desperation to his anger, as though vying emotions drove him close to madness, and his voice was furious and hard.

"Do not defy me, Angelique! You have seen my wrath and my method of punishment. The same fate awaits you if you insist on being stubborn!" He threw her away from him with such force that she fell to the floor. His eyes flew wide as he stared down at her, his fingertips quivering.

"Listen, my girl, and listen well! You are no longer your mother's daughter, or my daughter either, for that matter! Living in Martinique is hard for us all. Why should you escape these difficulties? Now . . ." and he took a deep breath and evened his tone ". . . I need you here. Desperately. You have a new role in life, which you can fulfill with pride. I suggest you do so. I beg you to do so."

He walked to the door and closed it behind him. She saw the bolt fall and heard the iron clang as it dropped into place.

chapter

6

She did not know how long she wept, and how long she slept afterward because she had been drugged. The slaves woke her and gave her food, and she slept again. There were times when the moon rose over her window and she crept to the casement and saw it glimmer on the curve of the sea. There were times when the sun streamed in and turned the stone wall beside her bed to a muted gold. But mostly she hovered in a gray twilight, too desolate to force herself awake when the opiates wore off, and more than willing to fall back into a fitful dozing rather than suffer the pain of separation from her mother.

There were times when the slaves carried her, or prodded her, down the tower stairway and into the sanctuary, where they placed her on the altar and she sat in a stupor while the men danced and chanted around her. Sometimes she felt she was not alone on the platform, that some unseen presence sat beside her. She remembered being dressed and adorned with chains and shells, like a statue decked out for a celebration. She did vaguely remember seeing her father, a look of displeasure on his face, but she was barely affected, having no idea why he would give her such a look.

There were times when her mind cleared, and she felt less like a ghost sitting in the chair by her bed, or in the bath, or before the mirror, but these moments floated past and disappeared in the flow of days.

She dreamed of the sea. She remembered how different it was beneath the surface, near the reef where she would swim for hours. She dreamed of the sea creatures hovering in their dappled world, heedless of changes in light or weather, rocked in the irregular rhythm by the dip and push of the surge, their colors gleaming, their bright eyes staring. She dreamed that she was one of them, her rounded body and limp legs forced into the shape of a fish. She would flutter gently as she slept.

She dreamed of her mother. In her dream, her mother was always moving, her body lithe as a palm tree danced by the wind. Different expressions flickered over her face, like sunlight sparkling on the surface of the lagoon. She was as happy as she was beautiful; love and deep joy flowed out of her. Angelique dreamed of the feel of her mother's hand stroking her, and her fingers combing through her hair.

There were days when they pinned flowers in her hair, blackened the rims of her eyes, and placed her in a curtained chaise which was carried by four black men through the slave quarters. Tucked in her tent, she could see gaping faces with eyes wide, wonder in them, as children and their mothers gazed upon her in amazement. On the floor of her carrier were bits of fruit and candy, which she tossed listlessly to the throng, vaguely aware of the commotion her presence caused. But she always watched the hubbub in a trance.

The ceremony became more familiar. She stayed hidden in the room behind the altar while the drums pounded and the chanting rose in pitch. At times even she was mesmerized by the timbre of the drumming, like the sound of thunder in the sky. After she appeared on the platform, the wild dancing became less frenzied, and the slaves became more gentle, as if their grief dissolved in her presence. The men surrounded her, their gleaming eyes fastened to her, and she felt clothed in their adoration. Often their hands would reach up and touch her feet or her fingers. It did not frighten her, for they softened when they touched her and became less angry.

There were times when she herself could not help being drawn into the frenzy. The odors of the candles, the perfumes, the sweating bodies, the smoke and flickering lights, the incessant drumming, sucked her into the spell being woven around her. She would feel pulses of heat that poured into her and out of her, and she would be aroused by her need to take into her body their betrayal along with her own. Then she would plunge into a well of despair. Her fists would clench, her form would grow rigid, tears would stream down her cheeks, and she would scream in agony, then, finally, go limp, fainting into grief.

*   *   *

Early one morning she woke with a clearer head than usual. She heard Thais lift the latch and enter stealthily with the tray of food. The dawnlight was glowing at the window, and the sky was lavender. Morning birdsong was faint in the air. Thais's dress was sprinkled with faded flowers, and her hair was tied in a blue scarf. She turned and smiled a little nervously, seeing that Angelique was awake.

"Well, chile, you wake up? Mornin', an' no rain be comin' down. You gone be eatin' now an' get a solid meal in you belly. Today you be goin' to town." Thais eyed her nervously. "Come along now, dearie. I gots to put you in the rose-colored dress. You like that? You a little mo' awake than usual, ain't ya? You be a good girl, now, y'hear?"

Angelique pushed the plate of food off the table, and it clattered to the floor. Thais gasped.

"Oh, Lord. What for you do that?"

"Because the food makes me sleep all the time!"

Thais looked guilty. "Well, now, that may be true, honey," she said. "But it be for the best. Frog when he sleepin' don' know the snake come. Now you gots to eat, or I be's in big trouble!"

"But I want to be awake. How long have I been sleeping? Weeks? Months?"

Thais sat beside Angelique and placed an arm around her. Her heavy body made the bed sag, and her soft face hung under her liquid eyes. A faint, but not unpleasant odor came from her, an odor of smoke and pig fat. She started to speak but, instead, threw her two hands in the air and looked up to the ceiling.

"Oh, Lordy . . . Lordy . . ." she exclaimed as she rubbed her rounded thighs and sighed.

Angelique suddenly remembered a dream from the night before. Her father had been in her room and he had come to her bed and stared down at her angrily. "She is too drugged!" he had said. "She must be more awake for the ceremony. She's like a zombie! Sleepwalking!"

"Why do you drug me?" she asked Thais.

"Listen, my little one, listen to me. What was I supposed to do? You's a crazy l'il thing, you is. You ran from Suzette. An' you scare the dickens out o' me." Then Thais's words came flying in a rush. "The Massa he be angry and hollerin' at me. He say, 'Why she so sleepy!' and I say, 'She gots to be, or she run off!' 'But she no good,' he say, 'she go droopin' that way, she not lookin' like the goddess, or nuthin'.' An I say, 'Well, you tell me to keep her clean an' not let her run off. You say she run off and you take off my hide.' An' he will, you understand. When you run down the stair that first night, he beat Suzette. Beat her bad. Oh, she hate you now. She got a hard heart for you, and you best look out when she be around. She say, 'Give her the nightshade, put the verbena in her juice!' So's I puts the powder, just a little, to keep you mindin'.'"

Thais was becoming more agitated. "But the Massa, he not happy either way, you see. He want you more spunky. The only reason you are awake is that las' night he tol' me not to give you none o' the drink! An' today, you gots to go into the town and Massa Bouchard wants you to be lively. So, we gots to watch

you so's you can't run off." Then she sighed and gave
Angelique a hug. "The truth is, I's glad to see you's
awake." She rose, moved to a walnut wardrobe, and
opened it. "Looky here at this pretty dress."

Thais took out a pale rose-colored frock from tissue paper and laid it on the bed. It was made of
watered silk taffeta, embroidered with leaves and
green trailing stems that curved around the neckline
and traveled to the hem of the skirt. The bodice was
lined with tiny pleats, and satin roses were worked
into the gathers of the sleeves. The dress was not new.
Little tucks at the waist and the faint traces of seams
let out and taken in again showed that the dress had
been worn by others. Still, it was the prettiest dress
Angelique had ever seen.

"You been to Carnival, honey?" said Thais, coax-
ing her out of her shift.

"Carnival? Oh, my mother takes me every year."

"Everyone, slaves, massas, all the mulattoes be
there. This dress come all the way from Paris, France.
What you think about that?"

The dress slid over Angelique's head with a
swishing sound, and the silk stuck to her skin. She
stroked the fabric with her fingers, drinking in the
rosy color. It was the first color of the morning.

Thais adorned her lavishly. She fastened golden
bracelets made of tiny bells around Angelique's wrists
and ankles. She arranged flowers, creamy frangipani
and snowy tuberose in her yellow hair. A scarlet
amaryllis fell into her lap. Angelique looked into the
center of the flower and studied its fragile petals, its

delicate inner parts. She touched the tip of the pistil, and the pollen dust settled on her finger.

She turned to Thais. "Please don't make me sleep anymore."

"Oh, Jesus, honey—"

"I want to be awake."

"Well, I hate it, yes I do. I be so sorry to see you like that, and you such a young thing. But you know seven year no wash the speckle off the guinea hen. You be goin' to run off, I jus' know."

"No, I won't run away."

"You promise me?"

"Yes. I promise."

"You do this for me."

"And for Erzulie."

"What about Erzulie, sugar?"

"I want the goddess to come to me. If she thinks I am pretending to be her, then maybe she will come into my head, and I will know her."

Thais stared at Angelique, a poignant look on her face, and then her expression softened. She drew the child into her arms and held her close.

"Maybe she will do that," she said in a low voice. "Maybe she get jealous and come. That would be jus' like her, too. And then you be fine."

After a long wagon ride, Angelique and Thais reached Saint-Pierre. The sounds of Carnival, flutes and whistles, drums and songs hummed in the air. There were throngs of people, not only slaves dressed in costume or in their hand-me-down finery, but also the *blanc*s, watching or taking part in the joyful celebration. Angelique was hidden in her carrier, and her father surprised her when he came to the curtain and looked in.

"Stay out of sight until nightfall and the worship begins," he said in a sharp voice.

The cavalcade began, and she was jostled by her bearers as though she were riding on top of a lame donkey. It was hot in the carrier and hard to breathe. She could hear drums, gourd rattles, and tambourines, shouting and singing and the sound of many footsteps. She longed to see it all. She clung to the bamboo structure of her crate and could not resist peeking through a tiny opening in the drapery. A great number of slaves surrounded her carrier, waving white flags and banners with the pierced red heart, and chanting, *"Erzulie, nain, nain."*

She saw a group of slaves, skulls painted on their black faces with a white paste. These living skeletons played flutes made of bamboo and danced with abandon, chanting a song to the god of the gate. One of these macabre creatures stuck his head into her carrier, and she drew back in fright, but he laughed rudely and danced away.

They passed the grand theater, and, on the beautiful curving steps, she glimpsed other slaves in white pantaloons, ruffled collars, and pointed hats. Their cheeks were painted with rosy rouge, their eyes circled in kohl. Then she saw something amazing: a handsome group of mulattoes decked out in what must have been the abandoned finery of landowners: European silk dresses and feathered hats, satin shoes with bows and striped waistcoats, and, most shocking of all, glittering jewels. She could not imagine who they were, but they were as exquisite as a painting come to life.

Deep drums and shouts announced another crowd of white-robed figures carrying a much larger platform than hers. Teetering on the top of the platform was a large effigy, fashioned out of straw, but clothed in black. His huge face was painted yellow, and three red horns protruded from his head. He was the King of the Carnival, and she remembered how frightened she had been the first time she had seen this paper giant with his toothy grin.

When they reached the part of the town closest to the wharf, they turned down the road toward the woods. She peered out at the docks, where groups of fishermen and sailors were coming to join the fete. There was a tall ship in the harbor flying a flag she had never seen, with red-and-white stripes and white stars on a field of blue, and near the largest warehouse she saw a group of soldiers in scarlet jackets. They shouted and dashed to catch the parade. She tried to follow them as they were caught in the crowd, and she was reminded of a school of red fish feeding in the current, moving as one creature, scattering then regathering as they wove the seaweed with their bright forms. The soldiers thrilled her, and she leaned out farther not to miss the flash of black boots and white waistbands, or the gleam of brass buttons and silver swords.

The platform carrying the giant effigy wobbled down the road in front of her. The carriers careened back and forth in a swaying motion, letting the clumsy figure fall perilously close to the ground before right-ing it again, and shouting back and forth to confuse and discourage evil spirits. Now the soldiers, slapping and shoving one another, ran behind it, and called out, "Ah-h-h-h-h-h . . ." each time the figure tilted. Angelique realized as she drew closer that the militia were actually teenage boys. Their boisterous banter betrayed their ages, and she saw several loose shirttails and muddy breeches. She longed to keep watching them, but she feared her father's wrath and sank back into her dark casement and pulled her curtain closed.

When she felt the chaise set down on the ground, she dared to peek out again. The whole procession had entered the forest, and they were now in a large clearing with an enormous bonfire ready at its center. Her enclosure was set back in the trees, and Angelique ached to descend from the carrier; it was cruel torture that she must remain out of sight. At least there was so much happening that she was not the only attraction, she thought.

Torches lit on tall posts flamed in front of the dark trees. Drums were set up before the bonfire, and several drummers began to beat out their infectious rhythms, booming, brittle, or staccato.

Sudden cheers rang out from a group of men, and she strained to see what caused their excitement. In their midst, two rust-scarlet cocks leapt and fluttered, their bloody talons slashing the air. A cockfight! She leaned farther out and realized her entourage had wandered off. Only Thais was drawing a white sheet over four poles to make her altar. Her father was nowhere in sight.

She saw the soldiers again only a short distance away. One was tall and slim, with a trim mustache and a small beard. He seemed older, an officer, for his uniform was in good repair and a sword hung at his side. The others huddled near him, crying out in disbelief or amazement at all they saw. She overheard them call him by the name Jeremiah, and realized he was in charge of this unruly gang. He smiled and nodded, cupping his chin in his hand and treating the boys with familiarity. One handsome boy in particular seemed a closer companion than the others; she saw the officer grin at the youth and tousle his curly hair.

Then the two turned and looked toward her carrier, and the boy stared at her with great curiosity. He made a move to approach, but the officer must have called him back because he suddenly turned, and she heard, "Here, here, you scoundrel! Come away from there!" She was surprised to hear English spoken.

She pulled the curtain open a little more. The young man was standing by the officer, and speaking quietly with him, nodding in her direction. The older man shook his head vehemently and put an arm about the boy's shoulder, leading him away. She was still watching when the young man looked back, and this time he caught her eye. For an instant he remained still, gazing at her with a sense of amazement. Then he did a very odd thing. He pursed his lips and, lifting his chin, kissed the air in her direction.

At that moment the torch was laid to the bonfire,

which erupted in fire, flooding the giant effigy with flame. The garish yellow face seemed to glow from within, the eyes like coals, the mouth slowly opening in a diabolical grin. Leaping bodies waving torches tumbled into the circle, chanting their hypnotic song, glowing limbs undulating with the drums. Angelique pulled the curtain shut and closed her eyes until the cadence entered her body and the throbbing was the beat of her own heart.

"Hallo in there."

She started. The whisper was near, just outside the drape, but it was a boy's voice, teasing and intimate. She shrank back at the sound, pulling herself into the corner. She waited, afraid to breathe, only to see the curtain slowly part as a shaft of light fell on her face. She snatched the curtain closed, but in a moment the drapery inched open again, and this time she did not move.

"Hallo . . ." he whispered. "I just want to look at you." He was standing quite close to her, an impudent expression on his face. It was a wonderful face, finely formed, with piercing black eyes, strong brows, and a scattering of freckles across his nose.

"I've never seen a real goddess," he said.

She was terrified that her father would return at any moment, and she stared at the boy, not knowing what to do. He was smiling, and his teeth were very white, and there was just the hint of a downy mustache on his upper lip. Brown curls tinged with gold fell loosely on his forehead, and his dark eyes flicked over her face as though he were looking at something wondrous. Suddenly he grinned a grin that would have been wicked if it had not been so mischievous. Finally she found her voice and whispered in English, "What do you want?"

"Why to talk to you, of course. What do you think?"

"You are not allowed to speak to the goddess."

"But you aren't a real goddess, are you?"

Heat rose to her face, and her fingertips tingled. His words made her angry.

"Yes, I am! I am Erzulie, the goddess of love."

He threw back his head and laughed. "What a jolly good prank! Better than the man who could make fire! Jeremiah said you were dangerous, that I should not come near you. So naturally, I couldn't resist. But, look at you. You wouldn't harm a rabbit."

"Why don't you believe me?"

"Why? Because I can see in an instant, even with the paint around your eyes, that you are a real girl, flesh and blood. And you are such a dazzling creature that I don't mind in the least. Ah! What a great adventure!"

"Go away!" she wailed, but it was more of a sob caught in her throat. He was the first person, other than Thais and her father, to speak to her in such a long time, and he was so familiar and so brash, that her throat tightened until the muscles in her neck hurt.

At her distress, his smile faded instantly, and a look of grave concern shadowed his face.

"Oh, I'm so very sorry. I didn't mean to frighten you. I was the one who was supposed to be afraid! Oh, come, come, please don't cry. You really mustn't."

But the tears fell onto her cheeks, and she was helpless to stop them as she tried to swallow but could not get past the choking lump in her throat.

Before she knew what was happening, the boy had climbed into her carrier and pulled the curtain closed. For a moment it was dark, and she sat paralyzed, aware only that his warm body was very near and that he smelled of the sea. Then she could see his face even closer than before, and he frowned and spoke haltingly.

"I—I—is it because I am a soldier? You mustn't mind this silly uniform. It's only from my school. Perhaps you think I meant to insult you. Well, it's true, I did. And I'm the very devil." He smiled at her again, and, taking the end of his shirt cuff in his fingers, he dabbed at her cheeks. Finishing that, he stared at her, newly dazed. "Why, your eyes are the color of cornflowers. And they are so big and worried. I suppose you think we came to fight the French and conquer your island."

"Are . . . you from England?" she said in a small voice."

"No. New England, silly! The fine state of Massachusetts. I came with my schoolmates on a seagoing excursion, to learn all about sailing and boats. I wanted to go to Africa, but my father refused permission. He's afraid of the middle passage, you see."

"And . . . did you learn anything?" she asked in a small voice.

"Oh, yes. That sailing is the hardest kind of labor, and tedious besides, crashing on the waves all through the night. I was seasick the entire time. Jeremiah brought us to the islands, but only the English ones of course. We heard there was Carnival here at Martinique. I begged him that we might be allowed to come. And I'm very glad we did, because I was able to see you, and . . ." He lost himself a moment in looking at her, then he blurted out, "I say! Has your volcano ever erupted? What is its name? Piley, or Paley?"

Angelique, amazed by his presence, and drowning in the unexpected flow of words, realized he was waiting for a reply.

"Pelée?" she said. "No . . . but, when the god is . . . awakened, he turns over, and . . . Pelée rumbles and spits fire!"

"Oh, I should love to see that! Wouldn't it be fun? Like Vesuvius! Everyone buried in lava, caught instantly in the act of whatever they were doing—and preserved forever—picking bananas, or sweeping the floor, or using the chamber pot!"

He laughed, delighted at his own joke, and Angelique smiled a little because she thought of Thais frozen in stone in that very position. The boy stared at her again.

"Would you like to see my treasure?" he said. He reached into his top breast pocket and withdrew a small sack. "There is a ship in the harbor at Saint Thomas that belongs to the Great Mogul from India and carries women! And silks embroidered with gold! My uncle, Jeremiah, the lucky codger, has gone aboard. And, this . . . is what they have in India." He leaned closer and poured a small handful of loose jewels into her lap, brilliant colors, apple green, amethyst, amber, and deep red. "He gave this lot to me. What do you think?"

Angelique gasped at the jewels and gazed at the boy in total wonderment.

"Look at this one," he said. "It's called a moon-stone. See?" He took her hand and placed a pale white stone in her palm. "The moon is captured there." And he rocked the stone slightly so that she could see the bright flash. "Do you see it?"

"Oh, yes!" She looked at him, astonished, then back at the stone.

He folded her fingers around it. "It's for you," he said, "to remember me by." And then he leaned in and kissed her softly on the cheek.

"Barnabas! Are you in there?"

The boy cocked his eyes at her and placed a finger across his lips.

"Come out of there this minute!" came a furious voice.

The boy scooped his jewels from her skirt, grinning at her as he stuffed them back in the sack. Then he tumbled head-over-heels backward out of the chaise and fell onto the ground. He was jerked rudely up by the man called Jeremiah and set on his feet.

"My God, Barnabas! Are you a complete imbecile?" His voice was more fearful than harsh. His eyes flew to Angelique's face, and he frowned and looked anxiously about him, before railing at the boy in a fierce whisper. "I told you how dangerous it was! If they caught you, they would kill you and think nothing of it. You would never see it coming. A puff of invisible dust! And that would be the end of you."

Barnabas winked at Angelique to show how absurd he believed this threat to be. But Jeremiah took him by the collar and practically pulled him off his feet. "Come along, young man. Back to the ship with you before I lose my temper." Angelique could hear their voices fade as they moved away. "How could you do such a foolish thing? Good Lord, Barnabas, don't you know you are in my charge? My brother would see me shot!"

And the last words she heard were the boy's. "They've made her into a silly idol, and she's only a little girl. What will become of her?"

She held the moonstone in her fist for a long time, and it was sticky with sweat before she was able to open her fingers and look at it again. She tipped it until its moon danced. Quickly she reached for the *ouanga* and pulled it loose from her neck. She untied the knot and placed the moonstone beside the tiny snake's skull. Then she tied it all up again.

Late that night, when the ceremony of Erzulie began at last, she stood in her rose-colored gown, with her golden hair falling about her. While thousands of candles starred the darkness, and the slaves sang to her and laid their powdered gifts at her feet, she wondered whether he was there and imagined that she saw him, standing behind the swaying crowd, watching her with his merry eyes, the boy whose name was Barnabas.

chapter

7

B arnabas set the journal down in absolute astonishment.

   He remembered well his first trip to the
islands. He had gone with Jeremiah when he was a
young boy—Jeremiah whom he adored, and who had
betrayed him in the end. He recalled, in a jumble of
images and colors, the creaking merchant ship, the
lush green islands, the fragrant, caressing air. He could
still picture the Carnival in Martinique, seeing magic
performed for the first time and—it seemed incredible—could it possibly be? The pagan creature hidden
in her chariot—the "living goddess," whom he had
found so fascinating, and so poignant—was Angelique?
He remembered now that the whole journey home he
had imagined himself to be in love with her.

   But his sharpest memory was his discovery on his
return to America. The decks of his father's ships
were crowded with their contracted cargo, barrels of
rum. One night on the voyage back to Boston, he and
his classmates had decided to peg one barrel and

drink like real sailors, tasting the golden elixir that poured fortunes into his father's pockets. That was the night when, after the others had fallen asleep, and his head reeled with rum, he had crept beneath the decks. Down in the wet and shuddering darkness, he had seen dozens of slaves crammed together and moaning, their black bodies chained together.

A soft tap on the door broke his reverie. It was Julia. Quickly, he hid the journal beneath the other books on his desk and rose to greet her as she opened the door.

"Let us we be off to Collinsport," she said briskly. "I've brought the car around."

"Yes, of course. Good of you to come."

She hesitated, watching him, sensing something in his manner.

"Are you all right, Barnabas?"

"Of course I am. What do you think?" He was uncharacteristically gruff, which surprised them both.

"I only thought, perhaps, we should make it some other day."

"But we must go back by the Old House. Check on the wreckers. They must be fairly far along by now," Barnabas insisted.

"I can do that for you, if you would like."

"Oh, for heaven's sake, don't be so solicitous, Julia. I'm really rather tired of being pampered. And seeing that anxious look on your face. It's most unbecoming."

"I'm sorry. . . ." She sucked in her breath, but held her tongue. Barnabas reached for his jacket and, in doing so, knocked the books onto the floor. The diary fell among them, and Julia frowned.

"You haven't been reading that, have you?"

"No! Well, I . . . glanced through it. It's really not very interesting."

"Barnabas, for the love of God, give it to me. It has already soured your mood and made you irritable—"

"Not in the least, my dear. Don't be absurd. I'm not at all irritable, as you say. And I must insist you leave off this nattering. It's getting on my nerves. As for the diary, I intend to burn it as soon as I return."

"I see." She took a breath. "As you burned the Old House?"

"What . . . ?"

"Barnabas, how else could the fire have started?"

"Julia, I do believe you have lost your senses."

Julia hesitated a moment, staring into Barnabas's eyes, before she turned away. "Forgive me. I don't know what possessed me to say such a thing. Shall we go?"

Roger droned on and on. Barnabas realized he was a captive audience of one at a lecture, and that Roger was in sore need of a partner and an admirer. He was a man of spiteful opinions and fierce energy, philosophizing, moralizing, content to pursue his topic without response. Barnabas stared at the aristocratic face of his cousin with its finely chiseled features, and he listened to his mellifluous tones, but in truth he felt terribly weary as Roger contemplated business ventures, capital, and investments.

Barnabas knew he should value any opportunities Roger presented. Why did his passions remain unstirred? Was it a symptom of his cure?

His eyes drifted to the window, where even in the manicured landscaping outside Roger's waterfront office, spring had strewn her lavish bounty. Beside the water, a magnificent cherry tree stood heavy with blossoms, its black branches sleeved in tissues of pink. The two opposing textures, one like jagged coal, and the other as delicate as the dawn, caused him a peculiar spasm of depression.

Bees had found the flowers, and they were mad with buzzing, thousands of them, drunken with nectar, and their humming filled his brain with a dull roar. He suddenly felt terribly lonely, and with a start, he recognized an old yearning: He wished he were in love.

He forced himself to listen to Roger.

"Now that you have recovered, Barnabas, I must tell you how anxious I am for you to come on board. We have several, what would you say, 'irons in the fire,' and a few broad-reaching involvements to be made more secure. Who is to do it, if not you? Carolyn would be a first-rate executive, if she so chose. However, unfortunately, she still shows no interest. She is bored with trading and feels, I'm sorry to say, that the textile mills are . . . ahem . . . unsanitary and 'unfair to the workers.' Of all the absurd positions to take. Collins Enterprises! David shows some promise, and one hopes that will be his field when he matures, if he ever matures. At any rate, you would do well to investigate all the Collins's ventures and not take things for granted. Times change. Carolyn and David must be provided for; investments don't just happen, they require planning and risk. So, what did you have in mind?"

Barnabas was jarred by the question. "What do you mean?"

"Why, to do, Barnabas, to do? Surely you don't intend to live off your fortune, or the Collins family fortune . . . such as it is."

"I—well, I thought, naturally, to become a member of the board, make some contribution on the executive level—"

"What sort of contribution?" Roger persisted.

"I beg your pardon?"

"What unique talents do you feel you possess? You have traveled a great deal, I know. What was your profession, actually, in London? The law?"

"I—well—business, I suppose. As a matter of fact, I have not needed to toil on a daily basis. There is a substantial amount of property," Barnabas explained.

"Land?"

"No . . . jewelry, antiques, furnishings . . ."

"Have you any notion of how quickly such objects, however precious, lose value. Have you made investments?"

"Uh . . . yes, of course." Suddenly Barnabas felt annoyed. "Roger, I resent the implication that I would not carry my weight. I have a large fortune which rests in England, and have no intention of living off of you, as you say."

"Well, now, my boy, calm down. I don't mean to

pressure you, but nothing like a new involvement to get the blood flowing, if you get my meaning. What do you say?"

"To what?" Barnabas asked.

"To a new involvement. I declare, Barnabas, do I even have your attention?"

"Sorry, Roger. My mind was wandering. Perhaps I should return to the Old House and see whether the wreckers have come. They had still not arrived at noon—"

"Oh, hang the wreckers. Now listen, Barnabas. Here's a word for you. *Tourism!* Great profits to be made in tourism, you know, they come in hordes— from Germany, the Orient . . . everyone wants to see the world!"

Barnabas began to wonder if the interview was ever going to end, for Roger showed no sign of slowing down.

"Travel is now the great middle-class occupation. Overweight Midwesterners in Bermuda shorts, or Japanese businessmen with expensive cameras—no sensitivity for the culture, without a clue about history, collecting countries as they would bottle caps or baseball cards! Nevertheless, it's a well to be tapped. What would you say to a four-star hotel! A first-class resort!"

Roger paused. Barnabas felt his head swimming from the onslaught of words. Roger lowered his voice and spoke conspiratorially. "We still, as you may or may not know, have property in the Caribbean. A sugar plantation fallen to wrack and ruin, but up on a cliff with a spectacular view, I'm told, of the sea."

Barnabas was jolted by the word: *Caribbean.*
"Really?" he asked. "Where?"

"Why, in Martinique, of course, French West
Indies. We once traded sugar there. We had ships, lost
them all after the revolution. The estate came into the
Collins family in the late eighteenth century and
nothing has ever been done with it. It was purchased,
I believe, by one of our illustrious ancestors for his
bride-to-be. The marriage never took place, I'm sorry
to say. She died mysteriously. But, we still have title to
the land. All the way back to the king of France!"

"And nothing has ever been done with it? Why is
that?" Barnabas asked, his attention fully on Roger
now.

"Politics, my dear man, politics. And lack of workers. But, I've just received carte blanche from the
French government. They welcome such an endeavor.
So, we need someone to go there, arrange for an archi-
tect, a contractor, find laborers, and . . . naturally, I
thought of you!"

"Uncle, I don't think I could take on such a mon-
umental task—"

"Come now, Barnabas! Mustn't be a slacker, my
boy! I can see you have a sense of these things! A love
of fine furnishings, as you say—antiques! Imagine it!
A grand hotel! You could travel to Europe, purchase
the decorative arts—rebuild it from the ground up—
breathe new life—apparently there are statues, parapets—"

There was a knock at the door, and Julia burst in
breathlessly. Her face was grave with concern. "Roger!

Barnabas! There's been a dreadful accident. On the road to Collinwood. Two men have been killed!"

Julia gripped the steering wheel as they drove down the road toward the Old House, searching for some sign of the accident. The sun was low in the sky, and they were driving into its glare.

"It shouldn't be much farther," she said, her voice shaking. "The police said it was before the crossroads, just past the covered bridge. In the stretch up ahead, don't you think?"

Barnabas squinted, then raised his hand to his forehead, shielding his eyes from the glare. "I can't help but feel that this is somehow my fault," he muttered.

"Barnabas, that's absurd."

"I know, but I arranged for the demolition and—"

"Goodness! I can't see a thing!" she cried as she braked the car almost to a stop. The dust on the windshield flared in the setting sun, obscuring the road. It was as if they were enveloped in a cloud of fire, golden haze gilding the glass. They inched forward, and, once the glare faded, they saw the wreck.

There were two police cars with their red lights twirling, along with an ambulance. Several policemen were huddled beside the embankment of the river. Julia stopped the car, and she and Barnabas got out.

The flatbed truck which had been carrying the bulldozer was upside down in the river, its wheels in the air, looking like a dead elephant. The cab was a blackened hulk, smashed flat; only the river had prevented the fire from spreading when the gas tank exploded. The tractor was lying on its side in the bushes, its wheels twisted and its bucket completely separated, tossed beyond the trees, as if it had been a boy's toy discarded in a sandbox.

"When did it happen?" Barnabas asked.

"Early this morning," said Julia. "The police didn't discover anything until an hour ago, but the burned metal was already cold to the touch."

"You mean we drove right by them today on our way to town and saw nothing?"

"How could we have seen it? The bridge is in the way. They were in the riverbed." She paused. "We couldn't have saved them, Barnabas."

"How do you know? We could have tried to do something." He looked down at the truck. "Poor bastards. What a waste!"

He stared dully at the two dead men. They had never made it to the Old House. Something had stopped them along the road, something he should have known would be there. One body was being loaded on a stretcher, but it was difficult for the paramedics in the rocky riverbed, and they stumbled with the weight. The other victim was still in the upside-down cab, his blackened face just visible, his mouth hanging open in a silent scream.

Barnabas had begged leave to retire early. Dinner had been a wretched affair, and he had felt only irritation with his family, their hypocritical concern for the men who had been killed in the accident. Elizabeth had called it a "tragedy," surely a misconception, for the drivers had been innocents, hired to perform a service, and they had carried no hubris. Any guilt was his own guilt.

The pall that hung over the family was the same unspoken sense of destiny and inevitability that Barnabas had experienced in other generations. Little was discussed, no sense of outrage or search for rational explanations heated the conversation. What was said was a set of lukewarm euphemisms about death; all were painfully conscious of what was not said: The family carried a curse. Misfortune came, and had always come, relentlessly and predictably. The Collins family kept itself apart from the community, kept its secrets buried away, and never knew release from Fate's avenging hand.

Out of sheer boredom he had withdrawn from the superficial discussion at the table, distracted with thoughts of his upcoming marriage.

Several days earlier, before this latest set of events, Julia had accepted his proposal with delight. They would set a date soon and planned a honeymoon in Singapore, where Julia knew of rare blood elixirs which she felt might preserve Barnabas's cure. Still, he was troubled by thoughts of sexual consummation. He had embraced Julia affectionately many times, held her hand as they talked, even kissed her lightly on the lips in greeting or parting. But he had never really kissed her—with passion. Sometimes he could feel her restlessness when they were alone together, an urgency to her response when he hugged her good night, an unspoken signal in her gaze. Soon, he must make love to her.

He did not feel precisely reluctant, although his performance as a lover gave him some concern. As a vampire, arousal had been a response to quite different cues, and he felt out of practice. Still, Julia was so clever, and so supportive, she was certain to ease that transition as well. He was, he told himself, still a young man, vigorous and hungry for life. He liked her lithe body, with its jaunty step and quick movements. Energy—passion—would return, he felt certain. He was more like an addict recovering from the insidious drugs which had shaped his personality for so long; now he would have to rediscover what he once had been without them.

He closed the door to his room, relieved to be alone at last. The books lay on the floor where they had fallen earlier. He lit the lamp and reached for the journal. Only when he opened the pages to search for his place did he relax. He realized that he had been longing to return to the diary ever since he had set it down.

He found himself reading a list of magical spells, charms, and notes for what seemed to be African ceremonies.

> Cult des Morts *of a* papaloi *priest*
> > *To call up the spirits*
> > *a crossroad at midnight*
> > *a candle made from honey wax and a swallow's liver*
> > *a loaded gun with earth placed upon the shot*

The spell is:

"Upon the thunder's rumbling may all the Kings of the Earth kneel down."

To put a woman to sleep that you may know her secrets

   a toad killed on a Friday

   place the head the heart and the liver upon her left breast

   Whisper:

   "Oh, my love, my love, my very love, hover near me, whisper to me."

To call up the Dead—Prise du Mort

   a bag of wild acacia

   a wooden cross and two stones

   four white candles—Signaler at four points

   A gun fully loaded

   Go to the grave at midnight and make this appeal:

   "Out from Pelée's fires must thou come because I need thee sorely."

When the dead appears do not run away but take three steps backward and sprinkle perfume on the ground between you.

Erzulie's needs:

   An enamel basin, soap in its wrapper, an embroidered towel.

   Sugared sweets, perfumes, and a white handkerchief.

Three wedding bands and necklaces of gold
and pearls.
The sky sound and thunder. Rain.

Things needed for a spell:
the tongue of a bird
the heart of a toad
honey wax or tallow
a mortar and pestle
a gun with shells

Needed to cast a spell over another:
clothing worn close to the skin
any growing hair
blood
nail clippings or teeth
excrement, semen, blood

Which, when eaten, instills desirable qualities:
The heart—courage
The liver—cunning and immunity to knives
The brain—accuracy in aim
The eyes—foreknowledge
Flesh of a child—immortality

chapter

8

Angelique missed the sea so much she thought her body would break in two. The bite to her life was gone: the cold plunge in the morning, the sizzling sand at noon, the coral's scrape, the sting of the jellyfish. She was shrouded in the thick dullness of gray walls and heavy air, hot and damp inside the tower. Without the breeze from the sea to freshen it, the air was like flesh, so palpable and smothering that her skin was always clammy.

Months passed, and the loneliness of her life became suffocating, then deadening. She filled the long hours of the day staring out the three barred windows. Set deep within the walls, each of the narrow slits had a wide sill where she could crawl up and press her face against the grate.

One window looked out upon the road back to Saint-Pierre. She tortured herself with thoughts of the long journey and how she had fallen to sleep so trustingly on her father's shoulder. She wondered if she could find her way home if she did somehow discover a way beyond the walls.

Another window looked over the cliffs that fell to the sea. She often thought of Barnabas and wondered whether he had sailed safely home. She could hear the waves crashing on the rocks, but she could not see the surf or shoreline, only the broad expanse of the great deep, with its changing shades of slate and indigo.

A third window framed a view of the inner courtyard, and it was here that she kept her vigil. If she rose early, she could see the slaves turned out of their quarters in groups of thirty or forty to toil in the cane, dragging their tired bodies over the hill before the overseer's whip. The dog-drivers shouted and cursed so loudly that even from such a distance, she could hear their threats. Her father's new cane fields lay spread out against the horizon, straggly and sparse, green in some plots, tasseled in others. She wondered if his crop would be a good one and whether this would make him any kinder to her.

Within the courtyard, she could watch the comings and goings of the slaves who cared for her, Thais and Suzette, and others who brought supplies, food, and flowers. The two women hung out wash, as her mother had done. They also fed and watered the animals used for the sacrifice: white chickens, goats, and sometimes a dog. From this window she could also see the broad lattice arms of the tattered windmill, groaning in its feeble efforts to spin. Below, scattered about the courtyard, were wooden troughs for the cane juice and a shed for the kettles, all abandoned. She thought it must have been many years since this was a fully working plantation.

Angelique had one occupation that consumed more and more of her thoughts. Each time a ceremony was held in the chapel, she was kept in the dark room behind the altar. Long frightened hours listening to the drums had given way to curiosity and then discovery. She was allowed a candle so that she could abide the darkness, and with that faint light she began to inspect the grimy shelves cluttered with amazing paraphernalia.

There were many clay pots tied and sealed with wax. There were also several large sacks of white powder, which seemed to be a mixture of cornmeal and ashes. She found enamel bowls, pitchers, and platters; an assortment of daggers, machetes, cane blades, and scalpels of several sizes; tins of powders, jars of salves, and boxes of herbs; little sacks of sea urchin needles, lobsters' feelers, and octopus beaks; piles of grasshoppers, millipedes, and various insects she didn't recognize; glass jars with rubbery pieces of flesh floating in water, trailing bits of limp skin; embryos of small animals; claws and pincers of giant beetles; dried toads, lizards, scorpions, and snakes. Some of the objects she had seen in her mother's possession, but most were unfamiliar and fascinating, and she combed this macabre collection as though she were sorting through a queen's treasure.

Inside a carved wooden box, she found, wrapped in silk, a beautiful kris, encrusted with bright-colored stones and jewels, its blade as sharp as a razor. She held it in her hand, turning it over in wonder, before she carefully wrapped it up again.

The most exciting discovery of all was a pile of books stacked in the corner. Most were moldy, thick with dust, the pages glued together from dankness. Some contained strange designs she could not decipher: odd circular pictures, crosses and curls drawn in fine calligraphy. Others were ledgers with lists of property bought and sold—slaves, kegs of rum, barrels of sugar—with all the numbers added and subtracted in columns. She amused herself by searching for mistakes in the addition.

But there was one book that was more precious than all the rest. It was leather-bound, gilt-edged and tied with a cord, and when she opened it she found long descriptions of ceremonies, chants, and songs.

The chants were written in numerous hands, so the whole must have been collected over time. Some were in Spanish, others in French, and a great many were in African dialects, with English words or Christian phrases tossed in here and there, all very difficult to decipher.

The African words would be repeated many times, naming the *loa* who was to perform the magic. The ceremonies were endlessly fascinating, and she silently read the words over and over, listening to the sounds in her mind. She also found quill pens and ink in jars, still usable. Since the book was heavy and the pages large and stained, she began to copy certain spells in her journal, mostly for amusement, the better to read them over in her room.

Thais always slept in the tower with Angelique, on a wooden bench beside the wall, but after a time the slave became more trusting, or perhaps less vigilant, and the door to the room was sometimes left unlocked for part of the day. When the slaves were off on errands and the castle deserted, Thais would allow Angelique to come down the stairway as long as she remained within the inner courtyard. Like a caged cat, she began to explore the perimeter of her prison.

The outer door to the chapel was always bolted, and the grounds were surrounded by the wall and the moat. One entire side of the castle rose high above cliffs, with sheer walls that fell away to the sea. Angelique easily rediscovered the underground tunnel to the chapel where she had gone the first day. There was a narrow ledge beside the water, and she was able to climb in secretly, staying dry, and read from the book or copy more pages. Finally, she smuggled the heavy volume up to her room and kept it hidden under her bed. After that, when she studied the book or wrote in her journal, she kept watch at the window facing the courtyard.

One day when she was sitting at the window, she saw a new slave girl come out of the kitchen. She was about the same age as Angelique, slender as a palm shoot, and she had glowing copper skin. She appeared with a large bucket and drew water from the well. Then she poured the water over one courtyard flagstone, got down on her knees, and began to scour it with crushed cane stalks, singing a simple African song in a high, thin voice.

Angelique watched the slave girl intently, her narrow back leaning over her task, her sharp elbows sticking out of her ragged dress, and her rounded pink heels turned to the sky. After a few moments, the girl lifted her head and watched a frigate bird flying under the clouds until it was a tiny speck and disappeared from view. Then she sat back on her haunches with a sigh, and made the print of her hand on the stone as the water dried. She began to slap the stone in quick little rhythms as though the paver were a drum. This occupied her for several minutes until a butterfly circled her head and she leapt up and chased it around the yard, an action that led her to dance. She began to skip and twirl, her small arms over her head, and her perfect limbs burnished with gold.

"Chloe!"

The shout from Suzette returned the girl to her flat-footed, gawky self, and she crouched and began to scrub once more, but not for long. The next bucket she raised from the well spilled over her feet, and she splashed in the puddle until it spread under the bread oven scaring out a green lizard. At once she was down on her hands and knees, creeping up on it, and poking it with a finger until it skittered away. Angelique's heart ached to become her friend.

Angelique realized that Chloe must be sleeping in the kitchen. Early in the morning she would be there, drawing water, singing her monotonous little song. Then she would spend the day washing the stones, or scrubbing pots from the fire. Some days she stayed inside, perhaps helping with the food, but she almost always appeared in the evening to sit on a step, eat her bowl of soup, bat mosquitoes from her eyes, and watch the sun go down over the edge of the sea.

One morning when the girl was at the well, Angelique took a bun from her breakfast tray and, stretching her arm as far as she could through the bars, tossed it to the ground. It landed at Chloe's feet, and she dropped the bucket chain, jumped back, and looked up quickly, squinting.

"What's that! Is the sky fallin'?" she cried. Then, glancing back at the kitchen to make sure no one saw her, she ran and retrieved the cake, brushed it off, and took a bite. A smile spread across her face, and she squinted again, this time toward Angelique's window. Lifting her hand, she gave a quick little wave.

That evening Angelique decided she would wait until Thais was asleep and slip down to the kitchen. She hid a good part of her dinner in a cloth. Then she lay awake far into the night, until the stars were as bright as millions of fireflies, and Thais was snoring. The windmill was creaking more than ever, blurring all other sounds, even the pounding of her heart, when Angelique lifted the latch to her door and slipped into the stairway. She was glad there was no moon.

The girl was curled up on a pallet under a huge chopping block in the dark kitchen. The minute Angelique appeared at the door, she woke, sat up, rubbed her eyes, and stared, knowing better than to move or make a sound.

"Chloe . . ." Angelique whispered. The girl shrank back against the wall and pulled her legs up to her chest. "Don't be afraid. I only—"

"Esprit!" Chloe whispered.

"What? No. I am not a spirit."

"*Mystère. . . ! Mystère!*" Chloe hissed, her eyes wide with fear.

"Don't be afraid," said Angelique softly. "I won't hurt you. Look at me. I'm real." Chloe only pulled herself more into a ball and whispered harshly.

"Don't you come near me! Suzette said I must never, ever, talk to you, or . . . you will eat me!"

"No! I won't eat you. I only want to . . . to . . . ."

"Erzulie! If you touch me, I will die!"

Angelique hesitated, then sat down beside the chopping block a little apart from Chloe. She waited a minute or two, listening to their breathing, then, opening her cloth, took out a piece of roasted pork and began to nibble it. She could feel Chloe's eyes on her.

After she had chewed for several minutes, she slid a piece of the meat over to the other girl. "I brought you something," she said. Chloe hesitated, then snatched it up. Both of them ate without speaking, sucking on the fatty bones, and making little slurping noises, until each became aware of her vulgar sounds and began to giggle. Angelique, afraid they would be discovered, put her hand over the girl's mouth and bit on her own fingers to stop herself, but they shook with sputtering and choking, until they both ached from trying to stifle their laughter.

"Your name is Chloe, isn't it?" Angelique whispered. The girl hesitated a moment, then nodded.

"Mine is Angelique."

"I know you. You lives in the tower." They sat in silence for another moment.

"How old are you?" Angelique asked.

"I dunno. Ten, maybe."

"Stand up."

Chloe rose warily, and they stood back to back. Angelique reached up and patted their two heads. "I think you're only nine," she decided, feeling superior. "But that's good."

"What you mean, good?"

"We can be friends. Even though I am almost eleven."

"Oh, no, I can't be your friend. I can't play with you at all!" Chloe's eyes grew wide with fear.

"Don't be silly. We'll meet at night when everyone is asleep. Don't you see? I have no one to talk to, and I have been here more than a year."

"Wha' for you pick me?"

"Oh, Chloe, I wished for a friend. I've been so lonely, and now you've come, and I'm so glad."

Chloe smiled a little to herself. "I likes the meat a whole lots," she said softly.

"Good. I have to go back before Thais wakes up."

"Oh, Lord. Go. Go now. Hurry!"

"But I'll come again tomorrow. I'll bring you some more dinner. And you can bring me . . . some mud."

"Some what?"

"Some mud. So we can make something." Angelique gave her a little hug, and dashed back across the dark courtyard.

The next night Angelique and Chloe crept quietly through the underground passageway to the little room behind the altar. Chloe brought clay from the riverbed. They lit a candle, and they whispered and laughed together for hours, making tiny lizards and turtles, cows and chickens and goats.

After that night, the room became their secret chamber. They created the whole plantation out of clay, with huts for the slaves made from tiny sticks and grass for roofs. They fashioned the tower and the great house and the castle walls. Soon there were small slave figures set at tasks, planting cane or pounding the stalks.

Every night, Chloe brought more clay as well as seeds and shells, leaves and berries, to enhance the village. Angelique fished though the drawers of her wardrobe and found bits of fabric and leather, wisps of lace or pieces of embroidery to decorate their little people. They made up stories and portrayed all the roles—overseer and planter, slave and child—moving the figures around and bouncing them up and down when they spoke.

Chloe seemed to carry none of the weight of her slave's existence. She was lively and lighthearted, and her enthusiasm for doll play was boundless; she sometimes took over the game.

"Get that slave outta here!" she would holler in the cruel voice of the overseer.

"No, no, Massa, don't put him in the ground!" she would cry for the slave.

"Dig the hole, you bassards, and stick 'im in it!" she would growl, and she would bury her shaking little figure up to his neck in dirt, all the time crying, "Oh, no. OH, NO! Don't put me in the hole!"

"Leave his head stick out, and bring me the honey!" the master would snarl.

"Oh, no, Massa, not the honey! Please not the honey!"

"Pour it on his head and bring me the bucket o' ants!"

"Oh, no, Massa, not the ants!"

"Pour on the ants so's they bites him good, bite his eyes an' his ears an' his neck an' his nose!" Chloe would become possessed and screw her face into a cruel mask when she pretended to be the overseer. And Angelique would join in, becoming the helpless slave.

"NO! NO! The ants be bitin' me! They be eatin' me all up!" she would cry, thrilled with a mixture of horror and fascination. She could not imagine such cruel tortures. She thought Chloe invented these dramas, and she was in awe of the girl's imagination.

It was Chloe's idea to make the dolls. Both were brown because the clay was brown, but one had Angelique's blond hair, and one had Chloe's little black braid. The hair was cut from their own heads. The clothing, as well, was ripped from their own dresses, and sewn in place, to make them more authentic. Eyes were tiny stones and mouths were slivers of seed, and they argued over who was to use the seed with the most perfect curve for a mouth. They pretended the dolls were sisters and made them beds with pillows and covers so that they could sleep side by side. Then they made a tent of silken scarves and cotton pareus and they would lie down beside the dolls and croon to them, songs their own mothers had sung, until they knew one another's songs and could sing them all by heart.

During the day, Angelique read from the book. She remembered many things from her mother's teachings and from the prayers of the nuns at school, but she wanted to know so much more. She asked Chloe if she knew about *loas*.

"*Loas?* There be many, many *loas*!"

"Oh, please, tell me all their names."

"All them? Well, there's Brava Guede, who's the best *loa*; he care for the chillen. An' Guede Ratalon. He digs the graves!"

"Who is Legba?" asked Angelique.

"Papa Legba be Maître Ka-Fu. He open the gate so's all the other *loas* come in!" Chloe spread her delicate arms when she said "O-o-o-o-open!" then she bowed down to the ground. "But when they call the Keeper of the Gate in this chapel, they say "Kalfu . . ." and she tried very hard to pronounce the word, *Carrefour*.

"Yes! I've heard them say that!" cried Angelique. "Why is it different here?"

"'Cause the voodoo be bad here . . . it be *anga-jan*!"

"What do you mean . . . *angajan*?"

"Baka, here . . . duppy . . . evil spirit . . . take ti-bon-ang, the soul! Like *Cochon Gris*—eat the pig, and drink his blood!"

Chloe's imagination ran to the fantastic. Angelique would listen to her and think of the little red crabs scuttling in and out of their holes, so hard to see and even harder to catch.

*   *   *

Angelique decided to try something from the book, but there were many things she needed she did not have. One night she said to Chloe, "Can you get me a toad, or a little frog, a *coqui*?"

"Why you want a toad?"

"To make a spell."

"What you mean—spell?"

"It has to be alive."

When Chloe brought the toad, Angelique turned it on its back and stroked it until it was hypnotized. Then she took one of the smallest knives and opened its stomach.

"See," she said, "there's the heart."

"That the heart? Oh, yeah! I sees it beatin' like a little drum."

"And which part do you think is the liver?"

"The what?"

"We need the liver. We need to eat them both," Angelique said.

"What you want to eat it for?" Chloe cried.

"For courage and cunning."

"Well, I ain't eatin' no frog's liver, I don' care what."

"You must," said Angelique, poking in the frog's insides. "I think this must be it." She pulled out a tiny slick organ and offered it to Chloe, whose eyes grew wide with disgust as she shook her head vehemently. Then Angelique cut out the heart, and holding the two bloody bits and slicing them into two small pieces, she recited the African words she remembered from the book. With a grimace, she placed her portion in her mouth and swallowed. Chloe watched, her face squeezed like a dried-up papaya. Angelique offered Chloe her share, but she refused.

Angelique tried to force it in her mouth, but she wiggled away, shrieking, "I don' want none o' that! Stay away from me! You got the blood and the slime all over your fingers!"

"We're going to do the spell now," Angelique said, "but yours won't work because you didn't eat the heart."

"I don' want to eat no heart."

"Then take up my doll and let's begin." Angelique reached for Chloe's doll and blew, then breathed on its face. "You are Chloe," she said softly, "and you are alive." She looked over at Chloe. "Do the same with mine." Chloe grabbed the doll with the yellow hair.

"You is Angelique, an' you is alive," she said without much enthusiasm. Still, she loved to pretend, so she tried to believe it. Angelique handed her a piece of black string.

"Tie it around the throat," she said.

"Why?"

"It's the spell. Do it."

Chloe fumbled with the string and managed to make a slipknot.

"Now say, 'Carefore tinginding oo-oo. Me hot me bas-e.'"

"Say what?"

"Just 'Ting-in-ding-goo . . .'"

"Ting-a-ding-goo . . ."

"Me hot me bas-e."

"Me hot. Me bas-eh?"

"Now pull the string tight. See if it chokes me."

"Chokes you? Why you want it t'choke you?"

"To see if the spell works, of course."

Chloe tightened the string, watching Angelique's face for any sign of choking.

"Tighter," said Angelique, frowning.

"If I pull it any tighter, it'll pull off your head!"

"Do it! And say the words!"

Chloe tried her hardest, she chanted and pulled the knot tighter, and just as she had predicted, the clay head of Angelique's doll popped off and toppled to the floor. Angelique sighed with frustration. "It doesn't work," she said. "I'm doing something wrong."

"What you want to do spells for anyway? That's for the *houngan* to do. Spells is dangerous. Besides, you need to make the *vévé*."

"What's a *vévé*?" Angelique asked.

"It's the picture of the *loa*, made with the white flour. An you di'n't ask Papa Legba to open the gate."

"Let me try it on your doll."

"I don' want to try it. Let's play sumpin' else. Let's dance!" She threw down the doll and, rising to her feet, began to spin. But Angelique was determined, and she took the string and wrapped it around the neck of Chloe's doll.

She placed the doll on her knees and blew on it again. "You are Chloe. You are alive," she said. Then she began to chant the spell softly. "Carrrrey Forrrrrey. Ting-gin-din-goo. Me hot. Me bassssey."

Her hands were still sticky from the frog's entrails,

and she wrapped the string around her fingers to get a better grip. Chloe was still humming and twirling, and Angelique began to pull very slowly, staring down at the little doll, which looked up at her with its pebble eyes and kinky braid. Her hands felt stiff and her mouth was dry, but she said the spell again, pouring all the force of her breath toward the little neck.

Suddenly she felt a sizzling spasm, like the tremor when she touched a certain kind of jellyfish, and then a ripple of heat at her shoulder bones, which seared her back to her buttocks. A flicker of fire curled like a snake in her belly, writhing and then thickening, and her throat burned as a bitter taste soured her mouth.

Chloe stopped still. "It workin'!" she cried. "It workin' now!" Her eyes flew wide and she reached for her neck and screamed. "It hurts! It hurts my t'roat!"

Angelique froze in disbelief, staring at Chloe, who was truly in pain, holding her neck with her hands and coughing.

"Stop it! Stop the spell! Pleeeese! I can't breeeeeathe!"

Angelique tried to pull her hands away but her fingers were tangled in the string, and jerking and tugging made the knot go tighter. Chloe made a thin screeching sound, and gagged, tearing at her throat and clawing at the air.

"Ow-h-h-h-h, Papa Guede! It . . . hur-r-r-rrrts!!!!" she gasped, barely able to make a sound. "Papa Guede . . . save me . . ." she whispered. Then she bent over and coughed, a raw, hacking cough, as though she would vomit, but nothing came from her mouth.

Angelique dug frantically at the loop of the string, but it refused to come loose. Chloe moaned and rocked her body back and forth, clawing at her neck, tears popping from her eyes.

Angelique crawled to her knees, scratching the ground for the knife she had used on the frog. Her fingers found the blade and she grabbed the doll. Her hands shaking, her nails digging into the hard clay, she eased the point of the knife under the string and jerked. The first time it slipped, but the second it cut! Chloe fell over in a small quivering heap, and stared up at Angelique with anguished eyes that slowly glassed over as she lost consciousness.

Angelique dragged Chloe into her arms and held her close. She could feel her small bones collapsed beneath her skin and smell her warm, spicy odor.

"I'm so sorry, Chloe. Oh, Chloe, please don't die," she sobbed, convulsed with spasms of dread. "I didn't know it would work. It worked so fast! Please, Chloe, wake up!"

But Chloe lay still and unbreathing, her neck loose, and her body as limp as kelp. Angelique grew frantic, and she looked helplessly at the shelves of bottles and vials as she searched through her mind. The spell! Another spell! There had to be one! Something, there was something, what was it? "To revive a strangling beast." That was it!

She struggled to remember the words. Different words. Christian words. They came to her in part, and then she remembered more, and she began to pray over Chloe's still form.

"God who was born. God who died. God who came to life again. God who was crucified. God who was in the cave. God who was pierced with the dagger! Save her. Save her!" She sobbed the words over and over, kissing Chloe's face, wet with her own tears, and breathing into her mouth. "You are Chloe. You are alive."

There was a faint moan, and Chloe opened her eyes. With a cry Angelique clasped her to her breast and wept hot tears of relief.

"Oh, Chloe. I'm so sorry. Please tell me you forgive me!"

"Them . . . spells is . . . evil . . ." whispered Chloe. And Angelique kissed her again.

"I love you, Chloe," she said. "I love you!"

Angelique held Chloe while she slept, watching her small breast rise and fall. Her thoughts were spinning. The spell had worked, so easily, and the force had entered her and ignited her energy. What was that power? "Charge," Chloe called it. Those simple words? Pushing the column of her breath? The book! Some of the rules in the book were correct. The doll with the clothing that had touched Chloe's skin; the hair was Chloe's hair. But Chloe hadn't succeeded with her spell. Why had she?

Her thoughts confused and frightened her. There was something else: Chloe had died, and she had brought her back to life? No. That couldn't be possible. And yet . . . She felt exhilarated, astonished by a skill she knew she must possess, but which she did not in any way understand. This was the "something" her father had spoken of. But what did he really know about her? And what did she know of herself?

It was dawn when the two girls crept back through the underground passageway, and morning birdsong was in the air. Chloe clung to Angelique, recovered but still frightened and unable to speak, her throat painfully sore. They emerged from the tunnel, and they were ready to cross the courtyard when they heard horses approaching at a gallop toward the gate to the main road. Angelique grabbed Chloe's hand.

"Hide! Back here!"

The two girls ducked behind the side of the chapel just as the great iron gate whined open and Angelique's father and another gentleman planter rode into the central courtyard. She remembered his name. It was Luis Desalles. He had been there the day she had been chosen.

The air was still, without a breath of wind, and even the long arms of the windmill hung silent. The hooves of the restless horses rang on the stones, and the men spoke in low voices, their voices thick with drink.

"You're Satan's whore, Bouchard! The whip is the music of the Negro! The whip alone will make him work. Hell's brutes!"

"No, you are wrong! They must have their dancing. The Negro is naturally superstitious. They are beasts, obsessed with her. I can barely keep their hands off her."

"What the devil do you mean?"

"They forget that I am there! And sometimes I

must pull out the sword! But they know in their cunning brains what is coming, and they will wait." He laughed bitterly.

Angelique and Chloe hovered in the shadow of the wall. The sun was rising, and a long shaft of light crossed the courtyard. They were afraid to move and could only cower against the stones. All the courtyard lay between them and the kitchen. The planter Desalles continued in slurred words.

"They are all morally and temperamentally unfit. Last week, Valentin threw himself into the big vat, just as it came to a boil—ghastly sight. And, just yesterday, Bence, my new boy who seemed so promising, climbed a breadfruit tree and jumped. Broke his neck, the bloody fool—"

"—And they use any means to take vengeance! I—I was flogging a slave and the madman swallowed his own tongue! Choked himself to death!"

Chloe coughed, then covered her mouth, but neither man seemed to notice as Desalles droned on.

"Villainous women—absorb their unborn children like herd antelope. One of my females, about to give birth—one day I see her, full with her baby, and the next—poof! Her big belly disappeared!"

Bouchard's horse clipped toward the chapel, and the girls hugged the wall. Chloe stared at Angelique with frightened eyes.

"My worst nightmare," Bouchard was saying, "I have to rerig the blasted windmill here. The new grinders haven't arrived yet from France. If the cane comes in early, I shall lose it all." The horse's hooves came nearer. "See what a pissing bind I'm in. That's why, on Sunday, I give them their damned ceremony, and then . . ." His voice was syrupy with rum. ". . . Erzulie . . . my little treasure, hidden away. What would I do without her, Luis?"

Angelique felt Chloe tugging at her sleeve. She turned to see the face of her friend contorted in a grimace as she motioned to her throat. Angelique instantly seized her by the head and buried it in her skirt, but Chloe exploded in a spasm of muffled coughs.

Bouchard barked in their direction, "Who's there?" Angelique and Chloe shrank farther back into the shadow, then quickly scurried around the back of the building. Hooves rang on the stones as the animal approached, stopped, and clipped again, more slowly. There was an agonizing wait until Angelique's father was staring down at the two quivering girls.

"What is this?" he growled at Angelique. "What in hell are you doing out here? Were you not forbidden to show yourself?" His tone was withering with contempt. "And to a slave!"

"Please, Father, don't harm her. She is . . . my friend."

"Friend? Don't you know she will betray us—if she hasn't already!"

"No! She would never do that."

"Why are you here—together—at this time of morning. Did you steal away in the night?"

"Yes, but no one saw us. No one!"

"For what purpose did you run off?"

"Only to . . . to play—"

"Play? Play what? Where?"

"Games, Father, make-believe—in the little room beneath the chapel—"

Her father's face turned purple with fury. He leaned from his horse and snatched Chloe up by the hair. She shrieked as he threw her across the saddle and, catching her around the waist, he galloped with her kicking figure across the flagstones and into the kitchen. Monsieur Desalles sat frozen upon his horse, gazing at the scene in stupefaction. He roused himself enough to call out.

"Here, here, Theodore. Don't harm her belly. Remember, you want her to breed someday."

Angelique ran to the kitchen door in time to see her father leap from his horse with Chloe still under his arm, her arms and legs flailing. He reached for a pair of coal tongs that hung on the wall above the sink.

Brandishing the iron tool, he called out, "Luis! Give me a hand here! Hold her head!"

Angelique grabbed at her father's coat. "No! No! Father! Please don't hurt her! Please, I beg you! She's done nothing! I'll die if you hurt her!"

Her father turned and glared at her, his eyes black hollows and his teeth clenched. "You'll die if I don't!" he hissed. "You heedless—reckless girl! Leave off those mewly tears! Don't you know what you have done?"

She leapt upon him, clawing for the hand that held the tongs, but he flung her away. Desalles was at the door now, and Bouchard cried out to him. "Hold her back! Damn the fiend!" Chloe screeched at the top of her lungs and Angelique, her head reeling from the blow and hot tears blurring her eyes, scrambled to her feet only to feel Desalles's hard grip on her arm.

"Thais!" her father yelled for the maidservant, trying in vain to hold Chloe who was scrambling and kicking. "Thais! Come down here, at once!" Then he muttered, "Blast your lazy black hide!" under his breath, vainly trying to still the wriggling girl.

Desalles had both Angelique's arms fast in his wrenching grip. Her father set the pliers on the chopping block and, grasping Chloe by the hair, held her head flat against the scarred wood, prying at her mouth with his thumb and fingers as she mewled and struggled.

Thais appeared, groggy and witless with terror, at the door of the tower. "Thais! Help me here! I will pull out her tongue! I will! I'll see that she never, never speaks again!" Staggering with drink, he cursed, "Bloody wretches, defy me, will you? I'll bash both your heads in before I'm done!"

"Let me go!" Angelique found her captor's crotch with a kick.

Doubling over in agony, he released her with an oath: "Damned slut!"

From the corner of her eye, she saw her father lift the dreaded pliers, and she flung herself on his arm again.

"Off me, you hellish creature, leave off!" he cried. But both she and Chloe, now like wild hyenas, bit down: Chloe on the fingers that pinched her slippery tongue, and Angelique on the side of the fist that held the tongs. Angelique felt her teeth sink in the flesh and the warm blood leak into her mouth, but like a rabid dog she held on even as blows smashed her head and she heard the pliers rattle to the ground.

Then her father, dragging both attackers like a bull beleaguered by lion cubs, raging with oaths, lumbered into the courtyard. He shook Angelique off with a curse and a kick, and she fell to the earth, rolled, and lifted her head to see her him lurch for the well at the center of the courtyard, with Chloe still under his arm.

She knew what he was going to do.

"No!" she screamed. "NO-O-O-O-O-O-O!" Crawling and stumbling, desperate to stop him, she grabbed for his leg, his arm, but too late. He lifted the squirming, howling girl above his head and hurled her over the edge. Angelique slammed into the rocks of the well wall, reaching, screaming, "Chloe!" and stared agonizingly down into the gaping hole. She heard a thin wail and felt the chain vibrate as though struck, and she screamed "Chloe!" again, her cries resonating with the falling girl's, bouncing, echoing in the cavern—like ravens' fading caws when they sailed over the trees into the rain forest—and then silence.

chapter

9

Thais tried but could not console the grieving Angelique, who sat clinging to her window. Her tears fell freely, while she stared at the forsaken well, as though she could draw Chloe, like water, back from the dead. She was numb with anger and despair, and her only thoughts were of her mother, how she must see her again, that hers was the only embrace which would lift this crushing pain.

It was late afternoon when a cart came through the gate and stopped by the well. A muscular man in leather descended from the cart with a young slave boy at his side. After looking into the well, and after much muttering and considering between themselves, the man pulled a long rope from the cart and tied it around the boy's waist. The boy then climbed onto the bucket and crouched there, his bare feet curled around the edge, and the man proceeded to lower him, inch by inch, down into the chasm.

A feeble, misguided hope fluttered near Angelique's heart, but as the man waited, the horse only clipped the pavement and the sun sank in the sky. There was no sound or movement from the dark hole. After a long while the chain finally gave a rattle, and the man leaned in and tugged on the rope, hauling the boy up to the top of the well wall. He was dripping wet and clinging to the rope as he climbed out and jumped to the ground. Then the two looked into the bucket as the man raised it, the chain rumbling and the pulley creaking as it turned.

When the bucket broke the air, it bore Chloe's limp form draped across the rim like a clump of brown seaweed caught on an old anchor. The man swung her off and tossed her to the earth as though she were a sack of feed. Angelique turned to Thais.

"Please, Thais, let me go down," she said softly. "I need to see her. To tell her good-bye." But shaking her head, Thais rose, took up a coverlet from her bench, and moved for the door.

"No, missy, you stay here. Like you shoulda done all along," Thais said. Then she left the room to help Suzette prepare the body.

Angelique turned back to the window. Chloe lay on the stones she had washed so many times, her face hidden under her arm, the ragged dress clinging to her delicate form and her perfect limbs modeled like clay from the gray earth. Angelique remembered Suzette, who had fallen on the same spot, beaten, but alive. She watched as Thais and Suzette silently wrapped the body and carried it into the kitchen. The man spoke to them, telling them to fetch him something, and Thais nodded.

Suddenly it occurred to Angelique that the man was not a servant and did not live on the plantation. His leather jerkin and boots marked him as a journeyman who had been called upon to save the well, someone who would have such knowledge, someone, perhaps, from Saint-Pierre.

The man turned and followed the slave women into the kitchen. Without thinking, Angelique dashed for the door, which Thais had forgotten to lock, and ran down the stairway into the courtyard, ignoring the slave boy, who stared at her in astonishment when she appeared. He made no sound and no move to stop her as she raced to the cart, scurried up the wheel like a rat, and dropped into the back.

She saw in a flash that it was a sailmaker's wagon, for canvas and ropes lay about in piles, sewn with grommets and loops of twine. The odor of the sea was strong, and the sails heavy, but she burrowed under them, tucking herself into a corner under the debris.

She heard the man shout to the boy, "Here! Here's soda and cornstarch. Pour these in the well!"

She waited, afraid to breathe for long agonizing minutes, certain her absence would be discovered, until, finally she felt the cart shake, then lurch, and the whip crack.

Slowly the wheels began to turn. The iron gate screeched and the bolt clanged, and at last, from the even rolling, she knew they were on the road.

The horse was spirited and took off at a good clip, to where she did not know or care, as long as she was free of the plantation. Her heart quickened at the thought of what might lie ahead: the longed-for reunion with her mother, the safety and love of her childhood, and the sea. She could not wait to be in the arms of the sea once more.

The pain of Chloe's death, her sleepless night, and the exhilaration of her escape all gathered around her, like phantoms, as she curled beneath the sailcloth, numbed into a stupor, clinging to one thought—her mother's warm embrace. She pressed her fingers into the *ouanga* still at her neck, her mother's charm, and, remembering the cart that had carried her to the plantation, fought sleep as if she could hold back the tide with her outstretched hands. But she finally succumbed and fell into a dark well, clawing at the cold walls as she slid into unconsciousness.

She dreamed of Barnabas. The curtain opened, the light poured in, and he was there, dripping wet, laughing, climbing in beside her, jostling her, pushing her to the corner of her carrier. He spilled the jewels into her lap and took them up again, his hand grazing her thighs, and his fingers carelessly brushing between her legs as he gathered the baubles from the folds of her dress. It took forever to expose them all, for some had hidden their bright colors in the creases, and each time he found one his feather touch comforted her. Then he kissed her on the neck and the lips, and he was so close that she felt the beating of both their hearts. He whispered to her, "Goddess," and his hand reached under her skirt and stroked her, and his fingers found places that quivered to life with his touch.

Angelique woke in the dead of night. Someone

was shaking her, and she sat up with a start. The cart
was still, parked in an empty shed, and the slave boy
stood over her, peering down.

"What you want, girl?" he whispered, his warm
breath close to her cheek.

"Where are we?" she said, sitting up and looking
around.

"We's home. The Massa's goin' in the house, and
he leave me here to coil them ropes."

"Home . . . where is that?"

"Why, gal, we is at the dock. In Saint-Pierre! We
brung you the whole way. What you goin' to do,
now?"

"Did anyone see me?"

"I din't tell nobody you was there. I din't say a
word to nobody. I knew you was tryin' to escape!"

"Are we really in Saint-Pierre?" she asked, not
daring to believe.

"Thas' right . . ."

"Oh! I have to go," she said, climbing out of the
cart. "I'm going to find my mother. I know the way
from here."

"You goin' alone?" he asked, surprised.

"Of course. It's the harbor road, only a furlong
beyond the caves. The house is on the cove,"
Angelique replied confidently.

"You ain't scared to go alone?"

"Why should I be?"

"I dunno. I guess nothin' would scare you. The
way you jump in that wagon! You din't run like a dog.
You run like a pig! You run for your life! But there be

bad things on the road. Robbers and run'way slaves. An' buccaroons! I'll jus' put these ropes away and come with you for a bit," the boy offered.

"I don't want to wait for you," she said. "There's no moon, and no one will see me." With that she scampered toward the dock. But the boy was fast on her heels.

"Trouble is," he said breathlessly, "they sees a white gal with a black boy, and I be in big trouble. So's I jes' hang back a bit behind. You go ahead, but you no worry. I be followin' right after."

The boy spoke not another word for over half an hour as they trudged along the road in the darkness. Several times she cried, "Go away!" and tried to run ahead and lose him, but he seemed glued to her and increased his speed whenever she did. Finally, she let him be.

The night was warm, and billions of stars hung suspended in the black sky, some high in the dome of heaven and some hovering just over the sea. The music of the easy-rolling surf was a siren's song, and the longer Angelique walked the shore, the more she ached for the water's sweet caress. Finally, she ran to the edge of the foam. When she saw the stars themselves swimming in the inky waves, she could bear it no longer.

"What you doin'?" the boy called.

She ignored him and plunged into the first breaker that rose up to meet her. The warm surge sucked her under, and she tucked and tumbled in the roll of it, curling into a tight ball, then thrusting like a supple seal under the next wave. She floated, at home now, more so than she would have been at her mother's side, for the sea was her soul's birthplace.

When she crawled out on the sand, breathless and exhilarated, the boy was sitting there, waiting for her.

"You swim like a porpoise," was all he said.

"Do you have a name?" she asked curtly as she sat down near him.

"Cesaire," came the reply.

"And I suppose you are the sailmaker's slave."

"No, miss, I ain't no slave. I gots my papers."

"You're free?" She felt an odd pang of envy when she said the word.

"Yes, miss, Massa give me my freedom, or at least, I earned it, sewin' sail. I been bustin' my fingers for ten year, made a hundred sail, an' I have all o' them strainin' in the wind right 'bout now."

"Then you still are indentured," she said smugly. "Just as I thought. You are certainly not free."

"Well, that show what you don' know. I been to sea already, as a sail maker's mate. An' someday I be like you—travelin' home—to Africa," Cesaire said proudly.

"Africa! What fine dreams you have!"

"I come over when I was a baby, down in the black hole. But I be goin' back befo' the mast, you wait an' see. That was a top royal mizzen you was hidin' under. An' I made that sail. It go to a ship in the harbor on the morrow, a schooner from America."

"America?" cried Angelique. "Is the ship from Maine, do you think?"

"Well, I don't rightly know, but it's an interloper, come every season to trade tobacco for rum an' guns. An' it take on illegal slaves."

"I don't believe you made a sail for that schooner," she said, "or you would know whether it came from Maine. Everything you said just now was probably a lie!"

She rose and began walking again, following the path around the lagoon. As it was after midnight, and there was no one about, Cesaire had given up hanging behind and now walked beside her. All they could see was the sea's glimmering foam, the long pale road, and the dunes rising to the jungle; all they heard was the sucking of the tide and the thousands of frogs singing, *"Coqui! Coqui!"* from the bush.

"What make you so bitter?" Cesaire asked.

"That's none of your affair," she said hotly. "Why are you watching over me?"

"Why, I thought you might destroy yourself. You was runnin' away, ain't that right?"

"Yes . . . so?"

"What from?"

She thought to tell him but couldn't answer. The harsh lesson of secrecy was driven too deep.

"Why was you there at that castle?" he persisted.

"It belongs to my father, Theodore Bouchard."

"Did you know the l'il girl who drowned?"

"Yes. I did," she said, and after a pause, added, "She was my friend."

"Why for she do that?" he asked, surprised.

"Do what?"

"T'row herself in the well?"

"But, she didn't—"

"That Monsieur Bouchard say she was horse to the goddess Erzulie, who mounted her and drove her to do it. Tha' she was driven' mad by the *loa*, and she t'rowd herself in the well."

"No, that's not how it was at all! That shows how stupid you are to believe such a thing be—" Angelique began, when suddenly she caught her breath in mid-word and her heart skipped a beat.

Far back down the road, a horse was coming at full gallop. She looked around wildly but Cesaire grabbed her arm and pulled her into a ditch beside the path, then crawled in beside her, under the tall grass.

There they lay, breathing in the dark, waiting as the hoofbeats drew nearer and thundered by their heads only a few feet away, before clattering away into the distance. Angelique was so terrified that she was afraid to move and lay burrowed under the sharp reeds, close enough to Cesaire to hear both their hearts beating like hammers. Finally, he spoke in a whisper that made her jump.

"He gone now. He din't see nothin'. We's like rocks in the stream, me an' you, me black and you silver, and both of us, hidden deep under the water."

She sighed and let the fear flow out of her.

"How much more to your home?" he said.

"I don't know," she answered. "It can't be far now, but I can't tell in the dark."

"Mebbe you should wait 'til mornin'. Then there be people on the road, comin' an' goin', an' you won't be so suspicious-lookin'. I could sleep a bit, could you?"

"I'm not tired," she said dreamily. There was a long pause.

"Has you bin with a boy yet?" he asked softly.

"What do you mean, 'been with'?"

"I means . . . alone . . ."

She was about to say, "Like this?" But her pride stopped her, and she remembered the night Barnabas had climbed into her covered chaise.

"Yes . . . once," she said.

"Only once?"

"Yes . . ."

"Well, tha's how it be with me, too. Once. She live in Saint-Pierre, and her name Tippi. Tippi, the jewel o' the night."

They lay in the grasses and looked up at the stars glimmering in gossamer curtains.

"Thank you, Cesaire, for not giving me up," said Angelique.

"I think you is a brave girl," answered the boy.

"Why do you say that?"

"I see you. You's got the heart to take what you think is yours. An' that be the bes' thing there is. You sees your chance, and you grabs it. Is your mama learn you that?"

"I don't know. . . ." She sighed.

"Well, that brave heart, it'll give you fortune and give you pain," he stated knowingly. "You know that?"

"No . . ."

"A lotta things come to you, an' a lotta things be lost to you. Once you choose a brave heart you gots to keep yer courage up, 'cause it be a hard load to carry. Hurricane take the frigate bird's roost and the crow kill his babies, but he be flyin' still."

Angelique heard these words as she drifted off to sleep, and with Cesaire there with her, she felt safe for the first time in a long while.

Suddenly the boy was shaking her, and saying, "I gots to go now. I gots to go back before I's found out. Can you find the way?"

She sat up. Dawn streaked the sky, and the sea rolled in on the golden sand, soft and blue, with foam cleaner than milk.

"I see the cottage!" she cried, scrambling to her feet. "It's there across the lagoon."

"That l'il box . . . way over yonder?"

"Yes that's it! That's my house! Oh, thank you, Cesaire!" She threw her arms around his neck and kissed his cheek. "You've brought me home!"

He stared down at her, and she up at him, and they saw one another clearly for the first time in the morning light. He was coal black, and his eyes were ebony, and he spoke in a shaking voice.

"Tell me your name. I want to think of you. When I's gone to sea."

"It's . . . Angelique . . ."

"Well, good-bye, Angelique," he said, "and good luck." He turned and started back up the road toward Saint-Pierre.

She worried about the late-night rider. Could it

have been her father? But the little house sat alone on the sand, and as she came around the curve of the beach, she saw no horse. Her heart began beating with exultation, as she imagined her mother's face, hearing her cry of happiness, feeling her mother's soft bosom against her cheek. Never, never, would she leave her again.

But as she drew closer, she felt a stab of dismay. The lustrous banana trees were hanging limp and torn, and the garden that had been so fresh and green was dried to bare earth. The once-coral house was now pale as the sand it stood upon, and the lavender shutters were fallen away, except for one, which dangled from a single hinge. The thatch of the roof was flattened and gray over the leaning porch, and the door stood open to a deserted room.

She drew nearer and walked up on the stoop. The house was empty of life, as if no one had ever lived there. She wandered inside and stood a moment in the room that seemed so small now, dusty and abandoned. A breeze stirred at the door and swept a cloud of sand across the floor.

"Mama?" she cried, unable to comprehend this nothingness. "Mama!" she screamed. "Mama!"

She walked to the back door and slowly pushed it open. A horse snorted, and she heard the thud of a hoof in the dirt. The animal was tethered to a broken banana frond, his tail switching flies, and he was rubbing his muzzle vigorously against his leg. When he saw her, he lifted his head, and looked at her, blinking. Beyond the house, fan palms dipped feathery fronds, like giant wings obscuring the brush, which quivered now, then was still. She froze as her father staggered out of the trees, fastening his trousers. He jerked his head toward her and scowled, and when she saw his murderous visage, the blood rushed to her face.

There was an eel that lived in the second reef beyond the caves that triggered a fear so primordial that she shuddered whenever she saw it. She felt the same repulsion now as she stared at her father, who was red-eyed and swaying. She knew the eel's crevice, and always kept a distance, sometimes glimpsing its fat snout and stark eye when sunlight streamed through on its hole. Her mother said that eels were lazy and would never chase her, but she felt certain this one would bite, for it had rows of sharp teeth and an evil practice of rhythmically gnawing at the water, an action so sickening, it spiked a prickly buzz under her arms and pulsed a painful throb between her legs.

These same sensations jolted her now as her father took an awkward step in her direction.

Once, late in the afternoon, when she was floating over the huge brain coral behind which the eel kept his cave, she saw the creature emerge to forage for food. First the head, then the long rubbery form—ten, twelve feet in length—eased out and slithered through the bright coral, scattering a group of angelfish and darting quicker than a snake through the sand. She had stared down, afraid to breathe or to kick, as she was now, staring across at her father, paralyzed with a fear she did not comprehend.

He blinked at her, as though she were not real,

then his drunken brain seemed to grasp that she was there. His face was contorted with rage, but he grinned slowly.

"Run away from me, will you?" His voice was hoarse and strangled in his throat. "I'll have your skin off your bones, I will!" He took a lurching step. "Damn you, and your impudence! What does it take to keep you locked away! You're the Devil's slut, you are, and I'll beat it out of you before I'll give you up!"

For a moment she thought she would faint, and she made a helpless swimming motion with her arms, pulling backward on the air. But he sprang for her and had her in a vise before she could move or cry out. She knew he was more a brute beast than a man as he pressed her to him, forcing the breath from her, and smothering her face in his shirt. She felt him tremble as though her fear had spilled into his body and under his heaving breast she sensed the anguish of his frustration.

"Why do you despise me!" he cried, rum slurring his speech. "Betray me! Defy me! Do you want to kill me?" He wrenched her away from him and dug his fingers into her neck, twisting them in her hair, and pushing her down.

She cried out in terror, her heart thundering. Then she heard his belt sing in the air, and she was Suzette, as the hot flash seared her back, and she was Chloe, as she plunged into blackness before the next blow came, and she saw the eel again, his gaping craw opening and closing, inching out of his crevice, just before the dark water swallowed her up.

chapter

10

Angelique was dressed in the white gown for the ceremony. The drums had been throbbing for hours, but Thais did not come to take her down, and it was almost time for her to appear. Then it was Suzette who came for her—Suzette, who despised her.

"Come on now, you, and don' give me no trouble."

They walked down the stairs and into the room behind the altar, and Angelique was surprised to see that, after all these months, the clay figures were still there. The little people, the trees and huts of the plantation, were all where they had left them. The Angelique doll was lying headless on the dirt floor, with the Chloe doll beside it. She stared at the toys but felt nothing, neither remorse nor grief. It seemed strange to her that she had played such a silly game.

When she took up Chloe's doll, the beady little eyes looked at her, and she had a sudden impulse. She pulled off a piece of the kinky black hair, and, reach-

ing for the knot around her neck, she untied her
ouanga. The moonstone gleamed within the wad of
herbs beside the snake's skull. She stuffed the wisp of
hair into the sack, pulled the string tight, and hung it
back around her neck.

"What you doin' with that?" Suzette asked, suspicious. "Sit down, now, and be still."

"No," Angelique said spitefully. "Don't tell me
what to do!" She smashed the toys with her foot, kicking them aside, until all the clay was crushed back into
dust.

The drumming in the chapel pulsed and flooded
the chamber with the sound. She could hear the
shouts rising and becoming more insistent, invoking
the mysteries and summoning the spirits:

"Carrefour! Saint Michael! Grand Père Eternal!
Luc! Marc! Louis! Baron Cimetière!" the worshipers
chanted, repeating each name in a sonorous cry. On
and on they sang in monotonous litany, until she
began to hear, "Ela Freda! Saint Vierge Marie! Erzulie
ge Rouge!"

"Go on, now, it's time," said Suzette.

Sullenly, Angelique climbed under the curtain.
Her mind was brittle tonight, and she was bored by
the ceremony. She watched coldly, impassively,
thinking to expose its secrets.

Chloe had told her of the *houngan*, who was the
leader, and she looked to see which one he might be.
Her father was nowhere in sight, but she noticed an
older man with grizzled hair who shook a sack of
white meal onto the ground, lacing thin lines in a fan-

tastic design. He raised a clay jug and sprinkled a yellowish liquid on the four corners of the pattern. Instantly, the drums came to life, bright and palpitating, and the *houngan* chanted and, above his head, shook a long, slender gourd dripping with beads and small bones. The bodies of the dancing slaves were coated with a thick white paste, their dark skin gleaming through pale streaks, their candles flickering.

A huge fire smoldered at the foot of her platform, and yams dusted with flour were tossed upon it to be cooked. The smoke and acrid odor rose to her nostrils.

Then she heard a terrified squawking above the sound of the pulsing drums, and a dancer leapt forward, carrying a white chicken dangling by its feet and flapping its wings. He wrapped his hands around its legs and broke them with a sickening, cracking sound, then placed the chicken upon his head, where it struggled a moment and fell still, its red eyes staring. It was almost comical, like a feathered hat, until the *houngan* reached forward and plucked off the head, which came free of the body as easily as if it had been severed with an invisible knife. The blood spurted down the dancer's face.

Angelique leaned in and listened closely, trying to understand his babbling. All the *loas* were listed in the book, and she wondered if she would recognize which one had claimed him, riding him like a horse and raving gibberish from his mouth.

She watched him with cold fascination, trying to decide whether he was putting on a show or was truly taken. When he drew nearer to her, she saw that his eyes had rolled back into his head, and he stared up at her with creamy slits. The blood streamed over his glistening forehead down to his soft mouth, and the white paste clung to the sweat, which trickled in rivulets upon his chest.

Suddenly she started as a small stone dropped on the platform in front of her. Instinctively, she reached for it and took it up. It was warm and smooth, copper-colored, and although the man's eyes were empty and as yellow as pus, and his lips did not move, she heard him whisper, "Chloe, Chloe, Chloe . . ."

A sigh seemed to pass through the other worshipers. They backed away as if he were something evil, and fear was palpable in the air, like an odor. He swayed and reached for her, his face in an eyeless mask. A croaking sound coming from his throat, his long fingers grazed her legs. Even as she shrank back from his touch, she felt an itching tingle travel through her body, as though tiny bugs were crawling on her skin.

Suddenly he quivered and sprang onto her altar, and the drums rumbled like stormy breakers in the sea caves, echoing, fading, and when he leaned over her with his eyes still blind, like a lover to kiss her, flames flew from his lips!

As she gasped and pulled back, she felt that the flames were cool, like ribbons, fragrant with perfume, enveloping her in waves of crimson and gold. They were leaves—petals—in such masses that she thought she would drown in the tumbling blossoms. She laughed, rising from the mound of delicate odors. Reaching down, she gathered the petals into her arms and tossed them like rain into the air. She saw them float down on the worshipers, who had become passive, and stared, each face beautiful and elegant as if carved from ebony.

The drums entered her body, and she began to dance, first as she had danced with Chloe, swaying slowly as a child in play, then more sensually, invitingly, as for the first time she sensed her body's curving hips and budding breasts. She was dancing on the loose fabric of her gown, and she was naked before them.

At that moment the spirit entered her, enfolding her in a glowing mist. Erzulie sang strange sounds from her mouth, and Angelique writhed and quivered, clawing at her own breast and sobbing with a deep sadness as she fell, trembling in the power of the *loa*. One by one, the worshipers approached and leaned into the platform and touched her, kissed her, their lips brushing her arched feet, her tensed legs, their hands pressing her thighs.

She was not the child Angelique, but the goddess Erzulie, as she eagerly welcomed their soft mouths, tongues entering her. There arose a quiet, ghostly silence, as the enraptured lovers tasted her exuberant innocence and were enthralled by the source of life. She raised her hips and groaned, longing for some release, but she was caught between the god's possession and man's devotion, and the nibbling and tonguing only tantalized her more.

Finally, with an anguished cry, she drew her knees together, her fists clenched, and her face contorted in pain as sharp as knives. She whimpered like a child, tears streaming from her tightly shut eyes, her body jerking in torment. The worshipers murmured solace and whispered among themselves, and they stroked her until she slept.

When she emerged from her trance, she had lost all memory of her possession except the tingling mind-flutter of a mysterious dream.

The next morning, Angelique sat by her window staring across the courtyard to the slave quarters. The day was cruelly hot, the sky a blinding blue. She looked out over the cane fields that were now like waves of foam, taller than the men who disappeared within them. This morning, a thrilling idea hung in the branches of her mind.

The spirits were real. She had never doubted it, but now she fully accepted the corporeal existence of the *loas*. She longed to know more. She felt a kinship with the slaves, for, like them, she was a prisoner of violence and fear. She envied their volatile natures, their easy access to the gods, as she turned inward for escape.

After that day, the ceremony became an obsession. For long hours she recited and repeated the incantations softly to herself; the mournful chants became melodies she kept in her head. All her time was spent poring over the *Book of Mysteries*, struggling to translate the several languages and decipher the spells. The pages revealed secrets of ancient African magic. Angelique studied each set of rules, memorizing syllables and sounds.

In the room behind the altar, she studied the formulas of potions and searched through the jars on the shelves for the correct ingredients. She arranged them and hoarded them, still uncertain as to their purposes.

Suzette watched her dully. "What you doin'? Leave that stuff be."

"Look the other way if you don't like it." Angelique spoke gruffly, and continued to taste and sniff all the powders and juices.

"You is an impertinent chile."

"I am not a child anymore."

She dreaded her father's presence. She often woke in the night, when the creaking of the windmill invaded her dreams, and the screeching sound was like the voice of a demon; she would be cold with sweat, her heart racing, thinking he was there.

After bringing her back to the plantation he had ignored her, except during the ceremony. She hoped that as long as she remained hidden and performed her duties as goddess, he would leave her alone.

She sensed how valuable she was to him, and to some of the other planters, who had begun to toy with African voodoo in darkest secrecy. On Sundays they worshiped in church, but at midnight they came to the dancing.

One day when she was lost in her studies, she heard a man's voice on the stairs and felt a jolt of fear, thinking it was her father. Quickly, she shoved the book beneath her bed, but when the door opened she was surprised to see a stranger. It was the Jesuit priest, Father Le Brot, who had spoken to her the first day, after the trial with the dogs.

"Angelique," he said kindly. "M-m-may I come in?"

She simply stared at him, dumbfounded, unable to answer. He seemed an emissary from another world. He nodded to Thais to leave them and walked to where Angelique was sitting; to her astonishment, he took her hands. He was a rotund little man with a balding head and a red face set on a fleshy neck that bulged over his collar. His bright eyes and jovial smile could not hide a self-important mien, and she remembered that when he spoke he had a tendency to stutter.

"H-h-h-how are you, my dear? I've b-b-b-been thinking about you, and-and-and wondering how you were s-s-s-sustaining your ordeal."

The use of the word *ordeal* angered her, and she was instantly suspicious. If her father had sent this man to test her, then he was a fool, for she would reveal nothing.

"It is not an ordeal to be Erzulie," she said coldly, rejecting his condescending tone.

Father Le Brot sighed deeply and motioned for her to sit at her small desk. He took a seat in the chair opposite her, and she felt him searching her face for traces of sorrow or weakness. She would show neither.

"What do you want with me?" she finally asked. "Why are you here?"

"I have c-c-c-come to pray with you," he said.

"Why would you want to pray with me?"

Her memory of the nuns in the Catholic school was dim, but she knew that their mournful prayers had always made her feel guilty. The nuns had taught her to read, but they had also droned over her as though she were doomed.

"Because I have great concern for your immortal soul, my child. You are living in a den of iniquity, and participating in pagan rituals that are the work of the Devil!" the priest intoned.

"The Devil?" she gasped. "I have not seen the Devil."

"The dancing and the frenzy, these false gods, the sacrifices . . . my dear, you must know, that is the Devil's doing, and that they are demons from Hell!"

"I know no such thing!" she cried hotly. "You think the Devil is everywhere!"

He calmed. "Do you w-w-want to make a c-c-confession?" he asked her gently.

"No. I have nothing to confess," she answered. She did not trust this man and was becoming impatient.

"Then p-p-pray with me," he said, taking her hand again.

"I don't want to pray," she answered petulantly, then rose and walked away.

Father Le Brot looked surprised, but his face softened.

"No, no, uh-uh of course you don't," he said. "How f-f-foolish of me. You-you-you s-s-s-say your prayers with the s-s-slaves, do you not? And t-t-tell me, my dear, are their p-p-prayers answered?"

She considered this question. What was the nature of their prayers, she wondered. Did the slaves pray for freedom and a safe return to the homeland? It seemed they asked for nothing, only life and ecstasy, and the chance to lose themselves in the dancing.

"They pray to me," she said.

Father Le Brot looked befuddled and shook his head. She was pleased to have bewildered him. "And the planters pray to me as well," she added, with a touch of arrogance. She thought she saw the priest's gaze flicker as though she had confirmed a suspicion he held.

"The planters come to these . . . these d-d-dances?" he asked.

"Sometimes," she answered. "Erzulie grants wishes if she chooses."

Father Le Brot rose and began to pace. Angelique watched his black habit flow about him, and she could see the sweat in the folds of his neck. She thought the priest's robes must be uncomfortable in the heat. He was deep in thought when he spoke.

"These planters who come to these rituals, well . . . in m-m-many ways they are as . . . as ignorant as the s-s-slaves. The franchise of civilization has invested them with neither c-c-compassion nor humility, and they turn to these primitive ceremonies out of d-d-desperation."

"They know Erzulie will give them something God will not."

The priest placed his folded arms under his round

belly and drew himself up as though he were making a proclamation.

"My dear child, how little you understand. God's great gift is life everlasting. For those who have faith, the treasures await in heaven. These g-g-greedy men are gamblers who crossed the sea because others before them had made fortunes in sugar. They were not gentry in France. They were renegades and s-s-second sons, who had no land or fortune to speak of, and Martinique is a p-p-place where they thought they would live like kings!"

His pontificating bored her, and Angelique became intrigued, watching the sweat dripping down his face, wondering what he wore beneath his gown to make him so warm. She understood him perfectly. He was afraid of the Negroes, like all white men.

"Oh, they come to Mass and profess piety, and, ah, yes, are quite ready to condemn heresy, but in truth, they have little true allegiance to God Almighty and no interest in the Hereafter. The wealth they yearn for is here!" he continued. "And one way or another, that wealth rests in the hands of the slaves! The planters see this, and yet they do not see this. They fear the slaves and need them, both their sweat and their heathen superstitions. Without workers, they are helpless. So black men swarm these islands, their numbers growing every day."

Father Le Brot was becoming impassioned and, amazingly, he had lost his stutter. Angelique thought the priest looked like a spotted puffer fish who had become alarmed.

"Every hour! And still they want more! They bring the poor creatures in ships of doom! To plant more cane! And harvest more sugar! And the blacks will not work, so they beat them to death and bring more! Already these misguided whites are outnumbered twenty, thirty, to one! And in the end God will not own these islands, they will belong to the Negro. It is the Devil's plan, and the Devil has planted the greed in the heart of the white man."

He stopped, out of breath, and stared at her, his eyes bulging. Then he seemed to regain his composure and, somewhat embarrassed, spoke to her in a gentle voice.

"I'm sorry, my child, I know these things are all a mystery to you and that you are helpless to change them. It is for your own soul I came. You must consider your immortal soul, Angelique."

"Where is my soul, Father," she asked. "Is it in my heart or in my head?"

"It is, my child, the invisible part of you that lives after death."

A cloud fell over her mood. Why would this priest speak to her of death? She was protected by her father and fed by the slaves. Nothing threatened her. Even the walls of the tower were thick and would provide safety from hurricanes. She decided that Father Le Brot was only speaking the words she had heard at Mass, words that always warned of doom and damnation, and yes, of the Devil. He began to stutter again.

"You are in grave d-d-danger," he said.

"Why? What kind of danger?"

"From the ceremony."

Her suspicions were true. The priest was threatened by the voodoo rituals because he had never seen one, or he would have known that she was the center of the dancing and the embodiment of the spirit. He had come to frighten her because he was afraid, but she would not be frightened.

"There is no danger," she said. "My father has seen to that. No one would dare harm me."

"Your father?" inquired Father Le Brot, raising his eyebrows. "Who is your father?"

"Monsieur Bouchard."

The priest seemed astounded. "I-I-I didn't realize," he stammered, "that Theodore was . . . that you are his d-d-d-d-daughter!" He threw his arms to the sky. "Oh, Lord in Heaven, preserve us!" With that he hurried to leave. But he turned to her at the door.

"I'll be b-back to see you," he said hastily. "Think about what I have said. I will pray for you. And . . . oh, I-I nearly forgot! Mercy me, what will b-become of me if my mind does not improve! I b-b-brought you this!" He returned and placed a small book on the table. "I thought you might like it," he said. And he exited quickly.

Curious, she walked over and looked at the book. The words on the cover read *William Shakespeare, Plays and Sonnets*.

chapter

11

Every morning when the bell sounded, Angelique rose and ran to the window. She watched the slaves drag their tired bodies to the field, slaves who had sometimes worshiped her the night before. She remembered the drumming that had brought their souls to life. She had thought about the things Father Le Brot said and was ashamed of her haughtiness. Never did she really believe that she was the source of the power; she knew it would have been the same without her. She was transformed by the slaves' adoration. The drums came from Africa, as did their deep faith in the spirits. The magic they evoked sprang from within them.

She knew she was only one embodiment of the goddess of love, and the *loas* floated in the air, longing to be called, as Chloe had called Guede the night she had died and lived again. They circled, waiting to descend, tempted by food or sacrifice, and when they came, they entered a dancer and spoke though him. Angelique began to yearn again for Erzulie.

Erzulie will protect me, she said to herself at night when she fell asleep, and in the morning when she woke, and at midnight when she walked into the chapel. She began to plan the invocation. It would be simple and imploring. She only wanted the goddess within her once more, embracing her, drawing her in waves of pleasure.

She waited until Thais was asleep, then crept down into the courtyard and, under a sky without stars, drew the *vévé* on the flagstones and lit the candles. She had flowers—amaryllis and tuberose—for color and fragrance, and cakes she had saved for days.

She also had a prize, a white pigeon she had trapped at her window with weeks of crumbs. Finally, he had become so tame that he cooed to wake her in the mornings, and she was able to reach out and touch his trembling feathers. That morning she had stroked him, and said softly, "Come, little dove, don't be afraid." When he was most trusting, she had tightened her grip around him, caught him, and wrapped him in a velvet cloth.

Now she had him pressed against her breast, ready for Erzulie. She looked at his quick darting head, his bright eyes, and felt the life within him quivering. She hoped this would be enough.

She took a knife and, with great care, pierced the throat of the living bird, and while it still jerked and thrashed, let its blood flow into a cup. Standing in the center of the *vévé* with a candle at each corner, she began to chant, softly and cunningly, "Erzulie-

Severine, Belle-Femme, La Sirene. Erzulie Boum'ba, Freda Dahomin, Ge Rouge."

She plucked the feathers from the bird, still soft and warm, and tossed them into the air like pollen. Swaying, turning, she scattered the dust from a potion she had made of herbs and bone meal in the sanctuary, then, closing her eyes and shivering, she stood and drank the blood.

She raised her arms, and cried, "Erzulie, Goddess, I call thee from within the thunder's rumbling, and out of the fires of Pelée. I beseech you to enter me, as I kneel to you, Mystère, Madonna, Mbaba Mwwana Waresa . . ." With that she fell to her knees and waited, her head bowed.

At first there was silence, then only the fluting frogs, and, far off, the sound of the sea. She felt weak and unprepared, then wholly unworthy. All at once, her body began to tremble with a tingling heat rising from her feet and flaming through her torso. Her mind fixed on the image of a tiny spark, which grew and flared as though the atmosphere was fractured into swarms of colors, and she could see the molecules of the air dancing around her in splintered rainbows.

There was a humming sound, as if the ether were alive, a living thing, pulsing and breathing, and its fingers caressed her, singing and moaning. The humming grew, piercing and vibrating, and reached a peal of sound that was excruciating, a gathering rumble, rising in pitch, expanding, exploding in the crashing boom of the thunderclap that she thought would rupture her brain.

A mist filled the courtyard, and voices whined like wind, dissonant, eerie. She smelled the odor of dead fish that had rotted in the sun. There was a figure, a human shape, but not of a woman, not Erzulie, that wavered in the gloom, a man's shape, robed, but not robed, sinewy, shadowy, flickering like a flame, but dense, with corporeal form: arms and legs and a face as smooth as alabaster. Ebony hair fell in waves across his forehead and down to his shoulders.

He was standing in a heaving chariot, legs spread, hands on the reins, and floating before him in tumbling arcs, were velvet horses, dark and muscular as the midnight sea. The vision oscillated, took shape, then vanished, only to return again.

And Angelique whispered, "Who are you? Why have you come?"

His voice was like the wind rushing across the water. "You called. You dragged me from my dreams, the centuries of sleep. But you are still a child, Angelique, too young. I see your flowering talent, and I long to capture it and draw it with me into the center of the world, but not yet, not yet." And he lifted and sank as he spoke, his voice brushing her ear, then floating away into the channels of darkness.

"Who are you?" she asked again, but she knew, in her deepest core, with a knowledge that was of her flesh and not her mind, that he was Lucifer, or some god of Evil, and that she had mistakenly summoned him.

"You don't remember?" he whispered, his breath smoky.

"No! I did not call you," she whispered. "Why did

you come?" She panicked. "I don't want you here!"

"Come?" he said, his voice a sigh. "Come, my darling? Yes, come with me, let me . . . touch you, feel you . . ."

He sprang from the pitching chariot and walked on the stones, and beneath the dusky robes Angelique glimpsed cloven feet and a barbed tail. He drew closer and hovered near her, flowed over her. She felt a cold stab like a finger of ice, ripping her, thrusting into her, and his kiss was like frozen sand.

She pulled away. "Don't! Don't touch me! Leave me!" she cried. "I don't want you! I never wanted you!"

He sighed like a wave retreating, sucking the swirling foam, and his face grew dark. "I will never leave you," he said, his voice like Pelée rumbling, "and you are still too young to choose. But remember, I am there, and I alone protect you. I alone love you, and I have always loved you." He faded, and his voice grew thin and distant. "I will never fail you," came the hushed echo. "And I will never desert you." The last word was as deep as a tremor in the earth. "Ne-ver-er-er-ererrr . . ." And he was gone.

After that night, Angelique lost her passion for the ceremony. A deadening dread permeated her mind, and she no longer craved Erzulie, or knowledge of the *loa*. She was unresponsive on the platform, and the moaning of the slaves gave her neither terror nor joy. All day she feared that her father might come to her, and every night she slept fitfully, imagining the return of the mysterious Dark Spirit.

She woke one morning to find Thais standing on one window seat, pulling the heavy tapestry curtains closed.

"Why are you doing that?" she asked. "I like the sunlight."

"Time to cut the cane!" Thais said. "We gots to move you out of the tower. Slaves comin' to mend the windmill an' install those new rollers, brought all the way from France!"

"Must you cover the windows?"

"Massa say you gots to stay hidden. Don't you go near the window, now, y'hear. He don't want all those people to see you."

"Did you say I'm leaving?"

"That's right."

"Where?"

"Why, to that place you been wonderin' about. Massa say put you in the little bedroom on the third floor."

"In the plantation house?" A shiver ran through her. Being anywhere close to her father was her deepest fear.

Thais seemed to sense her uneasiness. "But not today, chile. Too many people aroun'. We goes tomorrow. So's you gather up what you want to take with you."

Later in the day, Angelique heard shouting in the courtyard and, with Thais nowhere in sight, crept to the window and peered out from behind the curtain. There was a great commotion below. Slaves unloaded a wagon pulled by oxen, and a huge set of wooden wheels with deep grooves were set beside the tower. Her father, on horseback, directed another group of slaves to carry the third crusher inside, and Angelique could see a great cog gear still on the wagon, lying under several shiny copper pots.

Suddenly, she felt a vibrating inside the tower and realized that the huge post in the center of her room was turning. Too long out of use, it whined in complaint and slowly revolved, jarring the structure as though an earthquake were shaking the walls.

Outside she could hear slaves climbing on the windmill, hammering on the broken lath. One of the enormous fans swung downward over the window, blotting out the light. Through the fabric she saw the figure, lithe and slender, of a boy. He was stretching a new sheet of canvas over the vane. Angelique was admiring his agility as he clung to the huge rack, the canvas flapping in the wind, when she realized it was Cesaire.

She pulled the curtain aside a little more to make sure. The vane completely covered the window, obscuring the courtyard, and he was clinging to the frame like a tree frog, oblivious of the height, deftly tying off a piece of rope.

"Cesaire!" she called in a harsh whisper. He jerked his head up and looked around. "Here! At the window!" He swung closer to the tower and propped a foot against the stone, peering into the dark room and squinting. When he saw her his face lit up with a smile.

"My God! Angelique? Is that you?"

"Yes!"

"What—why you here?" he asked, dumbfounded.

"I didn't escape."

"What you mean? You no find your mother?"

"No. And—my father—made me come back."

"Oh, so . . . you are . . . alone? Shall I come inside and see you?"

"Oh, no!" she whispered. "And move away from the window now. No one must see you talking to me. No one is supposed to know I am here."

He frowned. "You mean you are a—"

"A prisoner."

His face clouded, and he shifted his position on the wall, trying to find a way to be closer to her. He grabbed the window bars from the outside and hung precariously, one foot still on the vane.

"How can I talk to you?"

"You can't." She began to feel frightened. "Please, leave now, Cesaire, move away, before someone sees you. My father is a ruthless man. He—"

A harsh voice rang out from the courtyard, and Cesaire quickly kicked back from the wall and, clinging to the vane, rode it down to the ground. He ran for a cart and pulled loose another piece of canvas. Once more he looked up at her window, winked at her, then moved away.

Late that night she heard a strange sound outside. Cesaire had climbed up on the vane and was tapping on the bars. Thais was sleeping, but Angelique was afraid to risk a conversation, so she made a motion to him that she would go down and ran for the stairs. Seconds later she was in the courtyard.

"Cesaire?" she called out in a breathy whisper.

"Here!"

She looked toward the edge of the flagstones, where the wall fell to the sea. He was sitting on the low balustrade.

She ran to the edge of the parapet and sank to the ground at his side. "I mustn't stay," she said. "It is dangerous for me to talk to you."

"Look." Cesaire pointed to the small inlet directly beneath them. The night was warm and hazy with starlight, and she could look out over the entire expanse of the sea. A long, thin peninsula reached an arm around in a curve, hugging the lagoon in its embrace. Even in the starlight she could see the breakers crashing on the outer reef, but the little inner harbor was calm where the rocks fell straight down to the deep water.

"What?" she whispered.

"There! There be your schooner from Maine."

She could just make out a shape in the darkness, a ship at anchor, with two tiny lights on board, gleaming like stars fallen into the deep. "Are you sure?" she asked.

"Ah, yes, I know all the boats. None of them get by me."

"Why is it here? Why isn't it in the harbor in Saint-Pierre?"

"Aw, 'cause she be hidden away. This little bay make a good anchor to wait for morning. She through the Passage, and now she take out across the sea with the morning tide. None of those bigger boats come in here. They be in sad trouble when they cross that reef. But this little barque, she sail fine before the wind. She skim the water like a bird."

"I wish I were on that boat." Angelique sighed wistfully.

"No, you would not want to be aboard her. She is a stolen barque, and tho' she move like a guileless girl, she is a whore."

"Why do you say that?"

"Because she carry slaves," he replied matter-of-factly.

Angelique stood up, walked to the edge, and looked down. "I wouldn't care," she said. "A slave is what I am."

"Gal, you don' know what you say. Someday you leave here."

"My father won't let me. And, besides, I have nowhere to go. I don't know what happened to my mother, or where she is." She looked at Cesaire's frowning face. "And—and I can't talk to anyone," she said, sinking down again, her heart aching as she looked behind her. "If my father found us like this, he would . . ." She shivered. "Do you remember the girl in the well?"

Cesaire nodded, his eyes bright.

"Her name was Chloe. We played together in secret. My father found us one night, and he . . . he . . ." She rose suddenly. "I can't stay here any longer, Cesaire. I should not have come down. . . ."

"Wait," he said. "I has something to tell you. Do you know what is comin'? Can you feel it in the air? Listen."

The waves pounded on the rocks, and, back behind them in the jungle, the frogs fluted. Far off she could hear drums, but that wasn't unusual. A night without drums was rare.

"You mean the drums . . ."

"Yes. The drums sing every night. Of rebellion."

"Rebellion?"

"They be escaped slaves living on the mountain, maroons, drawin' their strength from Pelée. They sneak down to the slave quarters at night, and they tell the slaves, "Rebel!" They preach to them of freedom."

"Freedom?" She loved the sound of the word; it was the most beautiful word she knew.

"When rebellion come, all the *blancs* be killed. They burn the great house—all the buildings—to the ground. That's what I come to tell you."

"Don't the owners suspect anything?"

"When the fox cannot reach the grape he say him no ripe. Listen! Them's Eboe drums. Your father's slaves all be Eboe. You know how they got those yellow eyes?"

Angelique remembered Chloe, her copper skin and golden green eyes, and she nodded.

"They be timid, melancholy people, feel desolate so far from home. An' in Africa? They are cannibals!" She shuddered, and he laughed to see her so frightened, his teeth white in the moonlight.

"Are you . . . Eboe?"

"Naw, gal! I be Mandingo! See my hair—so soft and silky. "Aw no, I no Eboe, no way!"

"Then you don't know those drums."

"I know enough. Listen to me. It's their history. They rise up one night and set the fires. When the time comes, I let you know. Then you can warn your father, and—"

"Warn him?" She caught her breath in her throat and felt the lump of pain when she tried to swallow. "I will never warn him! I hope the slaves do come and burn the plantation!"

"What . . . ?" He was dumbfounded.

"And leave him dead! Good-bye, Cesaire," she cried, backing away. She turned and ran back to the tower.

chapter

12

When Angelique woke the next morning it took her a moment to remember where she was. Thais had awakened her in the early hours, moved her to the plantation house, and locked her in a third-floor room.

Angelique looked around at her new surroundings: a rude bed, a dresser, and bare floors. She ran to the one small window and looked across at the tower and the storing sheds.

There was great activity in the courtyard, with many slaves at work. Her father was storming about—cursing, complaining, waving his arms, and pointing toward the tower. She was amazed to see that the windmill was turning briskly and that the doors of the crushing room were thrown open. Slaves were easing the rollers into place so that the gears on their crowns meshed.

Suddenly one of the men gave a cry and several workers inside her tower room bellowed in response. At that moment, the windmill shuddered and moaned. It moved heavily under the load, and the great rollers beneath it began to revolve. A great cheer rang out, and all those present gathered to see the powerful mechanism at work. Even her father seemed relieved. He stood apart, his arms crossed and his feet in a wide stance, watching the crushers grind against each other.

The thought of seeing her father face-to-face, now that she was living nearer to him, made her shiver with fear. She resolved to be as still as a hermit crab in a new shell, watchful and cautious. She wondered when the next ceremony would be, and she suddenly thought she should take from the secret room various powders she might need to protect herself.

As the day progressed, Angelique began to wonder whether anyone would come for her. She did not have her books or any clothing, other than what she was wearing, and no one had brought her any food. She went to the door, tried the lock, and, to her surprise, found it crude and easily forced with a pin. But she ventured out no farther than the hallway, which was dark and deserted. On the inside of her door was a drawbar and she realized she could bolt herself in.

All at once she heard cries from the courtyard and ran back to see two oxcarts lumbering through the gate, laden with cane. Twenty or so slaves unloaded the cumbersome grasses, then carried them to the crusher and, with much shouting and awkward thrusting, forced them between the rollers.

She glanced at the sky and saw a long plume of dark smoke rise from the stack. Through the windows of the curing house she could see flames reflected on the round bottoms of huge copper kettles. In the excitement of that first day of harvesting the cane, she had been completely forgotten.

Finally, late that evening, Thais appeared with a tray of food. She was exhausted, her clothes were filthy, and she collapsed wearily upon a small stool and dropped her head to her breast.

"Thais? What's happened to you?" Angelique asked.

"I be made to cut cane, chile, and it destroy me." She held up her hands; they were swollen with cuts and bloody welts. Angelique drew in her breath.

"Why must you go to the fields? You are supposed to care for me."

"We's all go; we's all walkin' before the whip now." And she looked up at Angelique with sorrowful eyes.

Angelique realized that the demands of the harvest would consume the time and energy of everyone on the plantation, and she would be ignored.

Before many days had passed, she began an exploration of the empty mansion. Most of the rooms were deserted except for an occasional ornate table or carved bench. Dust lay in the corners; mirrors were dim with grime; candles, streaming with globs of melted wax, hunched in unlit candelabra; and the shutters were closed to the sun. But the castle had once known grandeur, she could see that. There were floors inlaid with parquet or mother-of-pearl, leaded stained glass in arched stone windows, and, in some of the rooms, great tapestries hanging on the walls.

Compared to the gloom of the castle, the courtyard swarmed with life. From the hour before dawn, when the conch shell was blown, until far after midnight, the slaves toiled. The work fell into a grueling pattern. The carts came from the fields, rumbling up to the windmill, straining under the load of cane. Stacks rose in great piles against the wall; the crushers screamed and clattered; the windmill groaned; and the tall smokestack spewed forth its noxious gases into the turquoise sky.

Thais proved too old for the field and was stationed now at the fires. She would come into Angelique's room with the sweat pouring from her body, her clothes drenched, and the sweet smell of molasses emanating from her skin. Always she brought some simple meal, and always she was dragging her feet with weariness. One evening she moved so slowly, Angelique looked at her with concern.

"Thais? Is something wrong?" she asked.

The poor slave woman began to weep. "He beat me," she said in a voice that was barely audible.

"What ? Where?" Thais slowly pulled off her shirt to show her back. It was crisscrossed with bloody stripes.

"But, why? Why would he do that to you?"

"They call the order to strike, but it too late. The syrup turn hard as a rock, and is lost. I say, do it now, but the man in charge, Lazairre, he pull the bead between his finger, and he say no, not yet. Yes, I tell him, yes! Now! But he no do what I say and the foam get so high it boil and overflow the vat. Lazairre burned, and Massa say beat me, for ruin the batch."

Angelique felt a pity beyond words in her heart, and she went to Thais and sat beside her, laying her head in Thais's lap. "Poor Thais," she said. "I am so sorry for you. He is a hard and vicious man, and I hate him."

A thought flashed across her mind that might give Thais some consolation. "Do you know, Thais, that there is rebellion in the air?"

The slave made no answer; there was only a tightening of her muscles and a short intake of breath. Angelique looked up at her expectantly, but Thais only sighed.

"No, chile, no rebellion. Slaves rebel, they be hanged, or shot, or worse. When the slaves rise up over Trinité way, they call in the militia. No hope against *backra*. No pride against guns. All be dead now, twenty brave slaves massacred. Last maroon caught, he hung out in a cage to dry."

"But the drums! Don't you know what they say? I heard them again last night!"

"Drums sing like Pelée mutters, big talk, no explosion. Chile, the slave be doomed to labor to death, and the cane be his burial ground."

Angelique sat with her arms across Thais's lap and felt her heart shrivel. She had a sudden image of the stonefish, so venomous, so difficult to see, mottled and covered with mucus that looks like slime. She thought of how he lay on the bottom in the sand, with real rocks around him, covered by the same scaly growths, invisible until some unsuspecting shrimp fluttered past. Then a spine like a dagger would fly out, a silver needle from within the false debris, and death would come. She decided her heart would be like the stonefish. She would wait, and the dagger in her heart would stay hidden.

One morning Angelique heard her father ride out the gate on horseback quite early, and, wondering why the day was so still, she ran to the window and saw that the mill was shut down and the vanes were turning slowly in the windless air. Slaves sat about on the ground, exhausted and morose. It was deadly hot, and she was restless and even more bored than usual.

She decided to seize the opportunity to wander through the castle and, after an hour or so of searching, found herself outside her father's chambers. Tempted by the possibility of discovering some clue to her mother's disappearance, she pushed open the heavy door.

She saw a large, dark room with a huge, canopied bedstead. Rumpled sheets were strewn upon the mattress, and the curtain was frayed velvet, hanging at an angle across the frame. A chair was buried in filthy clothing, and, slung over the back, was the foul-smelling coat her father often wore. The imposing desk was covered with papers.

She glanced through the letters, harboring some faint hope of discovering her mother's whereabouts.

One short note complained: "Sugar not selling.

No boats. Suggest you retain molasses for rum."
Another, signed by her father, requested "patience,"
saying "the cane is too old, and shows little juice,"
"excessively hot," or "I cut too late, and it piles before
the mill and sits, losing its sugar. The workers still
don't have the way of it."

Farther down she saw "A pivot of one of the
rollers came loose, and I have had to stop the mill. . . ."
"Desperately need new large rollers . . ." "A set has
been found in Saint-Pierre for the horrendous sum of
1300 francs." She tossed the letter aside indifferently
and continued to search but found nothing about
women sold into slavery, no word of her mother—
only the lonely miseries of a man in the sugar trade.

The terror began one night after the mill was back in
operation. For days, the slaves had been driven to
work all night, feeding cane to the crushers' insatiable
maw.

This particular night, Angelique woke to screams,
and ran to the window to hear several slaves cry out,
"Stop the mill! Stop the mill!" They ran toward a lone
slave, who was flailing with one arm, while the other
was somehow caught, jammed in between the cylinders. He must have fallen asleep at his post, she
thought in a daze, and his hand went into the gears.

Her father staggered out into the courtyard, his
arms over his head, his voice thick with sleep, cursing
and raging, "What? What happened? Why the devil
did he do that?"

"Massa, he caught. We gots to open the rollers!"

"What? No! I tell you I won't have the mill shut down. Keep going, you wretched imbeciles! Find an ax! Cut it off!"

The windmill thundered and the crushers whined as the slave bellowed, and Angelique saw the ax rise and fall. The bloody stump whipped upward and jabbed the air, before the agonized man gathered his maimed arm to his breast and fell to his knees, his fellows about him in a terrified huddle.

Angelique watched as they carried him off, and when she returned to her bed, she lay awake, her mind a jumble of terrors. The air was vibrating with heat and the sound of the windmill, like an enormous press, with sharp scales, scraping her skin and flattening her bones.

Suddenly she heard someone walking in the hallway outside her door, and her heart gave a thump. Something was sliding on the wood, scraping and moving, and she could hear faint, ragged breathing. She crept to her door and bolted the drawbar, then lay in fear, staring at the closed door, not moving, not daring to make a sound, until her muscles ached for relief. The breathing wheezed, and an unseen hand jiggled the latch. For the first time since her imprisonment, she was glad for the bolt, which held, and, after a long moment, she heard the sound of departing footsteps.

After that night Angelique could sense the slaves change; they were sullen and restless. Though the overseer beat them, all their energy force had been drained. They moved slowly, dragging their feet, and the stacks of cane piled up by the wall, uncrushed. The drums throbbed before dawn, when the sky was still dark, and the moon had set.

One midnight her father and several other planters tore into the courtyard on horseback. They went into a room behind the curing house and came out with muskets in their hands, shouting to one another, their voices crazed with rum and rage.

"They've killed them all!"

"Wife and three daughters!"

"Slaughtered!"

"Set fire to the cane!"

Amid vicious oaths and clattering hoofbeats, they were off once more, thundering down the road.

Angelique woke to a low whistle, ran to the window, and looked out. Cesaire was standing alone in the courtyard, lit by the fires from the boilers.

"Angelique!" he called. "Come down!"

"I can't," she called back. "I dare not!"

"All's safe," he cried. "Your father be at the next plantation, seeking vengeance. I must talk to you!"

A few moments later, she crept out into the night. It was the first time she had been so close to the threshers, and she was staggered by the size and noise of the machine. Weary slaves, stripped to the waist, their muscles quivering, fed the unwieldy stalks into the cylinders, and juice trickled out into a lead-lined gutter that flowed into the curing house.

"In here!" Cesaire shouted, and dragged her

toward the boiling room. Thais and another older slave woman were leaning over a great copper kettle stirring the golden syrup. They were so numb from tiredness, they never raised their heads. Bubbles blistered the surface of the molasses, and white scum collected around the edges. The air was dripping with steam. Looking around, Cesaire finally pulled Angelique to the far corner.

"The rebellion is coming!" he said, his eyes wild, and she could see the sweat on his forehead.

"My father has gone off to join the militia," she answered. "He came back for muskets."

"No, no, that is nothing," he said. "The foolish slaves at Sainte-Marie make plan to take over the plantation there. They be crazed with hatred. Like idiots, they leap ahead. All for silverware! Ah, yes, and they pay with their lives, poor souls."

"Will they all die?"

"Yes, all, all. Still, it is a lucky ruse. The soldiers will massacre them and think they have smothered the fire."

"Then there is to be no rebellion."

"Aw, gal, you have no dream like this one. Maroons in the hills be arming slaves all over the island. Plot rumble deep, like fire at Pelée's heart. Tomorrow night at midnight, they set fire to Saint-Pierre! Hundreds, thousands, maybe, kill all the *grands blancs*. It be the time for the black man. He get his own back now."

"Will they come here? To this plantation?"

"You are doomed, gal, unless your father rouse

his slaves to defend it. You think they fight for him?"

"Never. He treats them like animals."

"So this plantation, too, will light the stars in the sky. You must warn him."

"I will never warn him!"

"Listen," he said patiently. "There is a little path down to the bay, and I will have a boat waiting there for you. Even if Pelée overflow, and rage fire down his sides, you be safe in the water."

"Are you sure? Won't it be dangerous?"

"Angelique, gal, I'm standin' here in this spot telling you all this because I don' want see you come to no harm. Them crazy slaves will rape you, and then they will kill you. You must do as I say. Warn your father. As soon as possible. No matter how much you hate him, you don't want to see him die, do you?"

She didn't answer, but she thought perhaps he was right.

"I will wait for you tomorrow night," he said. "Don't be afraid."

chapter

13

It did not seem possible for Angelique to fall asleep after this terrifying news, but somehow she drifted into the deepest level of consciousness, a dreamless slumber in the cavern of night. She woke to see her father's shadow hanging over her.

Her eyes flew wide at the sight of his leering face. His smile was lecherous, and his breath reeked of rum. Clumsily, he reached for her, and she shrank back from his grasp, even as she felt his rough hand graze her arm. He laughed, a hoarse rack, and stood up, his hands in his pockets, his legs spread wide.

"Get up now, dolly," he rasped.

"What do you want?"

"I came to tell you, your old father is a grand fighter, and you should be proud! Proud to be his daughter! Look! Look at that on my hands, and tell me what you see!" He smirked with self-satisfaction. "Do you know what that is? It's death, girl, human death! And these hands were in it!"

"Don't touch me!" she said, repulsed. "Don't come near me!"

"Why, Angelique, my angel, why do you hate me so much?" he complained, his mood shifting. "Haven't I been good to you? Given you lovely things?"

She didn't answer, but pulled herself into a fetal position, drew into the corner of her bed, and stared at him. She was conscious only of the waves of hatred flowing through her, filling her, like a murky pool of backwash rising in a cave with the tide.

"I only wanted to tell you, dolly. I saved your life tonight. Doesn't that make you like me better? Those bastards were coming for you, and I stopped them—I and my men—and wrung their wretched necks with these bare hands. God, it is a thrilling thing to kill a man, to feel his heart stop beneath your fist!" He stared at his hands, turning them over and back in wonder. Then he grinned at her again.

"Come give me a kiss for my pains," he said, and moved a step toward her.

"Stay away!" she hissed, her voice so deadly that it stopped him cold.

"What makes you so sour? Ah . . . I know! It's because you are my own kin, and you have my spite in you! By God, I like that temper! It riles me, but it sets me afire as well, it does. Come, give me a battle, my pretty, I want to feel you struggle."

He lunged for her and caught her up and pulled her squirming body against his, laughing and burying his face in her hair. She lashed out, clawing at him, fingernails scratching for his eyes.

Surprised, he fell back, the breath caught in his throat, but only for a moment, being too drunk to feel even pain. He drew back his hand and struck her a blinding blow across the face. She fell with a stifled cry, her head reeling, and he grinned down at her again. "You're a proud bitch, you are, but it takes more than that to stop me."

"I don't have to stop you," she said, her voice contemptuous, "because even if you kill me—and you will have to kill me to hurt me again—you will not see the light of morning two days from now! You think you've won the battle at Sainte-Marie, but you are a fool. They are coming! Thousands of them! Tomorrow night! And they will burn this plantation to the ground and you with it, and I shall be glad to see you in the fires of Hell."

He gaped at her, not comprehending, but stopped by her vehemence. "What makes you think that, girl?"

"I know!" she said. "The killing tonight only gives you false confidence! You think you have triumphed over them, but you are wrong!"

"Who told you this?"

"Cesaire. The sailmaker's boy."

"Free Coloreds!" said her father in a scathing tone. "They're behind all this! But—" He stopped and glared at her. "How did you talk to him?"

"I didn't," she lied, knowing she had him now. "I listened at the window, and I heard him tell the slaves at work in the windmill. He said if they would not defend you, you were doomed."

"You heard all that?" The liquor drained from his face, and his visage became grim and anxious.

"Tomorrow night," she said. "The slaves all over Martinique will burn Saint-Pierre!"

It gave her great satisfaction to see her father's face blanch at her words, and his lips tremble. He stared at her a moment, then turned and staggered from the room.

The next morning the mill was shut down, and the slaves were not at their posts. The courtyard was deserted, and she could hear music coming from the direction of the huts. She knew her father had given the workers a free day. Thais brought her breakfast, then sat on her stool, shaking her head in sorrow.

"Las' night be bad," she said in a low voice.

"I know," Angelique answered. "Sainte-Marie."

"Many dead, many in jail. So much bloodshed. What we goin' do now? We jus' find strength to fight back, and we be cut down by the soldiers."

"Don't you know what's happening tonight?" said Angelique.

"Yes. I know tonight they be a ceremony," answered Thais. Angelique was jolted.

"Tonight? No! Not tonight!"

"Yes, Massa ride off early this morning. He told me make you perfect in every way. I be goin' to the tower right now to fetch the white gown."

"I won't do it," Angelique said.

"What you mean? You won't do it. You crazy, chile! Why you such a little fool?"

"When he comes back, tell him if he says I must pretend to be Erzulie again, I will come outside and show myself to them all. I'll tell them it's all a lie!"

Thais's mouth fell open, and she stared at Angelique with complete bafflement. Then she rose and scurried to the door, locking it behind her.

Angelique wondered whether the things Cesaire had told her were true. Conflicting worries racked her brain. Was there really to be a revolt? She wondered if she should have told her father the plan. This might have been her chance to escape, but not if the slaves found her first and treated her like a white planter's daughter. Would her father keep her safe? Fight for her life? What was he doing now? Would he alert the militia? And would they even believe him?

She had a sudden longing to return to the room behind the altar. She went to the window and saw that the grounds were deserted; even Thais had disappeared. Angelique eased the lock and dashed through the corridor and down the stair.

Once in the room she realized that it had been months since she had performed the failed ritual to call up Erzulie, and it seemed strange to feel the familiar pulse quiver through her when her fingers touched the sacred powder of the *vévé*. As she sifted through the paraphernalia on the dusty shelves, she felt that something had changed. Various objects no longer seemed mysterious, but instead, perfectly useful.

Unconsciously, she began matching the items— bits of insect and leaf, the jars of salves, and boxes of herbs, little sacks of sea creatures, even the fleshy masses within the smoky jars—with the words of the chants and the instructions filling the pages of the book. Somewhere in her heart she felt sadness over the loss of Erzulie, and she wondered if she had been unworthy of the goddess.

Something flickered in the corner of her mind. She reached for her mother's *ouanga*, which still hung at the hollow of her throat. Inside was the tiny skull, the moonstone, and the snippet of Chloe's hair. These things kept her safe. *I will not perform the ceremony,* she thought. The memory of the dark figure was too terrifying, and she knew that somehow they were inextricably joined.

She found herself drawn into the great leather volume once more, newly bewitched by the words. Something hovered over her, like a great bird, and she felt comfort and peace beneath its wing. Deeper and deeper she plunged into the sounds of the chants, rolling the songs over in her mind. They seemed the secret writing from the beginning of time.

Tiring at last, she rose to leave, but stopped, and once again took the jeweled kris from its case, turning it in her hand to see the stones catch the light. After running a finger along its keen edge, she wrapped it up again and placed it in the box. A piece of dark paper or black ash fluttering high in the corner of the room caught her eye. Drawing closer, she gasped when she saw that it was a bat, dangling upside down from the rafter. Its wrinkled wings were folded across its back, its fur gleamed, and its beady red eyes stared at her with calm recognition. Shivering, she left it there and crept out of the room.

Later that day, when she was writing in her journal, there was a knock at her door. The key jingled, and when the door opened, her father was standing there. Her muscles stiffened, but to her surprise his demeanor was contrite, even remorseful. The inferno deep within his bulk seemed quieted now, and he stood before her with his head drawn into his shoulders and his huge hands dangling at his sides.

"May I speak with you, Angelique?" he asked.

"I won't perform the ceremony," she said. "It's stupid, deceitful. I'm sick of it. I won't do anything for you, ever again."

"I have decided to let you go," was his answer.

She was stunned.

"You are right," he continued. "I have misused you, and I regret it. You have every reason to resent me. But I have much to fear today, and I only ask your help one more time."

"No," she said. "I hate you! You are cruel and a murderer! You can't make me do it"

"Listen to me, Angelique. I have found your mother. She is working at the plantation at Trinité, as a physician in the slave hospital. I will take you to her myself, tomorrow."

Angelique could not believe his words. Joy surged through her body.

"My mother? Really?"

"I beg you to do this for me," he said, his voice

steady. "I have been to Saint-Pierre to alert the authorities. Perhaps this plot can be avoided. But the slaves are restless, obviously . . . eager for revenge. I suspect what you heard might have had some truth in it."

He paused and turned away from her. She could see beads of sweat dotting his forehead. He reached for a handkerchief and pressed it against his brow, his movements slow and heavy.

"I have promised them a ceremony," he said, "and I will sacrifice a goat. I have promised them *tafia*, all they can drink. They are so simpleminded and depraved, my hope is they will be caught up in their frantic dancing and won't turn against me, but instead turn on their own kind."

At that instant, she heard the drums begin, and she recognized the tambour of the ceremony, the Maman deeper than a beating heart and the Cata, brighter and sharper than birdsong. She felt a quickening within her. Faintly, she heard the chanting, and the calling of Legba; wisps of smoke from the ritual fire seemed to curl in her nostrils.

He lifted his eyes to her, like polished coals. "If you will appear in the ceremony," he said, "I give you my word, I will return you to your mother."

"All right," she said simply. "I will become Erzulie one more time."

The night was still, the air warm and moist. It was near midnight, and the drums were pounding more frantically and insistently than ever behind the doors of the chapel. Thais prepared her for the ceremony, and

Angelique looked at the gray head and stooped shoulders of the slave.

Thais's spirit is broken, thought Angelique, as Thais bent over her, fastening her dress.

The woman's body was heavy, and she groaned when she had to stand. The harvest had broken her, long hours over the kettle, stirring, skimming, pouring, breathing the hot vapors. Angelique harbored a fleeting thought of taking Thais with her to Trinité, caring for her, as she would now be free to care for her mother.

Thoughts of her mother flooded her mind, and she felt the tears brimming in her eyes. It was three years since she had seen her. She had grown, and her mother might not recognize her. She was tall, with hips that curved softly above her long, slender legs. Small breasts swelled on her chest, and her shoulders were bony but broad. Downy fur had begun to grow between her legs and under her arms.

As she smoothed the white gown over her flat stomach, the dress felt tight beneath her armpits, as if it had been made for a much smaller girl. Angelique was struck suddenly by something she had always known but never given much thought. There had been other goddesses before her.

"Will they choose another Erzulie?" she asked Thais.

"Yes, chile, when you be a woman."

"But this is my last time," she said. "My father is letting me go tomorrow."

"What you mean last time?" Thais cried, her voice sharp.

"He has promised to take me back to my mother."

Thais's face underwent a sudden transformation, and she rose and clasped Angelique by her two arms.

"What you mean? What you mean—let you go? He won't let you go!" She raised her hands and let out a wail. "Oh, Lord God in heaven, help us." A harsh sob followed her plea.

"Oh, Thais, I will miss you, I really will. Please don't cry. What is it? Oh, Thais, you mustn't grieve so. I'm glad I'm finished with this."

"But, chile, you don't know. You can't know, what's to happen to you now."

"Yes I do know. I'm going to see my mother. I want so much to be free, to walk through the streets of the village—talk to other girls, to run on the sand, and swim to my caves—maybe meet some nice boy and tease him and make him laugh! Oh, I'm so happy. You have no idea how lonely I have been! And now it's all over— Thais, what's the matter?"

Thais was sitting with her arms around her stomach, staring out and holding herself, rocking as though she were in pain. She looked at Angelique, and her lips formed words that made no sound, *The sacrifice!*

At that instant Angelique heard a cart rumbling on the courtyard stones. She ran to the window and saw Father Le Brot scramble down from the wagon, with a lantern held before him, and move toward the door of the plantation house. His plump body filled the folds of his habit, and she could see his wooden cross bouncing upon his breast. Not thinking, she reached for the charm at her neck and pressed it with her fingers.

Almost immediately her father was at her door. "What are you doing?" he glowered at Thais. "Bring her down."

Thais simply stared at him with an expression of such contempt and sullen refusal that Angelique thought she must have lost her senses.

Her father's scowling face darkened with rage. "Come!" he growled, and seized Angelique by the arm.

They were halfway down the staircase when they met Father Le Brot, huffing on his way up. They practically collided with the priest, who lifted his lantern to reveal his round and perspiring face.

"Oh, Bouchard!" he cried out in great consternation. "I-I-I have come to tell you that you m-m-m-must not do this dreadful thing!" But Angelique's father brushed by him with complete indifference, nearly knocking him off the riser. Pulling her by the arm across the entrance hall, he dragged her through the open doorway.

The rotund priest ran after them, shouting, "B-b-b-blasphemy! Sacrilege! You c-c-c-call upon the Devil for your v-v-villainous, c-c-c-cowardly hungers, and the Devil will come! He will come to you, I promise you that, Theodore Bouchard! Your soul is lost! Do not sacrifice your own daughter to the powers of evil!"

Angelique was astonished by his vehemence, and wondered at a faith so fearful and so resistant to other spirits in the world. Once again she thought of how greatly the priest feared the *loas*.

"Off with you, you meddlesome old fool! Go back to your stinking Mass with the body and blood of Jesus Christ upon the altar. What is the difference, tell me that? Your hypocrisy makes me laugh!"

"Theodore, I beg of you!" cried the priest, and threw himself in their path, raising his hands in prayerful supplication. Angelique was amazed to see tears running down his cheeks. Her father pulled back his booted foot and, with a vicious kick to the head, knocked the good man to the ground. His lantern clattered on the stones, and the flame sputtered out.

"Father!" she cried, struck by his cruelty, and tendrils of fear began to snake around her heart. He jerked Angelique across the dark courtyard toward the chapel.

The worshipers were in full ceremony, and she was met with the rush of heat from their writhing bodies and the bone-numbing resonance of the drums. The naked black dancers enveloped her in a dark cocoon, and she trembled at the power of their adoration. She felt a sullen lust emanating from them, colder and more frightening than ever before. Her father dragged her to the altar and forced her against it.

The fire was bright coals, the porcelain platter lying before it, clean and shining, and she thought of the goat that should have been tied for the sacrifice but was not there. Panic fluttered in her breast. The chanting rose in mournful dissonance, the songs sorrowful and repetitive. The flames of a thousand candles threw shadows on the walls. Suddenly, she felt her father seize her hands and wrench her arms behind her. She cried out in pain, as, with a quick twist of a rope, he bound her wrists.

A chalice was raised to her lips, but she took one sip and let the burning liquid flow back into the cup. She did not want to be drugged. She shivered, feeling the ropes tighten. Why was she bound? And then, in one shattering jolt, she understood. A colder fear than she had ever known took her in its grasp.

She saw their eyes as if for the first time, burning with hunger, and their faces frozen in expressions of dazed expectancy. She felt their fingers grazing her legs and prodding her thighs, and . . . something else was there, some other dark presence, icy hands groping, slithering beneath her skirt. . . . Some being was near her, nearer than her skin, and a voice like the wind moaned in her ear, "I am here . . ." But the pounding of her heart drowned out the sound.

At that instant, through the smoke, she saw a familiar wooden box fly open and a hand reach in and grasp the kris. As the drums thundered, the jeweled handle caught the firelight and exploded with vivid slivers of color. She was hypnotized by the kris, hard and shimmering, floating above her head, and then, as the chanting rose to a screaming pitch, she felt a sudden sharp stab of pain.

Incomprehensibly, she heard terrified screams—like those she had heard that first night when she waited in the tower, screams that had haunted her dreams—but this time the screams were her own.

Abruptly, she saw her father's face, warped with fury, his features blurred and twisted beyond recognition, as the knife plunged again, ripping into her flesh.

All at once she felt the floor beneath her split open and freezing air float up from under her feet, wrapping her in a sheath of ice. Visions of ink-stained pages flew past her inner eye. Her mind closed in upon itself. From beneath her twisted love for her father and the anguish of his betrayal, she summoned the power she knew was within her, a force ancient and tempered. From out of her lost childhood, she drew the magic, glittering and dark, that had lain dormant in her deepest core.

She spoke no charm or rune, but felt every nerve of her body harden and grow rigid as she became the kris, sharp, faceted, flung in the air. She heard her father cry out and saw his eyes grow wild as the kris came to life and twisted in his hand. She witnessed his horror as he forced it back, fought its downward plunge, but he might as well have tried to stop the lightning in the sky. Like an arrow loosed from a bow, she was the kris, and she rode it into his heart.

"Angelique!" a voice was calling, and a ray of light pierced the darkness. "Are you still there?"

"Yes! Cesaire!"

"Oh, good! I worry for you. Don't move! I be back!"

"Cesaire! Wait! What's happening? Are we safe?"

"Yes. I don't know. Just stay quiet. I come soon."

It was difficult to know exactly where she was. She was shivering, curled into a ball, and she had been waiting for what seemed like hours, hidden beneath the deck. The creaking of the boat and the gentle slapping of the water against the hull were mingled with the groaning of the anchor chain. The wind was a constant roar as the little schooner lifted and fell in place. There was another sound, close by and beneath her, of the moaning and muttering of human captives, slaves chained in the hold. The stench of human waste was putrid, almost more than she could bear, but the smell of wretchedness was even worse.

She pulled the hat Cesaire had given her down

over her hair, stuffing the curls inside. The ragged shirt and pants she wore smelled of him, and she dug her hands inside the folds of the fabric and pulled it to her nose to blot out the other, foul odors.

Clashing images of her escape, each thrown into high relief, as if illuminated by a bolt of lightning, flashed through her mind. She remembered seeing her father collapse at her feet and feeling the sanctuary become deathly quiet when the drums ceased. She saw the slaves draw back, stunned by her power, afraid she would strike them as well. And then, from out of nowhere, her bounds were loosed, a firm hand clasped hers tightly, and she was running with Cesaire through the chapel and out the wide doors.

As in any nightmare, her feet were like lead, and she was certain the maddened slaves, their desires inflamed and thwarted, were nipping at her heels, as they chased her across the courtyard. She and Cesaire hung for an instant at the edge of the parapet, the dark water swirling beneath them, before he cried, "Jump!" Then they were flying, falling for the longest of seconds, and plunging into the sea.

Buoyed by clouds of bubbles, she clawed to the surface. Cesaire was at her side, thrashing, barely staying afloat. "The ship is there!" he shouted, and she saw the long black hull riding the swell and the tall spars piercing the sky.

She swam, pulling Cesaire beside her. He sputtered, "You swim good enough for two," and they floated in an invisible current, buffeted by chop, as the swinging lights on the schooner's side rose up, then dipped from sight. They swam and floated, clinging together, until the moment finally came when they brushed against the barnacled wood of the hull. Exhausted, they found a rope ladder and climbed aboard.

The quiet on deck was unexpected. "Where is everybody?" whispered Angelique.

Cesaire was sprawled on the deck breathing hard. Then they heard raucous laughter from below in the galley. "They be gambling with Old Father Rum," he grunted. Finally, he sat up and looked at her. "Here, best put these on." He pulled off his clothes and gave them to her. "Better me naked than you. Seamen want no women on board, but one little black sailor like me be fine. Hide your hair so's you be a boy." He handed her the knitted cap he kept in his pocket.

She tried not to look at Cesaire's little penis, shriveled and gray, but she was struck by how skinny the rest of him was, shivering there beside her.

"Come on!" he said, and she rose to follow him across the deck until they found a small hatch, which opened to the hold.

"Climb in here!" he said in a low voice. "I'll go see if I can find the captain. They be expectin' me to come by dinghy, with a lantern and a big 'Hallo!' from your father, who was to pay for the right to come aboard."

She climbed down into the darkness. He shut her away and was gone.

She waited for long minutes, which dragged into uncertain hours. Once again she was hidden, forced to endure the impotence of imprisonment, but finally she had time to think about all that had occurred, and she was tortured by remorse. She had killed her father—she had driven the knife into his breast—an unthinkable crime. She had done it to save herself, but she had run away. Who would believe her now, now that she was completely alone?

She had no idea whether her father had told her the truth about her mother's being at Trinité, but she was terrified at the prospect of returning to Saint-Pierre. Several of the planters were aware of her true parentage; the priest also knew. Would she face charges of murder resulting in her execution—hanging—or worse, torture? And yet perhaps no one realized what had happened. If the slaves did revolt, her father's death might be blamed on the rebellion, and she would be free to pursue her life in Martinique. But how? Where could she go?

There was another nagging thought in the deeper layers of her mind. Her powers, still so new and unfamiliar, baffled her. Could she really be a sorceress? Sometimes she had been seduced by the ceremony, drawn in by the fervor of the worshipers, and the *loas* had seemed amazingly real. "I am in fear for your immortal soul," Father Le Brot had said to her. Was the power she possessed from God, or from the darker side, the side of evil? Was she, as Father Le Brot had warned, the servant of the Devil?

She could feel him now, down in the hold, with its abominable stench. The darkness was imbued with his presence, and the foul odor was the one she remembered, the stink of rotting flesh. She had only to think of him to feel him hovering, and if she was still and concentrated, his touch became palpable . . . intimate.

The moans of the slaves in their chains, woeful and forlorn, were like the music of the huge hollow pipes of the organ in the cathedral in Saint-Pierre—the low sounds, those deeper than hearing that vibrated in the bones. The mournful dirge became his voice—a lament sadder than any human cry, and in the murky air she saw the curve of the hull open and the seawater rush in, rising in a black wave that warped the space, filling it with a roaring sound that broke over her, before it was sucked back into the night.

She closed her eyes and listened to the sound of her heartbeat, quick and high-pitched. Then she heard another, deep and throbbing, within her, as though two hearts beat together. "No," she breathed, the hair rising on her arms. "Don't—"

"Angelique," he whispered, his voice like a rasp against wood. "Come with me now, come with me."

"Who is it?"

"I saved you. . . . I was there with you. . . ."

He was close to her now, and she felt the cold seawater leaking in through the hull where she sat, spreading beneath her thighs, the freezing fingers traveling under her clothes, creeping up between her legs. She stiffened and waited while he explored her everywhere, circling her waist, pinching her small breasts, caresses stinging with ice, until finally she heard a soft cold sigh.

"Come with me. . . ."

"Tell me who you are . . ." she whispered back.

A mirthless, patient laughter that might have been the scraping of the anchor chain echoed by her ear, as he murmured, "But you know who I am. You have always known, my lovely one. So why do you ask? If I give you a name, will you be satisfied?"

"Yes . . ."

"The one who lives for you, longs for you alone, the Horned God."

She shivered. "Dark One, leave me."

His breath was like Pelée's suffocating gases, oily, pungent, and she could see him now, as the velvet sea swirled into robes, and his thick arms grasped the staves. His eyes were flaming coals and his skin as smooth as obsidian, but his voice was the rolling pitch of the schooner as the surge crashed upon it.

"I empowered you. You are my servant now. And again."

"That was not you. I did that," Angelique insisted.

"How were you able to kill your father?"

"I felt the power within me. I made that choice."

"To use me."

"I do know who you are! Evil personified! Begone!"

The ship creaked and shuddered as though it had struck a sandbar, and the hull shrank back. The shining muscular shape merged with the wooden staves and became the moaning slaves once more, writhing in their chains, whispering: "You can never escape me. I am in your thoughts. Always."

She was restless now, and her skin had begun to itch. How much longer must she stay in this hole? The wait began to gnaw on her, and she was at the point of pushing open the hatch, when she heard footsteps overhead and voices. At once, her courage deserted her, and she shrank back behind the fat bundles of tobacco with their loamy smell. She could see dawn peeking through the cracks of the planking.

At that moment she heard the grinding of the anchor chain and the wheeze of the winch. The water throbbed beneath the hull, and she could hear shouts over the sounds of pulleys whining and canvas cracking in the wind. The ship was under way! The schooner lifted, hovered, and crashed as it plowed the waves, and she felt her heart beat with excitement. Where were they going? Where was Cesaire?

When she thought she could bear the suspense no longer, the hatch jerked open and Cesaire flung himself down at her side. He carried a small lantern. She was glad to see that he had found himself short pants and a jersey, but the best part was he was grinning from ear to ear.

"Cesaire! Finally! What's happening?"

"We goin' to sea!" he cried. "Gal, we gots such a good fortune."

"To sea . . . but where?"

"To the big island—Hispaniola! To the finest city—Port-au-Prince! And there, we grow fat and rich!"

"How long a voyage is it?"

"Ten days—two weeks."

"But why? I thought we were going to stay in the harbor until morning. What happened?" She beat her thighs with her two fists. "Oh, I hate it that I must stay down here with no way to tell what is going on. Can't I please go on deck?"

"That's just it! You can! You can come up. There be just one little thing."

"What?"

"We gots to cut your hair. They sees you's a girl, they puts us both ashore on the firs' li'l deserted island we come to."

"Cut my hair? But how can I cut it?"

"With this!" And he brandished a sailor's cutlass. Instantly, she pulled off the cap and let the golden ringlets fall below her shoulders. Taking up a lock, Cesaire sawed it until it came loose in his hand. He tossed it in her lap and started on another. The whole time he jabbered with irrepressible excitement.

"I jes' been atop the mainmast, raising the top gallant. Lord, it be the finest little schooner you ever did see!"

"Tell me everything that happened. You were gone all night. Did you find the captain?"

"I did! It were one close call, but I save myself with my intelligence! An' my fine climbing!"

"Oh, no. Did you risk your life again, Cesaire?"

"Firs' I sneak down the deck and listen through the porthole to the captain's cabin. I hear him say to his other officers slaves be settin' fire to Saint-Pierre and they lose the trade. They can't come in the harbor with the 'bacco they has on board, so they decides to take off to the other side o' the Caribbean. They wants more slaves than the ones they already gots. They argues and argues about it, an' they finally decides to set sail."

"When did you talk to the captain?" Angelique asked, as she saw another lock of hair fall into her lap. Cesaire bent over her and sawed away.

"Owoooo, that be the scary part. I's crouched there by the window, drinkin' it all in, and thinkin' what's the bes' plan, when along come a sailor and grab me by the ear! 'What you doin', boy,' he cry out like he got hisself a wild goat, an' he mean to roast him on a stick. I says, 'I gots permission to come aboard, sir,' and he say, 'From who?' an' I says, 'The capt'n.' So's he drag me, naked as a jaybird, down the ladder and into the captain's quarters! He tell the captain I be's a stowaway!"

"Oh-h-h-h, no. What do they do to stowaways?" Angelique interrupted.

"Well, he was about to t'row me overboard 'til I sing out 'I be mos' happy to climb the mast and rerig that torn royal, Capt'n!' I don' know if they be a torn sail or not, but I figures I take that chance 'cause . . . well, they always is! He didn't believe I could climb all the way to the top, an' he say black boys afraid of heights, so I says, 'Gimme the try!' and first light they all comes out to see me climb, or to see me fall, more like it, since it be such a fine sport. They don't know I gots the number for that!" Cesaire laughed, rocking back on his heels.

"Why didn't you come and tell me?"

"They keep me locked up down there, 'til mornin', so's I can't get back to you."

"Well, did you do it? Did you climb to the top?" she asked, her eyes shining with excitement.

"Aw, gal, what you say? You know me. I coulda

shinned up there so easy it make their mouths gape open and the wind fly in. But I does my best to give 'em a good show. When I gets to the top, I rerigs the mail royal, then, when they all got their necks crooked back watchin', I loose my grip and drop! I lan' on the cross brace, and just barely catch it, with one hand! Aw, it all make-believe, but it work good! They all so staggered, the captain say I can stay aboard."

"But what about me? How long do I have to stay down here in the dark? I can't bear it anymore!"

"Take it easy, gal, I do good for you, too. I tell him there be another boy like me hidden in the hold, and he laugh and smack me on the ear, whap! like that, and say I be the most insolent fellow he know! Then one of the young officers chime in and say they needs a boy in the galley, and he say yes that be so, let us meet this other lad who must be as reckless as you! He say, once we under way, come see him in his quarters. There! You look good. Put the cap back on so's your hair not look so spiky."

Cesaire and Angelique climbed out on the raked deck, and she blinked at the sight of the dawn. The ship was alive with sailors, some in the rigging and some at the lines, calling out and pulling hard. A couple of the men gave them a glance but, for the most part, ignored them, involved in the work of setting the sails and steering the ship. They were already so far from Martinique that she could see the top of Dominica on the far horizon, and the shining Caribbean stretched before them, with the sun rising to the right and the wind at their stern. All the sails were full and drawing, and the officer she supposed must be the captain was standing on the bridge looking down at the wheel, his hand on his hip and his blue jacket unbuttoned at the collar.

A moment later, she stood before him, filthy and barefoot, her cap pulled over her chopped hair and her head bowed.

"So, lad, the two of you have decided to stow away aboard my ship. You know that is a crime, do you not?" Angelique was afraid to look up and too terrified to speak. She merely nodded and continued to stare at the deck. "I would take you back to Saint-Pierre," he continued, "and turn you over to the authorities, were it not for the infernal rebellion. God knows where I would find the militia. Look behind you."

She turned to see, and, sure enough, several dark plumes of smoke rose from the hills above the harbor. So, they had done it! The maroons had staged a revolt, and slaves had set fire to Saint-Pierre. Her heart skipped a beat. Had they destroyed the plantation? Was Thais all right? She hoped if her mother was there somewhere that she was safe.

"Now see here, boy," the captain continued. "I had some lucrative arrangement to pick up planters and their families for safekeeping, but I have decided not to risk it with my cargo, so we are off with the morning tide and as you can see, already halfway through the channel, the wind on our helm. I should toss you into the sea, but you are in luck. We need a scrub in the galley. What say you to that? Is it agreeable?"

"Yes, sir," said Angelique under her breath. She

stole a look at the captain. He was a tall man with a full gray beard and deep wrinkles around his eyes. She caught sight of his right hand, which was missing the three middle fingers, and he crooked the claw of thumb and pinkie around the hilt of a sword.

"Very well. Work hard and help Cook, do as he says, give him no trouble, and you'll have a safe voyage, and a free one as well I might say, to Hispaniola. What I do with you once we are there depends upon your performance during the next ten days. Off with you, now!" He nodded to Cesaire. "This young monkey will show you the way. There are pots to scrub, I'm sure, and salt pork to pound thin. And we'll have our tea on deck. What a minute! What do you say to me, lad?"

"Thank you, sir," she managed.

The captain narrowed his eyes at her, and answered, "Humph!"

She scurried after Cesaire.

"Hurry up," Cesaire whispered, "b'fore he change his mind."

They ran past a group of younger officers, standing by the rail and looking back at Martinique, gesturing toward the fires. One young man, tall and well formed, with brown curly hair, glanced in her direction. At that moment the boat crashed into the trough of a huge wave, and the deck shuddered. Cesaire grabbed Angelique by the arm to steady her, but she cried out, lost her balance, and fell, sliding smack into a pair of legs.

"Oh, so sorry, sir!"

"Whoa! What's this!" he said, then seeing her all in

a tangle, he smiled and reached down to give her a hand. As she scrambled to her feet, she looked up. She was dumbfounded when she saw his face. She knew him! To her astonishment, she recognized the boy she had met at Carnival, the boy she had dreamed about and kept alive in her mind for three long years.

Unconsciously, she reached for her charm, where the moonstone still lay, and she opened her mouth and soundlessly breathed the young officer's name, "Barnabas."

He frowned at her and leaned closer. "What did you say, lad?"

"Oh . . . nothing, sir."

"I thought you said my name. Do I know you?"

"N-n-no, sir . . ."

"What are you doing here?"

"Cook's boy, sir."

"Ah, yes, that was my recommendation. I worried the captain might throw you in the drink." He smiled pleasantly. "Still haven't got your sea legs, I notice."

"No, sir."

"Well, see that you stay well below, where you belong. We might catch a squall, and you'll be swept overboard."

"Yes, sir. Thank you, sir."

Cesaire tugged at her arm, but the young man held her gaze. She remembered his eyes, dark and merry with mirth, and the flow of freckles across his nose. Familiar as well was his courteous and courtly manner.

"How old are you now, my boy?" Barnabas asked.

"Thirteen . . ."

"A good age, younger than I was when I first went to sea. And, by the way, you've no need to be mortified. My first time out, I clung to the safety line the whole time—for fear of falling on my face, and because I needed the whole span of the ocean to vomit in!" He laughed in a comradely fashion and gave her a smack on the shoulder as if he were sharing a joke, man to man.

"I don't get seasick, sir," she ventured, even though Cesaire was signaling her to hurry.

"Really? Ah, well, then I envy you, lad. Perhaps, sometime, you will tell me your secret."

She turned to descend the ladder to the galley, but he called to her again.

"Wait a minute, lad!" She looked back. He was staring at her more intently, and his hand went to his mouth. "There is something about you that is familiar. Where are you from?"

"Martinique, sir."

"Yes, but which part?"

"Basse Pointe."

"Hm-m-m-m-m, what is it? Those eyes . . . blue as wild asters . . . ah, well, memory plays such tricks. There's no way I could know you. But best luck to you on your first voyage. May you become a fine sailor!"

Cesaire pulled her into the galley.

15

"Barnabas! Wake up! I need to speak to you!" There was a pounding on his door, and Barnabas was jarred from his reverie. The diary lay in his lap where he had set it down in astonishment at what he had just read.

"Barnabas! Are you there?" It was Carolyn's voice.

He opened the door and found her standing in her robe, her hair disheveled, and a stricken look on her face.

"Carolyn, what is it?"

"Oh, Barnabas, it's Mother. She's had a fall!"

"Is she badly hurt?"

"I don't know. She woke up in the middle of the night, tried to get out of bed, and when she stood up she was suddenly very dizzy. She said all the blood rushed from her head."

"Where is she now?"

"Lying down. Julia's with her, and she asked me to fetch you. She needs your help."

"Of, course, I'll be happy— I mean. I'll come immediately. Tell her I'll be right there."

He shut the door and tried to concentrate on finding his slippers. Then he thought better of putting on a robe over his pajamas and decided to dress before going down. His brain was reeling from the journal. That terrible voyage—when he had been so young! The attack of the pirates—ruthless cutthroats, who put him in chains. The one with the scar, who laughed and said they could get good money for a "Collins" if they took him back to Maine alive. The black-hearted villain who wanted to kill him to see if his blood was actually blue. His total certainty that he was going to die. Then, the slip of a boy, filthy from the kitchen, who had set him free! He had never known who he was—the cook's lad, fleeing for his own life as well—fast as quicksilver—set him free, and was gone!

He pulled on his trousers and sat on the bed to tie his shoes. Snatched from the jaws of death. The scoundrels who guarded him deathly ill, retching in agony, and incapable of stopping his young rescuer, who was . . . impossible . . . too absurd a coincidence to even consider. Had her life and his folded in upon one another, as if there had been some hand of fate at work, before he had ever actually met her, known her, and . . . desired her . . . ? Incomprehensible!

In this confused state of mind, Barnabas presented himself in Elizabeth's bedroom. Julia was sitting with her, watching over the elderly lady, her own face lined with concern.

"Oh, Barnabas. Thank you for coming. I hate to ask, but would you mind . . . ? Willie has the car at the gate, and we need you to go into town, to pick up a prescription. She hasn't been taking her medicine—it's for her blood pressure—and I'm afraid she's had a bad spell."

"My own fault," Elizabeth said weakly, lifting up from the pillow. "I ran out of pills, and—"

"Hush now, lie down, dear. It's all right. Barnabas can get them for you," Julia said soothingly.

"Is the pharmacy open at this hour?" he inquired.

"Yes. The one on Main Street—Pierson's. I've already called, and they have it waiting for you."

"I shall leave at once."

"Thank you so much, Cousin," Elizabeth murmured from the bed.

"She should be fine once she has the prescription—"

"Say no more. I'm delighted to be of assistance," he assured them, and left.

It was near dawn when Willie brought Barnabas back up to his room. Julia, who had been frantic with worry, came running from her bedroom the moment she saw Barnabas staggering down the hall, his arm across Willie's shoulders.

"Barnabas! My God! What happened?" He turned and looked at her with vacant, red-rimmed eyes. His shirt was covered in dried blood, and fresh blood was streaming from his neck. He moaned and collapsed in her arms. Supporting his weight as best she could, she looked beseechingly toward Willie. "What was it?"

"I dunno," Willie answered. "He couldn't tell me. I think he was attacked by some kind of animal."

Barnabas reached for his neck, which was bleeding painfully. As the two of them placed him on the bed, Barnabas groaned and rolled his head.

"Will he be all right?" asked Willie.

"Let me look at him." Julia fought to keep her voice calm. "Do you have Mrs. Collins's medicine?"

"It's right here."

Willie held out a wrinkled bag, which was also stained with blood.

"I-I had to change the tire, after it blew, and—and the car was on a hill, so I had to find a rock to prop under the back wheel—"

"It's all right, Willie, I'll hear about it later. Just take Mrs. Collins the prescription. Oh, and throw the bag away first."

"Okay, I'll do that." And he lumbered out.

Julia leaned over Barnabas and unbuttoned his shirt, which was drenched in blood. He moaned and opened his eyes.

"Barnabas, can you tell me what happened?" He stared at her, dazed and unblinking, as though he were staring far off into space. "Barnabas . . ."

"Julia . . . I was followed by some creature," he whispered. "I-I didn't know what it was—some man— but not a man—he was too strong—some demon . . ."

"Was . . . he . . . dressed in a man's clothes?"

"A suit, I think, no . . . a cape. And he had the

strength of a . . . of a . . ." His voice trailed off, and he lay back with a shudder.

Julia went to the bathroom and returned with a large enamel bowl and several washrags, which she placed on the bedside table. Her foot struck a small object on the floor just beneath the bed, and she leaned over. She picked up the diary and held it a moment before the lamp. "Were you reading this last night?" she asked in a tone that betrayed her disapproval.

"What . . . did you say?"

"Were you reading Angelique's journal?"

He stared at the ceiling. "I told you it didn't interest me."

She put the book down on the bed and gently began to clean the blood from Barnabas's neck, afraid of what she might find. She wiped his wounds with the wet cloth, dipped it into the water, wrung out the rag, and wiped again.

Barnabas began to speak in a whisper that burned with intensity. "He came out of nowhere."

"Where were you?"

"Near the docks. I told Willie to take the shore drive. We were at the bottom of Canal Street, when we ran over something—something sharp, like a broken bottle—and the tire blew."

"Oh, that's an awful neighborhood, all warehouses, isn't it?" She had found a jagged tear just below Barnabas's collarbone, and he flinched when she touched it with the rag.

"Yes, I saw several derelicts—homeless men huddled around a fire in a trash can—so I said to myself, when I got out of the car, well, at least it's not completely deserted."

"You should never have walked there alone."

"Perhaps, but I was so preoccupied with obtaining the medicine, you see. Elizabeth was depending on me, and I sense the family has the feeling that I am . . . irresponsible."

"That's not true. Roger is condescending to everyone—that's his nature. You mustn't take it personally."

Julia was always so calm and sympathetic, he thought, always able to comfort and reassure. But there was something different in her mood at this moment, distant, removed. He grimaced from the pain.

"Here, you must lie back. Don't strain yourself. You don't need to talk."

"It seemed like such a simple task," he said impatiently. "Drive into town with Willie, pick up the prescription, and return. And it was necessary. Elizabeth needed the medicine. I couldn't imagine remaining with the car, waiting for Willie to change the tire."

"I understand. So then what?"

"I left Willie just as he was removing the jack from the trunk. You know, the street rises sharply there."

"Above the docks . . ."

"Yes. Well, I started up the block, thinking that when I reached Main Street, I would turn down it toward the pharmacy, which is only three blocks on the right."

"Can you sit up so that I can remove your shirt?"

Barnabas felt a slight irritation that Julia didn't seem to be paying attention, almost as though she thought what had happened was his fault. "At any rate, as I was climbing the hill, I reached a stretch of the sidewalk where the streetlights are out. It was extremely dark, and I noticed there were several large arched openings set deep in the wall."

"It's an old carriage house," she said.

"Really? Yes, well that's right, now that you mention it, the openings are large enough for carriages—arched brickwork and wooden doorways, quite deep. Just as I was passing one of the openings, I noticed a homeless man asleep there, on a pile of newspapers. I made a wide berth around him so as not to disturb him, but when I looked back at him, I saw that his eyes were open, staring out, and there was a large pool of blood on the newspapers just beneath his head. All of a sudden I realized he was dead!"

"Good Lord, do you think someone killed him?"

"I don't know. I was so determined to obtain the medicine, I just hurried on by. It was so heartless of me, so indifferent, to hurry off in that manner, but he was past help, and I thought Elizabeth might be in dire need. I decided I could call the police once I got back to Collinwood."

"He was probably in some kind of brawl."

"Perhaps, but he was lying on newspapers."

"He was dumped in the doorway?"

"Yes. Well, at any rate, I finally reached Main Street, and even though there was no traffic at that hour, at least the storefronts were brightly lit. I was hurrying toward the drugstore—I could see the Pierson's sign flashing on and off—when I thought I heard someone behind me."

"What do you mean?"

"Walking. Footsteps. But footsteps completely in sync with my own, because when I stopped, they stopped; and when I walked on, I heard them again."

"Perhaps it was an echo. Sometimes the street will do that."

"That's exactly what I decided, because when I heard the footsteps strongly ring out, I turned around. And there was no one there!"

"It must have been terrifying."

By then the basin of water was red with blood as Julia continued to wring out the cloth and wipe Barnabas's chest and upper arm. She went into the bathroom, poured the darkly tinted water into the toilet, and filled the basin again. When she returned, she began to work on the ugly rips in the skin of his neck.

"At any rate," Barnabas continued, even more agitated, "I made it to the drugstore and, happily, Pierson was ready with the prescription. Seems the usual pharmacist was ill. He handed over the pills, while inquiring after Elizabeth and making comments on the possibility of rain tomorrow. Just as he was ringing up the price on the cash register, he glanced at the store's front window and gave an involuntary gasp. I swear to God, all the blood rushed from his face, and he looked as pale as a corpse!"

"What was it?"

"That's what I asked immediately. 'Do you see someone there?' But in less than no time, he came to his senses and shook his head.

"'Ah, it's nothing but the odd spirit out this time of night,' and he laughed as though it were a joke. But I noticed an abrupt change in his demeanor because he hurried me to the door and, after letting me out, pulled it shut with no further ceremony, bolted it, and drew the shade. Almost instantly the lights were flipped off, and I could see him walking quickly to the back of the store, where, I suppose, there is a rear door on to an alley."

"It was as if he were frightened of something," Julia suggested.

"Yes, and a moment later I heard the engine to his automobile and immediately thought of asking him for a lift."

"Of course! If he had decided to lock up and leave, he could have taken you back to your car."

"An old Packard came out of the alley, and Pierson turned into the street with such alacrity, he actually crossed over the curb with his front tire and screeched off at great speed. I never had an opportunity to wave him down."

"What a pity!"

"Still, I told myself it was only a few blocks, and Willie should be finished with the tire by now, so I walked, or jogged, back to Canal Street and turned onto it. Right away, I began to hear the footsteps again."

"You didn't pass by the body of the dead man."

Julia had become caught up in the story.

"No. I intentionally came down the other side, continually looking back over my shoulder and trying to catch sight of the infernal stalker, and I suppose, once or twice I glanced over at the corpse, but I was not conscious of what lay to my left, some dark wooden buildings—"

"Stables," she informed him.

"What?"

"Those are the old stables, those wooden buildings, just opposite the carriage houses—"

"Exactly. And I was foolishly oblivious to any open door, or dark corner, when—from out of nowhere—came this . . . fiend!"

"Oh, God . . ."

"He wore a black cape, and . . . he leapt upon me from behind, or—when I think back—above. Yes, he dropped from above, onto my back."

Julia was speechless, her mouth agape.

"His strength, Julia, was so out of proportion to his size, which was human—not giant—yet he seemed to float above the ground—to rise up and fall on me again—ripping at my neck with his . . . long nails, or—worse—with his teeth!"

"What did you think he was?"

"Why—a robber—I had no idea what. I tried to shed him, but he clung to my back like a great . . . ape . . . his breath hissing and his teeth gnashing. And then, of course, I knew the worst."

"Barnabas—you don't mean—he must have been—"

"A vampire."

"Oh, my God, did he . . . ?"

"He drew blood, but he did not . . . feast."

"There was no—"

"No deep penetration, no loss of consciousness, I never felt him enter. Have you found anything?"

She turned Barnabas to the window, where the cheerless sun was shrouded in thick clouds, and in the light inspected the several wounds, now cleaned of blood.

"Deep cuts, rips, but no fang marks. You were fortunate. How did you get away?"

"I don't know. He was clumsy, perhaps . . . new . . . inexperienced."

"Or it could have been . . . your blood—the elixir in your veins—that repulsed him."

"Yes, you're right. That may have been it."

Barnabas was suddenly very tired. He sighed deeply, and his shoulders slumped. Julia placed a bandage over the cuts.

"I think you were saved. But I should administer an injection, just to make certain." She crossed to her medicine bag, withdrew the hypodermic needle, drew the fluid into the capsule, and came to Barnabas's side. As she injected the serum, she said, "You must rest now. I'll stay here with you. I won't leave you until you're asleep."

"Bless you, Julia," he said, looking up at her with gratitude. "You're all I have in the world. You know that."

He lay back, and she pulled the covers up to his

face and kissed him. Then she sat beside him until he fell into a fitful slumber. More than once he moaned and thrashed, or cried out, and she was obliged to calm him with soft words and a hand stroking his forehead.

While she was sitting there, she glanced over and saw the diary lying on the bed where she had placed it. Hesitating a moment, she leaned across and took it in her hand, opened to one page, then another, shuddered, and set it down on the bedside table. But after a moment she reconsidered and, checking to see whether Barnabas still slept, took it up again, slipped it inside her jacket, and tiptoed from the room.

chapter

16

Caught in the twilight between sleep and waking, Barnabas was prey to torturous flashes of memory as he was transported back to the summer of his eighteenth year. They saw the fast moving frigate on the far horizon, her three masts swollen with sail. As she drew near they could view through the spyglass, the flag of the Spanish Main flying above her topsail and the dreaded skull and crossbones furled beneath. There was bedlam on board his own vessel, sailors manning the cannon and firing the powder. But the guns were ill set, and the balls flew wild. She came at them steadily, and though they turned and fled before the wind, she caught them easily, and the pirates swarmed aboard, shouting oaths, flashing cutlasses, grinning like devils.

Had he fought gamely? He believed he had—but rashly, recklessly. He had a fierce memory of slashing the cheek of one of the beasts and hearing him howl in surprise. The melee was a blur of swords, bellows of pain, and, yes, he remembered thinking the buccaneers were no gentlemen because they would not stand and fight like soldiers, but engaged only to distract, so that one of their depraved comrades might sneak up behind and stab a good man in the back. He remembered blood on the slippery, treacherous deck, and a severed arm—and could it have been?—a head! sliced clean off by a prodigious blade. He had been determined to keep his back against the mainmast, the better to hold the ruffians at bay. He remembered beating the air with his sword in a futile attempt to ward them off.

But their numbers had been too many, and they overpowered him and lashed him to the mast, where he was forced to witness his shrewd, resourceful captain—that same courageous gentleman who had lost three fingers to buccaneers once before and still prevailed in that battle—cut down by the bloodthirsty bastards, like a bull slaughtered in sacrifice.

At first he had no explanation for why the pirates had seen fit to spare him. But, after the ship was lost and his comrades were all dead, he heard the outlaws arguing among themselves. One of his fellow officers had bargained for his own life—only to lose it in the end, for there was no honor among those thieves— with the information that there was the son of a wealthy merchant on board worth a magnificent ransom if spared and brought back alive. Some of them had believed it.

The pirates had thrown him into irons alongside his captured slaves. He was forced to lie with them in chains, down in the hold, wallowing in their offal, listening to their moans. He had then endured such humiliating shame, and such heartrending remorse, that he believed it had been enough to transform him once and for all into a man of integrity, with an irrevocable sense of justice.

But what use was that at the time? He had been convinced he was going to die in the full knowledge that his family's corrupt enterprise, the trading of human lives, had brought this punishment upon them all.

How long had he been captive? The days had run together into one long night of hunger, thirst, and wretchedness of body and spirit. Until finally, he had felt the ship swing into calm water and had heard her anchor drop. They came with sniggering jests for the slaves, but left him there, he felt certain, to die.

Then the unexpected had occurred. He could still see the boy bending over him, telling him that he would protect him, that he had nothing to fear. And what had the boy done? He struggled to remember. Was his memory perverted? Had he really seen him stalk and capture . . . a rat? Did he actually crawl along the inside of the staves reaching into the putrid water of the bilge until he caught the swimming creature? He could still see the boy's slender figure silhouetted in the opening of the hatch, with the limp brown body in his hand.

Later, when the boy returned with a companion, a young slave, he had the key, and he had unlocked the chains. Then his young rescuer had led him past the two guards, who lay retching on the deck, tankards of spilled rum beside them. While the slave watched, the boy had taken him down a ladder to a waiting dinghy, equipped with an oar.

Unbelievable! She had saved his life. Barnabas was wide-awake now, and he was burning with curiosity. The memories he had dredged his mind to discover provided too few details. How had she done it? The rum! That was it! She was already a witch at thirteen, and she had made a potion and poisoned the rum.

He had to know if he was right. He sat up, wincing from the pain in his shoulder, and felt around for the diary. It was not in the bedclothes or on the bedside table. Julia had said something about it before she had washed his wounds. She had asked him if he were reading it. Had she put it somewhere?

He fell to his knees and, nearly collapsing from weakness, searched beneath the bed, then back through the sheets and the quilt. It was gone!

He staggered across the room, the pain crying out against movement, and desperately explored the dresser, the table by the window, the chair, the desk. Nowhere! Furious that he could not find it, he ripped the sheets from the bed, piling them on the floor. How could it have disappeared? Julia. Of course. Julia had taken it! He made for the door and shouted into the hall.

"Julia!" He shouted again. "Julia!"

She came from her room, a worried expression on her face, but he knew her too well, and could easily perceive guilt flickering beneath the concern.

"What is it, Barnabas? Are you all right?"

"Julia, what happened to the diary? What did you do with it?"

"Pardon?"

"Angelique's diary. Where is it?"

"I thought—but you said you didn't care about it and I-I didn't want it there in your room, so I—"

"You what?" he demanded.

"I removed it."

"Where is it?"

She hesitated a moment, looking at him with a mixture of anxiety and censure. "So you were reading it," she said.

"Yes, yes," he responded irritably. "What if I was."

"Barnabas . . . the diary is evil—"

"Nonsense—"

"Angelique's hatred, and her jealousy, motivated the curse almost two hundred years ago. You yourself have admitted that to me. Tonight you were attacked— by a vampire. I cannot imagine that you would want any force of evil near you, influencing you—"

"How dare you—"

"Barnabas, listen—"

"How dare you intrude where you are not wanted—take it upon yourself to choose what I read and don't read. Can't you see that it's a violation of my privacy!"

"But you said—"

"Don't you think I am capable of determining whether a child's journal has power over me? Don't you think I know, by now, what evil is?"

"I only think you are vulnerable in your present condition. Remember, I am your doctor, and I decide—"

"You decide nothing! You are my doctor, yes, but you are not my mother!" He saw her flinch at his words.

"Did you burn it?"

"No. I was afraid to burn it."

"Where is it?" He was barely able to keep himself in check. Incredibly, she stood her ground.

"I do not intend to tell you—"

"Don't you understand? I must know!" His frustration, all out of proportion to the situation, overcame him. He was suddenly so enraged he found himself standing over her with his fingers dug into her shoulders, shaking her, squeezing hard. "Where is it!"

"Barnabas, stop! Please . . ."

Abruptly he let go and backed away, astounded at himself. What was happening to him? He stared at his hands in bewilderment.

"Julia," he said in a quivering voice, "I'm so sorry. I don't know what came over me—why I became so angry." He walked to the bed and sat down, lowering his face into his hands. When he looked at her again his expression was drawn and miserable. "It's just that I—please understand—I must have it back. Please . . . forgive me."

Julia sighed. "All right," she said. "If you must know, I'll tell you. I buried it—in the graveyard— under her tombstone."

*   *   *

His mind blurred by pain, Barnabas staggered across the lawn. The rain had been falling for hours, a steady downpour. He had left without an umbrella and was soon drenched. He walked, hunched over, the spark of determination the only bright fire within him.

He was desperate to read Angelique's account of the battle. She would describe him, reveal his actions and how he had been valiant, generous of heart. Her words would restore him, bring back his vigor and courage. He would be able to see himself again, through her eyes, youthful, optimistic, "merry" she had called him, and "courtly," the young man he had been so long ago before his decades of depravity. His heart ached. Damn Julia!

His clothes were now wet to the skin, but there was a certain comfort in no longer resisting the rain and letting it have its way with him. The exertion had eased the stiffness of his wounds, and the deluge of falling drops had grown pleasurable. He thought of Angelique.

Their first passion had been in the rain, the warm tropical rain that fell like silk in Martinique. He remembered her face as he kissed it, soft and wet, her lips full of sweet water. He had held her against him, feeling her bones beneath her dripping garment, and she was all liquid flesh enveloping him. He remembered lying with her in the falling water, a stream flowing beneath them and the sky opening above. Her breasts were slick, the nipples taut as swelling seeds, and his hands swam in her warm wetness, as their bodies floated into a river of currents, their limbs slipping together. He could still feel the rain pounding against his back, as she opened her legs and a deeper whirlpool sucked him in as their bodies and the rain and the river were all one.

He reached the gate to the cemetery. At that instant the sky was rent by a great bolt of lightning, and a rumbling clap of thunder shook the ground at his feet. The statue of the angel was illuminated in that split second, hovering over her tomb on the other side of the graveyard. A heartbeat later Barnabas stood beneath her supplicating figure, and in the drenched earth, he could make out the spot where the sod had been disturbed.

He fell to his knees and dug with his fingers, pulling back a loose mound of grass and some easily dislodged debris. Then he felt it; the diary was there. He wanted to weep when he saw it lying in the mud, a pool of water collecting around it as the rain fell upon it, the pages soaked through, and the leather cover blackened and ruined.

A flicker of hope offered the chance that some of the pages could still be saved, and he reached for the book. But at that instant, he saw what he had become. His resolution and fortitude, his devotion to his new life, had given way as easily as the mud beneath his knees, and he was staggered to realize he had fallen prey to his detestable obsession. Once more, she had him! He was caught in the spell of an irresistible liaison, and once again he was willing to sacrifice all virtue, even the generous heart of a woman who loved him, for his contemptible desires.

Julia had freed him of all that. What in God's name was he doing? At the very instant he had the opportunity to live as a man of integrity, he was willing to throw it all away? Had he not been tortured enough? What could he possibly gain from the diary other than one more fantasy of illicit pleasure. Julia had been trying to tell him that, and he had been unwilling to listen.

Angelique's childhood had been tragic, but she was evil, there was no denying that, and he had always fought against her. He had always struggled, in utter self-loathing, against what she had made him. How could he have considered any other path? Resisting her had been the only source of goodness within him, and it was goodness he now craved with all his being—the peace that only a guilt-free heart could bestow.

Leave it there! Suddenly a feeling of great relief rushed over him, and a swelling of pure happiness flooded his breast. Trembling from his decision, grimacing from the feel of the cold, slimy sod, he placed the dirt and muddy grasses back on top of the book. Then he stood, pressed the earth down with his boot, turned, and, with an unsteady but determined step, walked away from the graveyard.

chapter

17

*P*ort-au-Prince! The loas hover over the city as though the very air were the breath of spirits. They whisper, *Freedom.* The city swarms with blacks, maroons, quadroons, mulattoes, men and women of splendid, glossy colors, their hearts high with rage. Rage gallops through the streets and down the back alleys. There is no Christian God here. Africa reigns with her pulsing power, avenging ancestors, gods of blood. At every doorway there is a wrinkled charm, on every sweating chest a trinket of bones hung from a thong of flesh. Altars with blood on the stones, feathers, and fur dried on the walls, guard every courtyard.

I saw him on the dock, Negroes swarming around him. I moved closer, as though drawn by a magnet. He was making fire. He danced, his black body gleaming wet, and where he stomped there was smoke, and when he turned and hurled his fist at the ground, the flame sprang up as he bid it to do. I was envious. I stayed with him the whole day.

That night they lit the sacrificial fires, and he began the ceremony I thought I knew so well. But it was not the same. He is a true channel for the spirits. They come to him *instantly. After he was in deep trance, he took up the sword. The drums were like thunder in the sky. He quivered where he stood. His long grass skirt swayed and lifted, like seaweed under the surge. When the sword was red-hot from the coals, he pulled its razor edge against one arm, then the other. He carved with delicate precision upon his chest, his neck, his tongue. He lifted the blade and sliced his open eye. No blood flowed. No welts, no scars. His eye remained whole.*

The pages were separating now, under the gentle warmth of the hair dryer. Julia had let the book dry for several days, wrapped in towels, and then at last she had begun to pull the pages apart. It was slow, tedious, frustrating work. Much of the diary was lost. The ink had faded into watery rivulets as tears on a love letter would streak the words written there. Some of the pages were like tissue, limp and fragile, tearing easily into ragged strips like bindings for wounds. But there were other sections she could read clearly.

Abruptly, he leapt into the fire. I watched as he pranced on the coals, digging his feet into the bright embers, while the drums raged. He spun and cavorted, riding a burning broom, for he was the horse now, and he galloped in the fire-brands in a mad frenzy, until I was certain his feet must be burned, and all the while my own body crawled with a stinging rash. Then, at last, he collapsed, exhausted, his chest heaving, sitting with his legs crossed under him. The soles of his feet were gray from the ash but firm and unblis-tered. Unable to resist, I touched one foot, and found that the skin was cool and dry. I offered him water and he took it in his cupped hands and smiled at me.

Julia shuddered. But she did not doubt the veracity of what she read. Simply, she feared it. Nothing in her nature craved this magic or responded to the powers that brought it into being. She was more fascinated by the medical explanations. Skin was thick. Sweat repulsed the heat. Faith and speed were strong allies. Sleight of hand was always possible. Witch doctors were clever.

I followed him to his home, for I had nowhere else to go, because I wanted to be his slave, and because he led me there. He lives in a hovel among hovels, built into the side of a hill, with a dirt floor, and a ragged rug for his cot. He has no food or water. Others feed him because he is a great hougan. And because he is a renowned Bokor, I knew they would not question a white girl living in his house, if only I could convince him to let me stay.

I said to him, "Teach me to make fire."

He asked me why I thought he should teach me. What I had seen. And I told him everything I knew. I told him of Chloe and of Erzulie and of the last ceremony, when I had turned the knife in my father's hand. I recited the chants from the book of runes, and I told him of the spells I had mastered. And he listened quietly until I had finished. Then he said, "You know nothing, my child. Your knowledge is only of the mind, you have no intuitive skills. I cannot waste my time with you."

He said I could remain one night, and then I would have to leave. I asked him where I should sleep, and he pointed to the ground near the back wall. I asked for water, and he shook his head. No water, he said. The Negroes were not allowed to use the well in the square. They must walk several miles for water, out of the slums and into the country.

I woke just after midnight because I heard the sound of a stream flowing. At first it was muted, but then it became distinct.

When the day came, I told the houngan *I had found water. He said that was not possible, that they had tried to dig several wells, but had no success. I said, "The water is here, behind this wall, where you had me sleep. Dig here."*

He called several men, and they started to dig. They found the underground stream the first day. The water poured out like a silver flame, and the houngan *said, "All right then, tonight you come with us."*

The meeting place was at a crossroads, at a small village in the country. There were several thatched huts, and thousands of candles lined the cross in four directions. People came swiftly, like shadows on little paths through the cane, or over the trees. They wore bright costumes of the Soukougnan, *who shed its skin, and* Loup-Garou, *the werewolf. The* Bokor *said, "This ceremony is Bizango—blood sacrifice." Each man danced in the motions of his animal, strutting cocks, barking dogs, grunting pigs, even demons with tails and horns. I do not know how they transformed themselves. They called Carrefour, not Legba, and after he was fed, Baron Cimetière.*

I was pulled to the center of the circle with a frightened little goat and thought he was the sacrifice. I began to bleat with him and fed him leaves with my own lips to calm him, but his eyes were wild. The drums stopped, and they all drifted away stealthily, like leopards. They had long cords in their hands, cords the Bokor *said were cured intestines and very strong. When the victim was brought back he was a man, but he was turned into a cow before they killed him.*

Page after page Julia carefully, skillfully, peeled back. Her tools were her surgeon's scalpel, scissors, and small tweezers, all taken from her medicine bag. But so much of the book was gone. She wondered whether returning the diary to Barnabas in this ruined condition would only disturb him more. Sometimes she could save only a phrase.

The Bokor *has glittering eyes, and he likes a joke. He is a little wisp of a man, very black and scarcely five feet tall. He is thin and small-boned, with tiny hands and feet, and his face is as wrinkled as a sea cucumber in the sand.*

Julia's shoulders ached from her efforts, and her eyes were stinging from trying to read the blurred words. She had hoped she could save more. Perhaps if she let it dry a few more days, more pages would come apart.

He told me voodoo comes from Africa but the French call it voir—*to see, and* Dieu—*God, "to see God," but I said I have heard it means* voir dans, *"to see within." I thought it mattered a great deal which was the proper meaning, but he said it did not matter in the least. He asked me why I had memorized African invocations.*
    "You are not a Negro girl."
    "I have some of the blood in me."

*"Use your own language. The words don't matter.
Magic comes from the soul."*

> Eye of newt and toe of frog,
> Wool of bat and tongue of dog.
> Vampire, ghoul, bloodsucker, parasite.
> Drums, rum, blood.

"Tell me the three drums."
"Cata, Seconde, Maman."
"Why are they called those names?"
"I don't know."
*"Cata is mischievous, naughty, an unruly child. Seconde
is in the middle, the whole human spectrum. That is the ordi-
nary life. Maman is* voudun.*"*

Julia was deeply ashamed that she had taken the
diary. She felt the very least she could do was retrieve
it and return it to Barnabas in the hope that he would
forgive her. Also, the very next morning, as she lay
in bed before rising, she began to ponder the scien-
tific explanations for witchcraft—even as she had
immersed herself in the investigation and discovery
of the final solution for vampirism. A peculiar curiosity teased her mind. She had to admit to herself she
was fascinated with the supernatural and its antithe-
sis, its "natural" explanations.

*I said to him, "Can you kill someone?" and he said, "Killin'
is easy, but it is against the law." And I asked him, "Can you
make someone love you?" and he said, "You pays your money*

and you takes the consequence." Then I said, "Can you call back the dead?" and he said, "Yes, if they be feelin' mischievous. The dead love to be called. Unless, of course, they are zombies. Then you have yourself a slave."

Zombies! Now that was an interesting phenomenon. The living dead. Caskets opened and the body not decayed. Hair and fingernails had grown. Skin still flushed, rosier than in life, signs of rejuvenation, erect penis. Why had they used the headstone since ancient times? To prevent the corpse from rising. And why the multitude of ceremonies for the dead? That they might rest in peace in their graves. With the requisite objects, they might be willing to stay put: wine in jars, grains in bowls, coins for Charon in the mouth, poppy seeds for dreamless slumber.

A plantation owner came to the Bokor to buy some laborers, and the Bokor took the money. Then, with his face in a contorted mask, he mounted a horse backwards and rode it to the victim's door. He placed his lips over a crack in the door and sucked the soul of the victim out. After a few days the victim died. The Bokor took me to the graveyard at midnight, where the dead man lay in his tomb. He had the victim's soul in an earthen jar, and when he called out his name the dead man was obliged to answer because the Bokor had his soul. Then he passed the jar beneath the dead man's nose so that he could smell his soul, and the man rose up and followed him. At the Bokor's house he was given the red elixir that is the secret formula and became a zombie. Now he will work tirelessly for the lucky planter.

*   *   *

Zombie Powder:

Secure an entire afterbirth, the bag intact with part of the navel cord still attached. Wrap it in manchineel leaves.

Grind with a pestle:

bouga toad or unleached manioc

millipedes or tarantulas

seeds and leaves from poisonous plants

puffer fish stingers

human remains from a new corpse

A man who stole the secret of the Zombie Powder was killed by the Bokor's *hounci. He never knew they had found his hidden little bag. They took him in a boat, then, far from shore, they tied his hands behind his back and struck his neck with a rock, making a raw spot. Into the wound they rubbed a quick poison. He knew he was dead before he hit the water.*

The Bokor *said he made the Zombie Powder because it was easier than sucking souls through keyholes.*

Barnabas had not spoken a rational word to her since their argument; he had been so ill that everything he said was from the raging of the fever. He seemed to drift between penitent guilt and furious determination. "No more! No more!" he would cry, coming out of a disturbed sleep. Or he would grasp her hands in his and with wild eyes, plead with her to forgive him, saying, "Julia, stay with me, don't leave me!" Moments later he would stare off into space, and scream, "Get away from me! Stay away!" and she would shrink with fright, certain he was venting his anger on her.

The Bokor said, "I will not show you murder and death. These you have already seen. I have shown you life returning from the dead. And tonight I will show you how to murder Death itself. Tonight you will stake the vampire.

"The vampire has ivory teeth, elongated and sharp, to suck the life force, and he leaves his victims exhausted and spent. He is a self-absorbed being without sympathy. I have told you that all gods come from our imaginings, and likewise the vampire is born in the realms of our innermost thoughts. He is the manifestation of our deepest longing and our deepest fears. Dead, but not dead. Blood still within the body. The odor of the vampire is like the guano in the cave where bats breed. He has eyes like hollows of madness with which he can see colors of rich intensity. He has the hearing of a predator and far-beyond-human capacities of survival. He cannot be killed when he is awake; therefore, you must not wake him. He can only be murdered in the grave."

"What has made him that way?"

"The vampire bat has fed on him and poisoned his blood."

"Why does the bat come?"

"A curse—an enemy pronounces a curse, the consummate form of vengeance. It takes enormous power to make this curse. Great power and great hatred combined."

The sounds of the night were muted, and the candles gave a dim light. The sky was shrouded with clouds as we walked to the cemetery. Our footsteps were like the dead whispering. The Bokor motioned to the grave where the vampire slept. I saw the white cross and the coffin in the hole. The hounci were with me, because they wanted to take the parts, but they hung back in fear. "You cannot be frightened," he said. "All fear is weakness." He put the stake in my hand.

When I looked down on the vampire I was filled with wonder, for I could sense his mystery and his strength. His face was very white, like carved ivory, as were his hands, which were folded across his breast, and I could see the shape of his skull, and the bones of his fingers beneath his skin. His fingernails were long and yellow, and I could smell the odor of bat guano rising from his body. His coat was covered with dirt, and his ruffled collar with mildew and rust. He was sleeping so peacefully that I was suddenly reluctant to harm him.

The hounci moved closer. "Tonight you will murder Death itself." I placed the point of the stake against his chest and thought only of how thin I was, and wondered where I would find the strength to force it into his heart. All I had was the weight of my own body, and I raised up and pushed with all my might on the sharpened post of wood, feeling it pierce the fabric of his coat and the layers of his skin, each section giving way with a little jerk. The monster groaned. The stake struck a rib, and I slid it down to find a softer entrance.

At that moment the vampire opened his eyes. His hypnotic stare sent a terrified quivering through my body. I could feel him draining my strength with the force of his will as his eyes burned into my soul, then he reached up his powerful hands and grasped the stake. His mouth opened to form the words to stop me, and his lips drew back to reveal the fangs, gleaming white and covered with slime. I could push the stake no farther.

Then the Bokor leapt upon my back, knocking the breath out of my chest as it struck the end of the post. Our bodies slammed into the vampire, and, as the stake slid into his heart, the blood spurted forth and covered me. I lay upon him, my face next to his face, my breath sucking the prolonged death rattle of a windpipe choked with blood.

Julia shuddered. She remembered how Barnabas had returned without the diary, his clothes in an awful condition, shivering and soaked to the skin. The wounds had reopened, and he was weak from loss of blood. She was worried that the bite of the vampire would cause a relapse, for Barnabas appeared to be fighting an inner battle between opposing demons, his emotions in turmoil, and his very nature feeding upon itself.

Most of the time she was certain he had no sense of who or where he was, and he raved about a ship attacked by pirates and lying in chains. Other times he seemed calmer and spoke to someone in a gentle voice, someone he loved.

Unable to stop herself, Julia continued to dry out and try to read sections from the diary.

The Bokor spoke to me often, and he was always discouraging. He liked to tease me and torture me with his riddles.

"*Do you still wish to become a voudun mambo?*"

"*Yes.*"

"*The choice is not an easy one, and the journey once begun bears no returning. Will you go all the way?*"

"*I will not be left behind in shallows and in miseries.*"

"Why would you want such a thing?"

"I believe it is my destiny."

"Destiny is only what you believe." He giggled. He liked turning a phrase on its ear. This time, I was determined to make him listen.

"I mean, I have gifts, and knowledge."

"So does everyone."

"Will you teach me what you know?"

"Voudun is confusing and cumbersome. It will not make your life better."

"I need something to protect me."

"Voudun will only make you more vulnerable."

"But won't it give me power?"

"Power is unwieldy. You want to control things, but voudun is not control. This is why I know you will never be a mambo. You are a white girl. How can you look into the African soul? You only want your way, like all vain females. You want tricks, silly little spells. You want to play with others like they are toys. This is not power, but only fiddling and foolishness."

"I will tell you why I am so afraid. I have begun to think that I am bound to the Devil."

"The Devil?"

"Yes."

"And you want to be free of him."

"Yes . . . free . . ."

"But the Devil is only another loa, and not a very interesting one at that. Another luminous spirit. The loas will never harm you unless you let them. Feed them and give them drink, and they will never bother you. Strike the vévé with the asson and the loa is obliged to descend. You know that.

All the gods are only our own imaginings, and the Devil is no different."

"Are you certain?"

"I am certain of nothing."

"But I have seen him and spoken to him."

"I did not say that he did not exist."

"Then how can I free myself?"

"All right, answer me this. What is witchcraft, if you don't already know?"

"You have always told me. It is interference, meddling."

"How does it work?"

"You find the weakest point, and that is the place you fling your power."

"So, you have just answered your own question. That is how you free yourself."

"The Devil has a weak point? What is it?"

"Is he not the Horned God?" The Bokor giggled again, his little sea-cucumber body shaking.

"What does that mean?"

"Ah, you are still too young to know. He is always a cuckold. You must not fear him. As long as you fear him he has you."

"Then why does he tell me that my power comes from him when I have taught myself these things and suffered to know them?"

"That's easy. Think of what you just said."

"Ah, that is my weak point."

"Exactly. He knows how proud you are. He is trying to tell you something you already know. You have several choices. What are they?"

I thought about this for a time, then I answered.

"To live an ordinary life and never be what I was meant to be. To make little spells. Or to choose voudun."

"Once you choose voudun there is no ordinary life."

"What if I only choose good magic, like my mother. She was a healer."

"Ah, yes, good magic. But there is no good magic. It's all interference, and therefore evil. That does not mean it isn't distracting." And he giggled again.

"Stop these ridiculous riddles. Tell me the truth!"

"But the truth is the riddle!" And he jiggled with laughter. At least he was enjoying himself.

"So if I become a witch—"

"You are a witch already."

"If I practice only what I know, and am not proud, will he leave me alone?"

"No. Because what you know is meaningless. And now we have come back around to the beginning of our conversation. Listen to me, Angelique, and I will tell you the truth as you call it. Everything I say to you you will forget, because you will not understand. But I will tell you anyway, and perhaps one day you will remember it. Death is the only power, and the Devil is death. All voudun has death at its center. When you accept death and cling to nothing in life, your power will emerge, and voudun will guide you.

"Can you do that? Can you achieve indifference? I think not. I think you will always be obsessed with something. You have not the character of a mambo. You will cling to life and ignore the death it springs from. You will seek love, and it will turn to jealousy, then revenge, because deep beneath all your rainbow colors is a dark pool of despair, and because your way is the way of desire. You say Erzulie is your goddess, but

*her mirror side is Erzulie-Rouge. Which will it be? The lily
or the rose? Perfect innocence or profound understanding?
The great voodoo goddess has Death sitting by her side. The
moment surrounding the moment. The magic within the
magic. The power is in the mirror. It will be many years
before you realize, if you ever do, that you will be doomed by
your obsession, and that the greatest power is in desiring
nothing."*

chapter

18

Angelique was so filthy it seemed impossible for her to be light-skinned. The grime had entered her pores, and her skin had turned the color of ash. Soot was lodged beneath her fingernails, and her yellow hair was hidden, wrapped in an oily rag. She was so thin, she folded when she lay down on the earthen floor, her bones loose in her tattered shift. Cesaire would never have recognized her had her eyes not darted out at him like fire opals glinting in the dust.

"They told me I find you here," he said, his nose wrinkling from the odors of smoke and burning herbs. "But I not believe them."

"What else did they tell you?"

"That they tremble in your *hounfort*. That you are not cruel, but you are cruelly kind. That your magic be like the lightning, never know when it come, never know if it strike the mark. They say sparks fly from your fingertips, and that your potions are not safe, for sometimes you heal and sometimes you maim."

"Erzulie lies with me now, Cesaire. My skin is not a barrier to her coming. The *loa* enters me when I breathe."

"Erzulie—who is loved for her purity?"

"Oh, no, the other Erzulie. Her image in the mirror, Erzulie-Rouge, who is much more powerful, who feeds on men's souls."

Cesaire frowned and walked closer to where she sat.

"What are doing with these people, Angelique?"

"What do you mean? I live here."

"Why?"

"Where else would I go? I need the *hounci* to care for me and give me food."

"Is it so important to be a little goddess? To live in this foul place! Barrel of rotten apples give no choice."

Her eyes flared at his insult. "You think I am vain and proud. You know nothing. That's not the reason I am *Bizango* now. Erzulie protects me from him."

"Who? The *Bokor*?"

"No, not the *Bokor*. From him!"

Angelique rose and walked to the altar. Smoke rose from her garment as though it were made of ash. She stood there, her body willowy and strangely regal, gazing at the sacred table. A long copper-colored snake was crawling slowly around the clay jars and pots of decayed and powdered food, his undulating body circling lighted candles and flowing over piles of bones.

"I will make you a charm, Cesaire, a love-*ouanga*,

if you like. This morning I caught a hummingbird, and I need to use it before it grows cold. A love-*ouanga* just for you. Would you like that? Is there a pretty girl you want?"

She turned, and he could see the tiny bird in her hand, its iridescent feathers and scarlet breast. "I will need some of your blood and your semen." She reached for him, smiling suggestively. "Come."

Cesaire shook his head. "I need no charm from you today," he said, and with an effort pulled his eyes away from her, and looked instead at the painting above the altar. It was of a naked woman with large breasts, the lower half of her body covered with fish scales. On all sides of her were paintings of the Virgin Mary.

Cesaire came to where Angelique was standing. He saw that she was holding a doll made of dried skin, and she was embellishing it carelessly with a strand of human teeth. It had a tiny shrunken head with beady eyes and several pins protruding from its wizened chest.

"Angelique, I have come to take you back to Martinique."

"No. I don't want to go. I can't go back there!"

Cesaire shivered, and he looked up at the center painting again.

Beside the fish woman, a boat with a white sail rocked on curling blue waves. Beneath the boat was a chalice filled with crimson flowers, and the sky was painted black and sprinkled with stars. The woman was holding something, and when Cesaire looked more closely, he saw that it was a human head. It was then that he realized Angelique's entire altar was made of gaping skulls.

"Listen to me, girl. I have news of your mother."

Her eyes flew to his face, searching, revealing some hint of the child still hiding inside her.

"She in terrible trouble," he continued. "I thought you want to know."

"Where is she?"

"In prison."

"Prison! But why?"

"She be tried for witchcraft, and she have been condemned."

Angelique stared at him, unable to believe his words, as tears filled her eyes.

"I have a boat," he said. "Will you come?"

The weather was calm but there was a heavy, rolling swell, and the wind changed, forcing the schooner to run before it. A sulfurous exultation emanated from the sea, and more than once Angelique leaned against the rail and whispered, watching as the surface boiled.

Cesaire stood on the other side of the deck, and she knew he was frightened and thought he no longer knew her, that she was like a dark specter against the sky, and although she had let her hair down, and it was a pale cloud, it gave her no light. She could reach out and touch the Dark Spirit when the waves leapt to her hand. He was not of the sea, but he was within the deep, and she said to him, "Don't follow me."

*   *   *

She opened the gate to the prison and walked into the grassy court. The weather was changing, and ominous gusts of fitful wind caught the straggly palms by the prison doorway and whipped them into a macabre dance. The guard was sitting just inside the door, snoozing on a spindly chair, his head thrown back as he snored. She made a noise in her throat that woke him, and he shook himself and stood on wobbly feet to address her.

"Visiting hours ended an hour ago," he said abruptly. He was a large man, mulatto, with a red beard, and one of his eyes was blind, an opaque blue across the pupil, giving him a dismal demeanor as though he had only half a soul.

"I have come all the way from Port-au-Prince to see the woman who has been condemned for witchcraft. Please allow me to pass."

The tyranny of petty officials empowered him, and he sneered at her. "My orders is to allow no visitors. Come back tomorrow."

"What if I told you the woman I wish to see is my mother."

"I got no part in that," he said coldly. "Hangings every day, breakings at the wheel, executions by militia. I just guard the prisoners and, if I'm in the mood, throw them a bit of bread. Now be gone with you. I have my work to do."

Reluctantly, she turned to leave, and as she did she glanced behind his desk toward a small room, which she realized must be his living quarters. She could see a cot and a chair with clothes strewn about and a table with bread, cheese, a bottle of rum, and a thick tallow candle that had burned down and spread its wax in a yellow pool. She stared hard at the flame.

"Is that your room?" she asked, and when he grunted in the affirmative, she sniffed the air, and said, "I believe something in there has caught fire."

The guard let out an infantile yelp followed by a stream of curses when he turned and saw the flames springing from the floor. He lurched into the fire, tromping it with his boot, but to no avail, for it flared up in one spot, then another. It was attacking the bed-clothes when he grabbed a basin of water and threw it on the blaze. Angelique slipped by him without his noticing her.

When she entered the prison corridor and looked through the bars, she felt her heart lift to her throat. It had been four years since they had seen one another, but Cymbaline had not changed. She was sitting on a small stool singing to herself. Her glossy hair hung about her shoulders, and her golden skin glowed even in the gloom of the cell, as though the light from the one small window emanated from her.

When she saw Angelique standing outside the bars, her black eyes flashed suspiciously at first, then widened in disbelief as she slowly shook her head, and a profound expression of utter pathos melted her features. She lifted her arms, and as Angelique reached through, she pressed the girl to her, sobbing, "Angel, oh, my Angel, my daughter—my precious child."

"Mama, oh, Mama, I thought I would never see

you again. I've missed you so much. Why are you here like this? What happened?"

But Cymbaline was unable to answer. She merely held Angelique's face in her two hands and kissed whatever she could reach between the bars—cheeks, chin, forehead, lips—her words trapped in her throat. Her fingers traveled over Angelique's face and hair as though she did not trust her eyes and needed to touch her to believe she was there. All the while her tears flowed.

"Oh, you are so lovely," she whispered at last, "so tall, your body so strong—a woman now, I see."

"I'm fourteen."

"And have you learned many things about life?"

"Of life, I still know very little, only what you taught me, Mama, but I have been to Port-au-Prince—and I fear I have learned the secrets of death."

"The Devil Island—the spirits there are powerful. Sit down here close to me as you can get, and tell me everything. I want to hear—I know you fled Basse Pointe, during the rebellion."

"Mama, my father tried to kill me during the ceremony. All along he wanted me for that. He lied to you. He never meant to raise me as his daughter."

"The bastard tricked me. Oh, I was a fool to have believed him. I am sorry for your suffering."

"I slew him, with his own dagger."

"Is that true?"

"Yes."

"And then you sailed to Hispaniola?"

"Ten days on a privateer. Halfway across, we were boarded by sea beggars, set on plunder. Their clothes were stained with blood, and they carried knives and bayonets. Mama, they murdered almost everyone—officers, sailors, even the cook! They spared my friend Cesaire because he was a Negro and he could sail the ship."

"How did you escape?"

"They only let me live because I had been working in the galley, and they needed someone to prepare their meals. The drunken fools never knew I made a brew from a rat's tail and whiskers that I put in the rum, a potion that burned their insides and made them blind."

"Ah, yes, fatal vomiting from the hair. I see you have become a sorceress."

"What would you have me do?"

"No more and no less than I have done."

"They called you a witch."

"They say it is witchcraft, but it was not witchcraft. It was the manchineel tree."

"But everyone knows that is poison. What did you do?"

"Let's just say they caught up with me at last. I was three years working in the slave hospital at Trinité, a very big plantation. I birth babies, set broken limbs, stop sickness in his tracks. Often they say of me 'witchcraft' when I was only a dedicated healer. "

"Then why were you unhappy?"

"There was an overseer, a greedy lustful man who would not let me be. In the early years I never worried. I thought my place in the hospital was secure. I was necessary. I was needed. And when the overseer troubled me, I put the green worm in his drink to dull his lust.

"One night, he was drunk, mean drunk, and he caught me out in the yard. He pulled me into the bushes but I scraped my fingernails on the manchineel tree. While he held me down, I dug my fingernails into his back. The villain goat thought he was pleasuring me until the poison set. I heard him scream in agony when he died."

"And they accused you of murdering him?"

"That is what is so contrary, it mocks their tribunal. They found me guilty of not saving him. I could not do it. I would not give him any medicine. You see, they want me dead. For many reasons."

"So what is your sentence?"

"Oh, sweet darlin', you don't want to know.

"Tell me . . ."

"Not too bad. They give me a painless death, because of my service."

"What?"

"The gallows."

Angelique felt the blood spin in her head. "When?"

"Two days hence."

"Oh, Mama . . ." Angelique sucked in her breath, unable to speak, and her eyes burned. Cymbaline reached through the bars.

"Angelique, my darling, do not grieve. I could ask for no gift as fine as this one, to see you again before I die." Although her eyes brimmed with tears, she was smiling as she reached for the girl's hand and held it tight. Angelique's chest ached with a dull pressure, as though she had been holding her breath for too long underwater. She hesitated, then spoke in a quivering voice.

"Mama, I have brought a secret dust with me from Port-au-Prince. If they knew I had taken it, they would kill me."

"What is this thing?"

"It is a powder that produces a deep sleep, so deep it seems like death."

"You don't mean Zombie Powder?"

"Yes."

"Made from corpses? I don't want Zombie Powder!" Cymbaline withdrew, horrified.

"Mama, Mama, come back! The powder does not bring death, only the sleep of death."

"But the Zombie is pitiful and crazy because his soul is taken! He walks the world in a lifeless trance, trying to get his soul back. Death is far better than that."

"No, the taking of the soul is a ritual the *Bokor* performs."

"How you know, Angelique?"

"I have seen it, many times. The powder is only for the sleep, and the madness comes from waking in the grave, the horror of it, being buried alive. But I can bring you back from the sleep. I will be the one who wakes you, and you will never know where you have been. I have seen this happen again and again. You must trust me."

"You want me to use this powder?"

"It is your only chance, and, Mama, look. I even have the antidote." She showed her mother the sacks with the two powders, one white, one crimson. Cymbaline recoiled in distaste.

"What has happened to you, child? Who has given you this evil thing, and taught you how to use it?"

"Mama, I have been with a famous *Bokor* in Port-au-Prince. I have seen the way the powder is made. I have seen the man rise from the dead. You have only to blow it from your palm and suck it out of the air. One breath, and you will lose consciousness. You will fall into a sleep so still and lifeless, they will be certain you are dead. They will take you out to the graveyard behind the morne and bury you in the earth." Cymbaline listened, shuddering in disgust.

"No! It's too horrible—to be buried and to be still alive? I haven't the courage. I could never bear it."

"When everyone has left, I will come, open the casket, and wake you. You will never know—it will be like a dream for you. And we will escape together. I will take you with me back to Port-au-Prince."

Cymbaline looked at her child as though she did not know her and shook her head, her eyes filled with worry and pity.

"Mama, there is no other way."

"Give me the powder," she said at last with a deep sigh. "I will think on these things you have said to me. I do love life with all my heart."

"I promise you, Mama. It will save you."

Cymbaline touched Angelique's face again and gazed at her as if to memorize her features.

"Before you go," she said, "I must . . . there is something I thought I never would have the chance to tell you."

"What, Mama?"

"Theodore Bouchard, that vile monster, I'm glad you killed him, he . . . oh, Angelique, I did you a mighty wrong. It was my greedy dreams for you that made me do it."

"What about him?"

"I lied to you. He was not your father."

"What? But how can you say that? The birth-mark on my leg is the same as his!"

"My child, a birthmark is an easy thing to fake, for someone like me."

"But why did you tell me I was his?"

"I thought he would become a powerful, rich planter, and he would give you a good life. He was willing, he said, to raise you up a lady. I am ashamed to say he was my lover, as black-hearted a villain as he was, and I lay with him many times. He wanted to marry me, but I tell him no. Still, I told him you were his daughter, and he believed me. I never knew he was *Couchon Gris*. I let you go to them—and you such an angel child. I did a very evil thing to tell that falsehood, and it makes my heart wretched. So, you see, I really deserve my woeful sentence."

"You mustn't say that!"

"I should pay for such a crime."

"Don't talk that way!" Angelique looked down at her hands, flexing the fingers. "Mama, who was my father?"

"I don't know. I truly believe he came from the sea. Remember I used to tell you you were born of water?"

"Yes, and I always thought it was true, that I was the child of the sea because I was so happy there."

"I'll tell you the story of the day your father came, and you decide. It was a peculiar morning and there was no wind off the ocean. The wind came from Pelée, scorching and harsh; the sky was sizzling blue, and the foam of the sea was like cream. I was gathering crabs, but I was seeing the air, fractured into rainbows, and the sand was like grains of gold. That's when I think a spell is coming because the air was so hot and still, and then I see the white bird standing, watching me, and I know I'm right."

"The bird told you?"

Cymbaline nodded. "I went up the beach a ways, but I was having trouble finding crabs, because all the little white shells on the beach had come to life and were moving. Then I saw the great turtle, so green and spotted, like a sea beast come up in the day. She had dug her hole, there in the daylight, where she had no business being, where she had no way to hide, and I came close and saw her dropping her pearly round eggs out from behind her tail. She swished her behind back and forth, back and forth, burying her eggs, and I know it is a spell."

"What happened?"

"Why, sure enough, a man steps out of the sea—golden like a god, eyes like pieces of the sky."

"And he was the one?"

"He stayed with me five days. We have love, love of man and woman, and when he goes, I have you inside me."

Angelique closed her eyes and had a vision of her mother, in a flowered pareu, walking in the foam—slender, her hair long and dark, her body supple and curved, and her pareu clinging to her, flowering her body. But most of all, she saw her shyness and her awkward, girlish movements, the woman a man would see, not the mother who was so wise and loving and held her to her breast, but the rippling girl walking in the sand, shy and smiling the way she would smile to a lover, moving like music in her bones.

The dead man hung from the gibbet. He turned slowly on the rope, and his eyes bulged in the contortions of death. The air was hot and drenched with moisture, but the sky was leaden and there was not a breath of wind. The sun hung, a red and rotting sphere, and there was a far-off rumbling, a subterranean grumble that meant a hurricane was on its way.

Angelique waited outside the prison with a crowd of mulattoes and békés who had come to watch the executions, and she tried to quell the panic in her breast. The guards removed the body of the slave who had just been hanged, and flung the empty noose back to the sky. A row of crude wooden boxes serving as coffins stood by the prison wall under the arcade.

There had already been several hangings that day, and the crowd was growing impatient. She saw only a few *blancs*, tradesmen, shopkeepers; but the judges were there in black robes, a shabby detail of French militia, and she spotted Father Le Brot standing near the scaffold to administer the last rites. She drew back, afraid that he might notice her.

"Do you know the witch?"

The voice startled her, and she turned to see a kindly brown woman with a baby on her hip. She answered her softly.

"She is my mother."

The woman sucked in her breath and let out a low sound of commiseration, then turned and whispered to her companions. They all looked at her with pained expressions, and another darker woman approached, her face lined with compassion.

"Your mother did no wrong," she said kindly. "This is an unjust sentence. She is a good healer. She birthed my child. All the slaves at Trinité loved her."

Another woman spoke in a low voice. "It was the planters from the Grande Anse who wanted to avenge that overseer—his drinking comrades in Saint-Pierre. Ever since the rebellion there has been tyranny, suspicion, and cruelty. Many are executed for no reason."

The sky darkened, and rain threatened as Cymbaline appeared in the prison arch, and began the slow walk to the scaffold. Angelique could feel her heart racing, and she glanced anxiously at the low clouds on the horizon, for she feared rain drops would wash the powder from the air.

Her mother was dressed in a long white shift that failed to disguise her fine figure, and her black hair fell in waves down her back. She was without ornament, but her beauty shone from the gleam of her skin and her lustrous tiger eyes, which raked the crowd and lingered on Angelique. Just the shadow of a smile passed over her face.

The thunder rumbled like deep drums, and the air was palpable, thick and hot, hovering like a pall. Cymbaline mounted the scaffold with her head held high, stumbled slightly on the last step, then stood tall on the platform, only her trembling lip betraying her fear. A welcome breath of a breeze ghosted through, caught the hem of her skirt, but fled before it had cooled the square, and the air was still again.

Angelique hoped Cymbaline had the powder in her hand. But something was wrong. Something was not as she had imagined it. Angelique was jolted by the sudden realization that her mother's hands were tied behind her back! How could she breathe the powder?

A black-robed judge read the sentence, his nasal voice ringing in the sodden air. "Cymbaline Harpignies, you have been accused of the crime of witchcraft, tried, found guilty, and condemned to death. Do you have anything to say?"

Cymbaline looked down at the crowd. Her dark hair framed her face, and her eyes were wide. "I beseech you people to hear me one last time. I have committed no crimes and have only defended myself from the humiliation no woman should be forced to endure."

Angelique saw the old anger rise in her. "You say

he was a white man, and because African blood runs in my veins, I had no right to strike him down. He was white, I admit that, but he was a vile and licentious beast, not a man at all. I will not call him a man, and any that seek revenge for his well-deserved death are the same brutal monsters as he!"

There was a murmur through the crowd as the judges conferred among themselves, then one nodded to the priest. Father Le Brot mounted the scaffold.

"She is a witch!" a man called out. "She does not have need of communion!"

The priest turned to the man, and said gently, "All are equal in the eyes of God, and all who receive the sacraments ascend to the Gates of Heaven."

Angelique could wait no longer. Hoping he would not recognize her, she pushed forward as the priest placed the wafer in Cymbaline's mouth, and when she reached the edge of the platform, she called up to him, "Father, give her a crucifix to hold."

Father Le Brot turned and frowned slightly when he heard the voice, but he did not look down.

"She needs a cross, Father," Angelique insisted urgently.

The priest looked instead to the judges, questioning. One hesitated, then shrugged, and Angelique breathed a sigh of relief when she saw the guard untie her mother's wrists, and the priest hold the crucifix up to her. Cymbaline looked at the wooden cross for a long moment, then her gaze flickered, and she saw Angelique beneath the platform. Their eyes held, and Angelique nodded to her slowly.

Cymbaline reached quickly for the cross, took it, and pressed it swiftly to her lips, releasing a wisp of white smoke into air. Then she clasped the crucifix to her breast. Her nostrils flared, her eyes grew wide, she looked at Angelique, and took a last deep breath, just as the hangman lifted the noose. At that instant her eyes glazed over, she wavered, then swooned, and fell, crumpling to the wood. Her arm flew out, with the cross still in her hand. As the astonished crowd hovered around her, her breathing slowly ceased.

As if in response, the sky darkened. The clouds belched rain, drenching the populace. The downpour hammered the still body of Cymbaline as the guard turned her over on the platform and peered into her face.

"Is she dead?" a voice spit out.

"Dead," he said, with bewildered finality, shaking his head, raindrops falling from his nose.

The crowd exploded, and angry demands were hurled at the judges.

"She was a witch! The crucifix destroyed her!"

"No! It proves she is a martyr. The cross was her salvation."

"Hang her nonetheless!"

"Her sentence was unjust!"

"What if she is a witch? She'll return and torment us!"

"That isn't true! Christ took her with him when she held his crucifix to her breast! She deserves a holy burial!"

"The witch must be hung! Or she will live again!"

But Father Le Brot intervened, and Cymbaline's body was lifted and carried back to the prison. There she was wrapped in a shroud and placed in the last empty coffin, which stood within the arched gallery. Sheets of rain blasted the stones of the square.

The funeral procession began slowly, winding its way toward the edge of town. The coffins were stacked on a heavy wagon pulled by two horses, and Angelique could see that there were many mourners, mostly families of the condemned and executed, some weeping, and others trudging in dull-eyed remorse. Her mother's coffin was the last one at the back of the cart, and Father Le Brot had tied the crucifix to the rope which held the lid to the box. Angelique walked close behind it, sometimes reaching out with her hand to touch the rough wood, as if to reassure herself that all was well.

The incessant rain fell in curtains, gusted by a treacherous wind which seemed to come from no one direction, but drove the rain sideways across the road, bending trees to the ground, then spun and whipped the grasses to tangled mounds. The roar was constant now, rolling in from the sea, and Angelique could hear the surf pounding from its great height on the beach.

Angelique watched as the coffin was lowered into the dark grave, which seemed to fill with the water flowing from a thousand rivulets newly created by the downpour. Rain spattered on the flat wooden cover.

The diggers could not shovel the dirt but were obliged to scrape the mud into the hole, struggling to cover the box with sodden lumps of earth. The force of the gale made it difficult to stand, and the two men leaned into the thrust of it as they labored. At last they were finished, and one man rested against his spade and wiped the dripping water from his face. As he stood and looked toward her, Angelique was surprised to recognize the prison guard, with his fuzzy red beard and the one cloudy blind eye that lent a dull malevolence to his gaze.

When the hurricane was mounting its worst assault, Angelique returned to the deserted graveyard with her shovel and, bracing her feet in a wide stance against the power of the roaring wind, began to dig. Palm fronds careened through the air, and dark coconut leaves sailed past her head as she bent to her task. Her arms soon ached, and her back flared with pain. She felt the wind as a physical body, buffeting her bony frame, so weak now from lack of nourishment in Port-au-Prince, and she staggered under each blow. Often her shovel came up with nothing but pebbles the stubborn gale blew back into the pitiful hole she was making, until, finally, she fell to her knees and began clawing with her hands, mindless of her bleeding knuckles as the rocks ripped the skin from her fingers.

The wind reeled, and the shed by the cemetery gate exploded and collapsed with a clattering crash as pieces of tile crumbled into bits and the wattle walls broke in the mud. It was as if the world were falling apart. Every time she opened her mouth to breathe, it filled with water, and she thought of the many times she had tumbled in heavy surf and lost her sense of the way to the top and had swum instead toward the deep. But now there was no surface to this foaming sea of air that beat her with punishing fists and filled her eyes with grit so that she could no longer see.

Still she dug at the grave, until at last she could feel her fingers scratching the wood of the coffin, and she began to pray softly, "Mama, don't wake, I am here, I am coming for you now, and I will lift you out, and this death will be washed away by this hurricane, and all we will remember of its fury will be our resurrection."

At last she had the earth cleared from the coffin, as the rain now aided her, washing the clods from the surface of the wood, and, with a surge of joy, she tore the crucifix from the rope around the box and stood and strained for a grip on the slippery surface of the wood as she lifted the lid.

Her first thought was that the water had penetrated the casket, because the shroud was so thin and collapsed against the bottom, but as she dug at the limp fabric a sickening dread wrapped its menace around her bones. She stared at the gaping receptacle in bewilderment. The coffin was empty!

"Mama . . . ! Mama!"

No! How could it be? Where was she? Staggering though the graveyard, stumbling, falling to the mud and rising again, she searched for another new grave, but the scattered debris from the storm covered every piece of earth, and there was nothing but bruised mud lying beneath ripped and mangled branches. She screamed, "Mama!" But the wind whipped the sound from her throat, and there was no answer within the roar. She fell to her knees and sobbed.

"Somewhere, because of me, somewhere in the bitter darkness, she must die . . . a second time . . . and she suffers now, is crying out for me now . . . and I cannot hear her, I cannot find her . . . no . . . Oh, God, please . . . no . . ."

She flung her arms hysterically into the shrieking wind and screamed with the force of the tempest. "What have you done to me? You have betrayed me! Answer me! Devil! Tormentor! Murderer!" The howl of the gale was her only answer, but she could feel him in the turbulent air, as surely as she could hear the two hearts beating within her, and she knew he had found the way to destroy her forever. She looked to the tumultuous sky, and with all her strength she called to him, "Save her! Show me where she is, Fiend! Satan! Where are you? Why have you abandoned me? Come to me!"

And at last the voice answered in the numbing roar, "I am here. . . ."

She spun and raked the darkness for him, but the furious deluge was all she saw. "Save her!"

"You are a disappointment to me, Angelique," said the deep, rasping monotone. "I did not move her body. Look to the one-eyed gatekeeper for that. You suffer from pride and crippling fears. You believe only in your own powers. You have rejected me, and now when it suits you, you summon me. I am weary of you. When your heart is stone, then I will come to you.

Until then, you will never know when your powers will fail you."

"I renounce my powers! Do you hear me? I want no more of them, forever and ever. They are no use to me! They only bring me heartbreak and despair! Leave me, forever, and take them with you when you go!"

If the screaming wind could laugh, he laughed, a high, earsplitting whistle, and he said, "As you wish, my child, as you wish! You have made your choice." And he was sucked away into the holocaust.

chapter

19

Barnabas sat staring out the window of his room at a day that bore all the beauty of a passing storm. Heavy clouds hung low in the sky, but the light poured around them, silvering their shadows, and bright rays shone down on the earth. The air had been washed by the rain, and, when the sun finally broke, the color of the grass was a dazzling emerald green.

It was two weeks since his collapse, and he and Julia now believed that the vampire's attack had not reversed the cure. Long days spent in bed had left him restless. He was so tense that it was impossible to sleep, and although he felt weak, he could not remain in his room for one more hour.

Julia was sitting at her desk, working on the journal. She had finally loosened a particularly thick section when she heard a knock on the door. "Yes?"

"It's Barnabas. May I come in?"

She ran to the door and opened it. "Barnabas, you shouldn't be out of bed."

He was propped against the doorframe, smiling, and she could see his complexion had some color.

"Oh, Julia, I'm bored. I wanted to ask whether I could go for a walk, and if you would join me. I don't think I'll need a wheelchair," he joked. "Perhaps I could just lean on your shoulder."

She blushed slightly. "What a charming idea!" she cried. "I'll come at once." As she was reaching for her jacket, he caught sight of the book on the table, glowing in the lamplight. He frowned at first, and when he realized what it was, he appeared quite disturbed.

"Julia, what do you have there!"

"Oh, Barnabas. It—it is Angelique's journal."

"But . . . you buried it!"

"I know I did. I'm so sorry. It was selfish and stupid of me." He stared at her, more in amazement then reproach, as she continued. "I've been planning to return it to you, Barnabas. I've been working on it. I saved as much of it as I could. But . . . the whole center part, I'm afraid, is gone, except for bits and pieces."

He walked over to where the book lay and looked down at it as though he couldn't believe it was there. "You read from the journal?"

"Yes . . . I must say she had a fascinating childhood. But so steeped in the supernatural—she was most definitely a witch, a trained witch, a voodoo priestess at fourteen. The parts I read were very disturbing."

"And do you still find it . . . evil?"

"I must admit I do. I realize it's only a record of her experiences, but they were depraved and spiritually bereft. Still, she suffered so much, I almost feel pity for her. She never knew her father and—it was heartbreaking—her mother died a horrible death because of her. I think she tried to give up her powers and live an ordinary life."

"But you still think the book is dangerous."

"Well I think it could be, yes. However, I've been reading it for several nights and . . . it's had no effect on me . . . other than finding parts of it repulsive. . . ."

"Are you saying that now you think it's all right for me to read it."

"I think . . . I should not have tried to prevent you from reading it."

"Well, the truth is, Julia, I'm not at all interested in the diary anymore. I wish you had left it in the graveyard."

Julia shook her head and chuckled.

"Why are you laughing?"

"Only because I spent so many long hours drying the pages and separating them. I may have been foolish, but I wanted to return the book to you so that you would no longer be angry with me."

"But, Julia, I was never angry with you. I am devoted to you and greatly indebted to you. Come, leave it there. Come for our walk, and let's not mention this ridiculous diary again."

Later that night, as was almost always the case, Barnabas found that he could not sleep. He knocked softly on Julia's door before opening it. She was deep in slumber, and he thought better of disturbing her.

Angelique's diary lay open on her table. The shape had changed. It was thicker than before, as the pages were warped, the leather cover was blacker and heavier, but the soft moonlight coming in the window fell upon the damaged volume, imbuing it with a ghostly glow. After hesitating a moment, he took it up and, silently closing the door, returned with it to his room.

His hands were shaking as he opened the book and began to read. An odor rose from the pages, of damp mold and the sea, but almost immediately images began to form in his mind, as though he were caught in a dream.

Cesaire found Angelique, prostrate and nearly drowned, beside the grave, and led her, dazed and unresisting, back to the sailmaker's shack. There she keened and mourned, to the very edge of madness, and only his sympathy and constant vigilance kept her from destroying herself. Her daylight hours were seared with guilt, her nightmares a tangle of ghastly visions. She had nowhere to flee, except into a drugged semiconsciousness which Cesaire induced with chamomile tea laced with *tafia*.

One day she seemed a bit better when she woke. She looked out the window at the new day with a pale, drawn face. She turned to him, and said, "Tell me, Cesaire, what happened at Basse Pointe?"

"Why, it has gone to the rats, gal. Everybody left— all the rebellious slaves—all dead. Plantation house deserted. People stay away, say there be roving spirits."

"Will you take me there?"

"Why you want to go back there, gal?"

"I want my books."

So Cesaire borrowed an old horse and together they rode up into the hills, she clinging to his back. There was solace in the closeness of his taut body, sprung like steel, and she buried her face in his hair, which was soft and smelled of dried roses. She wrapped her legs around the mare and let the easy gait rock her, loosening the binds of pain that twisted through her bones.

She had never realized the forest was so lush, trees reaching into clouds, the dark undergrowth crowded with broadleaf foliage, lianas festooned with orchids, and bright heliconia arching like scarlet birds. There were buzzings and rustlings in the thick patches of ferns, and intense heat rose from fetid pools between the bloodroot trees, where the great fanned buttresses spread into the swamp.

Every so often, a patch of sky would show through, and she would glimpse Pelée rising to a ceiling of mist, the steep sides smothered in green fur, and Angelique felt a longing she did not understand—as though the mountain were calling to her.

It was queer walking through the heavy gate, which hung open, and crossing the courtyard. Cesaire had been right when he said the plantation was deserted. The fine windmill revolved slowly like a ghost ship, but it was unhitched from its gears, and the crushers were silent. Stacks of dry cane lay scattered and wasted, the soft breeze rustling their papery stalks.

As Angelique climbed the silent stairs to her old

room, images flashed across her mind. Everything was the same; her books were exactly where she had left them over a year ago, lying in the dust beneath her bed, and she pulled out the journal, a few school-books, and the Shakespeare.

The room behind the altar seemed smaller and dingier than she remembered, but she carefully selected a variety of healing herbs and powders in small containers and placed them in a satchel she had brought for the purpose. The book of spells was lying in the corner, covered with grime, and she left it there.

Lifting the curtain, she walked into the sanctuary. She stood for several minutes before the altar, listening to the wind whistling outside the stone walls, and the utter, implacable silence within. For the last time she said good-bye, as she had beside her mother's grave, to all her dark powers.

"But I don't want to be a lady's maid!"

"Angelique, listen to me, you must go on. What else is there but life and a new adventure? You can't run the mill with water gone by." Cesaire sat with her as she ate the dried fish and biscuit he had brought her.

"Can't I stay here, with you?"

"There is nothing for you here." Cesaire held a paper in his hand, on which was written the name: *Countess Natalie du Prés.* "Look at this and think in your head. This be a good sign. A fine lady, from Paris, and you educated some, modest, and wise, just what they be wantin'."

"But, Cesaire, a servant . . ."

"Gal, everybody serve somebody. Those we care for keep us breathing, give us reasons to live."

"No. I want to stay here."

"You too good for this life. That's why I'm leaving here, too."

"You are? You're going away?"

"You know it be my dream to go to sea, and that's what I aim to do, gal. The pig no min' the mud he hunker in, but the birds gots to take to the air. "

The plantation at Trinité was elegantly kept and built on a grand scale. As Angelique approached the plantation house, she was almost blinded by the sun gleaming from the red-tile roof of the verandah. It was a fine, two-storied, plaster edifice, with heavy shutters painted green. A giant wooden wheel turning in a fast-running stream ran the mill, and the sparkling river wound through the pasture. There were four or five slaves— working in the garden, tending the fruit trees scattered across the lawns, and carting wood to the kitchen. Far off on the hillsides the cane fields carved the land into multicolored patches of mahogany, emerald, and gold.

The Countess Natalie du Prés sat in the wide parlor on a wicker chaise, sipping from a china cup. She wore a dress of magenta taffeta, and her hair hung in red ringlets. Her face was angular, with high cobra cheekbones, and she had an aquiline nose with flared nostrils. Her dark brown eyes fixed themselves disdainfully on Angelique, and she pursed her mouth when she spoke.

"'Angelique,' is it? But you are such a drab, uninteresting child. Why would I want to hire you? You're obviously an ignorant peasant girl with nothing to offer. Who is your mother?"

"She is dead, Madame. She worked in the slave hospital. Her name was Cymbaline."

"Ah, yes, I remember, tried as a witch." Her eyebrows drew together. "Do you take after her?"

"Oh, no, Madame."

"You don't dabble in poison, or practice witchcraft?"

"No, Madame. Those things frighten me."

"No, of course you don't. You're much too ordinary for anything having to do with the occult."

"But I will work hard, Madame, and I learn fast."

"No, no, that's not the point. I need a girl to be tutored with my niece. You would not be at all suitable. Can you even write?"

"Yes, Madame, and recite Shakespeare by heart."

"Oh, really? You recite Shakespeare? I find that very hard to believe."

"It's true, Madame."

"Indeed. Say a piece for me."

Angelique thought for a moment. "Which is your favorite play?"

"Are you trying to pretend you know them all? Or are you stalling because you have lied to me?"

"I will say something from *The Tempest* if you like."

"Go on."

Angelique took a breath and began softly, her

voice picking up the melodious cadence as she gathered courage.

> "Full fathom five thy father lies;
> Of his bones are coral made:
> Those are pearls that were his eyes:
> Nothing of him that doth fade,
> But doth suffer a sea change
> Into something rich and strange.
> Sea-nymphs hourly ring his knell,
> Hark! now I hear them, ding-dong, bell."

The countess was stunned. "Where did you learn that?"

"I was given a book of Shakespeare, Madame, when I was small."

"Well, yes, hm-m-m-m. Although memorization is not a sign of intelligence. Imagination and perceptiveness are the hallmarks of a fine mind."

"Yes, Madame."

"However, it's impossible to find educated servants on this island. Since I am in need of a proper maid, you might be trainable. And Josette wants a companion. It's the very devil keeping her at her lessons."

"I will study with her, Madame, and do my best to help her."

"She's younger than you are, and much prettier. For that she is indulged by her father. We will make a trial of it, that is all. I warn you, any sign of laziness or insolence, and you are out! You will move into the servants' quarters, but you will join Miss Josette in the library when her tutor comes, and if you prove to be a decent scholar, who knows? I may allow you to remain."

And so began Angelique's long term as a lady's maid. She lived an ordinary life, altogether uneventful, though she was comfortable and employed. Innumerable tasks occupied her from dawn until dusk, and only when she was alone in her bed at night did she have time to think of herself, of her memories and her dreams.

The countess was an exasperating employer, changeable and unpredictable, with a temper. She always demanded more than Angelique could accomplish and insisted on complete devotion to duty. Once a new requirement was met or a proficiency mastered, she took no further notice of it, but complained anew of some clumsiness or carelessness in a skill not yet achieved, her bright beady eyes darting about above her snake-skull cheekbones. She was never pleased and never complimentary. But even though she did not admit it, even to herself, she grew to depend on Angelique greatly, for she was, despite her fine airs, singularly lazy.

The countess had to be wakened at nine, with the opening of the drapes, and because she despised the hot sun, she was always bad-tempered in the morning. She wanted tea and cakes, but if the tea was too cool or too weak, or the cake too dry, she sent it back with a sharp reproof. She insisted that the silver tray be polished to perfection and the linen cloth pressed without a wrinkle. Otherwise, she would allow neither upon her bed. She complained incessantly about Martinique, "this dreary jungle festering with flowers and pestilence."

Her morning toilet consisted of a bath, the water infused with oils, and Angelique was expected to scrub her, but not too vigorously. After the bath came her powdering and her coiffure, an elaborate invention every morning.

The Countess du Prés considered herself royalty, and her soul's true home Versailles. Therefore, Parisian standards were the ones she followed. Even in the sticky heat of Martinique, she wore a full silk gown and petticoats, preferring to suffer the discomfort of the climate, rather than to dress, as she called it, "like a peasant."

Once the countess was attired and her room tidied, Angelique was released to go to the library. There, Josette's tutor would be engaged in teaching the gay but inattentive child her lessons. Poetry and language arts, music, some mathematics and geography were all presented, and Angelique found it was an easy task to set the model of an industrious student. She was fascinated by all subjects and applied herself with great energy. She especially enjoyed literature and was always disappointed when the lesson ended.

Josette, on the other hand, was more interested in playing hide-and-seek, dress-up, and make-believe. What she enjoyed most were the instructions in becoming a lady. Clothes and manners were her obsession, and she talked constantly of going to Paris and being received at court.

Still, Angelique had to admit she had charm. Her nature was warm and her incessant prattle was filled with kind remarks and bright comments on people and the world around her. She was affectionate and leaned in to touch others when she spoke to them, ensuring their constant attention, her words bubbling over like a fountain. She was gifted musically, and, despite an appalling refusal to practice, she played the pianoforte with ease, picking out the notes from memory and singing in a high, lilting voice.

As Josette loved everyone, she loved Angelique, and the feeling was returned with some reluctance. Both being in need of a companion near their own age, in time they grew close. Although the countess never allowed Angelique to forget her place, Josette was oblivious to the contrast in their stations and treated Angelique as a sister.

She was generous to a fault and would have given all her toys and clothes to her playmate had the countess allowed it. But then Josette was always receiving new baubles. Nevertheless, she was jealous of nothing, other than her own flawless complexion, which she guarded religiously from the tropical sun. She was seldom seen out of doors without a parasol, and she was like another flower in the garden when she strolled there, her red-brown curls tumbling about her shoulders and her pretty figure graceful beneath the curve of the umbrella.

Lunch was in the shade garden with the countess, and Angelique was obliged to serve. The Countess du Prés instructed Josette on the delicacies of proper decorum at table, complete with the niceties of conversation as to topic and modesty of comment. Josette's posture was corrected every thirty seconds, and the use and handling of each piece of silverware, saucer, and cup was considered with somber attention. Angelique, in turn, was educated on the specifics of serving an aristocratic table. The countess's intention was to prepare both girls for their proper roles in life.

In the afternoon, Josette was required to write her lessons or work at needlepoint, and Angelique's time was given over to spotting, pressing, and mending. The care and cleaning of all of the countess's and Josette's clothing and bedding fell to her. If the music or dancing instructor arrived, the girls would have a lesson, Josette receiving the special attention of the young lady of the household, with Angelique serving only as an accompanist or partner.

The countess insisted that dinner be formal, even though the necessities of dressing sometimes irritated Josette's father, André du Prés. Angelique was fond of André, who was a sturdy little man with a warm heart, if a bumbling and distracted manner. He was devoted to the management of the estate, which gave him no end of anxieties. But he managed well, and his slaves were for the most part content.

André respected the *Code Noir* and did not beat his slaves. He gave them good rations, days off, and plots of land for gardens. He maintained a hospital for them, and even had a tendency to forgive them when they broke his trust, treating them like naughty children. He had the sense to know he could not raise sugar without them, and all his fortune depended on them. Dancing was allowed on Sunday afternoons, and the drums were never ominous or threatening, but joyful, full of singing that lasted well into the night.

Since Josette's mother was dead and Natalie had agreed to come to Martinique to undertake Josette's education, André felt beholden to his sister and catered to her wishes, appearing for supper in evening jacket and waistcoat. He had wispy blond hair with heavy sideburns and a ruddy complexion, the result of hours spent riding across the plantation. His most prominent feature was a pair of twinkling blue eyes that flashed whenever he smiled or frowned, for he was both fond of wit and prone to vexation in equal measure.

Angelique did not serve at the evening meal, since there was a butler. She ate in the kitchen with the other servants. It was at dinnertime that she most felt her position. The family dined happily on Limoges porcelain with Waterford crystal, whereas the kitchen staff used wooden bowls and crockery. Angelique would close her eyes and pretend that she balanced a silver fork in her hand and her bitter cider was fine French wine in a delicate goblet.

As the months went by, Angelique struggled to keep the Dark Spirit at bay. She never again used even the simplest magic. When she was ill, she waited patiently for her own body to make her well again. If the countess was particularly annoying in her demands, Angelique pushed to the farthest corner of her mind any temptation to employ witchcraft. She was successful in the role of a servant. She followed her gifts and was eager to learn, applying herself to the lessons given by Josette's tutors, gaining as much if not more from the experience than her young mistress.

All for what? When the countess had hired Angelique, she had called her "drab" and "uninteresting," never dreaming what passions simmered just below the surface. And even though these passions were kept well hidden, they still flamed and made Angelique vulnerable to painful cravings. Since she had no true friends, she never revealed these feelings and was very lonely. None of the other servants were her confidantes. She kept to herself, not simply because she was too proud to associate with those she considered inferior. Even though she had laid sorcery aside, the time she had spent in Port-au-Prince made the other servants' conversation seem trivial and vacuous.

Yet her passions must needs go somewhere, must feed and nourish some fruit. And jealousy grew in her heart like a tree with intoxicating flowers. It flourished there, watered by tears of yearning. All the while she knew, especially when she reread passages from *Othello* or *Macbeth*, that jealousy was a grievous sin, an insane root that takes the reason prisoner. But try as she might, she failed to resist its poisoning influence.

On Sundays, the family attended Mass in the chapel on the plantation, and every servant and slave was required to attend. Sometimes the service was conducted by Father Le Brot. If he noticed Angelique seated with the du Prés household, he never acknowledged her, but she could not look at his small round body and jovial countenance without feeling deep gratitude that he had tried to save her life.

Only once did she imagine he was staring down at her from the podium, and she trembled when she heard the homily for the day. It was based on the tenth and last commandment: "Thou shalt not covet thy neighbor's house, nor his wife, nor his manservant, nor his maidservant, not his ox, nor his ass, nor anything that is thy neighbor's."

The priest seemed to be speaking directly to her as he continued to read from Exodus. "And all the people saw the thunderings and the lightnings and the noise of the trumpet, and the mountain smoking: and when the people saw it they removed and stood afar off . . . and Moses drew near into the thick darkness where God was . . ."

Angelique had seen Pelée smoking and smelled the sulfurous vapors that rose out of coned fissures near the top of the volcano, fetid air that caused little birds to fall from the sky. The villagers always said the god was turning over in his sleep, but Angelique was afraid, for she believed in her heart the god of Pelée could only be the Evil One. The sermon seemed aimed at her that morning. How could the Father have known that Angelique had envied Josette from the very first day?

*   *   *

Saturday was market day and the most exciting day of the week. Angelique and the driver left in a small cart before dawn, the Atlantic thundering at the high shore where Trinité still lay sleeping. She never tired of riding down out of the hills early in the morning and always caught her breath when she saw the sea and the moon-shaped harbor of turquoise, with its necklace of pearl white sand that was Saint-Pierre. Looking back, she could see the towering amphitheater of mountains, with Pelée rising out of the forest, its head in the clouds.

Her throat tightened with anticipation as they drove into town, and all her dreams were reborn in Saint-Pierre's steep, winding paths. The narrow streets were bright with color, and sharp angles of sunshine gleamed on the red-tile roofs.

The city had once been the haven of buccaneers and still offered its safe anchorage to trading ships from all lands. She always looked for a schooner with the American flag: a blue field with red-and-white stripes. Vessels of all sizes and shapes circled the cove, and the wharf bustled with activity. Saint-Pierre was the center of culture for Martinique, and the shop windows displayed fine jewelry, silks, leathers, and luxurious furnishings.

Angelique especially loved the huge cobbled square of Place Bertin, with its graceful fountains and elegant plantings. Her heart always soared at the sight of the handsome theater, three stories high, with seven arches formed by ionic columns in bas-relief and twin carved-stone stairways with wrought-iron railings. Often there was a troop of traveling players or a company of dancers performing, usually from France, and the posters advertising the enticements within made her mouth water.

It was therefore a thrilling day when André du Prés announced that he had purchased a brick house in town on a lovely tree-shaded avenue. What had been a fairly staid life in the country now took on renewed promise. Arrangements for moving into town occupied the entire family for months. The first night Angelique slept in the new house she lay awake staring at the ceiling of her small downstairs room.

She was tortured by the awareness that there was so much more to life. Since she had renounced her powers, she lived with a memory of the untapped potential that lay within her. What did it matter that she had, through ingenuity and perseverance, maintained a firm discipline against sorcery, if the future held no promise? Her soul was imprisoned, and she often felt that she had never left the lonely tower room at Basse Point.

Coming to live in Saint-Pierre renewed one pastime that bought great joy to Angelique's life. On Sunday afternoons, freed from her duties, she took to wandering up the beach beyond the harbor and swimming in the sea. She would shed her clothes and take to the reefs once more, diving into the deeper pools, exploring the mysterious horizons of the ocean floor. The coral was lovelier than ever, elk horn, finger, brain, star, and flower, rich hues of copper and ocher, mauve and maroon. She rediscovered the undertow, breathing, swirling, the current pulling and curling the fans and grasses, and the curving coral reaching up, rounded, lumps of gray-green, etched into tiny mazes.

She found a wide sandy shoal that was covered with red starfish, thousands and thousands as far as she could see, delicate pearls jeweling their pointed arms. She swam through a school of blue tang, their false eyes taunting her as they skimmed around her. She ached as she watched the creatures, lively and free, fondling and feeding in the coral, and once again she was happy there.

There was a beach at which she sometimes swam where a deep channel lay between the shore and the reef. If she wanted to reach the coral beds, she was obliged to swim across this empty space of sea, which held a strong current. The bottom fell away swiftly, and she would look down into murky water, which seemed to stretch forever, with only swirling flicks catching the sunlight near the surface. It took many long minutes to cross the channel, the blackness slowly increasing as the water grew deeper, more dark and foreboding, before the bright coral again sprang into view.

When she lay in bed at night she sometimes felt she was crossing that channel, swimming and swimming through a watery purgatory, as indiscernible depths loomed beneath her and the current tugged at her feet.

chapter

20

One afternoon Angelique wandered so far up the beach that she saw her old cottage in the distance. She hesitated a moment, susceptible to a mixture of painful feelings, then broke into a run and did not stop until she could see the porch, the yard around it, and the roof with a fine new thatch.

At first she thought the house was covered with giant spiderwebs, until she realized it was draped with finely woven and gauzy fishing nets, hanging from several tall stakes. She noticed baskets and tubs strewn about a well-tended garden plot, an outdoor fireplace, and, nearby, a rough-carved wooden chair.

She crept up to the door and peeked inside. The interior looked unfamiliar, and the house was certainly inhabited. The sleeping corner was a pile of quilts, and most of the front room was cluttered with fishing paraphernalia, poles and spools of line, nets and sewing tools, weights and hand-carved lures. The kitchen had a few copper pans, some pots hanging on the wall, and tins of crackers and salted beef lying on the table. A man's clothing—a jacket and several plain shirts—were draped on the one straight-backed chair. She was surprised to see a small shelf of books and writing paper on the table.

When she came back out the front door and looked toward the sea, she saw the fisherman. He had pulled his boat up on the beach and was lowering the sail, which flapped and shivered in the wind. She stood and watched as he tied the sail to the boom and tended his lines, coiling them and twisting them in fluid motions. Then he leaned beneath the rudder arm and pulled out a strong rope, slinging it over his shoulder. Attached to the line were three or four long tarpon, their silver sides reflecting like metal in the afternoon sun. The fisherman was bare-chested and barefoot, and, as he drew nearer, she was astonished to see that he was only a year or two older than she.

He stopped when he caught sight of her standing by his door, and he looked down the beach to see whether she was alone. Satisfying himself that she was, he nodded to her and came closer to the house. Lowering his catch into a tub of salt water, he washed the brine from his hands.

She could see that he was strong, his body lithe and well formed. His skin was darkly tanned and salted with a fine mist of seawater, and his muscles were fluid and shadowed. His hair was a sandy color, his face was gilded by the sun and finely featured, and his eyes, when he looked up at her finally, were a mossy shade of green, the color of his fishing nets.

"What do you want?" he said at last. "Are you lost?"

"No," she said. "I was walking on the beach when I saw the house."

"You might call it a house now," he said defensively, as though he thought she might take it from him. "When I found it, it was a pile of scattered timbers. What you see here, I built, all alone. I only thatched the roof last week."

She looked down at his feet, which were long and veined, and she could see the bones moving as his toes hugged the sand.

"Once I lived here," she said, "when I was small." And she added hurriedly, "I mean, it was once my house—before it fell down and you built it all again."

"You lived in a magical place," he said simply.

"Do you know the caves?" she asked.

"The caves? Of course. I go there often."

She was startled by a feeling of joy in finding a kindred soul. "And the rooms where the sun streams in—"

"Where the rain has streaked the boulders with long, rusty stains—"

"And the pools are so clear the water is only a whisper of light."

The boy looked at her a minute, then shrugged, and said, "I must clean my fish. Come, you can help me."

The boy went into the house and returned with a small knife and a basket of limes. He jerked his head to beckon her over, and she walked to the tub, which had a broad slab of driftwood and a skinning blade lying beside it. He handed her the limes and the knife.

"You can squeeze out the juice for me," he said.

She waited while the boy slapped the first fish on the slab and used a long blade to open the stomach down the creamy underside. The red guts spilled out onto the sand. The faint scent of the eggs rose to her nostrils as he scraped against the bones, turning the fish with an easy flick and carving off the head with a snap at the gills. His movements were deft and concise, and she was caught by the delicacy of his wrists and arms, the supple muscles, and the long slender fingers digging the crimson heart and lungs from the slick insides of the fish. She watched the pliant motions of his shoulders and back as he dipped the tarpon in the water again. Then he slid the fish over to where she stood and nodded to her, as though she would know what to do.

She cut a lime in half and pressed it between her palms, letting the juice flow over the skin of the fish, tasting the fresh tang in the air.

"That's good," he said, smiling. "It takes a lot." There were amber glints in his mossy eyes. They worked for the best part of an hour, until the sun was low in the sky and she knew she would have to leave to be home before night. He made no offer to walk with her, but he said, "Will you come to the market on Saturday?"

"Yes, I am always there, shopping for the household that employs me. I am a lady's maid for the du Prés family."

"I will be selling my fish. Look for me, and I will give you a livre for your work."

She ran all the way home, the sun flaring the sea to flame as it sank beneath the horizon.

Saturday came, and she found him, perched upon a splendid cart, his fish limed and salted, selling briskly. He barely looked up when she drew near, but after a few moments, he motioned to her with an easy gesture of his wrist that sent an odd ripple though her. She came behind the cart, and he turned from his fish and placed a coin in her hand.

"Come and see me again tomorrow," he said, and returned to his customers. She held the coin as she walked back to her basket. When she opened her hand and looked at it, it smelled of fish.

After that, Angelique walked the two miles around the cove every Sunday. Before she reached the boy's house, she took off her maid's dress and wrapped a pareu around her body, tying it at the neck. She felt more comfortable in the role of an island girl.

His name was Thierry, and he had been living alone for three years. His father had been a fisherman in Marseilles, and had come to the islands indentured, but both he and Thierry's mother had died of *le mal de Siam*, the yellow sickness. Thierry treated Angelique as though he had always known her. Sometimes he did not come back from his day of fishing until almost dark, and she had to leave before seeing him. Those days, she would tidy the cottage or tend the garden while she waited for him, singing to herself.

On other days, when the wind was calm, he would not go out at all, and they would swim together in the reef or wander through the caves, pointing out to one another the colorful creatures beneath the surface. They could watch for an hour as a hermit crab dragged its new shell into a niche in a rock. If they saw a peacock ray lift from the sand, they would swim down and caress its velvet skin. They would hide from one another in the thick kelp, or float along the tops of anemone forests, pricking the delicate tentacles of the living flowers and seeing them shrink away to nothing. They would steal up on nurse sharks basking, or taunt wobbegongs in their sleep, watching them flounce away, ruffles fluttering like ladies' dresses. Some days they would sit in the dunes, and she would read to him from the Shakespeare, and he would lie on his back and gaze at the sky.

When he took her out in the boat with him, she sat in the bow and watched him fish. Her eyes would wander over his limber body as he leaned into the rudder, his head tipped back to gauge the wind in the sail. She noticed the taut muscles in his legs as he straddled the width of the boat, tossing the net, then gathering it in under him with long easy tugs, the foamy mesh flashing with flipping sardines and the odd goatfish for bait.

He began to touch her casually as he leaned over her to reach for a hook, or to rest a hand on her knee, calling her attention to a frigate bird overhead. Whenever he brushed against her or grazed her with his fingertips, it felt warm at the spot, and a tremor fluttered through her body. All week she would think of the touch and remember exactly where it had been, trying to re-create the tremor.

They began to explore one another in the most innocent manner, as though to each the other was only another new and amazing sea creature pulled in by the tide. They sat in the shallowest pool of the caves one day, under the boulder that leaned out above them as though it would topple over and crush them. Thierry slowly pulled Angelique's wet pareu off one shoulder and stared at her breast, then cupped it in his hand, tracing its small round shape with his fingers and touching the nipple hesitantly as it grew taut, like an anemone flowering its silken flutes.

He kissed it, exploring its shape, and she felt the warmth of his mouth over the cold firm tissue and his tongue quiver around it. Then he replaced the cotton fabric and tied it at her shoulder. He did not touch her again, but he looked at her, and she let herself sink into the green depths of his eyes, all the while feeling the easy slap of the gentle edge of the whole living ocean curled beneath her body.

All week, as she worked at her various tasks, she imagined him, untangling his nets in the water, mending his hooks, salting his catch. She felt they worked in unison; she stood when he stood, or lifted when he lifted. She thought of little else than his taut body and his slender hands, with their motions so deft and sure, and every time she remembered his careless touch, her body pulsed.

The following week he removed her pareu as she

lay in the water, her body half-submerged, and he looked at her shifting shapes in the flickering liquid, and stroked her as though he were trailing his fingers in the sand, leaving goose bumps where his hand had been—down the length of her arms, across her breasts, over her belly.

He touched the flat of her stomach and pressed her thigh, then he lifted her leg and pushed it aside so that he could see, faintly beneath the water, the curved shells of her buttocks, and the fluted gills between, which he grazed with his finger. Then he gently probed, discovering for the first time a sex so different from his own.

She rose up and saw what she thought was a long white fish beneath the water, waving slightly, and they both were curious as she cupped her hand around it, feeling the silken flesh with her fingertips, astonished at its tautness as it stirred within her hand like a live thing. When Thierry lifted it out of the water she leaned in and kissed the tip, then drew it farther into her mouth, closing her lips around it and tasting the salty sea.

And still they had not kissed each other's mouths like lovers.

Finally, one Sunday, Thierry suggested they take the boat, for the fishing had been good all week, and he hated to miss a day. She ached to return to the caves and continue the tantalizing finger play in the pool, and she was somewhat piqued that he was more interested in profit at the marketplace than in the delicious intimacy they had begun. Still, she had grown used to the aching fire that flowed though her body, and it seemed that nothing would quench it, so she helped him push the boat into the surf and, running beside him through the foam, leapt aboard.

Thierry yanked at the mainsheet and wrapped it around the cleat, pulling the sail to the wind and easing the little skiff into the waves. The eager craft rose and fell on the swell, in a lulling motion that at once relaxed and disturbed her. She watched Thierry's face against the sky. The soft curls on his forehead stirred in the wind; his tanned cheeks were freckled and his mouth soft. All his fine features seemed carved from some rare, golden wood. She thought he was a beautiful boy. He turned and looked at her with his green eyes for a long moment, and she felt her heart jump.

The boat did not move quickly, as the breeze was not strong, but it had covered a considerable distance from shore when the wind fell off quite suddenly and they were becalmed. Thierry loosed the sail and, going forward, raised a little jib, but the canvas flapped listlessly in the still air. He stood staring out at the sea, so oddly calm, and, following his gaze, she could see an oily scum swirling on the surface of the water. It was silent but for the sea slapping and a bird's wild cry far off on the island.

Thierry shrugged and turned to his hooks, setting a piece of cut tuna in three of them, piercing the red meat with the silver barb, and letting out the line. The stern line he tied to the anchor hoist and the bowline he wrapped around the rudder post. He kept the third line in his teeth as he pulled in the jib and, never looking at her, unhooked the sail. He folded it and placed it across the bottom of the boat. Then he lay down on the sail, took the line from his mouth, wrapped it around his ankle, the better to feel a strike, and reached for her. She went to him eagerly.

They lay beneath the lazy, drifting mainsail, staring up at the cerulean sky. The shape and motion of the boat, arrhythmic, tossing, lapping on the water, forced their bodies together, and she drifted into the bliss of the rocking cradle as they kissed for the first time, tentatively, tasting, barely brushing lips, tongue, softly exploring salty mouths. They were pressed so close that she could hear their two hearts beating, hers a rapid flutter and his, deeper and stronger, as though it, too, were beating inside her chest. But as she heard it, a sudden cold throb of fear flickered through her.

He felt her tense, and said, "I don't want to hurt you. If we do this, we are pledged and will belong to one another. Is that what you want?"

"I want to live with you forever," she said, as the wave of panic subsided.

"Yes," he said. "I, too, want to be with you always."

She arched her body into his, reaching around to feel his hard shoulders. She ran her fingers down the vertebrae of his back, pressing each one until she reached the rise of his buttocks. She let her hand continue into the crack, moving until she felt the rippling there.

Thierry trembled and pushed her legs open with his knees, kneeling slightly over her and looking down at her. She felt him nudge her between her legs, then press harder, as she lifted her hips from the bottom of the boat to meet him.

What happened next was a confused blur, but Thierry felt a tug at his ankle, then a jerk so vicious, he was almost yanked from the boat. He sat up quickly and reached for the line, first drawing with his arms and shoulders, then standing, his penis erect and his tensed body braced against the other gunwale, as he backed all his weight into the rope, easing, then hauling, with practiced skill, as he set the hook and dragged the fish toward him. "It's a marlin," he shouted. "A big one! We have a fortune on the end of this line!" He laughed, a giddy laugh, and grinned at her, his eyes acknowledging the conflicting thrills of the moment.

Angelique watched as he played the fish like a toy, and she rose and curved her body behind him, helping him pull, easing the reluctant creature closer to the boat.

"Why doesn't he jump?" asked Thierry once, and shook his head. "This marlin wants to hide his face."

Then the line went slack, and Thierry overhanded it into the boat quickly, the rope coiling at his feet. "I think I've lost him," he cried, but the fish suddenly loomed beside the boat, and they saw that it was not a marlin but a great black shark, its long sickle-shaped tail whipping back and forth, its sail fin cutting the surface of the water. Angelique's scalp went tight with creeping fear as she and Thierry stared down at the great fish skimming the surface, and she saw the red eye looking up at her out of the black head lurking beneath the plane of the water, with the sleek undulating shape flowing back and forth.

"Cut it loose," she said to Thierry.

"Why?" he said, "A shark is a good catch, once we've tired him. And look at the size, almost as long as a man. There's good meat there."

"Cut it loose, I tell you," she said, her heart pounding and the cold fear snaking. "It's evil. The fish is the Dark One, the Devil."

"What? Are you crazy, girl? I won't give up a catch like this. You should know better than that if you are to be a fisherman's wife." And he leaned back against the line and looped it around the cleat, then pulled her against his naked body and laughed, as though she were a superstitious child.

But she tensed, jerked away from him, and said, "Thierry, I saw the red eye of the Devil." She fell to her knees and scrambled for the knife she knew he kept in the hole under the rudder.

Just then the fish turned and sounded, heeling the boat, and Angelique lost her balance and crashed against the ribs of the skiff. Thierry whipped off the cleated line and held on, as the fish tunneled through the deep, raking the rope through the boy's hands and ripping the skin from his palms as he braced, and yelled at her, "Come on! Help me hold him!"

But the line whistled and flew through his fists, the loops at his feet eaten up in seconds. Before he could reach for the end, the line still wrapped around his ankle caught, and he was lifted and pitched feet-first from the boat, yelling, twisting, and grasping for the gunwale, clutching, loosing, his eyes wide with surprise.

Angelique grabbed one of his hands and held on with a fierce grip until she was slowly, torturously pulled with him over the rail and into the water. She swam down, down, deeper and deeper after him, until she caught his outstretched hands. Then she was under him, her fingers clutching at his body and he clinging to her, as she turned, her lungs exploding, and swam toward the surface.

She could feel his hands clawing, traveling the length of her body, darkness closing in on her. She was sure he had her, but he was pulled the other way as well, and he could not hold on to her. Finally, she felt him slip away. She turned and saw his face disappearing though the gloom, his anguished eyes and hollow mouth open in a swallowed scream.

She broke the surface with an enormous gasp and stared wildly at the empty sea, slimy with trails of froth sliding over the lacquered surface. She took a deep breath and dived again, piercing the dismal haze, plummeting farther until she could bear the pain no longer and was forced to turn for the light. Many more times she dived, each dive deeper, until the sun motes disappeared and nothing but inky blackness surrounded her. She found no sign. The jaws of darkness had swallowed him up.

Exhausted, she heaved for the boat and pulled herself over the rail. She collapsed in the bottom, wheezing and choking, filling her aching lungs, numb with disbelief. She thought of her fine boy and what pain it was to drown, then she shuddered, staring up at the sky with sightless eyes until she fell into a swoon.

While she lay in a stupor, she heard out of the water slapping on the hull, "Angelique . . . it is time. . . ."

She moaned as her mind rolled with the sound. "Why . . . ?"

"Did you think I would let you love him? You are a witch. Remember? Never may you love."

"Why have you killed him? You are heartless, evil . . . cruel . . ."

"To save you," came the lapping sound. "To save you from human weakness."

"Murderer," she whispered. "Fiend!"

"I have chosen you as my bride," he answered. "How can you deny your destiny? Talent such as yours comes only after centuries of scarecrows and charlatans. Through you, I will be revered and adored, and the greedy souls of men will fall under my power."

She lifted herself with great effort and looked across the water. "I will never go with you! I despise you!" she cried.

The Devil rose out of the sea on the side of a huge swell, his horse's nostrils smoking froth. The little boat rode the surge, hovered on the crest, then fell with a shudder. She clung to the rails as she watched him descend from his chariot and cross the water, his robes floating on the waves, his hair tangled with brine.

"Leave me! Begone!" she cried desperately.

He reached for her, and his marble face was gentle and beautiful, like Thierry's, but she knew it was a trick, and she shrank back as he covered her with his freezing shape.

"My sleek and glossy girl," he whispered in her ear. "You are born to the oldest breed. Worship the Earth Goddess and live an ordinary existence. Yours will be the pain of childbirth and the humiliation of old age. Or come with me and be my consort, and together we will fly the dark night."

"I do not want you!" she cried, pushing him off, her hands entering into the modulating surfaces of his shape. Fervently, she said, "The strength of my power is my own. I taught myself. My knowledge did not come from you. And you cannot take it from me."

"Then call him back . . ." There was a moment when the Dark One floated off, and the wind gusted and blew the chariot into the sea, but the ebony chaise rose again, and he was standing within it. "Call him back, Angelique. You know you can."

She hesitated, then said dully, "No. I will not."

"Someday," he whispered, "you will serve me, you will rejoice in that service, and that will be your triumph. I own you, and I have owned you since the night on the altar when you destroyed your tormentor. You made your choice, that night. Immortality beckons. Turn and come."

And slowly, he disappeared beneath the waves.

chapter

21

It was a bright summer afternoon. A delivery carriage stopped in front of a fine town house in Saint-Pierre, and a mulatto courier walked to the door carrying a large package. Angelique, wearing a simple frock and a ruffled cap on her blond curls, came to the door and opened it. When she saw the box she frowned, then pressed a coin into the driver's hand and took the package without a word or a smile.

"Angelique?" The girl turned when she heard her name and saw the countess coming into the hall from the drawing room. She was dressed in one of her ridiculous Parisian gowns, with a long, flowing back. Perspiration had darkened the fabric under her arms. *I'll never get those spots out,* Angelique said to herself. The sausage ringlets that Angelique had set that morning were already limp from the heat.

"Did Josette's gown arrive? Let me see!"

Angelique set the box on a bench beside the stairs and lifted the lid. The dress in the carton was water taffeta in a clear shade of turquoise blue.

"What is this?" The countess was not at all pleased. "This is not the dress I ordered. It was meant to be wine-colored, embroidered with pearls."

"But . . . it's a beautiful gown, Madame," Angelique said with astonishment.

"It's atrocious! Josette would look dreadful in that hideous aqua. It's the ugliest color in the world, and besides, the dress is much too plain for the ball. Oh, I am greatly distressed. That is my reward for making a purchase in Martinique! Those free coloreds are not to be trusted. And to think the woman claimed to be a seamstress."

"What shall we do with the dress, Madame?"

"It must be returned at once. Catch the driver."

Angelique ran back out the door and looked both ways up and down the street, but the carriage had disappeared. She stood a moment, gazing at the wide verandahs of lemon-colored houses, and the gardens filled with scarlet-flowering trees. Bright angles of light streamed over the red-tiled roofs, the coral walls, and the lavender shutters, but a shadow fell across her eyes as if she were remembering her childhood dreams.

For an instant she imagined herself running after the carriage, flinging herself against the door, and leaping inside to be whisked away to a new world. She took a deep breath, drinking in the fragrance of the sea, then she shuddered and wrapped her arms about her waist. How restless she was! Her bones felt weak, and vague discontent descended over her spirit as she turned to reenter the house.

Josette looked out from the parlor, and when she

saw Angelique her face broke into an impish grin. "Angelique!" she whispered. "How could you leave me alone with that tyrant? Come on!" Her dark eyes glowed, and her chestnut hair tumbled about her shoulders.

"I can't. I must speak to the countess. I believe she needs me to go into town."

"Will you come! Honestly, I can't learn the dance without you."

A moment later Angelique was poised reluctantly opposite her mistress as the dance instructor, a foppish young man, sat at the harpsichord and eyed them both with disapproval while he counted out the steps. Josette rolled her eyes at his instructions, and Angelique hesitantly moved through the round with her.

"And one, and two, and turn, and bow," he shouted in a thin, nasal voice as he banged tunelessly on the keys. The girls performed the movements gravely. Josette moved with grace, her slender body supple beneath her white-organdy gown and her carriage erect. Angelique, the coarse skirt of her maid's dress swishing at her ankles, mirrored Josette's movements precisely as they curtsied, smiled, crossed, and turned, and thought only what a waste of time and effort it was for her to learn the dance at all, since she would not be going to the ball.

"No! No! Not to the left!" the instructor cried impatiently, lifting his narrow chin. "What is the matter with you, Josette? Go the opposite direction, or you will find yourself without a partner! And then it will make no difference how pretty your face is, because it will be so red!" He rose to demonstrate, assuming a feminine air and raising a fidgeting hand to Angelique's. "And, dum, ti dum," he quavered, becoming his own piano and marching off the quadrille with style. "Titty dum, titty dum, titty dum dum dum!"

At the word *titty,* Josette burst into laughter, and collapsed on the chaise, her gown a froth of ruffles.

"Oh, Monsieur Beauregard, please let us rest a while. Too much dancing makes my head spin!"

"And if you do not know the steps by Saturday night, what then?" he snapped.

"This is Martinique, Monsieur. No one will know the steps. Besides, everyone will want to dance the calenda!"

"Oh, Mademoiselle, how scandalous!" he cried, his Adam's apple bobbing in his skinny neck. "That would be far beneath this distinguished family, I hope."

"Why? Didn't you know the Catholic nuns were caught dancing the calenda! Isn't that true, Angelique?"

"In the chapel on Christmas Eve," Angelique agreed in a soft voice. "They were most embarrassed. But, Mademoiselle," she cautioned, "many of the guests will be *gens du colour,* and they will shun the calenda for the reel."

"Oh, they do put on such airs, the *nouveaux riches.*" Josette laughed. "Those women will wear more jewels than the countess!"

"And masks, to hide their copper skin," Angelique added.

"And what about the militia, Mademoiselle?" intoned the dance instructor. "The young men who are here from France. I believe they will be well schooled in the quadrille."

"*They* are coming?" Josette asked, suddenly more serious.

"Mademoiselle, yours is the richest and most powerful family in Martinique, and it is your eighteenth birthday. It is time you conducted yourself like a lady." Monsieur Beauregard seated himself again at the piano. "No more of your procrastinating. Up, up, up!" He began to play. "And, one and two . . ." But when he turned around, the two girls had fled.

Late that night Angelique was working in the kitchen. All the silver candelabra needed polishing before the ball, and the task had fallen to her. When that was finished, she had the great linen tablecloth to press: the stove would have to be lit to heat the iron. And she must rise early to do the week's marketing. With the celebration only two days hence, the household was in a turmoil. The clock had just struck midnight when she heard a tentative knock at the servant's entrance. She was surprised to see a small black boy standing on the walk.

"Excuse me, miss," he said in a shy voice.

"Yes."

"Is this the du Prés household?"

"Yes, it is. How can I help you?"

"I's lookin' for the young lady who lives here."

"Josette? She's gone to bed. Shall I give her a message?"

"No, miss, the lady I wants, her name be Angelique."

"Oh, well, I am Angelique. What is it?"

"Please, miss, my father sent me here to find you. My little sister is close to dyin', and she need your help." Angelique looked back over her shoulder, then stepped out into the night and closed the door behind her.

"I cannot help her," she said. "You must send for the doctor."

"We got no money to pay doctor, miss."

"Then one of your witch doctors—"

"My father say he once know your mother, when she work at Trinité. That you learn the magic from her. Please, miss, he sit weepin' by the bedside, his old hat in him hand. I think he die, too, from cryin'."

"What is the sickness?"

"Stomach all bloated and hard like a big coconut."

"If you wait here, I will fetch you some herbs." She turned to go back in the house.

"No please, miss, you come, too!" he cried plaintively.

"What is your name, child?" she said kindly.

"Nicaise, miss."

"Listen to me, Nicaise. I have given up any magic. Long ago, after my mother died. It is not a good magic, but an evil one. It comes from the dark side, not the light. Do you understand?"

Nicaise clung to her arm and began to cry. "Oh, please, miss, don't make me go back to my father, his eyes so full of tears."

"But it is better that your father's love cure your sister, or that her own light see her through. Children are strong. The magic always demands a price."

"Oh, miss, you don't mean that. What evil can there be in curing a little child? Don't make magic. Just come and touch her. Please. Just come and touch her hard ol' stomach!"

Angelique felt her heart go out to him. "All right. I will come. I must at least get my bag. Wait here."

A quarter of an hour later she was following Nicaise through the streets of Saint-Pierre, with only one lantern to light the way. When they had walked a short distance, she saw a large building on the right with all its many windows lit, and as they drew nearer she could hear music and laughter. They were in the district of the soldiers' barracks, and young men were up late drinking in the tavern by the corner. Three soldiers were sitting at a table very near the window, and they wore the scarlet jackets she always hoped to see again. As she passed, she could even overhear snatches of their conversation, raucous from the effects of rum.

"Ah, the *belle affranchie*, '*La Martiniquaise*,'" one intoned, "island girls, sweet, ripe, and ready for the picking!" Angelique was surprised to recognize an American accent and stopped a moment, looking through one of the panes.

"Martinique is famous for its women," another said. "There must have been one good-looking tribe in Africa, and they are all its descendants!" Rude laughter all around and pounding on the table wearied Angelique, and Nicaise tugged at her sleeve. "Come, miss, we needs hurry." She was about to turn away when she heard the American accent again. "The women here have great charm," the voice said, "but no fortunes."

"Well, you don't marry them, Barnabas!" spoke the soldier opposite, raising his glass. "The day will come when you will pledge yourself to one woman for your entire life—that is if you don't die on your voyage home. So live, for God's sake! Live while you can!"

She gasped, her breath stopped in her throat. Could she have heard the name correctly? She turned back to the window, transfixed, as the young man rose. She was able to see him clearly in the lamplight.

It was he! The boy called Barnabas! Strong now, and ruggedly handsome, his eyes were still lustrous, and his black curls fell across his forehead in the same rakish manner. He wore the tight-fitting jacket of an officer of the navy, heavily braided with gold, and his white-plumed helmet lay on the table. She smiled, overjoyed to see him alive and happy. So he, at least, had escaped, she thought with a tremulous excitement.

She had never known whether he had saved himself after she had led him down the ladder to the skiff. And he was here once more! In Martinique. The clever, dashing boy she had kept alive in her dreams.

But he was an officer and of distinguished birth. Considering her position, there was no way to make his acquaintance. Besides, dalliance with any young man was forbidden to her forever.

Reluctantly, she pulled away and followed Nicaise. There were no longer any cobblestones, and the street had become a dusty alley twisting through stubby trees and one-room hovels crowded together. When they reached the shack, Angelique stepped through the low doorway and smelled a pungent odor. Raising her lantern, she saw the child lying on the cot.

The child's father lifted his watery eyes as Angelique leaned over the sick girl, who was wrapped in rags and dripping with sweat.

"Fetch me some water," she said to Nicaise, "and some clean shreds of cloth."

When he brought the water she did not wait, but tore off a piece of her petticoat and dipped it in the pail. She began to wash the child, cooling her, wiping the face and letting the water drip into her hair. The girl's eyes were vacant, but tiny golden earrings flashed on her ears. She was slender and perfectly formed, except for the bloated stomach, and Angelique could not help but think of Chloe's delicate brown limbs. She could see immediately that it was hopeless.

"It is a bad fever," she said to the father. "It will either break, or she will die. Continue to bathe her and blow on her wet skin. We must keep her cool." The humble man took the rag and began to do as she had ordered, his veined hands trembling and his mouth muttering with hope. She turned to Nicaise. "Go to the well for more water. I want it to be clean and cold."

Turning to the light of the lantern, she opened her bag. There, on top, she saw the amulet, her mother's charm, which she had left off wearing years before. She held it a moment between her fingers. She could still feel the tiny skull and the moonstone, small and hard. Impulsively, she tied it again at her throat.

"I need to boil water," she said to the father. Then she extracted the pouches, sniffed them, and emptied several powders into her hand. Her movements were quick and efficient, but they belied an inner trepidation. While the father built a small fire on the ground, she waited, trying to quell her misgivings. She was afraid that she might provoke the Dark Spirit.

Surely one good deed will not attract his attention, she thought, *if I call on no loas and recite no incantations. I will use only a simple remedy. That does not come from him. That will not draw him to me.*

Once the tea was brewed, she took the cup and went to the child. She lifted the limp head. "Drink this," she instructed. "It will make you feel better."

The girl took a few sips, and the father watched her every move from his crouched position on the mat. They waited in the lamplight, but after an hour, there was still no change. The child stared at Angelique with supplicating eyes, her mouth slack, her breathing a tortured wheeze. Nicaise stood by the door, his arms hanging at his sides. The old man began to weep.

Nicaise took a tentative step in her direction, searching Angelique's face with his eyes.

"I'm afraid there is nothing more I can do," she said to him.

"Touch her belly," Nicaise whispered. She looked at him helplessly. "Please, miss. Please."

"I can't."

"Please . . . just once."

Angelique took a breath, slowly reached out, and stroked the girl's swollen stomach, gently, calmly, fighting to keep her mind clear, but conscious of the spark igniting, just as she had known it would. She quivered as the once familiar flame fluttered in her gut; she flinched but did not smother it. She felt the fire streak though her body and down her arm like a sliver of lightning. The child convulsed, and a foul odor filled the air. When they lifted the rags, they saw she had passed a vile, liquid mass. In a quarter of an hour her stomach had softened and her skin was cool.

The father sat beside her, holding her hand, tears running down his cheeks. "I bless you, girl," he said in a quivering voice. "You have performed a miracle! How can I repay you?"

"In one way only," she answered. "This must always remain our secret. Tell no one I was here." She met the old man's gaze as he nodded to her silently.

Angelique emerged into the night. She was trembling, exhausted, but she felt more alive than she had in years. She raced though the narrow alley, hearing the music of running water. In Saint-Pierre, the sounds of water—fountains in hidden gardens, overflow trapped in the gutters, little streams that trickled down from the mountains—were always present. She skipped down a cobbled walk that broke into a waterfall of steps she could barely make out in the moonlight and descended into the dark boulevard.

Newly elated, her mind was consumed with a single thought. Was Barnabas still in the tavern? Would she have another glimpse of him? But her spirits sank when she saw that the barracks were dark. Then she heard some of the soldiers coming from the tavern, their laughter echoing in the empty street.

Her path lay in that direction, and the lamp still glowed at the corner when she passed by the drunken officers, her heart fluttering inexplicably, and, as she ducked beneath the flame, she turned toward them. The light fell on her face.

Catching sight of her, Barnabas stopped, caught his breath, and stared into her eyes, entranced, and puzzled, as though she were an unexpected vision conjured by the midnight hour. They looked at each other for a long moment before, unable to breathe, she pulled back into the darkness. But even as she retreated into the night, she sensed that his friends could not draw him away. She felt his eyes following her, as the moonstream on the water follows the lonely wanderer walking on the strand.

It was a beautiful morning, warmed by the sun rising over Pelée, as Angelique moved though the marketplace. Odors of flowers, sweets, fruits, and freshbaked bread perfumed the air as the shopkeepers set up their stalls. Carts of vegetables, hogs and chickens, donkeys laden with firewood, came pouring into the square.

Angelique, relishing the commotion, went from stall to stall, making selections. She had a courteous demeanor and grace unusual in a servant. She felt an unfamiliar exuberance and was aware of the cut of her plain lavender dress enhancing her slender body as she moved.

When she reached for mangoes high on a cart, she turned lightly on her foot, as though she were dancing. She felt her whole person imbued with a sprung euphoria. Glimpsing her reflection in the bottom of a polished pie tin, she could see her pale gold hair and her eyes, dark and luminous. Smiling to herself, she exchanged greetings with others, but maintained a reserve, a distance from the shopkeepers, as though she chose to remain in a separate world of her own.

Catching sight of a stall with golden apples, she was irresistibly drawn to the vibrant color. She reached for one and was turning it over in her hand, trying to decide whether to buy and eat it at once, or to take a sackful back to the house, when a man's voice spoke low in her ear.

"Surely the hand of Eve was not so lovely, nor her wrist so fine."

She spun around and looked up, straight into the face of Barnabas. Instantly the throngs of people surrounding them faded to a murky blur, and he alone was all that she could see. The boy with the freckles and merry grin was still hidden there, but now the features were finely formed and devilishly handsome. The eyes were dark and set deep, shadowed by heavy brows. They shone with a startling luster, so fixed on hers that her heart gave a leap because the gaze was so familiar and so penetrating. She felt the blood rush to her face, but managed a slow, secretive smile.

"Take care," she said softly. "The Tree of Knowledge bears bitter fruit."

Lightly, he grazed the apple with his fingertips. "Will you offer it to me?" She stared down at his hand, quivering as though the skin of the apple were her own.

"Why do you think this apple came from the Garden?" she asked.

"Because . . . wherever you are standing, my lady . . . must be Paradise."

She flushed again at the compliment, but turned away and began to place the apples one by one into her sack. When she had finished, she gave the coins to the farmer's wife. Barnabas never took his eyes from her.

"I have been watching you," he said, "move through the fair."

"And if this is truly Paradise, who are you?" she said, afraid to look at him. "God's first creation— made in His perfect image? Or are you that other fellow, the one that I should fear?"

"God's first? I would prefer to be your first."

"My first. And not my last?" she said, cutting her eyes at him. "Then it is a fool's paradise."

"I say, do I know you?" he asked abruptly.

"I . . . don't think so." Was it possible that he recognized her?

His forehead narrowed in a frown. "Those eyes of yours, like blue forget-me-nots . . . something about you is familiar. What is your name?"

"You will be disappointed, Monsieur. I am not called Eve. And since we have not been properly introduced, I think it would not be wise to tell you my name." She was amazed at her own impudence. But he was so forward, and he did not seem at all discouraged.

"I understand. Well, mine is Barnabas Collins. And it is an honor to make your acquaintance, Mademoiselle Mystery." He took her hand, bent to kiss it, then after a moment in which he looked into her eyes, turned her hand over and kissed the hollow of her palm. She pulled away, conscious of having felt the warmth of his breath.

"Sir. I warn you, take no further liberties."

"Dear lady, I only desire a stroll through the square on this new morning with a lovely woman on my arm. To me that would be bliss of the rarest kind. Will you at least take a turn with me?"

His tone was teasing, almost mocking, yet beneath the humor she sensed an eagerness that disarmed her. The brash young boy who had climbed into her curtained chaise so long ago was still there, but when she finally allowed herself to look fully into his face, she saw hidden behind the eyes a tormented urgency that moved her deeply.

She dipped her head to him and smiled. He took her arm, and they walked though the stalls and out into the quiet square. He led her to a great spreading fig tree beyond the arcade, and they stopped in its shade. The heavy branches formed a roof of silvery leaves that arched above their heads.

Finally, to break the silence, he said, "You're up with the sun. Are you shopping so early for your family?"

Unwilling to reveal that she was a servant, but not wanting to lie to him, she answered, "Yes. I always come early, before the crowds; the better to have my choice." She smiled at him again, then pulled her eyes away and nodded toward the sea. "Also, I am curious to see what ships have arrived during the week."

"Do you look for my schooner?" he asked. She was startled. Could he know that his was the ship she always longed to see?

"Why would I do that?" she said lightly. "I do not know your schooner, Monsieur."

"So, you are from Martinique?"

"I have lived here all my life." She could see that the stiff collar cut into his neck and that the red gabardine of his jacket pulled tight over his muscular chest. He had become a powerful man, tall, broad-shouldered, vigorous with energy. His stare was so intense that she felt uncomfortable, and rather than meet his gaze, she placed a hand on the thick gray trunk of the tree and glanced above her head. He followed her eyes up to the masses of green leaves.

"Oh, look, look where we are," he said with surprise, leaning in to her, his breath against her cheek. "It is the inside of a cave, a secret hideaway where we could live together and be hidden from the world."

The intimation of intimacy was clear, and she should have been offended, but somehow the flirtation seemed harmless enough, completely of the moment, and too pleasurable to cease.

A breeze lifted the branches, and a spattering of new green leaves floated down though the air. "Ah, yes," she murmured, feeling giddy, and faintly delirious. "Safe, until the storm."

"No, don't you see how thick the branches are?" he said, brushing a leaf from her shoulder. "This is an old tree, old and wise. I know this tree well. It is a personal friend of mine, and I have had serious words with this tree." Grinning, he scanned her face for some reaction to his raillery. "It has agreed to shelter us, and protect us, and never reveal to anyone our whereabouts."

"And just who is it we are hiding from?" she asked.

He shook his head slowly, and the smile that crept across his face suggested acknowledgment, as if he had met his match. As he leaned over her, she had a sudden memory of a painting she had once seen in the du Prés library, in a book of reproductions from some European museum: *The Soldier and the Maid*. She had studied this painting many times and savored all that it suggested. The naive peasant girl, holding her shopping sack against her skirt, looked up at the handsome man in uniform, who was obviously speaking to her in seductive words that stirred her passions and compromised her virtue. It was as if she were suddenly standing within the painting, but the soldier's intentions were not so transparent, nor the girl so innocent.

Angelique's heart was racing from attentions so irresistibly potent, not from just any man, but from the man she had held in her dreams for so many years, the man who, as a boy, had entered her sanctuary, seen through her disguise to the girl she really was, and laughed at her charade.

He had whispered, "You aren't really a goddess, are you?" She could feel the *ouanga* around her neck where the moonstone lay sleeping. He had been charmed by her then, and she had somehow trusted him. And she did now, as he was at this moment drawn to her again. She felt a thousand years of loneliness fade in an instant.

He crossed his arms and leaned back against the gray tree trunk. "You have not asked me why I am awake so early. Did you think I came for vegetables?"

"Not at all," she answered, taking a fruit from her sack and looking down at it. "I thought perhaps you had come for apples." Her eyes danced, and she bit into the yellow flesh.

He watched her mouth for a moment. "I did not go to bed at all last night. Life is too brilliant for sleep, don't you think?"

"I had a restless night as well," she said, savoring the taste.

"Really? Were you with your lover?"

"No, Monsieur, I have no lover."

"Ah, but you will. I can see it in your walk, in your eyes. You are a flame for moths."

"And do you compose verses for all the girls?"

"Poetry does not come easily to me, but then I have never before been truly inspired. What spell have you cast on me, my lady?"

"Why, none that I am aware of, Monsieur." She looked at him fully. His eyes lay in such deep hollows, lavender shadows encircled them. She took another bite as he continued.

"What if I were to tell you that I saw you last night, in the street, beneath the lamp, and you saw me as well. You remember, don't you? I am only here because, afterward, I could not sleep, but walked along the edge of the sea thinking. 'My God, what would it be like to be loved by such a woman?'"

She stopped at these words. "Monsieur! How can you say you have not been to bed when you spent your whole night dreaming?"

He reached for the apple, took it from her, and brought it to his mouth. "What was it disturbed your sleep?" he asked, chewing his bite slowly.

"I . . . don't think it would interest you."

"Why do you say that?"

"Because . . . it was not a frivolous affair."

"I am even more curious."

Once again she felt a wave of trusting warmth. "Very well, I will tell you, sir. I . . . was called to visit a young girl who was gravely ill. I stayed with her the night, and cared for her, and I . . . think I was able to . . ."

"To save her life."

"Yes."

"Are you a sorceress?"

"You jest, Monsieur."

"Forgive me. What I mean is, are you skilled in medicine?"

"My mother had a talent for healing."

"And you? Can you heal . . . with your touch?"

"I don't know. Perhaps you can tell me," she said. She hesitated a moment, thinking it might be imprudent, then placed her hand on his cheek. "Do you feel anything strange?" she asked. Her hand trembled at the prickle of his beard.

He closed his eyes, the same delicious smile playing over his lips. "Ah-h-h-h . . . passing strange. Your hand is cool, but where it lies, there is warmth. . . . I'm certain I feel a tingling—"

She snatched her hand away, her face burning. He was vainer than she thought and dishonest as well.

But he only smiled his tender smile, obviously entranced. "I have always heard that the women of Martinique were beautiful," he whispered, brushing her arm, "but I never knew, until now, how true that was." He leaned in to her. "Will you let me kiss you?"

She could smell the sweet odor of apple and longed to lift her face to his. But she pulled away. "You trifle with me, sir, once again," she said. "You have already kissed my palm."

To her surprise he held out his own upturned hand. "Then you must repay the transgression," he said. She was startled to see how large his hand was, with long, slender fingers. "My hand is yours. Do with it what you will."

She placed her own hand beneath his and smoothed his fingers open. She felt she had been holding her breath for several minutes, and that her body would catch fire if she moved. Somehow she managed to say, "Perhaps . . . I should read your fortune."

"Please, do . . ."

She stared down, thoughts whirling in her mind. Her vision blurred, and she could not look for the truth in the lines. Reading palms was child's play; she wished to speak words from her heart. "I see a ship far out at sea," she began, "and great turmoil on deck. You were threatened with death, and you risked your life many times to save your comrades. You suffered greatly, but never abandoned courage, and you were never less than valiant and bold."

He stared at her in amazement, then his face clouded. "You could say such things about any sailor, and they would be true."

She frowned at his palm, then shook her head. "What?" he asked. "What else?"

"Seasick?" she asked. "A seasick sailor?"

He threw back his head and laughed. "How could you know that? That has always been my secret." He nudged her. "Tell me more."

"I see you are impulsive, moody, and there is a temper." She frowned. "Such irreverence for custom and authority. You like to break the rules." She looked up and he nodded, urging her to continue. "You are also a born leader, resourceful, generous, and keenly sympathetic to those in difficulty. Tell me? Why are you always so harsh with yourself?"

His eyes darkened as though she had struck a chord, but he shrugged, feigning indifference.

"I see another man beneath all these idle jests," she continued, now looking into his eyes, "one who yearns to explore life's deepest mysteries . . . a passion for tenderness which has long gone unfulfilled . . . and . . . a hunger for love. You have a tempestuous nature which must not, at all costs, be thwarted. If it flowers in your heart, you will find great happiness."

He stared at her, amazed. "Who are you . . . ?"

"Is it all true?"

"Not a word of it," he said softly. But his eyes were glittering, and he seemed to be forcing a smile. "As a fortuneteller, my dear, you are an amateur."

"Very well, then, if I do not engage you, Monsieur, I shall be on my way."

Barnabas turned pale. "Dear lady, you must believe that I meant no ingratitude. It's only that . . . please, please, forgive me. I am a . . . blundering fool." He paused, then said, "It is my deepest wish to call on you, and meet your family."

Her heart shrank when she heard his offer. "That is impossible," she said in a tone she hoped was disdainful. "I am afraid you have exhausted any opportunity you might have had to call on me."

She turned, but he moved in front of her. "Mademoiselle, you must believe me when I say I meant no unkindness. I was only pretending to think my fortune was ill read. It . . . it was more accurate than I was willing to admit. I-I know it is all a trick, but—to be truthful—I don't know how you were able to look so clearly into my soul. Please tell me that I may wait on you, in order that I might demonstrate, from this moment forward, the utmost civility."

She looked at his face, the expression so fervently sincere, as the absurd jumble of words tumbled from his mouth, and knew she must tear herself away before she kissed that mouth and humiliated herself beyond all saving. She turned and ran, the sack of apples bouncing against her thighs.

He watched her go, but this time he did not follow her.

chapter

22

The carriage finally pulled away, and Angelique turned and went back into the house. It was quiet now, after the family's hysterical departure for the ball. She climbed the steps to Josette's room, where stockings, camisoles, petticoats and shoes, ribbons and capes were scattered on the furniture and floor, carelessly strewn about in the excitement of dressing. Automatically, she rearranged the crumpled rugs, smoothed the bed, and collected the discarded articles of clothing, folding them carefully, and storing them in the wardrobe. Going to the vanity, she replaced each piece of jewelry that had been tossed aside. Every item was lovely and whispered of Josette's enchanted existence: an ivory cameo—a birthday present from her father; the diamond cross—a family heirloom; a necklace of garnets and pearls—ordered from Paris by the countess.

She realized at this moment how much she envied Josette, who never seemed to notice if something was precious or fine. It was not remarkable that

Josette was so loving, for she moved in a world without want, and her actions had no consequences. Even though she was invariably generous and kind, she was still protected by her station, and she carried the unconscious arrogance of the upper classes, the presumption of privilege.

At first Angelique's tears only burned behind her eyes and formed a lump in her throat, but as she smoothed the cover of the jewelry case, she saw the dark spots blooming one by one on the pink-satin wrapper.

She was irritated with herself for succumbing to self-pity. She told herself these were only lifeless objects, but she knew it was not the possessions themselves as much as what they represented, things she so desired: comfort, promise, and most of all, affection.

Five years she had worked now for the du Prés family as the countess's maid, and it seemed this would always be her life. She lived each day from dawn to dusk struggling for contentment and seeking to forget the past. The encounter with Barnabas at the market had inflamed her appetite for change. His looks, his words, promised ecstasy, and she was left with only dissatisfaction. Would the joys of love always be denied to her?

She folded a silken nightdress and placed it on the pillow. Josette attacked her life with eagerness. Each day brought new and unexpected delights, whereas the life of a servant was always one of arranging and preparing the lives of others. The work was invisible, never noticed or appreciated; only the unperformed task received remark. And all the objects one touched, the basin, the quilt, the fork, the shoe, all belonged to another, existed for another's pleasure.

Wealth was like a smooth river one floated down, Angelique thought. Josette was always receiving gifts, and she had been given so many presents that day, her birthday, tokens from admirers, friends of André's, total strangers seeking his goodwill. Some had not even been opened, and others had been exclaimed over and set aside. Josette was not to blame for her casual attitude. She could have any trinket in the shop window, a trinket that was then often discarded without a second thought. The hardest thing for Angelique to bear was this waste—like a piece of sweet cake with only one bite taken, the rest left on the plate.

About to leave the room, Angelique noticed on the floor the box containing the rejected turquoise gown made by the seamstress in Saint-Pierre. Impulsively, she took the dress from the box and held it to her before the mirror. The color swam to her eyes, setting them aglow. Moments later, she had it on.

The fit was not perfect, for the bodice was cut small; her breasts swelled at the low neckline, and the waist was so tight she could hardly fasten the hooks. The dress had been made for Josette, who was slimmer, but the gathered sleeves floated off her shoulders, and the skirt, which the countess had not even bothered to uncover, was yards and yards of shimmering fabric, the azure floating in her eyes. She dabbed a bit of Josette's rosewater on her neck and lifted her hair high on her head.

*   *   *

She did not remember leaving the house. She knew only that moments later she was in the street. The theater was blocks away but she started out, walking in the direction of the ball, trying not to think of what she would say if the family saw her. Gathering determination made her reckless. She didn't care. She would think of something. She had a right to be there. And she had taken nothing, really, not a ribbon or a jewel, only a dab of cologne and a dress no one wanted. The crickets and little frogs sang in the warm night. Soon she could hear the music, and before many moments had passed, she was in the square.

The flagged courtyard in front of the theater was crowded with buggies and traps, and horses were tethered to every lamppost. A great gathering of excited and noisy Negroes pressed in at the entrance; they had come to gawk at the *blancs*; *békés*, who were the only white Creoles descended from old colonials; and mulattoes invited to the ball. The mob parted to let her pass, sighing and murmuring, and seeming not to notice that she had come alone and on foot. She was simply another fine lady to them, she assured herself, and her heart beat faster.

She trembled at the thought of the countess, or André, catching sight of her, but bright orchestral music and the buzz of voices drifted down to her, drawing her farther. Climbing one of the great curving stairs, her skirt floating over the marble steps, she held her head high. Moving inside one of the arched doorways, she paused a moment in the darkness of the overhang.

The theater was overflowing with noisy celebrants. All the well-dressed planters and their families were there, but they were overshadowed by groups of dazzling mulatto ladies dressed in lavish gowns that seemed more designed for the Opéra in Paris. Lustrous dark hair was piled high with flowers, and jewels hung at necks and ears. Many of the women, and their equally resplendent escorts, wore masks of feathers or lace, covering their faces, but revealing flashing eyes and painted lips.

Angelique realized every property owner and merchant in Martinique had received an invitation. André du Prés was notoriously open-minded in such things, mostly because he was shrewd enough to realize it was to his advantage to accept all newcomers in the world of business, whatever their color. But her heart skipped a beat as she caught sight of several people she recognized. They were Monsieur Santurin, his wife, and their two horse-faced daughters, who sometimes came to visit at the du Prés household. Terrified that she would be noticed, she slid into a group of glittering ladies of color; one particularly glamorous matron seemed to notice her uneasiness and gave her a sly wink.

"Would you like a mask, my dear?" she inquired. "I'm leaving with my escort and have no further use for it. And . . . it matches your dress." Angelique looked at the mask. It was made of the iridescent feathers from a peacock's breast. A mask—such a delicious means of disguise!

"Thank you," she said, and placed it over her

face, slipping the tiny wires behind her ears.

The dancing began again, and the orchestra was ragged but enthusiastic as it launched into a polka. Suddenly the entire room was filled with recklessly swirling couples. A slave boy moved through with a tray, and she reached for a cup of rum. Without thinking, she lifted it to her lips and drank it down, just as the rollicking melody ceased and the cry went out for the quadrille.

Suddenly she felt a strong arm about her waist, and an awkward young man pulled her into the long double line which was forming across the hall. It was then she caught sight of Josette surrounded by suitors at the far end of the ballroom. Angelique was loath to be on the floor where she could be seen so easily, but before she could duck away, the music of the slow promenade began, and she was forced keep her place, to curtsy, cross, and turn again, and again, each time meeting a new partner.

Somehow in all the riotous brilliance she had missed the scarlet jackets. The tenth time she spun, she saw the brass buttons and the buttonholes stitched with gold before she looked up into the face of the man who was next. She was stunned to see it was Barnabas.

"Aha! A mystery woman!" he cried when he saw her mask, and he took her hand firmly and marched her down the row. He stepped back and bowed extravagantly to her curtsy, but the moment he looked into her eyes, he recognized her.

"It's you!" he said, incredulous. Angelique crossed

behind him, swept on by the motion of the dance, and Barnabas continued to follow her with his eyes as she passed farther and farther down the line until the quadrille was finished. Then, in the space of a breath, he was at her side, taking both her hands in his.

"By God, you won't run away this time," he said, "because I will not let you go. Ah, this is a dream! I prayed you would be here." Violins began to play. "Listen," he said, "a waltz. And I have you. Dance with me!"

"No, I do not wish to dance, Monsieur—"

Her words of resistance were swallowed by the burst of the strings as he whirled her into the crowd. At first she was too nervous to keep up with him, but every time she missed a step, strong as he was, he picked her up and set her down again. The music surged, and the dancers swirled around them. Finally, she abandoned herself to the rhythm and seemed barely to touch the ground. She could feel his body as he held her and the strength of his thighs as he moved. The odor of his body was musky and heady. When it was over she fell against him, drunk with the tempo of the music. Then she looked up at him; he was grinning.

He led her out onto the balcony, and they stood together, caressed by the balmy night air. "Take off your mask," he whispered. "I want to see your face." He reached for the wires and gently pulled them away, revealing her features. As he looked down at her, he began to chuckle to himself.

"What is it?" she said.

"I was thinking of the poor girls I've abandoned. I signed so many dance cards."

"Then go to them."

"I want to be here with you."

"There are not many balls in Martinique, and—"

"I have a secret to tell you. When I saw you for the first time, late the other night, beneath the tavern lamp, I followed you home."

"Did you? I am shocked, sir. What did you see?"

"I watched you go in the side door of your house. I waited to catch a glimpse of you, and I was rewarded with the sight of you at your window, braiding your yellow hair in the candlelight."

"You should not have spied on me. Why did you do that?"

"Let me ask you something. Do you believe it is possible to fall in love at first sight?"

"I believe it is possible for some, Monsieur. However, I'm afraid that love and I are not happily acquainted. In fact, we are bitter enemies."

"Enemies? Really? Aha!" He drew back and stood at mock attention. "At last, I have my calling. I will become your champion, and it will be my duty to vanquish all your foes."

"And if love be the only adversary I own?"

"Then I shall force love to submit, bend to my will, or I shall run love through." His eyes were dancing as he made a thrust with an imaginary sword, his arm brushing her skirt before he placed his weapon in an invisible sheath.

"So you would murder love to possess it?" she asked.

"Yes. If that's what is necessary."

"But . . . then you are left with nothing," she observed. And she was sobered by her own words.

"Or, everything . . ." he whispered, leaning in to her. At that moment she had a vision of another face burnished by the sun, a face she had tried to forget.

Barnabas cupped her chin in his hand. "Oh, you are puzzling. What is it about you . . . secretive . . . fascinating. Something mysterious sleeps in you. I haven't been able to stop thinking about you."

Images of Thierry, struggling to hold the gunwale of the boat, the slimy sea empty of life, the Evil One in his dark chariot, flashed though her mind. What had she done? She had been so immersed in the delights of flirtation, she had forgotten her dire constraints. Selfishly, she had allowed Barnabas to pursue her, and now he was in grave danger. With a sinking heart, she realized she could continue this insanity no longer.

"What you see in me is something you should fear," she said quickly.

"As one always fears, and longs for, a new adventure."

"What if I were to tell you that I am . . . that I am not what you believe me to be."

"What I believe? I don't know what I believe. I know if I were to dream of a woman, in all her beauty and mystery, that woman would be you."

"I am not like the other girls in Martinique. I was not raised in the common way." She struggled for clarity, but her thoughts were blurred by his closeness. She felt him place him arm around her waist.

"I already know there is no one like you."

"You speak of love," she blurted out, "but could you love a sorceress?"

"A what . . . ?" He leaned back to look at her more clearly.

"It is true," she said breathlessly. "You even asked in jest if I were . . . that strange creature. Your instincts were right. You must believe me when I tell you that because of . . . certain restraints on my actions . . . I-I have been forbidden . . ." She stopped, floundering in the awareness that her words were meaningless to him. How could she explain the Dark Spirit who guarded her, especially when he, Barnabas, who was flesh and blood, was staring down at her, obviously smitten.

"You aren't really a sorceress, are you?" he said, and his arm tightened.

"But I am. I have traveled to the farthest vistas of the mind. I have performed spells that would terrify you."

His black eyes shone; he was intrigued. "Tell me one thing you have done and see if I am frightened," he challenged.

She hesitated a moment, thinking of the horrors she could never reveal, but knowing she must warn him away. Finally she said, simply:

"I possess the power to make fire."

He sucked in his breath and drew her to him. "You have already done that, my lady," he whispered. Her words had only aroused him. He lifted her against him, molding her body to his, and kissed her neck, breathing in the perfume of her skin, then, clumsily at first, and then more insistently, he found her lips and kissed her softly, deeply, with such longing that she thought her heart would break.

She was not aware of the murmuring crowds gathering outside on the terrace until she finally opened her eyes, breathless, her head reeling. There were excited voices, and several hands pointing toward Pelée, the volcano. She turned, afraid of what she would see. Orange gases tumbled from the top of the mountain, and explosions of sparks traced the heavens.

"Look," Barnabas whispered. "Pelée is breathing fire!"

"The god is turning over!" a woman cried.

A man shouted, "He is angry that he has been awakened."

Angelique felt a shiver race though her body.

"The god? Of the volcano?" Barnabas asked the man.

"The god who guards the entrance to the underworld," he answered. "Baron Cimetière. The god of death."

There was a sudden clap of thunder, and the sky was rent with brilliant arcs. Angelique's stomach clutched as she saw lava pouring down from the lip, radiant rocks tumbling in sparks and flashes of fire.

Barnabas was enchanted. "Look at it! Amazing! How does it happen?"

"Don't you know?" she said, trembling against him.

"I have no idea."

"These islands are all tips of volcanoes," she said. Somehow she had to find a way to tell him, but other words fell from her lips. ". . . mountains of a land beneath the sea, with meadows of sea grass and forests of coral . . ." He was watching her, spellbound. Why was she suddenly talking to him about the places she loved? "And . . . living in that world are the most beautiful creatures on earth." Her voice broke. "But beneath, there is a dark sanctuary, where Pelée lingers."

"What makes him so angry?" he asked, indulging her.

"Because . . . I am here, with you," she said, and her eyes filled with tears.

"I can see his fire glowing in your eyes. Ah, now I understand. He is envious, longs for you as I do, burns with the same desire . . ."

"Your ridicule mocks sincerity, Barnabas. What I say is true!"

He pulled her against him. "I believe you. Don't they say the gods envy mortals when they fall in love? This is the happiest night of my life!" Once again, his youthful fervor, his bold self-assurance, swept him past her vague words of caution.

"You must not tempt me, Barnabas," Angelique said finally. "I must never fall in love."

"Why do you say that?"

She struggled to speak, but her words were only enigmas. "Everything . . . in the world has its shadow. Grief . . . is love's reflection. Love is not for me, Barnabas. I learned that a long time ago."

"But you are so beautiful. You were made for love."

At that instant, she heard a familiar voice and

turned to see Josette moving toward the balcony, two young men bending over her, whispering.

"It's too late," Angelique cried desperately. "You must leave me alone. It's too late!" And she turned and ran down the stairs and away from him, into the night.

chapter

❧

23

The next afternoon, Angelique was upstairs in Josette's room repairing the petticoat to Josette's gown. Someone had stepped on the ruffle during the waltz and torn the hem. Angelique smiled to think that she and Josette had danced to the same music, and Josette had never known she was there. Angelique had returned early, before the family, and replaced the blue dress safely in its box. Her stolen evening was now a dream—a dream that would have no repercussions, and would never come to fruition. Still, she allowed her mind to linger on the pleasant memory, and she trembled when she recalled Barnabas's insistent kisses.

She heard voices downstairs, men's voices, and noted absently that André was receiving visitors. André maintained the du Prés plantation, but his real fortune was derived from his carefully timed loans to other planters. He was a shrewd investor and creditor to new landowners with reckless schemes that often failed, resulting in foreclosure on their property. Or, if their hogsheads finally shipped, he was repaid with high interest. However, Angelique had lived with the du Prés family long enough to know that André had a grave fault. He dearly loved to gamble, just as the man she had once believed to be her father, Theodore Bouchard, had done. Sometimes male visitors to the house came to collect on André's flagrant debts, livres lost forever at the table.

The ruffle was voluminous, and Angelique was sewing swiftly when she pricked her finger. Fearful that she would stain the white cotton, she rose and, sucking on her finger, wandered into the hall and casually leaned over the railing. André was talking with his visitor in the foyer, and when she saw the scarlet jacket, her heart jumped. Barnabas was here!

Of course, he knew where she lived. He had followed her the first night he had seen her, and now he was making good his request. He had come to call on her. At once she knew whatever vague hopes she may have harbored were dashed forever. She was startled to see that she was gripping the railing with both her hands. Her knuckles were a bloodless white.

As the two men entered the drawing room she could hear André sputtering effusively, "By my word, the Collinses! Absolutely I know of you, sir, and of your family, renowned in these islands, not to mention yourself, Mr. Collins. Why I should say you are something of a hero, are you not? Escaped from filibusters! I should love to hear that story! Bécè!" He was calling his houseboy. "Brandy! In the drawing room."

Angelique crept down the stairs silently and listened outside the drawing-room door. André and Barnabas were discussing the war in France.

"They've done it, haven't they? Poor Louis is gone! The best of kings and that most humane man, led to the scaffold by the ferocity of his people."

"And France has not known tranquillity since."

"The guillotine! My God, what a horrific scene that must have been. Did you know they want to bring one of the damned contraptions to Guadeloupe? An invention of the Devil!"

"And yet, in Martinique, sir, trade flourishes, now that the British are threatening to take over. Our ships have even been offered safe passage only until then."

"What a pathetic showing we will make. Don't you think? Martinique will fall without a whimper. I myself couldn't care less. I have been furious with the Republic. They have always thought the colonies existed for the benefit of the home country. You've settled your disputes over the divine right of kings. Ours are only just beginning."

"It seems calm enough here."

"It is the calm that precedes a hurricane."

"But last night's ball was the height of carefree gentility."

Angelique felt nausea in the pit of her stomach. She leaned against the wall to steady herself.

"Were you there?" André exclaimed. "Brilliant gathering, if I do say so myself. The theater was a splendid venue, all lit up like that."

"Even Pelée provided spectacular fireworks."

"Glorious! And it didn't cost me a cent! It was the

volcano paying tribute to my daughter on her birth-day."

"Oh, yes, your daughter, Monsieur du Prés. I believe I danced with her. Does your daughter take after you, sir?"

"In what way?"

"Has she blue eyes?"

"No, no, Josette's dark eyes come from her mother, God rest her soul. My daughter is chestnut-haired and uncommonly pretty—a delightful creature, the joy of my heart, and developing splendidly. She's had all the best tutors, that sort of thing—every decent influence a young lady would have had in Paris. Would you stay, Mr. Collins, and dine with us?"

"It would be a pleasure."

"Marvelous to have a gentleman from America to discuss the political scene. You and I must go hunt-ing. I have some fine new pistols. And I'd like you to meet Josette. I must warn you. You might very well fall in love with her."

"Do you have another girl in this house, who was also at the ball. With yellow hair?"

Angelique felt her throat tighten as André responded.

"No, only one, only Josette, I'm afraid. But I am certain you will be charmed with her. There is a ser-vant girl with light hair, Angelique, but she did not accompany us to the ball."

When she heard this damning sentence, Angelique felt her knees go weak.

"A servant girl." So now he knew, and that was

the end of her little ruse. She told herself she didn't care. She herself had rejected him, pushed him away out of fear. Even if she had not, he would most likely have used her to his own advantage, as wealthy young men are bound to do, and cast her aside. It was fortunate that he had learned of her station before she weakened and succumbed to any further advances. She could hear André's voice droning on the subject of sugar cane.

"We need an inexhaustible stock of human machinery to harvest these crops."

Servants, she thought. Necessary to spin out their masters' fine lives. Indispensable, invisible. And between those servants and their masters lay an ocean that could never be crossed. Enmity for her station stung her heart, and the old anger flared in her breast. Had she the wealth and the name, she would have marched into the drawing room and rejoiced at Barnabas's face when he saw her.

"How much longer before you will be forced to free your slaves?" Barnabas asked.

"Who knows?" answered André. "The river of brown blood runs deep, and grows broader every day. At times, my boy, I despair. Life is a transitory commodity to be ended in violence or prolonged in pain."

This last remark Angelique overheard seemed a woeful prophecy, spoken from her own soul.

She remained in her room during dinner, as she had not the strength to risk seeing Barnabas. Only once did she pass by the door to the dining room, on her way out to the kitchen. André was telling the story of his life, and his voice was warm with rum.

"My grandfather was a refugee, landed in Dominique with fifteen francs in his pocket. Today, my plantation alone is worth a hundred and sixty-seven thousand."

"To what do you owe your success?" Barnabas inquired politely. It was Josette who answered the question.

"Prudence, caution, and temperance," she said in a bright voice. "My father has always said that judgment and character are the deciding factors in acquiring a fortune, not the ups and downs of the sugar market."

"Shall I tell you my secret?" André added. "I never lend money to planters with colored heirs!"

Everyone laughed heartily.

Later that evening, as she was lighting the lamps, Angelique noticed that the oil in the hall lantern was low, and went to fetch the needed fuel. Opening the gate to the outdoor shed, she glimpsed a young man standing on the street in front of the house.

The moment he saw her he called out harshly, "Angelique!" In an instant Barnabas was at her side. "That is your name, isn't it? Angelique." He took her hands. "I've been waiting here for over an hour in hopes you would appear. I endured that interminable supper without one glimpse of you, and yet you were there all the time, somewhere in the house, were you not?"

He was trembling, and his face was drawn, as if he

were in physical pain. In the lamplight his skin took on a yellow cast, and his eyes were deeply shadowed.

"I must talk to you," he whispered. "Will you come to my room later tonight?"

"No, Monsieur. How could you ask such a thing?"

"I won't violate you. You have my word. You can trust me as a gentleman." She saw drops of perspiration standing on his forehead.

"Surely you know you ask the impossible. I have been flattered by your attentions, but now that you know the truth about me—"

"What do you mean?"

"That I am a lady's maid, sir, and not gentility. I should have thought you would have noticed in the market, by my dress—"

"Your dress!" he said, laughing. "You are exquisite! You have such delicate airs! You must be a . . . a princess, with your gait, and your form. I thought your dress charming. Don't Parisian *elegantes* dress in peasant costumes for amusement?"

"I wouldn't know, sir," she said, feeling her heart sink, "but now, please, excuse me. It's time I returned to the house."

"Angelique, please don't go. I beg you. I have been in agony since last night, trying to think of a way to see you again. I long to know more about you. If you won't come tonight, then tomorrow. Meet me at the tavern, or the theater, or, if you prefer, the cathedral! It doesn't matter. Only tell me that I may see you again."

She hesitated, and she felt him sense her resolve waver.

"Angelique. Please, say you will."

"In the square, by the fountain," she said. "I will be there tomorrow evening, at six o'clock."

The following night, when she arrived, he was waiting, and she was able to observe him a moment without being seen. He had one foot casually placed on the stone riser and was looking toward the sea. He had shed his uniform jacket and wore only breeches and a loose-flowing shirt of white cotton that complemented his finely molded features and dark curls.

The sight of him moved her in a way she did not expect, and her limbs went weak. Light falling on the fountain brightened the air around him, creating an aura behind his head, as water fluting from a cup lifted in the hand of Dionysus tumbled over carved acanthus leaves.

When he saw her, he stood up eagerly, his face lit with pleasure and his eyes caressing her movements as she approached. She felt that she was floating above the ground. He stepped forward and took both her hands, and she trembled at the intensity of his gaze. *People do not look at one another in that way,* she thought. *They live together for years and barely see one another.* But this look was intimate and uncomfortable, difficult to sustain. Yet she felt if she looked away, this feeling of time standing still would be lost.

"Walk with me," he said gently. "The night is so lovely." He took her hand and placed it around his arm. They strolled for a quarter of an hour without speaking, down the wide tree-lined avenue, then down a side street toward the wharf. He was a large man, much taller than she, and his stride was longer than hers. Every so often she was forced to take little running steps to keep up with him.

They stopped and looked out over the sea, where the moon had risen, causing its moonstream to flow across the water. They sat on a small stone wall that circled the strand. The air was fragrant with honeysuckle and frangipani, and the little coqui chirruped in time with accordion music wafting from a gypsy band playing outside the theater. Barnabas gripped her arm, as though she could fly off into the night, and spoke to her in a voice that was deep, sonorous, with a slight rasp that gave his words the character of long-held and guarded secrets.

He told her of his life as the son of a shipbuilder in Maine, boarding school in England, and of his house in Collinsport, a town named after his family. He spoke of his years at sea, his many escapades, and he related to her a long, fascinating tale of having been captured by buccaneers. She listened with her heart brimming, but said nothing. This brush with death had changed him a great deal, he said. It had transformed him and given him whatever moral character he now possessed.

He poured out his life to her, confidences she had not expected, that he had been deeply ashamed of his family's ownership of slaves, and of how he had always felt estranged from his father, neither ever

approving of the other. He spoke of a desperate loneliness, a distance from his comrades. He told her that
he had been reckless and foolhardy all his youth, not
because he was prone to bravado, but in an effort to
escape a furious aversion to all that was his own
world.

She shared her life with him as well, at least the
parts she could reveal: her childhood by the sea, the
bond she felt with the ocean. She spoke of the little
convent where the nuns taught her to read, her cama-
raderie with Josette, sharing tutors as well as the
schooling of a Parisian countess. She entertained him
with her knowledge of the intricate mechanics of
making sugar on the du Prés plantation, somehow
able to render humorous, even ridiculous, the trials of
raising cane. She spoke of her love of Shakespeare and
other English poets she had read, and she told him in
confidence that she had always kept a journal in
which she recorded all her thoughts and memories.
He drank in every word, making generous comments,
and encouraging her to continue. He seemed all the
while to be the victim of an inner turmoil, a kind of
intoxication he repressed with a tremendous effort.

They had been walking for over an hour when he
stopped before an elegant town house. A little trap
and groom stood there, the horse tied to a hitch.
"These are my private quarters," he said. "I have dinner waiting." Her first thought was that he was going
in and would ask the carriage to take her home.

She nodded and turned toward the buggy, but he
stopped her and took her hand. "Please do me the

honor of joining me," he said, his eyes so dark and his tone so painfully anxious, she was amazed.

Candlelight beckoned from a beautifully appointed apartment hung with velvet tapestries and encircled with mahogany paneling. She could see a white cloth, the gleam of silver and translucent china. With tentative solicitousness, he led her to the table. She was keenly aware of his happiness in having her there and forgot everything in the easy embrace of refinement. It seemed that she had always known such a life could be hers. Luxuries she had only dreamed of were as natural to him as the sand to the shore, and he treated her as though she were in every way his equal.

She sensed his nervousness and was surprised when he poured her wine and clumsily tipped over her glass with the lip of the bottle. Cursing to himself, he mumbled an apology as the red bloomed on the white cloth. He covered it quickly with his own napkin, and she noticed, as she had the first time, his large hands, muscular and primitive, beneath the ruffled cuffs of his shirt. He looked at her to see whether she found him foolish. His eyes were wide apart, dark and lustrous beneath the heavy brows, fringed with lashes, and set deep in shadows. His nose was formidable, almost too large for a face that reminded her of pictures she had seen on Roman coins, endowed with character and strength, yet permeated with that human quality which suggested even leaders of great empires had ordinary cares.

After they had finished the dinner and were sipping the last of the wine, he leaned back in his chair and stared at her. The night was caressingly warm and moist, and the air between them seemed palpable and thick. Barnabas appeared calm on the surface, but Angelique was aware that there was a rushing of turbulent feelings somewhere deep within him, feelings that he held tenuously in check.

"You have told me that you will never love," he began. "Now you must tell me why."

She sighed. Warm with the wine, and languorous with the comforts of his apartment, she felt that her troubles were part of a dim past, whereas at this moment she wanted only to relish the delicious feelings that flowed through her body in waves.

"Is there someone else? Another man in your life who has claimed you? Some lover who has eclipsed all others?"

She could only shake her head. She looked at Barnabas. Somehow she had always felt she could trust him, even when she was a child and he had given her the moonstone, or when he had spoken kind words to her on the deck of the schooner. She struggled to answer him. Finally, she said, "Those I loved were taken from me. I have something in me that is dangerous, injurious, some dark power I don't understand. . . ."

"What makes you say that?"

"It was told to me once . . . long ago . . . by the . . ."

"A fortuneteller?"

". . . yes . . ."

He looked at her with such compassion that it seemed that all her griefs were only bitter dreams and she was waking from them.

"Oh, sweet lady . . ." he said.

Her eyes filled with tears and, try as she might to stop them, they flooded and fell down her cheeks. Inexplicably, when she had wanted so much to be strong, she was weeping, and he watched her until she found her voice, and said, "Why do you ask?" she said. "Why does it matter?"

"Because I have found the woman I want to love," he said with utter guilelessness. She was not certain she had heard him correctly. "I knew the moment I set eyes on you," he continued, "that I desired you, and since that moment I have been able to think of nothing else. I am only afraid that you will forget me after I return to America."

"I will not forget you. How could you suggest such a thing?" Unconsciously, her hand went to the *ouanga* at her neck.

His words tumbled out. "I must tell you that I have very deep regard for you. You are not only beautiful, you have intelligence and strength of character. And a quality few women claim . . . mystery. You are like no woman I have ever known; something in you stirs me; and all I know is that I long to possess you. Nothing else matters. I don't know how I can be more honest than to tell you my true feelings."

"I fear, Monsieur, that you may regret your generous words at another time—" She stopped, for he had fallen to his knees at her feet and was clutching her hand. "Oh please, do not kneel—"

"What about you, Angelique?" he asked, kissing her hands. "Do you have feelings for me as well?"

Her head was swimming; she had no idea how to answer him.

"I am deeply flattered by your offer, and I want to say yes to you with all my heart, but . . . I am afraid . . . that you have been caught in a storm—a reckless infatuation, that will clear in more sober moments."

She saw something dart in his eyes, a quick jerk as though he had heard something unexpected in her reply.

"This is . . ." she said softly, keenly fearful of being forward, "I am correct in assuming, am I not, that this is an offer of marriage?"

"Of course," he answered quickly. "Yes. Of course, it is, my dear, what do you think? I long for you. Oh, God, I love you! I want to live with you, and I don't want anyone else to have you."

"But we are separated by society's codes. The difference in our stations might cause you to change your mind in time—"

"Angelique, I have a fortune! Enough for both of us!" he said hurriedly, almost as though he were irritated by the need for explanation.

He stared at her a moment, then rose and went to open another bottle of wine. When he spoke again, Angelique could sense him struggling as though he were compromised by some battle raging within him. "My father's marriage is not a happy one," he said at last. "My mother is a fine woman, but he does not love her. I don't think he is capable of love. And so, unfortunately, she drinks."

"My . . . my father was a drunkard as well. He

was depraved and unpredictable . . . and very cruel to me—"

"I can't understand it! Often she is so drunk by the afternoon that she cannot come to dinner. She drinks because she is miserably lonely. And so is he! My father has amassed a fortune in shipping, but his heart is bankrupt. If human feelings were coins, he would be a pauper."

"Will I meet him?"

"I hope you will never be forced to meet him. You wouldn't like him."

He sat down again and took her hands; he appeared more at ease with his feelings. "I have come to value more subtle things," he continued now with great urgency. "I have sworn to have love in my life. I want a woman who is my soul's companion, and I believe that woman to be you. If you will have me, Angelique, I will return within a year's time, when I am due to come into my fortune. I will take you back to America with me."

"America! So far away . . . and, safe, perhaps. . . . I don't know what to say—"

"Then say yes."

For a moment she was transfixed, her head reeling with the conflicting emotions she was feeling. He had said he loved her, this man she had worshiped for so long. He had asked her to marry him. He was rash and wild, and perhaps did not know his own mind. The candlelight molded the planes and shadows of his cheek and brow, and his deep eyes searched hers for an answer. What could she do? Was it possible for her to escape the cruel forces that controlled her life? Where was the evil spirit who owned her soul? Had he abandoned her forever? It had been so many years. Was it possible that she was free?

She remembered the dawn over the ocean, when the morning mist obscures the horizon and the great deep is encircled by the haze. How sheltered and close the sea appears in the silver light. Once she had been caught beneath a huge school of moon jellyfish, their transparent bodies rising above her head, a thousand clear blue saucers floating pearly and translucent, their long tentacles swaying. She had been terrified by their beauty, but though she could hold her breath no longer, she could not bring herself to swim into them for fear of being stung. What had she done that day? Had she slipped through unharmed, or had the tide blown them all away?

"Say yes . . ." He bent and kissed her hands, and it was as if the gloom parted, and the sky gleamed with light. She was more frightened than she had ever been, but, unable to help herself, she uttered words she never dreamed she would hear herself speak. "Yes, I will go with you, Barnabas—"

"And do you love me? Let me hear you say it!"

"Yes, yes, I do love you with all my being. I have always loved you, and I will love—"

He swept her into his arms, and his kiss took her breath away. His lips tasted hers as though she were all sweetness, and he sucked at them and traced them with his tongue until her mouth melted into his.

"I want you," he whispered, his voice ragged with

excitement, and she realized he was shaking, as he pressed her to him and kissed her over and over.

His mouth moved down her neck and into the hollow of her throat, where she could feel her own pulse quivering. Then he fell awkwardly to his knees and, placing his hands around her, buried his face in the folds of her skirt. She could feel the heat of his breath through the fabric and sensed again his impetuous youth, and the violence of his passion.

He rose to his feet. Trembling, as though he would shatter with the fierceness of his desire, he said to her in a hoarse voice, "I will take you back now. I promised that I would not violate you, and I am a man of my word."

He crossed to the door, turned, and reached for her hand. But she stood as though in a trance, and after a moment he returned to her. His eyes were luminous and she thought he was as beautiful as a god when he sighed and touched the side of her cheek. "Come," he said, "before it is too late."

They had walked only a few blocks when it began to rain, and the underground streams of Saint-Pierre, which were its music and its secret life, sprang from every hollow and hillock and trickled into the gutters that ran along the street. "We should turn back," he said, but then, looking down at her, he shook his head and smiled. "I don't trust myself alone in that room with you again." With that he wrapped his arm about her so that she would not fall, and led her along.

It was a hard rain, warm and caressing, and they walked until they no longer cared how wet they became.

Their hair and clothes were dripping. A thought hummed in her head like the drone of a waterspout, and she realized she was holding her breath, deadly certain of what she knew was coming. Some diabolical catastrophe awaited her. She would slip on the wet pavement and fall to her death, or the sky would darken, and a bolt of lightning would sear her flesh. But there was no sound other than the pounding rain, and the path a little way in front of them was all they could see.

She began to feel as though she were caught in an underwater current, flowing down from the mountains in an inexorable journey to the sea. If she were going to be stopped, she wanted it to be now, before her heart was completely lost. Where was he, the Dark Spirit who had forbidden her to love? Why was there no sign? Suddenly, a reckless defiance gripped her. She would challenge him, taunt him into coming. And if he did, whom would he destroy? Barnabas was too strong, too merry. She looked up at him, and he smiled, his eyes glowing with fierce vitality.

Tempted by her look, Barnabas stopped her by the high wall of a garden in a deserted street. His hand reached around her waist and he pulled her to him. "Just one kiss . . ." he said softly.

Heedlessly, she fell against him with abandon, fear dissolving into itself. He pressed her against the stones, and, emboldened, she responded eagerly. He kissed her liquid mouth, drinking the rain as it flowed from her lips. Rhythmically, he kissed her, pushing against her, feeling her body beneath her saturated skirt. She felt her heart pitch against her chest, as deliberately she flung caution aside and dared the Devil to come.

Barnabas lifted her up in his arms and carried her a little way to where the wall rose up between the garden and the street. The water dripped from his face as he crushed her against his chest, and she could hear his heart thundering—not the deep bass, but a furious drumming, bright and hard as the rain. The sound frightened her, and she remembered when the surge swept her against the reef and she knew the coral would tear her skin.

She struggled to free herself, but he held her against him with such fierceness that she thought he would break her body in the strength of his arms. He searched until he found an opening in the wall and carried her through into the sheltered garden.

Then, as though coming from a trance, she found she was lying on a mossy step with a stream of water beneath her. Barnabas gathered her to him, still kissing her wet face. His back was naked to the pounding rain, her breasts slippery now against his chest, and he reached beneath her in the flowing water where her legs were bare, and she became the stream, rippling and sinuous against him. As he moved into her, she felt as though she had been holding her breath underwater for thousands of years until, finally, with a burst of air into her lungs, she was able to breathe at last.

They walked home in silence, and when they arrived at the house, he said only, "Meet me tomorrow night?" and she answered, "Yes, tomorrow, and tomorrow, and tomorrow."

"Good night, then, and may all your dreams be sweet ones." He kissed her softly and clasped her to him for a long moment, then turned and walked off into the night.

Once in her room, she went to the window and looked out. The rain had stopped, and the sky was clear and deep as the sea. Trembling, but defiant still, she waited, then uttered a prayer. "Power of Darkness, you have left me alone for so many years. Are you still there, watching over me? Are you as determined as ever to control my life and my heart?"

There was no answer. Only the brilliant stars in their orbits shone down on her, cold and silent.

The following night she went to Barnabas's chamber. As she felt her dress drawn off her, she wondered whether she had even existed before now, and her body seemed suspended in rapt expectancy. He kissed the insides of her palms, which floated over his face, and then her aching breasts, which sprang to his mouth. He stroked her soft arms until they moved around his neck, and he trailed his hand down her stomach and around to the bones of her hips, wandering slowly to her inner thighs. His touch sent waves of pleasure through her, so intense that she wanted to weep. Her body amazed her, and all the magic she had learned until now paled before these new secrets, so deep in her core, so vivid and rushing, that she lost all memory of herself and all desire to know or understand any other force but this: the all-consuming power of love.

chapter

24

For three enchanted weeks the lovers stole away at every possible moment, snatching private intervals together: a conversation in the marketplace, a walk on the seashore, an assignation in Barnabas's chamber in the early-morning hours. Often it was dawn when Angelique returned to the du Prés house and crept quietly in the kitchen door. Every rendezvous was sweet with the knowledge that the time they had was flying by, and that his ship would soon sail back to America.

Clandestine meetings were arranged in whispers, and the pain of not being able to reveal their love affair was a cruel impediment. But kisses in shadows were dearer than sunshine, and furtive trysts heady with ardor.

One afternoon when they had secreted themselves away beneath the wreck of a schooner on the beach, Angelique said, "I can't bear this hiding any longer. We will have to tell everyone someday. Can't we do it now?"

Barnabas said to her, "I want to tell the world about you. And I will, when I return. You must trust me. When my inheritance is certain, and my father can no longer reject me, then we will be free to love one another openly."

"Your fortune is not important to me. It's you I love."

"My darling, do you want us to be paupers?"

"Will you write to me?"

He thought a moment. "How can I do that? Wouldn't Madame du Prés discover a letter?"

"Is there no way I can write to you?"

"Where would you send it? My father . . ." He sighed and drew her into his arms. "The time will go quickly, and I will return. Let's not worry over trivial things. Will you forget me?"

"Never!"

"Nor I you."

The morning Barnabas's schooner sailed, the harbor was shrouded in fog. The schooner floated like a ghost ship on the swirling mist that covered the sea. As Angelique watched from the wharf, she thought the ship was like a painting, the sails white against white, their curved shapes like bleached shells as they drew away into a haze of nothingness.

Josette and Angelique continued their lives as companions, but with every season, a widening gap edged between them. Josette's life now included visits to other plantations with the countess, sometimes for weeks at a time, as the easily bored Parisian expatriate pursued stimulation and distraction in what she referred to as "this infernal jungle of an island teeming with unfortunate souls." Josette was invited to teas and balls in Saint-Pierre and found a group of wealthy young ladies who shared her station in life. Angelique was called upon much more than before to wait on Josette and attend to her needs, and she had increasing difficulty performing her duties as a servant, knowing she was to marry into a fortune. Time passed slowly for her, as all was heartache and longing.

Josette as well seemed far more drawn into herself. She spent hours alone, playing the pianoforte and singing sweet and plaintive love songs, sketching at her tablet, or writing long letters to friends who were traveling abroad. These letters seemed to occupy more and more of her time, and she took to walking into town, or, if they were at Trinité, the long length of the tree-lined colonnade, to meet the post. Angelique longed to send a letter to Barnabas if only there were some way, and how she wished somehow one would come for her.

Often Josette's letters were the subject of intense conversation with the countess, who had become her confidante, as the developing young woman sought the advice and experience of a woman of the world. At times Angelique overheard snatches of conversation coming from behind the closed door of the countess's boudoir:

"You must be reserved, Josette, and not appear too fond. Remember the man loves the chase. Don't respond right away, but wait a week or two, then plead various occupations and family responsibilities which suggest merriment. Speak to him of exciting travel or essential social events, so that he will believe you are far too busy to be thinking of him. It's best to make him wonder how you feel. But always remind him of how delighted you are to have heard from him—someone you admire so deeply, or he might slip away!"

It was obvious that Josette had a special suitor, but she was secretive, and Angelique could not help but wonder which of the young men who came to call at the du Prés household was the happy gentleman. A planter from Lamartine had a strapping young son who sat in the parlor with his hat in his hands and appeared so besotted with Josette's beauty that he could scarcely utter a word, but simply sat watching her play the pianoforte with watery pain in his eyes.

A wealthy young landowner appeared to be Monsieur du Prés's favorite, since the two men conversed for hours when he came to call, and Josette waited patiently in the drawing room. André dearly loved bestowing business advice on the industrious young entrepreneur who seemed destined to make his fortune in sugar.

There were various gentlemen of whom her father did not approve, but he held his tongue and never berated her or pressured her, for he seemed to trust her implicitly. Angelique often wondered how it would have been to have had such an affectionate father, one who doted on her every whim. She envied Josette her parent as she envied her in every other way.

A wickedly handsome young officer met Josette often outside the side door of the house in Saint-Pierre, and Angelique could sometimes hear Josette laughing giddily at the remarks he made to her. Once she caught sight of him leaning in to speak to Josette while he had her trapped under his resting arm, and she felt a sharp pang of envy as she remembered the same scarlet jacket and Barnabas's hungry kisses.

It was the letters that came from abroad that seemed to make Josette deliriously happy, and she kept them tied with a blue ribbon and hidden in a locked compartment of her desk. Which suitor could it be? Saint-Pierre was overflowing with traders and merchants from Europe and America, and many came to wait on the young du Prés girl. Her father's wealth alone made her a magnet for gentlemen and fortune hunters alike. Finally Angelique decided that the devilish young officer must be the favorite, since his attentions had been so well received.

One day Josette met the carriage, and a letter had come for her that rendered her ecstatic. She ran back down the road, her dark hair in tangles and her skirts fluttering around her feet. She rushed up the stair and hid herself away in her room for the rest of the afternoon. That evening the doors to the drawing room were closed on a long, serious conversation between the girl and her father, and Josette emerged from the interview with a beatific smile on her face.

The following morning Josette called Angelique to her room and, embracing her for the first time in months, spoke to Angelique effusively.

"Oh, Angelique, I am so happy! I am betrothed!"

"Oh, Mademoiselle!"

"I have received an offer of marriage that has made me wondrously happy! Last night Father gave his permission, and I wanted to tell you before anyone else did. I am so in love that I think my heart will burst!"

"Who is the fortunate gentleman?"

"I can't say as yet; it's all still a secret. Father and his father must exchange agreements, dowry arrangements and the like, for he is a person of wealth and owns a great house in New England. Angelique, I am to be the mistress of a grand estate!"

"America?"

"Yes! I am going to America, for a while, although we will live on both shores, and my fondest hope is that you accompany me there. I don't know how I should ever do without you."

Angelique felt the usual pangs that were part of all her conversations with Josette, but she also hugged to herself the deliciously ironic coincidence that they might be neighbors some day. "I am so glad for you, Mademoiselle. You deserve every happiness."

"Will you come into town with me today to look at fabric?" Josette had an endearing habit of leaning into a person when she spoke to them and placing a hand on their arm to ensure their attention. She reached for Angelique and spoke with a serious voice. "The countess is insisting that my dress come from Paris, but the couturiers there are so unreliable now, ever since what Father calls the Reign of Terror. And

Martinique has Belgium lace! Wouldn't that be exquisite? Say you'll come!"

The next afternoon, André went hunting wild goats in the scrub with a few planters, and Angelique and Josette took the little buggy into Saint-Pierre and stopped in at the seamstress's shop. Josette was measured for her wedding gown, and the solicitous mulatto woman spread luxurious yards of goods for Josette to see. She took her time, considering each one before choosing a bolt of cream-colored silk that came all the way from the Orient. It had been secreted away for a decade, ever since an exotic trading ship from India had called in St. Thomas, and it cost sixty livres a yard.

The following week, Josette went for her first fitting. The sheen on the gown had the luster of pearls and so enhanced Josette's ivory complexion that she resembled a porcelain figurine.

Angelique folded away into her mind every detail of Josette's preparations, thinking the day would soon come when she would partake of these same delights. Before she knew it, it had been over a year, a long, agonizing year, since Barnabas had departed, and every morning she woke wondering when he would return to claim her as his bride. Working at her menial tasks, or walking in the garden, her hopes kept alive by anxious anticipation, she was always lost in delightful reverie, remembering their hours together, imagining her future happiness. She thought often of the seamstress's shop and fantasized of going there to purchase the fabric for her own wedding gown, a blue watered taffeta, pale as ice, she had seen on the top shelf. But she told herself she would sew real pearls to the bodice.

One afternoon, when she thought she could bear the waiting no longer, she passed the door of the seamstress's establishment on the way back from the market. She decided to order another dress, a dress she would wear when Barnabas returned.

From that day forward she saved every penny of her small salary and kept the coins safely stashed in a little purse. It would be the gown of a fine lady, fitted to her perfectly, and tailored with elegance and style, the first of many she would see hanging in her own wardrobe one day.

The day she was to choose the fabric, Angelique allowed her imagination full rein as her eyes feasted on the rich colors of silks and taffetas folded on the shelves. As her fingers stroked the lavish stuffs on display, she lost herself in the exquisite hues and remembered the shades of vermilion and lime, the corals of the reef where she used to swim. She chose a tissue satin of the palest gold, which tumbled like liquid metal against her hand when she lifted it.

While the muslin pattern was cut and pinned to her body, the seamstress bustled around her, her mouth filled with pins, patting and tucking the pieces into place, murmuring comments about Angelique's graceful form, all the time assuring her that the gown would be a lovely addition to her wardrobe. The fitting was an unexpected pleasure, for the seamstress was both skilled and courteous, and Angelique enjoyed standing near the window of the shop where passersby could see her being treated with the respect bestowed on a valued customer.

She was thinking of the years when Thais had dressed her as the goddess and pinned the flowers to her skirt, when she noticed a young Negro man stride by the window and turn into the square. Something in his gait and carriage was familiar, and Angelique moved closer to the glass to see whether he was a person she knew. She was sure she recognized him. She ran to the door of the shop, and called out, "Cesaire!"

The young man turned when he heard his name, and she knew she had not been mistaken. It was her old friend. When he saw her at first a puzzled expression crossed his face, then he broke into a wide grin as he walked back in her direction, his eyes lighting up.

"Angelique, gal, is that really you? An' all grown-up?"

"Cesaire! Yes! Hello. My goodness! I never thought I would see you again." She wanted to hug him, but all the pins prevented her, and it was just as well, for a white girl could not embrace a black man on the street in Martinique.

"What you doin' out here, gal, an' what's all this? You all pinned together in sailcloth?"

"I'm having a dress fitted, you silly thing! Oh, Cesaire, you've been gone for such a long time!"

"I seen the world, gal, an' the high seas between."

"Did you go back to Africa?"

"Africa, yes, and Venezuela, even Philadelphia! I stay in Guadeloupe when I'm not on board ship because the slaves be free there. Not like here, where *backra* look right through you if your skin be black. The planter fear the guillotine in Guadeloupe!"

Angelique could see Cesaire had grown into a proud young man, with skin like varnished mahogany and fiery eyes. He must have been thinking of how she had changed as well, for he said, "You are a fine young woman now I see, and rich enough to have your clothes sewn for you. No longer a lady's maid at Trinité?"

She dropped her eyes, wondering why she was ashamed to say she was, but just as quickly she lifted her chin, and said, "I am, Cesaire, still working where you left me, with the family du Prés."

"Then why this fancy gown?"

"Oh, Cesaire, my fortunes are about to change."

He smiled at her and cocked his head to look into her eyes. "Yes, I see clearly now. You be in love! Am I right?"

"How did you guess?"

"I know that look from other eyes. What do you think? I have had many a lovely girl to call my own, and seen that look before. So who is this lucky man?"

"Oh, you won't believe me when I tell you. He was on the schooner we sailed on to Hispaniola—the officer whose life we saved—remember?"

"Of course . . . and he was a gentleman."

"A fine gentleman who lives in Maine. Wealthy, and from a powerful family."

Cesaire's face clouded. "What you doin' lovin' a fine gentleman?"

"He has asked me to marry him! And soon, very soon, he is coming back to Martinique."

"But that is a dream, Angelique. An' you be in bad luck if you not give it up. Little island packet never catch the brigantine, even in high winds."

"It's not a dream, Cesaire."

He hesitated a minute, then said, "Just so you be happy, gal. I won't ever forget the little soldier who jumped into my wagon. I never knew before or since such a brave one as you. I don't want to see your heart broken." Then he looked back over his shoulder. "My ship sails on the tide. I only came ashore for these, they make in the foundry here." He showed her a handful of iron rings.

"Will you come back? Will you come and see me when you do?"

"I'm bound for France, Angelique, to work in a sail yard in Marseilles. It be many years before I see you again. Take care of yourself and remember to be wise!"

"Perhaps I'll see you in Maine . . ."

"Maine it is!" And he was gone.

Seeing Cesaire left Angelique feeling lonelier than ever, and now Josette had received the joyful news that her fiancé was sailing from America for a visit. A prolonged residence with her favorite friends at Trois Islets kept her occupied for more than a month, but as the time drew near for her gentleman's expected arrival, she returned to make preparations to welcome him into her home.

Pastries were baked, linen was ironed, silver polished, and a pig was fattened in the barnyard. The countess insisted on force-feeding a goose for pâté, although she bemoaned the fact that the geese in Martinique were an inferior breed. Crabs were kept in buckets of salt water, okra and sweet herbs were gathered from the garden, and even a turtle was penned for a savory soup. Angelique was caught up in the excitement as well, for she had become quite curious about Josette's intended, and her own longing was eased by her mistress's infectious delirium.

The afternoon the young gentleman arrived, Josette was unable to leave her room until Angelique had done her chestnut hair to perfection, fastened the garnet necklace at her throat, and stained her lips with crushed beet juice. As Angelique buttoned the back of Josette's organdy gown, the excited girl nearly swooned, and Angelique was obliged to catch her and hold her steady. "Angelique, I am so in love! I think I shall faint."

"You are beautiful, Mademoiselle. You will break his heart."

"Yes, yes! I must be beautiful, as beautiful as I can be, since I am not sure he will remember my face."

"How can you say such a thing? Of course he will remember."

"But he may not," Josette said as she finally gathered herself together, took a deep breath, and walked to the door. "You see, even though we have exchanged many letters—and he is a poet, his letters are so beautiful—still, I only met him once, and that was over a year ago. I am so frightened!"

Before Angelique could respond to this puzzling admission, Josette had dashed from the room and was descending the stair into the hall. Angelique followed her to the banister, looked down, and saw André waiting with a tall young man in an indigo-velvet jacket and brocaded waistcoat, with a well-built physique and close-cropped dark hair. He was presented to Josette, who curtsied prettily, and he bent to kiss her hand. The murmurings of their voices floated up to Angelique as they exchanged greetings, and André gestured toward the drawing room.

As the young gentleman followed after Josette, he turned and looked toward the stair where Angelique was standing. His eyes were black and penetrating, and they locked onto hers, as, at that instant, her heart flew to her throat. She felt as though her breath had been knocked out of her. It couldn't be true! Josette's fiancé was her own long-awaited lover, Barnabas Collins.

chapter

———

25

S everal days passed while Angelique remained in torment. Barnabas arrived each morning, and he and Josette rode off in his small carriage. From Josette's ecstatic descriptions, Angelique learned that they had visited friends at Fort Royal and Trois Islets, where other wealthy families owned small plantations. The area was more refined than Saint-Pierre and was rapidly becoming the center of society.

She combed through her memories, trying to understand what could have happened, unable to endure the enormity of her disappointment. Had he ceased to love her? It did not seem possible. Why had he had forsaken her for Josette? The pain of his rejection became more than she could bear, and each night she escaped to her room to weep piteously, welcoming the tears as relief from the visceral spasms of resentment and jealousy.

As time went by, she became determined to see him again, to speak to him, and to look into his eyes. She would confront him, force him to admit what he had done, that he had asked her to marry him for the purpose of making love to her, that he had seduced her and abandoned her. At least she would hear the truth from his own lips. Anger welled up in her like a wave until it had filled her completely.

She overheard Josette tell her father the name of the inn where Barnabas was staying, and she dispatched a short letter requesting an interview. She waited several days for an answer, meeting the post every afternoon in heart-wrenching expectation, but there was never anything for her. Each day yielded greater anxiety and an agony of mind brought on by bewilderment and incomprehension that moved toward madness. When another day came with no response, she decided that she would go to him that very evening.

Opening the drawer to her wardrobe, she withdrew the dress of golden satin and laid it on the chair. Among Josette's things she found jewels, a corset and petticoats, satin slippers and a shawl. She arranged her hair in the fashion she had so often created for Josette, softly curled and piled upon her head, and placed a pair of opal-and-diamond earrings in her ears. When she looked in the glass her eyes were a gleaming azure sparked by fire. She was satisfied that her appearance was that of a fine lady, with a delicate waist, a lovely bust, a mass of golden curls, and eyes that sprang to life when the diamonds in her ears caught the light. At that moment, the hatred storming in her heart subsided, and she was certain she would win him back. How could he not love her as she loved him?

The gown was silken against her flesh as she slipped out her door with a candle and moved quietly down the stair. It was after eleven o'clock, and the house was dark and quiet as she entered the back hallway. She tripped over a pile of jackets and boots piled by the door. André had, no doubt, been on a shooting party out in the surrounding country that day with some of the other plantation owners. She stopped when she noticed the leather case that contained his pistols. Hesitating, she knelt, set her candle on the floor, and opened the box.

The two guns lay in the velvet, handle to muzzle, fitted together like lovers. Unable to resist, she took one up and cradled it in her hand. It was heavy and cold, and the barrel glinted in the candlelight. The shot was still in the chamber. Impulsively, she placed the pistol beneath her shawl and opened the door into the night.

The night was balmy, the air thick, and a soft breeze stirred the long fronds of the palm trees. Passing the fountain where the water flowed from Dionysus's chalice, she thought of her first night with Barnabas, and her heart hardened with anger once again. She would have satisfaction, if nothing else! She found the inn and endured the salacious looks from the concierge, who pointed to Barnabas's room. Then, holding her breath, she walked to the door and knocked softly.

"Yes?" His voice revealed irritation at an unexpected visitor. The door opened, and he was looking down at her. He wore a silk robe, and she glimpsed the muscles of his chest, covered with dark hair, within the collar. She had forgotten how tall he was, how massive his shoulders. His eyes widened in astonishment when he saw her standing there.

"Angelique!"

"Yes . . . Barnabas. Did you not think I would come?"

He tried to cover his discomfort. "What a lovely surprise!"

Could she detect annoyance on the edges of his greeting? She was not sure. "I had to see you. I waited so long for you to come back to Martinique—to return to me, and now . . ."

"I-I know . . . I know. I'm so sorry, my dear," he said, stumbling over his words. It was then she realized he had been drinking. "I intended to see you, as soon as possible."

"Did you receive my letter?" She was conscious of the weight of the gun beneath her scarf, held in her two folded hands.

"Yes, yes, and I had every intention of responding. But . . . it's been very difficult. Josette is—"

"Are you betrothed to Josette? Is it really true?"

"Please, come in . . ." he said gently. He took her arm and, leading her into his room, shut the door quietly. Warmth spread through her body at his touch. He was breathing quickly, and she could feel the quivering in his hands where they gripped her. His disquietude gave her courage.

"Let me get you a glass of wine," he said in that resonant voice she remembered so well. "We can sit here beside the window and look out at the sea, and I will explain everything."

At that precise moment the swift beating of her heart subsided. She could feel the warm blood in her fingertips, and her limbs were effused with vitality, as though her entire body were no longer flesh, but pulsing light. She walked to the window, feeling her dress flow on the carpet, but did not sit. Instead she turned to him, the glow of the candlelight on her face, and stood like, burning flame, waiting for him to speak.

He looked at her for a moment, then, to her surprise, he said, "My God, you are such a beauty!"

And she knew, if nothing else, he desired her still.

"Your . . . eyes, are . . . hypnotic . . . I had forgotten. . . ." He jerked his collar closed and tied his robe tightly around his waist, then went to his cabinet for the brandy. A great gilt mirror hung behind the cupboard, reflecting the room, and she watched his back as he bent over the bottle. She heard the snifters clatter against themselves, as though his hands were shaking. It was then she took the pistol from her shawl.

The door of the cabinet failed to catch and slowly fell open again as he fumbled with the stopper. Noticing it, he slammed it shut with such ferocity that the wood shattered. He stood there a moment, obviously fighting for control, before he looked up into the mirror and saw that she had lifted the pistol and pointed it directly it at him.

He whirled back at the sight. "My God . . . !"

"Did you expect me to remain silent, Barnabas,

and accept your betrayal demurely, like a well-bred lady?"

"Please . . . my dear . . . put that away. . . ."

"I found this in André's gun case. Your intended father-in-law, Barnabas. How fitting, don't you agree? And I shall fire it, if I so desire. Tell me one reason why I should not blow a gaping hole in that deceitful breast, where the heart is already hollow!"

"Angelique, please . . . it's dangerous . . . truly . . . you don't intend to . . . please, sit down and . . . have a glass of wine. . . ." He looked at her, an expression on his face that was difficult to read, then he took a step back. His face sagged.

"Oh, very well, fire away," he said dejectedly. "I deserve it. Rid the world of a despicable scoundrel who will be happily released from these months of torture. . . . I should be more than glad if you would do for me that which I have not had the courage to do myself. . . ."

His words stunned her for a moment, but she was not fooled. "Oh, come, Barnabas, two women in love with you, and you want to die? I should think you would be appalled. When such an exciting life lies before you! Tell me the truth!"

"I am . . ." he said, taking a deep breath, "tentatively . . . betrothed to Josette."

"Tentatively? Does this mean you have made your choice? A shallow life, a life of duty, of catering to the whims and demands of a spoiled child, who is sentimental, to be sure, but all artifice. She is intended for a boy, some pretty gallant who will sit at her feet and feed her candy. Do you prefer her to—as you yourself put it—your soul's companion! A passionate woman who knows you, worships you, and will devote her life to your happiness? Tell me, then, and hurry. My arm wearies, and the weight is against the trigger!"

"Angelique. Look at me. Don't you know no one can take your place?"

She felt the room spin and closed her eyes for a moment. He saw her falter, and added quickly, "You must believe me, I have been tormented, stricken with remorse. . . ."

She lowered the gun, suddenly feeling weak.

"I have been dreaming of you, longing for you," he continued.

"But you didn't come" she said. "And when you did, it was not to see me. I love you. I am the one in torment. . . . I am the one who wants to die. . . ." She held the gun away from her, her arm aching and quivering, and it fell toward her own breast. He lunged for it and grabbed the barrel, struggling to wrench it from her grasp. Her eyes grew wide, and, suddenly, the gun exploded.

Barnabas screamed "No!" as the bullet shattered the mirror into shimmering knives that fell crashing to the floor. Angelique stood gaping at the dark wall where the glass had been.

"The mirror . . ." she cried. "You see! I've broken the mirror. . . ." She trembled so, she thought she would faint.

Coming to her, and taking the gun from her gently, he led her to a chair, then knelt in front of her. As she shuddered, he stroked her hands and her hair, soothing her, speaking in a tremulous voice.

"It's nothing . . . here . . . have some wine . . . calm yourself . . . try to drink this . . . you know I'm devoted to you. You have given me great happiness. . . . Will you listen to me?"

She took a taste of the wine, and he spoke to her softly. "The only explanation I can give you is that Josette's father suggested the marriage, which would be monetarily beneficial to our family. I never took the idea too seriously. To tell you the truth, I did not think she would have me. I only met her once. She never gave me any encouragement when I was here, and . . . and finding so much . . . joy with you. . . ."

He looked at her, his dark eyes registering his meaning. He was in turmoil, struggling to find the words. "After . . . I left Martinique, I had every intention of returning to you. But it was impossible for us to exchange letters and still keep our love affair secret. Whereas—Josette and I—wrote to one another, friendly notes at first. And then, after a time, I felt her affection for me develop."

Angelique stiffened and turned her face away. He hurried on, the words coming in spurts. "You must understand that my family has become extremely important to me in this last year, and I have come to recognize my obligations as the son of a wealthy shipping magnate. My father . . . has never found favor with my adventures . . . I thought I would come into my fortune . . . but my father has delayed the transmission of property, pending my . . . that is . . . you should be aware that were I to marry you, I would be stripped of my inheritance. I would be able to offer you nothing. He would simply see it as another of my degenerate escapades, an excuse to cast me out."

"Is that how you see me? Loving you for your fortune?"

Now that she knew what he was saying, Angelique became more aware of the way he was looking at her, a smoldering hunger in his gaze. He trembled, and his voice was ardent with feeling, as she studied the facets and shadows of his face, seduced as always by his passionate visage. She tried to concentrate on the simple pleasure it gave her just to look at him, when she had dreamed of him for so long.

He continued. "Whereas, this proposed union of our two families, Josette's and mine, was the first instance I can ever recall of his approving anything I have ever done, and, as the months went by, he began to assume that the marriage was a settled affair, or as he put it 'a connection that we cannot afford to pass up.'" There was an ever-so-slight bitterness to his tone. "As for Josette . . . she's young, innocent . . . she's fallen in love with me. . . ."

Angelique raised her eyes to his. "Josette is my mistress, Barnabas. Am I to travel with her to America? And carry my burning heart in my breast? Not speaking? Not saying a word? Is that what you expect?"

He shook his head, leaned over, and kissed her hands. She drew them away.

"Then say something more," she cried, "that I may despise you, for I want to hate you. When I look at you, I want to see only ugliness and deformity. Free me. Can you? Repel me. As cleverly as you pursued me."

He rose and moved away from her, and she stood as well, leaning on the table.

"I have come like the goat to the butcher," she said bitterly. "No matter how much I might bleat and kick, my fate has been sealed. What am I to do? If I demand love where none exists, I will only create greater antipathy."

He turned and looked at her as she went on. "Anger—although my heart reels with anger—will only drive you further away. I could be generous, I suppose, and forgiving, and relieve you of all culpability, but I will not do that. I will never forgive you. I wanted to see you dead!"

She could see the pain in his eyes as his face took on a gray cast. Her voice quivered. "No, there is no satisfaction for me here. So, why did I come? If you must know, it was only to look in your eyes and hear your voice again, to stand with you in the same moment in time. For you are my beloved. And the price I pay is forfeit of pride. This fleeting transport was purchased with humiliation, and shame. But I pay it gladly, for I did love you, and I love you still."

The candle at the window sputtered, and the flame threatened to fade in the melting wax. Barnabas went to the desk, took out another taper and lit it with the dying flame. He cupped his hand around the new light until it burned strong. Gripping it with his huge fingers, he forced the raw end into the soft wax until it was deep enough to hold.

"I am still as drawn to you as ever," he said in an anguished voice. A slight breeze floated in through the window, and the warm air caressed them both. "Being here in this room with you, seeing you now, feeling your mysterious presence, is like a dream."

"Why do you say these things? You insult me to offer hope! Tell me, is there any way for us to be together now?"

After a long moment he answered, "No . . ."

"And it is your wish that I leave you."

"Yes . . ."

"Then . . . good-bye, Barnabas."

She walked to the door slowly. She could feel his hunger following her as though he were reaching out to her with his mind. Placing her hand on the knob, she turned to him and looked into his eyes, thinking only what ecstasy it would be to feel his mouth on hers. She knew he would come to her if she willed it. She felt the flame within her as she held his gaze, and a feeling of radiant power flowed out of her.

"Angelique . . ." His voice was a ragged whisper. "Please . . . don't go. . . ."

The place high in the rain forest where the stream flowed from a hidden lake could be entered only through the water. The climb was torturous, up a giant stairway of silvered rock. Angelique looked back and laughed as she led Barnabas higher and higher, to where the cascade tumbled over their hands and feet, turning them fluid from the wrist and ankle down, and the mist was so fine it changed to liquid sunshine.

The forest surrounding was more lush than she had imagined; they had been climbing for hours, deep into the jungle, and it was a great relief to reach the top. Beneath the lip of the cascade they found a chamber, where the ferns grew in delicate skirts and the roar of the falling water obscured all other sounds. There, hidden from the world, they watched the light play upon the waterfall and, reaching out through the curtain, tried to catch the silver in their hands.

The lovers had spent many stolen hours with one another, hours of incredible bliss. The marriage to Josette was still planned to go forward, but Angelique clung to the knowledge that she would continue to belong to Barnabas whatever happened, as his mistress and beloved. She consoled herself with the belief that he would change his mind about Josette and that the marriage would never take place. At times she sensed his restlessness, or even his pangs of guilt, and the beginnings of anger would rise in her, but once he was in her arms, she knew he lost all desire to be elsewhere, and she always excused his moments of doubt as fleeting and unimportant.

Josette, oblivious to Barnabas's secret life, never ceased chattering happily about her courtship. How bitter it was to see happiness in another's eyes. As a result of Josette's innocent confidences, Angelique became aware that Barnabas had never even kissed her, and contempt soured Angelique's heart. Custom and propriety dictated that even an engaged couple never be alone together.

Barnabas rose and stood wide-legged on the precipice, his magnificent body silhouetted against the air, the waterfall flowing over him. Angelique was moved again to pity and rage. His beauty seduced her, but his insensibility to her agony wrenched her heart. As she watched him she had a flash of how easy it would be to send him to his death. How vulnerable he was, balanced there on the brink of life, unconscious of any danger, oblivious to any thoughts she might have. She could see from the arrogance of his stance that he felt he was a god looking down on the world.

She stepped over and placed her body behind his, leaned against him, and reached around, threading her fingers though his thick body hair. Once again the feeling came. One quick shove and he would be gone, tumbling to his death in this lush, dark wilderness. No one would ever find him, and he would torture her no more. She trembled with the thought and caught her breath, loosening her hands and placing them against his back. Then he turned, pulled her to him, and kissed her, and the falling cascade tumbled over them both.

As daylight waned, they lay in the grass while Angelique watched reflections flowering on the still surface of the lake. Somewhere in her deepest mind she remembered the *Bokor* saying, "Can you achieve indifference? I think not. You will cling to life and always ignore the death it springs from. You will seek love, and it will turn to jealousy, then revenge, because deep beneath all your rainbow colors is a dark pool of despair, and because your way is the way of desire."

She had never understood what he had meant. She only knew he was speaking of the magic she had rejected. All that was in the past. Now she was glad that she had chosen the ordinary life, free of sorcery, that she had renounced her powers and sent the Devil away forever. Indifference? She could never be indifferent to the joys of passion. The long, lonely years were over. All she knew was that she had found love, and that was all she would ever want.

"Look," she said, "there are two of everything. First—the clouds floating, then the rising peaks, repeating themselves in the water."

"Ah, yes," he said. "You are right—the lake is a mirror." All along the edge, the dark shapes drew from the dimpled sheen, their other selves.

"What do you see?" she asked him.

"Hm-m-m-m, birds flying sideways, pears cut in half, butterflies, skeletons—"

"—two hands—thumb against thumb, trees nodding to their twins—

"—scallop shells fanning open, orchids, a woman's sex—

"—and the moon has fallen into the water like a fish."

There was a pause. "I love you, Angelique," he said quietly.

She saw how each object along the lake's edge found a rhythm of its own desiring. She smiled, he beckoned, and now the dipping moon, caught in a ripple, became a white bone. He had said he loved her, and a bit of a verse floated into her memory. *Swear not by the moon, the inconstant moon . . .*

They lay together in the grass, and she thought, as he looked down on her, how nature loves her own likeness, like Narcissus adoring himself. And so she was shape to his shape as he moved to her, and they opened and closed like a new moth, fresh from the chrysalis, drying its wings for first flight.

"I cannot live without you," he whispered. "Say you will be mine forever."

chapter

26

Boston was, without a doubt, the most amazing place imaginable. The streets were overrun with people and carriages. Many fine buildings lined the tree-shaded avenues. Merchants sold everything from silver to vegetables in the market, and Angelique could not help but notice that class distinctions were far less important there than in Martinique. There were few slaves, although poverty was more apparent. The beggar and the tradesman both seemed to mingle on the street with all the finer sort, and there was energy in the air, a sense of promise.

André desiring one last holiday with his daughter, had sailed with her first to New York. There they would shop for her trousseau and he would show her the sights of the new nation's capitol.

Certain that Josette would already have arrived at Collinwood, even though there had been no message, the Countess Natalie du Prés finally decided to leave Boston with Angelique and embark on the two-day journey to Collinsport. She did not wish to arrive too soon and be unwelcome, but without the two of them there, Josette would have no servant or companion should they be needed. Angelique was overjoyed; her long wait of three months was almost over.

They began the journey early in the morning. Angelique, in dismay, peered out of the carriage window at the passing countryside. The rain fell on a bleak landscape of barren fields. They passed woods with low stone walls and tall leafless trees, their thin black branches etched against the white sky. She was unprepared for the grayness of the countryside, and for the cold. Her thin cape, donated at the last minute from the countess's wardrobe, barely kept the chill from her bones, and if her heart had not been beating so fiercely, she would have been shivering. Her hands were like ice, and her breath came in clouds, but a heat was raging through her body. She was afire with anticipation, waiting for that first moment when she and Barnabas would stand in each other's presence. She was certain she would collapse with happiness.

She and the countess spent the night at a small country inn, where it seemed the entire male population of the area gathered that evening at the bar to drink some warmth into their veins. The boisterous carousing lasted far into the night, and the countess and Angelique were grateful to climb into the carriage the next morning, if only to sleep. Late in the day, the route began to skirt cliffs that fell to a roaring sea, and the horses labored on the grade. The roadbed now seemed to be entirely comprised of large rocks, jolting the passengers mercilessly.

"I don't think I can bear much more," the count-ess complained. "This road is unforgivable; it's like rolling through a pigsty!" Angelique looked out and could see what seemed to be pieces of the sky flying through the air.

"Oh, look, Countess! What can that be?"

"That, Angelique, is hail! You've never seen that, have you?" said the countess disdainfully. "Such dreadful weather! The rain is turning to ice, and the road to mud."

When she saw the falling hail, a strange feeling came over Angelique. She had never seen Maine, with its raw shores, but something seemed familiar, some dim recollection of a time when she was not a child of the sea and her world had not been blue and gold. Her mind tried to stitch together these delicate tree branches, which were like pen-and-ink drawings on white paper, with the thick glossy green of the Mar-tinique foliage. But she gave up, and memory merged with reality. This was to be her home, this cold and forsaken wilderness that seemed to stretch on for such great distances. In Martinique, they would have crossed the island and back by now.

Suddenly the carriage lurched, and Angelique was thrown forward into the countess's arms.

"I knew we were in for some trouble!" the count-ess gasped, for they had come to a dead stop. The driver was whipping the horses, and they could feel the straining of the carriage and the jerking on the harness; however, the conveyance did not budge. After a moment, the driver opened the carriage door.

"So's, m'lady, seems we're stuck in the mud!"

"Well can't you dig us out, my good man?" the countess responded, thoroughly exasperated.

"I aim to, ma'am. We're not too far, only a half mile or so from the Collinwood estate, and once I have this wheel free, I'll take us there in no time, no time at all."

"Well, make haste, can't you. Before we freeze to death!"

So there was to be another delay, when waiting had become unbearable. Angelique could contain herself no longer.

"If it's only a little way, why don't I go for help?" she cried.

"What, girl? Don't be foolish," said the countess. "Why it's near dark and freezing rain. I think we'd best rely on the strength of the driver and his spade."

"But what if he is not able. We can't remain here the night. I could not let you suffer in such a way!"

"Nonsense, child. Here, pull that blanket over me, if you will—" But Angelique was already out of the carriage, gathering up her skirts to keep them from the mud, as she ran to the driver's side.

"Is Collinwood just down this road, sir?"

"Yes, miss, it's a pity we didn't make it before we ran into this deep rut here. The horses are weary, and—"

"What sort of house is it?"

"Why, it's the second house on the road, miss— set back a bit, with tall white columns and a round portico. There is another grand place we'll come to first, in the last stages of building, a great mansion, but—I say, miss, you're not going on foot, are you?"

But Angelique was already a hundred yards down the road, running, mindless of the mud on her boots or the rain falling on her shoulders. Her only thought was of the face of her beloved Barnabas. Her heart was beating wildly, and she felt that she would burst with eagerness to see him. Her mind was so full of the promise of exultation that she fairly flew over the distance, and it seemed only moments before she was standing beneath the wide columns in front of the large wooden door. She could hear voices within, arguing with some heat, and a man shouting.

"Love! Love is only a word in ladies' novels!" There was a male response, low, murmured, and the angry voice cried out again. "A *woman* is not a *future*!" What was this argument? Could it be between Barnabas and his father? Was it possible that he was talking about her?

She lifted the brass knocker and let it fall. The door opened, and he was standing there, in a wine-colored jacket, his dark hair falling about his beautiful eyes, which widened with astonishment.

"Barnabas!" Her heart leapt, and she felt she would faint from joy. She wanted him to pull her into his arms, but he failed to make any move at all, and simply stared at her, awkward, not speaking.

"Are you surprised?" she asked, her eyes dancing. She told herself that the presence of the other man, whom she had overheard but could not see, prohibited any immediate show of recognition.

"Astonished," he answered. "We didn't expect

the countess for at least a week." There was a quick
jerk to his eyes, a look behind her, a moment of hesitation. "Where is she? And why are you walking?"

"Oh, your roads, Monsieur," she smiled again,
embarrassed. She must look a strange sight, she
thought, her cape dripping, her hair in disarray. "The
carriage is buried in the mud—completely stuck!"

"How far back?"

"Too far for my mistress to walk," she said. But
she wanted to lean in, and whisper, "But not too far
for me to fly to your side." She felt girlish, giddy with
euphoria. She fixed her eyes on his, looking for the
silent message that he was as delighted as she.

But instead, to her disappointment, he asked her
in with some diffidence. As she lifted her hood, she
saw the room she had imagined a thousand times,
warm and charming, with fine appointments. He was
wealthier than she had supposed, and she realized the
ties of his family must be strong, but not as strong—
she told herself—as their secret pledge.

She turned to see an elegant older man with graying blond hair and prominent sideburns, standing by
the fireplace.

"Father," said Barnabas, "this is Angelique. The
Countess du Prés's . . . maid."

She curtsied. So, it had been his father with
whom he had been arguing. Monsieur Collins wore a
velvet waistcoat and a gold watch fob, and he had an
air of weary despondency underneath his irritable
manner. Angelique could not help but wonder
whether he had known some deep disappointment at

some time in his life. Barnabas asked that rooms be prepared. Then he said, referring to the countess, "I must go and fetch her."

"I will accompany you!" Angelique answered at once.

"That's not necessary." Was it her imagination, or was he afraid to look at her?

"Oh, but it is most necessary to my mistress," she said with a determined air, flashing him a look. She turned to Joshua Collins and curtsied deeply.

"It is a great privilege to be in your home at last," she said with a smile. But Monsieur Collins merely grunted and turned away, and she felt the stab of resentment she had known so often in Martinique. He treated her as a servant: invisible, ordinary, easily replaced. Anger welled up in her, and blood rose to her face.

She was none of those things, she thought. Now was her time, and soon she would throw off her maid's disguise. She was a beautiful woman, and once she had the dresses and the jewels, no one would ever fail to see that. She was certain that Barnabas would never find anyone to replace her in his arms.

The stable was warm. With the rain falling, steam rose from the bodies of the animals. The sweet smell of the horses, hay, and droppings, made her delirious. She remembered the joy of being at Barnabas's side, when all the world seemed enchanted, and the words that flew through her thoughts were like poetry. She stood while the groom and the caretaker harnessed the buggy, longing to look into Barnabas's eyes, but afraid to betray her eagerness. Then the buggy was ready, and she climbed in beside him.

To her chagrin, the caretaker heaved his obese body into the buggy as well. He carried an ax, and he saw her staring at it.

"To fell branches, to place under the wheel," he said in a thick voice, and Angelique observed at once that he was somewhat simpleminded.

"Good idea, Ben," said Barnabas. This Ben was strong as a bull; the muscles of his neck protruded from his shirt. He sat directly across from her and watched them both with a murky gaze, his presence forbidding any intimate conversation.

Barnabas reached for the heavy leather wrap and draped it over her and himself, giving her a quick smile that melted her fears. She could feel the warmth of his body beneath the blanket as the buggy trotted down the road, and she was drenched in happiness. She felt she could remain there for eternity, embraced by his dear presence, and be content. She closed her eyes and wished that time would stop, that the journey would last forever.

A few hours later, when the Countess du Prés arrived at Collinwood, wearing her enormous ostrich-feather chapeau and carrying a feather muff to match, Joshua Collins was disdainful, and she, in turn, was rude. They stood in the hallway verbally parrying with one another.

"The area in which you live is a wasteland of emotion and courtesy!" said the countess.

"Then I think you might have stayed in Boston if you dislike it so much here!" he retorted. Angelique rejoiced that the meeting was so strained, for this would only reflect on Josette. She had to smile to herself when the countess asked—

"Is it ever warm here? Does it ever stop raining?" She herself was wondering the same thing.

Once she was in her small room off the servant's hallway, Angelique looked around in contempt at the plain furniture and common brick fireplace. How quaint, she thought, to find an old spinning wheel long out of use, its skeins unraveled. Was it there to suggest that her place in this house was one of service? But this was no time to fret like a spoiled child; she must prepare for the visit she knew was coming. Opening her luggage, she chose a simple flowered frock, then arranged her hair at the mirror so that it tumbled in soft ringlets. She studied herself dispassionately. She would never forget the countess's words. "You think you are beautiful? Is that why I catch you looking at yourself in the mirror? You are not beautiful, Angelique. Josette . . . is beautiful."

She had not Josette's pale features, those of a patrician gentlewoman, but her face was well formed, perhaps the nose and mouth a bit small, but her eyes were deep and languorous. At this moment she thought she had never looked more desirable, for her skin was flushed and her eyes were soft with longing. She felt her senses quiver, aching for him, for his touch, for the melting warmth of his body.

She sat on the end of her bed and wrapped her arms around the turned post, easing her cheek against the smooth mahogany. Then she let her mind play with the images of their last night together in Martinique: the cascading waterfall, the spray and the surrounding mist, the darkness of the cave, the sweet-tasting water on his lips, the soft rain as it wet their faces and their mouths, the merging of their bodies under the flowing stream, and she felt a helpless throb in the deepest part of her.

When, at last, the hour grew late, and thunder rumbled in the darkness while rain fell between flashes of lightning at her window, Angelique could endure the wait no longer, and stole down the corridor. She climbed the great stairway and some instinct led her to Barnabas's room as there was a light beneath his door. She tapped lightly on his door.

"Who is it?" She heard his voice. It was a long moment before he opened for her, and she burst into the room.

"A ghost from your past!" she cried, and flew to his arms. "Oh, my darling, I waited for you. . . . I couldn't bear it! Not any longer!" She kissed him, her eyes laughing. "Why didn't you come? Were you too proud? Don't you know how I love you?"

She leaned in to him, pressing against him, limp with relief, sighing, whispering. "After you left the island, I dreamed of you every night, I heard you saying my name. . . . I so longed for this . . . hold me!"

She clung to him, her fingers digging into his velvet coat, and she kissed his face, his lips, sliding with a rush into her rapture. It was a moment before she felt him resisting, pushing her away. She kissed his mouth again, but felt no response.

"Ah, you taste of this cold house," she cried. "What is it?"

"I am not cold, Angelique, but I want to be. I have to be," he said softly. "I can't do this. I mustn't. Please . . . you must realize . . ." He lifted his hand in a limp gesture of embarrassment. "It was all a mistake." Her head reeled, and she felt faint, as if all the blood had rushed to her feet.

"What? What was a mistake?"

"It was . . . my weakness to—" he stammered, turning from her.

"To what?"

"To—to love you . . . it was wrong . . . I'm sorry. . . ." She saw he was in anguish, struggling with what he was saying. "When we were together . . . I still wasn't certain I was going to be married. . . . Josette loved me, but I never dreamed I would grow to love her in return. . . ."

"You love Josette? Josette is a thin-blooded girl! When you came to the door tonight. . . weren't you glad to see me?"

He looked at her a moment. "I was surprised to see you. I never expected you to come. I was confounded by your appearance, your eyes, shadowed by your hood. . . ."

She bit her lip, waiting for him to say what she longed to hear, but he did not.

"Please try to understand, Angelique. You and I

can never . . . there is no way . . . we could marry. I know I may have led you to believe that it could be possible, but my father . . ."

"Your father! What do you care about your father? He . . . is not you!" And she ran to him again, grasping his arms and looking up into his face. "Where is the man I loved—so rebellious and passionate? I never expected . . . weakness! Surely you will have the courage to tell your family what you want from life. You know you love me!"

Barnabas turned from her. "No, you are wrong," he said after a pause. "I did love you. You are a beautiful . . . fascinating woman, but . . . perhaps I do not have your brand of courage. I have other things, more important things, to consider. I know it is difficult for you to understand, but my duty is . . . is to my family."

She watched him helplessly, not comprehending, as he struggled to say more and could not. Then he seemed to grow resolute, and his eyes narrowed as he looked at her. "The truth is, I *have* grown to love Josette. I love her now, with all my heart. And if you value the power of love as much as you say, you will respect my feelings. Now, please, I'm sorry, I don't want to hurt you, but . . . I must ask you to leave."

"Leave?" she said grimly. "Before you regret all the foolish words you have just spoken?"

There was a long pause before he whispered, "Yes."

"You don't want me anymore."

There was another long moment of silence. "No."

Her eyes flooded with tears, and, too proud to let them be seen, she fled for the door.

Once in her room, she wept as though weeping would dislodge the crushing weight on her heart, as if a dull dagger was sunk deep in her breast. She wept until she was choking on her tears, coughing, sobbing, her chest heaving, and all the while she kept imagining that she heard his step in the hall, that the door would open and he would come into her room and take her in his arms. She felt her body ripping, as though it were being rent by the sharp claws of some cruel, indifferent monster. Disbelief was mingled with despair, and she realized that Barnabas's rejection, his coldness, his complete lack of feeling was the only reaction she had not expected.

She had been prepared to flee, to run off with him, to endure misfortune, to show sympathy for the loss of his inheritance, to remain by his side through all tribulations, to work, to slave, for him. She had imagined adventures, hardships, a return, at length, to the embrace of his family.

But she had never imagined this. She had never believed that Josette would be a significant rival. She had seen Josette as a means for her to come to New England—where she could be near Barnabas—simply as an instrument of their finally being together. She would have even endured their pointless marriage if she could have remained his mistress and beloved. How could she have been so blind? Nothing had prepared her for this emptiness, this unbelievable vacuum that was now her future. What would become of her? Where would she go? How could she remain here as a servant, seeing Barnabas every day, humiliated, invisible, watching him living beside Josette and making love to her.

She rose, went to the window, and placed her hand against the glass. It was so very cold. The dark trees twisted their bare limbs in macabre shapes caught by the lightning. The flame of the candle at her table flickered and died, and in the shivering darkness, lit intermittently by bright flashes, her mind began to wind through channels of possibilities.

What would induce Barnabas to falter in this resolution and succumb to his deeper desires? This fidelity to father and family was only a posture, an attitude he had adopted. Of that she was certain. Was there some way she could weaken him—distract him?

She had a facetious notion: perhaps some silly bit of magic would awaken him to his true feelings. She instantly regretted her idea; magic was no longer an option for her.

She returned to her bed, lay down, and stared up at the ceiling. Her mind began to search for solutions, and she grew calmer. One clear thought emerged. He loved her, and he had forgotten that he loved her; what was probably more true, he had decided not to love her. The surest way to clarity of mind was an encounter with death. Face-to-face with one's mortality, the human creature always realizes, in a flash of insight, what is truly important. A brush with death— that was it! That was what she needed to bring Barnabas to his senses.

The only problem was how to create such an incident, and she had abandoned spells and potions so long ago. Was it worth a bit of subtle dabbling? She had to be very careful; the last thing she wanted was to awaken the attention of the Dark Spirit. She had abandoned her powers, and he had left her alone; that had been their truce. But something small, unnoticeable would be so simple. It was tempting; she had to break Barnabas down in some way. She decided to be patient. And with these thoughts fresh in her mind, she finally fell asleep.

Opportunity presented itself much more easily than she could have predicted. Once again she embarked on her servant's duties with modesty and resolve. The countess depended on her for so many trivial tasks that she often wondered whether the woman would have been capable of dressing herself or arranging her own coiffure. There was no end to the mending, trimming, and removing of spots, not to mention selecting the perfect piece of lace for the bodice or jewel for the neck. Sometimes she felt as though she possessed all the expertise behind the stylish woman she served. Each day she released her to the world, transformed, elegantly arrayed, and only she knew what pains the transformation required.

The child Sarah, Barnabas's little sister, often came to Angelique's room to play. She was only six, but her presence carried Angelique back to her own childhood, and she remembered her time with her mother. She often thought of the man she had believed was her father and how defiant she had been. How obsessed she had been with learning the book of spells. Her determination and her courage had saved her then. It was difficult to believe that she had once been worshiped as a goddess and that Erzulie had embraced her spirit.

Sarah was an imaginative girl, capable of falling into the grip of the stories Angelique told so well. Her eyes grew wide at the descriptions of ceremonies, Negroes dancing on coals without burning their feet, of worshipers in deep trances singing and drumming. She particularly enjoyed tales of slavery in Martinique and of the soldiers who came to quell the uprisings. Once she brought a small wooden soldier from the nursery to show Angelique, and left it behind when she was called to dinner.

Angelique held the toy in her hand and looked at it carefully. It was painted wood, with a blue coat, a three-cornered hat, and a movable arm holding a tiny musket. She remembered, with a smile, the first time she had seen Barnabas in his uniform, how smart he had looked, and she knew in a flash that the toy had belonged to him when he was a child. She placed it in the pocket of her dress.

As plans began to form, and she became more hopeful, her mood grew cheerful. A line of verse sang in her mind: *Look like the innocent flower, but be the serpent under it.*

She even smiled as she retrieved the countess' shawl from the drawing room, stopping to admire the furniture, the gleam of mahogany and the texture of brocade, imagining that these riches would someday be hers.

She pulled the toy soldier from her dress and was staring at it, musing over possibilities it might have, when Jeremiah, Barnabas's uncle, appeared in the room. Angelique remembered seeing him in Martinique at the festival when she had first met Barnabas. She was immediately struck by his handsome face and his respectful demeanor. How different he was from his brother, Joshua Collins, who was so arrogant and abrupt, and from Barnabas, who was passionate and rebelliously volatile. When Jeremiah saw the doll, he seemed to recognize it.

"Do you know what this is?" she asked.

"A member of the regiment," he answered, and smiled. "An old soldier."

"Was it yours?"

"No. It belonged to Barnabas. They were his favorite toys when he was a boy. It should be in the playroom."

Her intuition had been correct. "Then I'll return it," she said.

"Very well." She thought she saw a flicker of interest in his eyes, but it faded almost as soon as it appeared.

"Shall I take it for you?" he asked, almost as if he wanted to make conversation. She could sense a strained melancholy in his nature, as if his life had no purpose, no source of vitality, other than his work at the shipyard. Perhaps, as the younger brother, he had been under Joshua Collins's iron fist of control even longer than Barnabas, even to the point that he, Jeremiah, had lost his taste for adventure. *How vulner-*

able he is, she thought. *Those who are resigned to a life without romance are most susceptible to love's beckoning.*

"I'd like to keep it for a while," she answered, "just to look at."

"Of course."

"It's such a fascinating little toy."

"Very well," he said, almost awkwardly. "Keep it as long as you like."

She held his gaze. Yes. He was the perfect foil. But his role would come later. For now the doll was almost all she needed, if she chose to do it, to cause Barnabas more pain and suffering than he had ever known.

That evening, Angelique sat by her window, gazing out at the night sky. The moon was wrapped in fog, and the moonstream flowed faintly upon the water. Here the sea was cold, she thought, and threatening, no call to warm embrace, only dark and forbidding. Nevertheless, she felt a longing for its force crashing against the shore. It had been such a long time since she had attempted sorcery, she wondered whether her powers lay dormant, or even whether they had shriveled and died. It was years since the Dark One had spoken, and she had repulsed him. But she did not need him now, not at all.

She took out the box she had brought with her from Martinique, undisturbed for so long, and yet she had not been able to leave it behind. She unwrapped the cloth and opened the lid. The tins were there, the vials, the small sacks. She shivered and slowly closed the lid again. There was a knock at her door, and she placed the box beneath her bed.

Angelique was surprised to see Barnabas standing in the gloom of the hallway. Never had he looked more handsome, with his silk vest and his fine white shirt with its poet's sleeves, falling to soft gathers over his strong hands. His black hair tumbled over his eyes, which burned like coals, and she could see from his stance, his head lowered, his legs spread, that he was attempting to present an air of cool composure.

"May I come in?" he said softly. She stood aside to let him enter with a rush of hope. She had known he would come. She needed no spells when she herself possessed such power over him.

"I want to tell you how sorry I am," he began, "and that I deeply regret what has occurred." Angelique waited, saying nothing, feeling her pulse throb in her throat. "I admit that I may have taken advantage of you and treated you with less than the respect you were due. But . . . surely, I was not your only lover, and Martinique was . . . an enchanted place. A place of dreams. I—what I have come to say is . . . I see no reason why we can't be friends."

"Merely friends?" she whispered.

"Yes, why not? You are devoted to Josette and she to you. All I want is . . . for us all to be content. Don't you see, our . . . love affair in Martinique will always be a cherished memory. I will never think of you without affection. But now, we both have different roles in life."

A new role in life, her father had said. *One you can fulfill with pride.* She would never forget those words—

words that had plunged her into a life of desolation at the whim of a heartless man.

"And what is my role?" she asked bitterly. "The countess's maid?"

Barnabas looked at her, a helpless pain in his eyes. "Angelique—"

"I am your servant," she said simply.

"No . . ."

"And you are my master."

"Angelique . . . please . . ."

"What do you truly want, deep in your heart?" she whispered. "At this moment?" She took a step toward him. "Why are you here?" She saw him tremble, and he lifted his hand to his mouth.

She thought of the many times that hand had touched her, those fingers had stroked her, as he now stroked his parted lips, the full lips that she had kissed with such abandon. He had told her once that he could live on her mouth. She could see how he struggled with his feelings, and her heart ached for him.

She went to him, embraced him. "I love you," she said tremulously. "I will do anything to make you happy." She kissed him softly, deeply. Her body lifted against his, and she whispered, "Think of those nights in Martinique. No one has ever loved as we do. You do remember, don't you?"

He gave a little moan, his hands reaching for her, clutching her, bending her to him. She murmured, her mouth near his ear, "If all those promises we made were sweet lies of the moment, nothing more, then lie to me again. What does it matter?" She let flow from her lips the silent utterances of her heart. "Lie to me again," she whispered, and pressed against him, feeling him weaken.

He lifted her into his arms and carried her to the bed, and she was amazed at his sudden ardor. His hands moved over her body, his fingers pressing the flesh beneath the fabric of her dress. She was in the sea, the surge rising, and the surf thundered in her ears. His kisses were savage and insistent, and his breath was harsh next to her ear, like the rush of the wind in a cave. His fingers groped for her skirt, and beneath it, and when he found her, she felt her body throb in response. His weight was upon her, crushing her and, even as she sensed, with a twinge of regret, that his desire for her had overtaken his reason, that she had tricked him, she still slipped into the rush of bitter release, drifted from her safe shore and rose to meet that sweet heaviness, folding herself under a huge arching wave that carried her, tumbled her, lifted her, and flung her into the deepest of all waters.

Afterward, she drifted in a quiet eddy before she turned to him and saw that his face was shadowed with remorse. She traced the shape of his cheek with her finger, thinking how he was changed after lovemaking and wondering why this was so.

She smiled, and whispered, "You see, nothing can keep us apart."

He rose and pulled on his clothes, embarrassed, uneasy.

She watched him, then said lightly, "I told you you cannot resist me."

"I admit you are difficult to resist—I lost . . . control—"

"When two people are in love, nothing can stop them from wanting to be together."

"I think . . . it would be better if we did not see each other again—alone."

"How will you stay away?"

"I will. I must. Josette is coming. Angelique . . . I love her."

"No, Barnabas, you only think you love her. You are trying to convince yourself that you love her."

"I am going to marry her."

"A marriage that will only be a charade. One week, and you will regret it. She will never make you happy."

He turned to her and looked down at her. His eyes were red, and there was a weariness to his tone that made her want to weep. "This was the last time for us, Angelique. Please believe me, and don't make it more difficult than it already is."

Her heart filled with a sudden hatred for him. He was weak and dishonest, and he had used her again. She had allowed him to do so, humiliating herself in a desperate effort to rekindle his love with his desire. She was a fool. "Go. Leave me. Leave me now," she said cruelly. He walked to the door, then turned.

"Is there any way we can be friends?" he said helplessly.

"Oh, Barnabas," she said in a low voice, "I will always be much closer to you than you think."

*   *   *

Word was received that the ship carrying Josette and André to New York had been blown off course in a storm, delaying her arrival for more than one week. Josette was anxious to join her fiancée, and, as André had further business in the city, he had sent her ahead with an escort to Collinsport.

The time for father and daughter together in New York was cut short, but Josette had managed to peruse the shops for the latest fashions. When she arrived at Collinwood, she was dressed in a wine-colored coat that fell to the floor, loose in back and flowing with a train. She carried a fox muff, and her hat, a bouquet of lavender and roses, perched on her chestnut hair, which lay in charming ringlets on her breast. Her face was radiant when she embraced Angelique with unabashed affection. Barnabas appeared, breathless, and while Angelique watched, her heart filled with envy, Josette went into his arms, and he kissed her with great tenderness.

"Josette, my love, welcome to your new home," he said warmly. It was impossible not to see that his devotion was genuine. He fairly glowed when he looked at her. Slightly self-conscious, Josette turned to Angelique.

"Has my luggage been sent up?"

"Yes, my lady."

"Then . . . would you see that it is unpacked?" Josette was gentle as always, never condescending or unkind, but the intonation was clear. She wanted to be alone with him.

Of course Josette was lovely, and so very sweet,

always insisting that Angelique was her friend, not her servant, and now she would again begin to confide in her, sharing her feelings about Barnabas. Angelique would be forced to listen attentively, giving solace, understanding, commiserating, although the poisoned fiend of jealousy was already curling in her stomach, spitting his sour taste into her mouth.

Once she was back in her small room, Angelique opened the drawer of her dresser and took out the toy. Her hand was shaking, and a numbness flowed down her arms. The little soldier was sturdy and ready for battle, as untroubled as the man he impersonated. The handkerchief, easily found among Barnabas's things, was cumbersome, too large, but it carried his monogram and would suffice.

"Wake up, little soldier," she said, her voice tense and uncommonly sweet. "The time has come for you to perform your duties. My mistress has arrived to prepare for her wedding. But there isn't going to be any wedding, is there?"

Carefully, she looped the noose around the little neck. "Just a little pressure," she said, "just a slight tightening of the collar." How she wished she could be there to watch, but she did not need to be; she could picture it all in her mind. Then she sucked in her breath and called up the pulse of fire. It quivered at once through her body, like a snake of flame, and danced down her arms and into her hands. How simple it all was.

There! It was happening! Down in the foyer, Barnabas was kissing Josette when he stopped, confused by the discomfort, then panicked at the jerk at his throat.

"Barnabas, what is it?" Josette cried, frightened, then hysterical, as Barnabas collapsed in the chair, clawing at his throat.

"I can't breathe. . . ."

Angelique pulled the noose tighter. She smiled as she felt the force surge through her, physical, pleasurable, almost as though she were with him, holding him, feeling him in her body.

"I—something is choking—the room is—growing darker—where are you—Josette?" He groaned, crashed to the floor, knocking over the chair. Josette screamed, helplessly bewildered. Servants were called. He was carried to his room. The doctor was sent for.

Several hours passed, and Angelique decided to look in on Barnabas. Josette sat by his bedside, weeping piteously. She looked up, her eyes rimmed with red.

"Oh, Angelique, what am I going to do?"

"How is he, Mademoiselle?"

"Much worse, I'm afraid. Even the doctor can't help him."

Angelique felt a quiver of pride. "The doctor came?"

"The doctor has said there is nothing medically wrong. It's . . . it's as if something attacked him . . . a look in his eyes, his hand to his throat—"

"Is there anything I can do?"

"Will you come and pray with me, Angelique?"

"Of course, my lady."

Angelique knelt beside her mistress, then turned to her, hands folded, as if with a sudden impulse, and said: "Perhaps, if you intend to pray, it might be helpful for you to have your medal of Saint-Pierre. Did you bring it with you?"

"Oh, yes! It's in my luggage."

Angelique rose as if to go fetch it, but Josette stopped her.

"Let me find it," she said breathlessly, obviously glad for an excuse to be away for a moment. "Stay and watch over him." And she dashed out. Once alone, Angelique looked down at her victim.

"Barnabas," she whispered, leaning in close to his face. "You are such a foolish man, and you look so pathetic." He was sweating, his skin gray, his mouth moving with no sound. She touched his throat lightly, and he opened his eyes. "What are you thinking?" she said softly, without rancor. She waited while he looked up at her, tortured, bleary-eyed, and struggled to speak. Then she said with amazing calm, "Is there anything you wish to tell me?"

"I'm dying," he rasped, his voice thin and strained. Angelique felt a pulse of fear. Surely he wasn't close to death. It was far too soon, and the handkerchief was not tied that tightly. She was reminded of something, some anguished, long-buried memory, and suddenly her heart began to beat faster.

"I am dying . . ." he said so softly she could barely hear him. "Death is all around me. . . ."

"No! No, you cannot die!" She leaned in close to him, her breath mingling with his.

"Angelique . . . please . . . help me. . . ."

"I love you! If you die, I will have no one!" Then the memory struck like a dagger.

Chloe!

She dashed down the hall to her room, her heart pounding in her throat. Her hands were shaking when she reached for the doll.

Chloe!

She wrenched at the handkerchief, but it was so tight around the neck of the little soldier that she could not tear it loose. Cold panic in her veins, she relived the nightmare, floundering in self-reproach. She killed the things she loved. She destroyed her chances for happiness. What would she do if he died? What would she do if she lost him? She would be alone!

Desperately she fumbled through her bureau, searching for scissors, a knife, nothing! She jerked at the knot once again. It had to come loose. It must. There was a sickening moment of helplessness, as her fingertips dug at the handkerchief, nails ripping with pain, and finally, she felt a loop loosen, and slipping a finger beneath it, she pulled it free.

In her mind she saw Barnabas gasp for air and breathe again with great wrenching gulps as Josette embraced him with joy.

"It was so terrifying," he said, clinging to her. "Death was . . . whispering to me."

Angelique sat numb with relief, staring at the doll in her hand. *How could I have been so careless?* she thought. *I must not ever harm him again. If he had died, I would have been left with nothing. It can't be a spell on Barnabas. I must find another way, some other means of disturbing the world around him, destroying his hopes, so that he will turn to me for solace, and then I shall be his.*

chapter

27

One morning, there was a carriage on the path and a great bustle at the door. Packages had arrived from Paris for Josette's wedding and the honeymoon, which was to take place in Martinique. The boxes were carried upstairs, and since Josette had gone into town with the countess, it was Angelique's duty to unpack them. As she pulled the strings loose, she thought of how she had changed since her arrival, as though her entire nature had been poisoned by jealousy. Never had her hatred of Josette been more bitter.

Under the soft embrace of tissue, she found silken underthings, petticoats of lace and satin, dresses of taffeta with exquisite embroidery, tucks, and flounces. There were gloves and shoes of fine doeskin and bonnets that were creamy confections of straw and ribbon and flowers.

One particular chapeau was so lovely that Angelique could not resist trying it on, and the moment she placed it on her head and looked at herself in the glass, she felt her heart sink. Her beauty was painful to her, so unrevealed, and she thought of the coral beneath the sea, gardens of shimmering color which, when ripped up and exposed to the sun, faded and grew dull, like the shade of her drab maid's dress. She gazed at her face beneath the hat, so becoming, so enhancing to the shape of her face and her eyes, and the hopelessness of her situation seemed more than she could bear.

It was at that moment the door flew open, and Josette appeared, flushed with excitement.

"They came! The packages came! From Paris! Oh, Angelique, let me see!" Josette rushed to the bed and took up a dress with silver-and-blue candy stripes, which rustled as it fell against her. Only when she came to the mirror did she see Angelique.

"Oh, how lovely!" she cried. "You look so sweet in that bonnet!"

Then she smiled impishly. "Angelique," she blurted, reaching for her arm, "let's try on all the dresses—together!"

"I couldn't do that," said Angelique. "They aren't mine."

"But then I shall give one to you," said Josette, impetuous as always, although a flicker shadowed her gaze when she realized she was being very generous.

"Where would I wear it, Mademoiselle?"

"Oh, I don't know. What difference does it make? Here. Try this one!" And she tossed a gray taffeta frock across the bed.

A few minutes later the two girls were admiring

one another as they posed in front of the glass, their slender waists nipped by corsets and their delicate arms draped in soft flounces. Josette pulled Angelique to her side and placed an affectionate hand on her shoulder as they stood before the mirror.

"Look at us," she whispered. "Are we not a pair? You are even more beautiful than I."

"That's not true, Mademoiselle. You are the beautiful one."

"But together we are all the comeliness of womanhood. You with your bright golden hair and me with my dark eyes. It's too bad one man can't have us both!" And she laughed with delight at this idea.

As Angelique gazed at their reflections in the gilt frame, she thought bitterly, yes, it was true. Josette was her reverse, not only in coloring but in nature. It was as if all the hatred in her own heart had sucked any possible enmity out of her mistress, so that the dark-haired girl was all purity, trusting and open, while her own character was corrupted by a force of evil that left her suspicious and closed to the world. She knew that these things would never change, and bitter tears sprang to her eyes.

"Oh, no, don't cry," cried Josette, and she ran to the bed and reached for the bonnet. "Here" she said. "I want you to have this. It doesn't matter if you never wear it. Take it."

"I can't. Really, I can't," said Angelique, shaking her head.

"You must, or I will become very angry," said Josette with a sly smile. And she clasped Angelique's hand and led her to the bed. "Listen," she said, sitting beside her. "We are going to find a nice young man for you. I can't bear to be the only one who is happy. Once I am married, I intend to make it my first order of business to marry you off as well. I shall become a matchmaker! And you will wear this bonnet, I promise you."

The time had come for fresh herbs, powders, and, most important of all, a helper, someone to fetch the things she needed. Angelique realized how reckless she had been, how easily she might arouse suspicion. Even the act of searching for deadly nightshade in the woods had turned up the feeble-minded caretaker, Ben, who crept up behind her.

"What are you doin' with them leaves?" he asked gruffly. She jerked back, startled and flustered.

"Looking for herbs. My mistress . . . likes them in her salad." She winced. *It is fortunate,* she thought, *that he is an imbecile; otherwise, he would never have believed such a silly story.*

"And what do you think that is?"

"Bay leaves," she answered smugly.

"No, it ain't. That's deadly nightshade, and it's poisonous."

"Poisonous?" She feigned astonishment.

"I seen cattle die from eating it, and they suffered a mighty lot of pain."

"Oh, I'm so grateful to you for telling me," she said, dumping the basket of leaves on the ground. She looked at him kindly. "You're Ben, aren't you?" He nodded. "I've seen you before. I remember when you lifted the countess's carriage out of the rut. Why, you have the strength of two men, and . . . and knowledge of herbs as well."

Just as she expected, he softened under her flattery.

"I know you, too. You're the countess's maid."

"My name is Angelique, and I hope we can become friends."

"I-I shouldn't even be talkin' to you. Mister Joshua Collins would have me whipped."

"I won't tell anyone," she said, touching his arm.

"Most women don't want to talk to me."

"Well, I like it. I like talking to you very much," she said, smiling warmly, seeing the idea that she was flirting with him forming in his mind.

Back in her room Angelique crushed two powders with a mortar and pestle, and poured in a potion of the nightshade she had retrieved after Ben had left, and a bit of her own blood from a pricked finger. Then she looked into the fire. She called Ben's name softly a few times, and it was only moments before he was knocking at her door.

He seemed bewildered when she let him enter, and he said, "I dunno what I'm doin' here."

"I wanted you here," she answered. He was dumbfounded when he heard these words, but he wasted no time. He grinned lasciviously and grabbed for her clumsily, but she danced out of the way, offering him the potion.

"First, drink this."

"And after?"

"We shall see," she said slyly.

Ben swallowed the elixir without hesitation, blinked, and stared at her in foolish stupidity.

"How do you feel?" she asked.

"Strange . . ."

"That is because you no longer have a will of your own," she said sternly. "My will is your will. You shall do whatever I tell you to do; you shall be my slave."

He tried to shrug this off as a silly female whim, but she could see by the blurred look in his eyes that the potion was taking effect. He staggered a little and caught himself on the arm of the chair, stared a moment at the floor as though trying to remember where he was, then lifted his eyes to her, stunned and worried.

"Now that you have drunk the potion, you are in my power," she said in a low voice. "And I will protect you from all evil spirits, even from death itself." She reached for his huge paw. "Yours is the hand I will use when mine is too small, your arm when mine is too weak." She laced her delicate fingers in between his thicker ones. "We are united by invisible bonds which can never be broken," she added.

Then she pulled her hand away and walked to her dresser, thought a moment, and turned. Ben was still standing there, watching her in a total stupor.

"I must have a spider's web from a living oak tree. Not a single strand of the web can be broken. Go and fetch it. Go now. I have important things to do."

Ben turned and walked out of the room without a word. When he returned he had found his voice; his manner was wary but a bit curious.

"I had to pull three down before I found one that was perfect," he said. "What you want it for?"

Angelique took the web, which was spun around a slim forked twig. "It's for a dress," she said. Ben's eyes lit up.

"A dress—I'd like to see that!" His lips were slack, and his words slurred, as though saliva had formed in his mouth.

"It's not for me. It's for this woman." She walked to a crude clay doll standing on her desk.

"She ain't got no head."

"It doesn't matter, because the woman is Josette. And the dress will be held to her body by a lock of her lover's hair."

"Where you gonna get a lock of Mr. Barnabas's hair?"

"Not Barnabas," she said, feeling a pulse of excitement as she smiled at Ben. "Jeremiah. Josette's lover will soon be Jeremiah."

Ben laughed, a full-throated chortle, which irritated her even further. Even though he was forced to do her bidding, he still continued to treat her with familiarity, as though they were equals.

"Jeremiah? You sure got that one wrong," he said.

"Tell me something, Ben. What does a man hate most in a woman?"

"I don't know much about women."

"But if you were married to a woman, what would you want her to be?"

"Why . . . faithful to me, I guess."

"And what would you do if she were not faithful?"

Ben became aroused with rage as he imagined this situation. "I'd . . . I'd kill her!"

Angelique smiled. "Barnabas won't kill her," she said. "But I can see his face . . . I can hear his voice . . . sending her home! And I will be the one who comforts him."

Ben was incensed. "You can't make her do that! I'll tell him!"

"You'll do nothing of the kind," she said scathingly. "If you open your mouth to say one word against me, you will never speak again."

She saw the full realization finally lodge in Ben's dim brain. His mouth fell open. "You're a witch!" he said in dumb astonishment.

Angelique smiled again at this simplicity of mind. "Yes. I am a witch. And you are my helper."

Late that night she sat before the fire and stared at the clay figure sitting on the desk. "Yes, Miss Josette, no, Miss Josette," she said bitterly. Her heart was cold as a stone, and she was filled with resentment. "She thinks she orders me about," Angelique whispered to herself. "But in this room I am the one who orders her."

She recalled the joy she had felt when she arrived at Collinwood. How foolish she had been, how absurdly naive. When had he ceased to love her, and why? Her own feelings of love had changed as well. What had been a warm and joyous devotion that had pervaded her whole being was now a tortured fixation.

Her love had become twisted into another shape, sharper and more oblique. It was as though a seed had turned in the earth, and showed a darker side to the sun, before sprouting a foul weed full of nettles.

Perhaps she had always been this way and had only repressed her true nature. She thought of her beautiful reefs in Martinique and the amazing life in the coral. She remembered now that the natives, when trolling for larger game, never ate any of the brightly colored reef fish if they caught them in their nets. The brilliant creatures with their dapples and ruffles carried a deadly poison in their flesh.

When would she learn that nothing would come to her without effort, that nothing was predictable. It was apparent that Barnabas had tired of her. She might be able to entice him into another hour's dalliance, but now he truly desired Josette for all her innocence and vulnerability. The familiar gaze, the deep affection in the eyes, the charming smile, he now bestowed on Josette, as though he were performing a role in a play and reciting the same lines with a new ingenue.

She had to admit he demonstrated a steadfast and determined attitude toward Josette, far more serious than he had displayed with her. Oh, how she regretted going to his room the night she wore the dress of gold satin. If only she had left things as they were, she might have won him back after he and Josette were married. But with no claim on him at all, she had given him everything.

She was not like Josette. She did not have the luxury of strolling through gardens, laughing with young gentlemen, confident that she was exquisitely gowned and coifed, knowing all who set eyes on her found her fair. Gifts came to Josette like rain from the sky.

Josette had no worries, nothing to fear. But all that was about to change. "I will make a life for her," she said to the empty room, "a life she will loathe so much there will be only one thing left for her to do. That is my bequest. That is my gift. And that is also . . ." she said with a melancholy realization, "my only choice."

After Ben came with the ring and the lock of Jeremiah's hair, Angelique had everything she needed for the spell. She arranged Josette's handkerchief around the doll and drew the strand of dark hair through the ring to distribute and blend the oils. It was the simplest of sorceries, and yet as she began to chant the old words, words from time's beginning, she suddenly grew faint. A shadow fell across her mind, and she seemed to be spinning in a whirlpool.

She gripped the edge of the desk to steady herself, and when her thoughts cleared she began again. When she spoke, the fire behind her flared up as though an answering echo. She felt the familiar pulse flutter in her shoulders and throat, and the words began to swim with the throbbing in her brain, as she smelled the acrid odor she remembered from long ago.

"The oil from Jeremiah's ring will bind the hair into a belt for the cobweb of love."

She drew the delicate spiderweb over the doll's

head, and the threads ripped and stuck to the clay. "The cobweb of love will trap Josette, and the strands of the web will be like iron." She closed her eyes and whispered, "Josette loves Jeremiah. Josette loves Jeremiah. Josette loves Jeremiah."

As the power pulsed, her body grew taut, and spasms of pleasure throbbed in her core. Then she was overcome by dizziness and fell into a faint. She lay by the fire for a quarter of an hour before she regained consciousness and remembered what she had done.

Things began slowly, but Angelique could not help being fascinated with the spell's progression. Josette chose a candy-striped dress that morning, one that was far too coquettish for her, but it fit her petite figure like enamel on a china doll. She then whimsically insisted on a bow for her masses of chestnut hair, which she left loose, falling about her shoulders.

Angelique smiled to herself when she overheard Josette begin a childish argument with Barnabas over whether she would allow him to kiss her. She was certain the effects of the magic were beginning, and she had only to be patient and wait. Josette was already making a fool of herself.

Angelique was intrigued when Barnabas asked her to meet him in the drawing room. Perhaps he was already tiring of his frivolous fiancée. But the moment she saw his face, her body stiffened. He was more angry than she had ever seen him.

"What do you know about this?" he asked her curtly, handing her a large square box.

"Nothing," she said simply.

"I think you do."

"Why? What is it?" she asked, more curious than cowed.

"A wedding present," he said with withering sarcasm. "See for yourself."

Angelique hesitated a moment, then, setting the box on the table, lifted the lid. What she saw made her blood run cold. Inside the box, staring up at her, was a skull, a white gaping skull, wearing a thick wig of dull chestnut hair! She stepped away in disgust.

"Is it from you?" he asked.

"Of course not."

"Obviously it was sent by someone who does not approve of our marriage."

"But how could I . . . I haven't been off the grounds since the day I arrived."

"Then what am I to think?" His gaze was so cold and contemptuous that tears sprang to her eyes.

"You act as if you don't even know me, as though you know nothing about me," she said, "when you know me so well." She felt a wave of desperation. "You know I would never do anything to make you hate me!" She fled the room.

Once back in her own chamber, Angelique went to the window and stared blankly out, struggling to compose herself. There was only one being she could think of who possessed such a vile sense of the macabre.

Had he always been there, hovering near, waiting for her to weaken? Her long years of abstinence and self-restraint meant nothing; they had disappeared like an interminable drought that is dissolved by one rainstorm. He had returned, and he would come for her, even though these were merely silly spells, what the *Bokor* had called "playing with toys." Yet they were enough. She turned and looked helplessly around her small room.

"Are you here? Are you with me now?" she whispered. She waited—not summoning, not quickening to the force—and listened. There was no sound, no disturbance in the air, nothing at all, only the silence that quivered with the beating of her heart. Was it worth it, risking his return? She had been a child when he first came to her. She had been too young to challenge him, and she had not known how to protect herself. Somewhere, deep within her core, lay the power to fight him, and she must reach for it. But first she must quit these foolish sorceries, which were not worthy of her talents and only disturbed the long truce that had guarded her soul. She promised herself she would not perform another spell.

However, her resolutions were futile. Much to her dismay, that night Josette passed down the hall on the way to Jeremiah's room. She wore a sheer lavender gown that was shamelessly revealing, and she was flushed. She walked as though she were in a trance. She was so intent on what she was doing that she never saw Angelique who had come to prepare her for bed.

Josette knocked on Jeremiah's door, and when he

answered, spoke to him in a voice that was low and
sultry. Angelique had no way of knowing what tran-
spired, but Josette came back to her own room deeply
upset and ashamed. She threw herself upon her bed
and refused to be comforted.

The spell had begun, thought Angelique, and
there was nothing she could do to stop it now, even if
she had wanted to do so.

The next morning Angelique saw Jeremiah in the
drawing room. He was troubled and introspective, but
he took advantage of the maid's presence to question
her about Josette's mood.

"How was your mistress when you left her?"

"Oh, very well, sir."

"Is she happy here?"

"Why yes, of course she is, very happy."

"You don't think she is in any way . . . disturbed?"

"Not at all. She is . . . exactly as she was at home."

She saw the insinuation hit the mark. Jeremiah's
jaw set, and he shook his head in resignation. He was
having difficulty believing what Josette had done. And
truthfully, how could anyone seek depravity in such
an unblemished character. Josette's unsullied virtue
was as obvious as the dawn.

Angelique felt a wave of pity for her, pity which
she buried away. Why should Josette escape the
whimsy of fate? She knew Jeremiah was intending to
tell Barnabas that his fiancée could not be trusted.
Barnabas's pride would be wounded and his arrogance deflated, but he would never accept Josette if he
discovered she was inconstant.

*   *   *

The conversation actually occurred that very afternoon. Josette, still humiliated by her actions, remained in her room and sent Angelique to say that she was not well. After delivering her message and enduring Barnabas's disappointed countenance, Angelique remained in the hallway, eavesdropping as he spoke with Jeremiah.

"Isn't Josette lovely?" Barnabas said. "Have you noticed how she listens, and how she moves? The only thing I don't understand is why she chose me. I don't deserve her."

Jeremiah murmured a few words, searching for some way to approach the difficult subject in the face of such adoration. "Perhaps you don't know Josette as well as you think you do."

"My God, Jeremiah, what makes you say such a thing?"

"You've always told me I had accurate perceptions of a person's character."

"And you sense something is wrong? Don't you like her?"

"Yes, of course I like her," he said with hesitation, adding, in spite of himself, "very much."

"She likes you, if that's what was worrying you. In fact, I think she is jealous of you, of our friendship. She deeply hopes that you will approve of her."

"And how do you think she will seek my approval?"

"Why, Jeremiah, how serious you are! She has no need to seek it! I think perhaps you are the one who is jealous. Am I right? Don't you think I am an exceedingly lucky man?"

Jeremiah hesitated, then appeared to forfeit his enterprise. "You are fortunate to be able to love so fully," he said finally, "and to trust so completely."

Jealousy flared again in Angelique's heart, and anger that her conjurations had not culminated in a revelation of Josette's improprieties. Frustration quickened her determination, and she decided to forgo her plan of having Josette endure the pain of unrequited love. It was time for Jeremiah to respond to, in fact desire, Josette's advances.

But this time she was hampered by an inner trepidation, an uneasiness that made the creation of the potion difficult. She found the herb she needed in the woods, and the catalyst was stored in her bag. Ben would take Jeremiah his evening toddy and, by her bidding, drop the potion in his drink. The plan was certain, but the execution frustratingly static. She found it difficult to concentrate; she knew she was using only superficial tricks, but she was afraid to dig deeper.

As she was working, the words of the *Bokor* flashed in her mind. *"Can you make someone love you?"* she had asked him, and he had answered, *"You pays your money and you takes the consequence."*

A love spell was tricky and disturbed the hand of fate. She would never use such a spell on Barnabas. He must come to her as he had in Martinique, because he wanted her, because he was devoted to her. She knew he loved her, and she had only to remove the impediments to that love. She had only to eliminate Josette as quickly and as painlessly as possible.

Bitterness, however, muddied the clarity of her thoughts, and a swimming miasma stirred in her brain, making her body weak. Her longing for Barnabas interfered with her capacity to make the choices that would bring about her aims. She was certain that casting this spell was the right decision, but she seemed to be losing her ability to focus. She knew only that she was determined to stop the marriage. Josette must run away with Jeremiah. Then Barnabas would realize how wrong he had been and how much she, Angelique, loved him. She clung to that belief with all her strength.

That same night, the two lovers met in the moonlight at the marble fountain of Diana, inexplicably drawn to one another. However, to Angelique's extreme vexation, the Countess du Prés surreptitiously followed Josette when she left the house. Worse, she witnessed, in the garden, beneath the statue of the Huntress, Josette and Jeremiah pledge their love in a stilted exchange and a hesitant kiss. The artificiality of their meeting convinced the countess, a vain but not a stupid woman, that Josette was acting against her heart's true desires.

As a result, Angelique began to encounter some difficulty from the countess, who had a natural resonance with the supernatural and prided herself on silly tricks such as the reading of tarot cards. These talismans of prophecy kept revealing, according to her, "an evil force" somewhere in the house. The countess could sense that Josette was so unlike her true self, except in the strength of her resilience.

Josette's character was of such faultless integrity that she was able to fight the spell unconsciously with every fiber of her being. The magic caught her and forced her into unprincipled behavior, but later she was disconsolate, plagued with guilt. She became moody and secretive, and the countess, in turn, became suspicious.

In spite of the countess's vigilance, Angelique was convinced that the spell would achieve her ends. She tried to control her anxiety, constantly picturing in her mind Barnabas's face when he realized that his Josette had betrayed him. She ignored his negligent treatment of her, clinging to the belief that he was repressing his true feelings. But the Dark One made another insidious appearance, almost as though he were taunting Angelique. The mark of the Devil's pitchfork appeared mysteriously on Josette's hand.

Josette was deeply alarmed as she stared at the evil symbol, rubbing it as though dirt had soiled her hand, but she did not feel more dread than Angelique, who instantly comprehended the origin of the mark.

"What could it be?" asked Josette in dismay. "It won't come off."

"I have no idea, my lady."

"Perhaps it is a bruise."

The mark was absurd and crudely drawn, as though the Devil were making some clumsy effort to aid Angelique in her endeavors. She found some pretense to look at it closely, and it was so ridiculous she almost laughed. Pressed to find some means to console her mistress, she said, "I had a mark like that when I was a child." How ironic it was that, in offering commiseration, she had spoken the truth in the midst of a lie. "I was able to remove it with rosewater," she added.

Giving herself over to her servant's ministrations, Josette allowed Angelique to rub the mark with rosewater. The cologne was from Josette's toilette, rosewater Angelique had secretly laced with the elixir of love. The tangled web of lies was gathering them all into its net.

The mark washed away, but the next day, to Josette's bewilderment, and Angelique's vexation, it reappeared, as dark as before, and it appeared on Jeremiah's hand as well. Angelique knew the two perplexed lovers would attempt to erase the pitchforks themselves, alone in Josette's room, and their furious scrubbing with the rosewater would come to naught, only unavoidable caresses and, finally, an inevitable embrace.

It was as though the Devil were assisting her now, working at her side, creating spells as foolish as hers to taunt her and harass her. He had made no appearance nor did he speak to her, but he was in the shadows, waiting.

chapter

28

A t last, André du Prés arrived from New York to celebrate his daughter's wedding. Angelique was curiously glad to see him, and he greeted her with civility, relieved to see a familiar face, although he was snappish and officious as usual, feeling ignored and put out when there was no one from the Collins family to greet him.

"Angelique, my dear," he said, giving her a cursory nod, "where the devil is everyone?" She smiled when she saw that for his visit André had purchased a handsome suit of dove-colored wool, which nicely disguised his round girth, and that he sported a matching top hat of magnificent proportions.

"I'll tell Josette you are here," she said, feeling for the first time a stab of guilt that this well-meaning man would be distressed by his daughter's behavior. When Joshua Collins came in from his study, André was awkward, intimidated by Joshua's impeccable manners. *So sad,* she thought, *when he, André, has far more money and property.*

But André was "rich as a Creole," and money made in cane was not considered "old" money the way shipping money was. According to Joshua, Caribbean planters were riffraff from Europe who had escaped their lowly origins. Still, Angelique thought bitterly to herself, Joshua was certainly not above the union that would bring untold riches to the Collins family, if not the requisite prestige.

André noticed immediately that his daughter was out of sorts. He could not have been more understanding and solicitous, and once again Angelique envied Josette her doting father, his sweet and undiminished affection.

That evening, over a fine bottle of French wine, the countess visited with her brother and told him everything that had occurred since her arrival in Collinsport, including Josette's untoward behavior. They were easy together, congenial, glad to be confidants once more, and Angelique was sent to request still another bottle from Joshua's cellar. Smiling to herself over what the patriarch's reaction would be when he discovered the loss, she stirred the fire and added a log or two, giving herself the excuse of lingering a few moments in the parlor.

"I'll be damned if she'll marry a man she doesn't love!" André blurted. "Which one of these chaps does she really want?"

"André, listen to me. I have come to believe, as ridiculous as it sounds, that Josette in under some kind of spell, that . . . there is a witch in this house, or some cruel demon, forcing Josette into the arms of

Jeremiah. They don't love one another, I'm sure of it. She acts as though she were in a trance."

"Hogwash! You know, Natalie, your imagination has been overstimulated by your time in the islands. Josette's always been a capricious girl, never known her own mind. I've adored her, and spoiled her, and, you know as well as I do, although many island dandies have courted her, she's never been in the company of real gentlemen. Barnabas is the first, and this Jeremiah is an obvious rival."

"He is Barnabas's uncle, and they have been the best of friends since Barnabas was a child. Whether you believe in sorcery or not, I think the marriage is in danger."

"Then call the damn thing off! Let's all sail back to Martinique, and the devil take the lot of them!"

"No, I think Josette and Barnabas should marry at once. The sooner the better!"

Angelique, holding the poker in the flame for too long a time, suddenly realized that it had become burning hot in her hand. She dropped it into the fireplace and stood staring at it, not knowing how to retrieve it. The countess turned to her.

"That will be all, Angelique. You may go."

She did not go farther than the hallway. She felt that her legs would not carry her as far as her room, and she leaned against the banister, her head swimming. The wedding was planned for weeks away, and she had thought there would be ample time to perfect her manipulations. The romance between Josette and Jeremiah was at a standstill. They fought it so desperately, and their sense of propriety was so entrenched.

"You mean have them marry before the elaborate ceremony they've all been planning so strenuously? I was led to believe this wedding was to be the event of the season. Haven't a great many guests been invited?" André was playing devil's advocate, and even through the door, Angelique could hear the warmth in his voice from the wine.

"I know," the countess answered. "Everything here is so controlled, so fastidious. In the tropics decisions melt like ice, but here the ice is always hard . . . and permanent."

"I don't know that I blame Josette," André was saying, something in his voice Angelique had never heard: something pensive, and slightly melancholy. She crept back to the edge of the wall by the door so that she could hear every nuance.

"Tell me, Natalie, now that you are older and wiser, as I myself am, what—when you were young— did you think of love?"

"Love, André? Oh, I don't remember. It—oh, very well, it was rapture! It was undeniable, irresistible bliss!"

"Yes, ah, yes . . ." he answered. "Irresistible . . . rapture . . . I have never told you this, Natalie, although we have been very close, but Marie was not my one true love. She was a devoted wife, and I was fond of her, I respected her. She came from a good family, as you know, and the match was presentable, arranged by both our families. I married to please Father, and, I must say, I never regretted my decision.

I actually grieved deeply when she died. She was a dear, sweet woman, and she gave me a delightful daughter who is the light of my life. But she was not the woman of my dreams."

"Oh . . . then who was?"

André sighed deeply. "I have never admitted this to another living soul," he said, "but the truth is, I don't really know. I was young—a strapping lad, even if I do say so myself—you would have been amazed. Ah, yes, young, and wild, and full of conceit. I loved to ride. Martinique was so untamed then, and I had a magnificent horse that I would take into the sea. Have you ever ridden in the surf?"

"No, I have not, never . . . dear God . . ."

"You can't imagine the feeling of being on a horse when he is swimming. This powerful animal, churning the foam, floating and digging for the sand, leaping over the wave, plummeting under the water, then galloping to the surface again. It is an unbelievable sensation! When I was on his back, I would feel like . . . like a god!"

"And how did you meet this woman?"

"What . . . ? Oh, yes, well, early one morning, I was galloping for miles and miles along the water's edge, a long way from my home, when I saw a girl, gathering shells, or scallops, by the line of the tide. I pulled the horse up and watched her. She was wearing a piece of cloth that was all the colors of the coral, and she was graceful, like a dancer, when she bent and lifted whatever it was she was finding into a basket on her hip. I can't tell you what came over me, but I was drawn to her. She was, well . . . irresistible, as though she were not real, but a vision I had to make out before I could turn away. It was as if I had seen one of those rare birds in the forest, you know what I mean, that is so beautiful, you creep toward it without breathing because you know how exquisite it is and you simply must see it."

"Yes, yes, I have done that."

"I remember, I dived into the sea, I think because I hoped I could swim closer to her without being observed. I must have been afraid she would vanish if she saw me."

"And you say I have an islander's imagination."

"When I walked out of the water she looked up and smiled and, you mustn't be shocked, Natalie, I could see she was quadroon."

"I was going to say . . . naturally . . ."

"She was honey-colored, with long black hair, and her eyes were like a tiger's. She was a real beauty. She didn't say a word, only turned and led me across the beach to her cottage, as though she had been expecting me. I walked behind her, and I can still remember her black hair swinging down below her waist in a luxurious cascade, and beneath it, that golden part of her that was below her waist but above her buttocks, and then the curving flesh that was wrapped in her pareu.

"She took me inside, and her cottage smelled of mint and bay leaf, and so did she, spicy, herbal fragrances. There were bunches of dried flowers hanging from the ceiling. She fed me, and cared for me, and . . .

and sang to me. I remember her honeyed songs. She was a goddess, in a dream—a flower, but not one of those tissue-paper flowers that are limp, and fragile— she made me think of an orchid, those up high in the tree that live on air—waxy, firm, the inside of a shell, with a sheen on her, her dark eyes, and her mouth like the delicate center of an orchid."

"Did you stay?"

"Stay? Of course I stayed. Days. Weeks. I can't remember. I only know she was the one woman I truly desired. She gave me . . . rapture . . . and I have never forgotten her."

"Why didn't you—"

"Marry her. Ah, yes. Well, one morning I woke up and she was gone. Like the idiot I was, I went home, and within six months I was a respectable married man and Marie was my wife."

"You never went back?"

"Can you believe it? I am a callous bastard. I never went back. I shouldn't say that. Years later, I was on that part of the beach, and I found the cottage, but it was broken-down and deserted. She wasn't there. No, Natalie, I never saw her again."

Angelique fell back against the wall, chills lifting the hair on her arms. Raising a hand to her face, she traced each of her features with her fingertips, then stroked her neck and wrapped both her arms about her waist. She could scarcely believe what she had just heard. André was her father! Of course! She had his eyes and his fair hair, and were it not for a cruel trick of fate, she would have also had his name. She had always believed she had aristocratic breeding, that in her heart and soul she was a lady, and now she knew it was true. Resentment flooded through her. Somehow the revelation only made her more disconsolate. Her true father!

The day had been bitter cold and dark, and the wind whipped the branches of the trees, clawing like specters begging entrance at the glass. Thunder rumbled in the distance, warning of a storm, and streaks of lightning pierced the somber sky. Angelique stood at her window and thought she had never seen a sun so bleak, so darkly impotent, as it shone weakly through the clouds.

Bitterness and hysteria fought for control of her emotions. The wedding had been rescheduled for that night, and she now believed there was nothing she could do. She had poured a new love potion into Josette's rosewater, but Josette disliked perfumes and had never used it. An offer to massage her forehead with the rosewater had been rejected.

Still, Angelique clung to the idea of marrying Barnabas herself, as though her whole life were at stake. Each cruel setback only drove her forward. Her mind was racing. Jeremiah! He was her only hope. However, only that afternoon he had promised André that he would leave Collinsport. What could she do? He had vowed he would take the first carriage out of town, hurriedly packed his belongings, and ordered his horse. Even though he knew Joshua would never forgive him, both he and Josette had recognized their shameless predicament and the imminent scandal that would tear the family apart. Bewildered and angry, he had made a gallant decision to sacrifice his career at the shipyards and renounce his claim on Josette, even though he was more strongly drawn to her than he had ever been to any woman in his life.

After a desperate search, Angelique found Ben chopping wood behind the house. With the storm coming, the house would need a good supply of firewood. He laughed in her face when he saw her, a sharp barking laugh. "There wasn't enough magic in that charm of yours! You didn't get him after all."

She gathered her cape about her and shivered in the freezing wind. "Listen to me, Ben. I need to make another spell. Get me something of Jeremiah's. Something small." Ben stood up, towering over her, and she could smell the stale odor of his sweat.

"Why don't you get it yourself?"

"What? I would never go into a gentleman's bedroom. A lady doesn't do such a thing, and Barnabas is never going to be ashamed of me!"

There was a crash of thunder, and the wind whipped the tops of the trees in a chaotic frenzy.

"Why do you have to hurt people?"

"I only hurt those who hurt me."

"What has Miss Josette ever done to you?"

"She has taken the man I love!"

"He loves her, not you! Can't you see that?" And he cackled again, and grunted, a feral sound in his throat. He infuriated her.

"Ben, you are stupid and backward! You don't

have the capacity to understand anything. Do you think the course of true love can never be altered? Barnabas will have every reason to stop loving her. She will belong to another man."

"Why are you doing this to him?"

She sighed with irritation. "I'm doing it because I love him."

Ben lifted the ax and drew his thick fingers over the blade. "Mr. Barnabas has been kind to me. I don't like doing something to make him unhappy."

"You underestimate me, Ben. I will devote my life to making him happy."

"Mr. Joshua treats me like a slave, but Mr. Barnabas said I can come and work for him when him and Miss Josette are married. I don't want you to hurt Mr. Barnabas or Miss Josette." He took a step toward Angelique, and she could see the hatred in his eyes, hatred he drew from years of helpless servitude. She had aroused that hatred when she forced him to obey her. Ignorant men, when angered, were dangerous.

"You're a witch!" he said, and she could see saliva dripping from his slack bottom lip. His eyes were bloodshot, and the muscles of his arm bulged through his shirt as he lifted the ax. "I'll kill you—"

There was a sudden sizzle of lightning, and a crazy spiral zigzagged in the sky behind him as the shattering crack of thunder caught him unawares. In that instant Angelique raised her hand and felt her body buck with the force of her will.

"Stay where you are, Ben," she said in a voice like ice. "Come no closer." She took a breath, and it was as if the electricity snaked through the ground beneath her and out her fingers. "You can never harm me," she hissed. "I have powers that protect me, and you are a greater imbecile than I throught if you strike with that ax. For the blade will turn, and you will rend your own skull."

Ben stood paralyzed, his ax arm lifted. He looked like a statue of a man set in the town square to honor the lowly workman. Only his eyes darted in terror. His lips moved, but he could not speak.

"Do you feel it, Ben?" she asked coldly, as he nodded slowly. "Do you understand that you can never harm me? Do you promise me that you will never threaten me again?"

He nodded again.

"Then I will free you." She lowered her hand, and Ben's body shuddered as he dropped the ax to the earth. He stood staring at her sullenly, his eyes dazed, as though his mind had turned to sand. "Now go, and get me what I need."

He turned and shuffled into the house.

Angelique remained a few moments, shaken and disturbed. The use of her powers had left her weak, and she was stunned by the vehemence of Ben's anger. A feeling of utter loneliness invaded her spirit. She looked at the bare limbs of the trees etched on the white sky and tasted the bitter air. The sun had disappeared, swallowed up in the haze, and icy blasts of the wind against the panes of the cold mansion rattled the glass like skeletons in their coffins.

Then she heard a strange twittering sound, as

though the air were filled with crickets, and shadowy shapes flew over her head in haphazard streaks, sputtering like tiny crows. They were bats, darting in frenzied pairs from the chimney, where she could see a gaping hole open to the sky. Bats lived in the chimney!

Something made her curious. She felt about for a loose brick and found a spot where the mortar had decayed. The brick slid sideways to reveal the cavernous interior of the chimney wall, and she could see the bats, fluttering, jostling one another for the light of the opening and ducking through to venture out into the early evening for a night of foraging.

Back in her room, Josette seemed to be her old self, elated, brimming with happiness, as she dressed for the ceremony; and Angelique was obliged to assist her, fastening the tiny buttons of her white dress, smoothing the lace and silk, arranging the flowers in her hair. All the while, Angelique felt that her bones were knives, and her heart pumped poison into her veins. She repeated over and over to herself, *André is my father as well; all this could have been mine. Barnabas is the man I have loved since I was a child, who lived in my dreams, who taught me love's mysteries. He is the lover of all that I am, my soul's companion. How can I let him go to her? How can I let him wed another?*

The countess sat on a chaise in Josette's room exclaiming over the dress. "My dear, you are exquisite! You make a beautiful bride."

Angelique was becoming frantic. Ben had stolen for her Jeremiah's blue handkerchief, and now she begged leave to return a moment to her room. "I have a little something I want to give you," she said to Josette, her voice weak as though she would faint.

Once alone, Angelique realized the handkerchief was much too large as she fashioned a clumsy rosette, desperately forcing it into the shape of a flower as the rain beat at her window. She returned to Josette's room and hurriedly reached for the rosewater. She sprinkled it on the flower, spilling it on the dresser and causing the handkerchief to become spotted and limp. It was an impotent spell, one that she was certain would never work.

"What do you have for me?" Josette asked sweetly. But she frowned when she saw it.

"It—it is an amulet, Mademoiselle, to bring you good fortune." Angelique forced gaiety into her voice and leaned to pin the rosette on Josette's dress. The drab blue cotton clashed with the delicate silk, and the flower looked lumpish and unwieldy. It was evident at that moment that Josette was fighting her own conflicting demons, for she reacted nervously, her voice strident.

"Oh, I couldn't possibly wear that."

"But why, Mademoiselle?"

"It's . . . well, it's too cumbersome. It doesn't go with my dress."

"But it will bring you happiness."

"Please, Angelique, this is no time to indulge in silly superstitions."

Angelique turned away, the agony of her desperation forcing hot tears to her eyes. Josette was astonished. "What? Why are you crying? Are you angry with me?"

"I had nothing to give you, Mademoiselle, for your wedding. Only something from my heart. And you hate it!"

"But, Angelique . . ."

"I-I have failed you."

Josette looked to the countess for support, but for once that arbiter off all things suitable felt compassion for Angelique, and she responded to what she perceived to be a tender gesture. "Oh, wear the little amulet. What does it matter? It will make her happy, and she has served you well."

Josette turned to Angelique, fighting her simple wish to have her dress flawless. Finally, her gentleness prevailed over her vanity.

"I will wear the amulet," she said.

"Thank you, Mademoiselle," Angelique responded, and she knelt and pinned the flower to the dress.

The wedding party waited in the drawing room for the bride to appear, and the minister, who had been called to the house with very little notice, became perturbed and then embarrassed for the bridegroom. The countess was dispatched to fetch Josette and she returned with a bewildered look on her face. "She isn't there," she said unhappily. "Josette isn't in her room. She's disappeared."

To Angelique's amazement, the spell had overpowered them, and the hapless pair had fled together. When it was discovered that Josette was missing with

Jeremiah, even though Jeremiah's departure had been expected, there was great consternation in the house. André was more than distressed, and Barnabas was perplexed when he learned that both of their horses were gone from the stable and the stable man revealed they had left together. He fought torturous suspicions, insisting that, "Jeremiah and I are like brothers. It is inconceivable that he would ever do anything to deceive me."

Nearly hysterical with worry for Josette's safety, Barnabas convinced André to search the woods even though the storm still raged. He took his pistols in case they found her kidnapped or in danger. But Angelique knew he would find nothing, and she prayed that when he finally accepted the bitter truth of Josette's betrayal, he could come to her for solace. He would be so changed, so contrite. As ashamed as she was of her meddling, Angelique felt that there had been no other way. The couple were probably married already and hidden away in some roadside inn. Besides, they were happy together now, and in love with one another, so what did it matter. She had only to wait for Barnabas to remember how much she had once meant to him in Martinique. Then she would have him in her arms again.

But the weary and disillusioned man who returned from his failed search scarcely noticed her when she appeared in the hallway. He had found Josette's shawl, torn and clinging to a tree branch, and he held it in his hands, looking down at it as though it were a talisman.

"Has there been any news?" she asked, feigning concern.

"Nothing of importance."

"You must take off those wet clothes and then you should rest. You must be tired after all that you've been through." She wanted to go to him, but the coldness in his demeanor stopped her. He looked at her and seemed to sense what she was thinking. Bitterly, almost resentfully, he said to her, "In spite of all that I've been through, I still love her. Do you understand that? No matter what has happened or will happen, I will always love her."

chapter

29

When Josette and Jeremiah returned, enervated and listless, they were unable to defend their reckless adventure, even to themselves. Barnabas, numb with shock, sought an audience.

"Are you married?" he asked in a dull voice.

Josette looked at him, her eyes brimming with tears. "Yes," she said helplessly, "we are married."

"I demand an explanation . . . of this perfidy . . . this betrayal!"

"We have none," admitted Jeremiah. "Somehow, we could not fight ourselves."

Barnabas was enraged. Seizing Jeremiah's glove, he whipped it across his astonished face. "Then you will fight me!" he cried. "I will avenge this dishonor!" Jeremiah bore the insult with stoicism. There was no choice for either but a duel.

All the family begged them to abstain, each attempting in his or her own way to plead restraint. But Barnabas was fixed, determined, and Jeremiah followed his lead like a man in a trance. Guilt so oppressed his spirit that he wished only to die.

Angelique tried as well to change Barnabas's mind, but he would not listen to her. On the morning of the duel, she was able to press upon him a medal which would protect him, and, almost not noticing, he allowed her to hang it about his neck.

However, as things turned out, he had no need for her charm. As the two rivals paced off the count and turned to face one another, only Barnabas aimed with intent to kill. When Jeremiah fell, Josette, her whole being wrenched by loss of her true love and the near death of her husband, turned on Barnabas in hysterical accusation. "You monster! You madman! You couldn't bear to see us happy. You have killed the only man I have ever loved!"

After the duel, Josette spent all her time at Jeremiah's bedside, weeping as though her life were over as well. Jeremiah's face had been blown away, and his head was wrapped in bandages. He never responded, never spoke again. Everyone in the house knew he would not survive, that it was only a matter of time until it was over. Barnabas could not bear to face Josette, and, as the days went by, he became more responsive to Angelique, if only to accept her many gestures of kindness.

One evening he sat, dejected and disconsolate, by the fire, and listlessly allowed her to massage his forehead. "You see," she said. "I can be useful!" She could feel the warmth entering her fingertips, and was elated by the pleasure of touching him at last, stroking him, drinking in his presence.

But Barnabas's mind was elsewhere; he seemed hardly to know she was there. "Is your headache gone?" she asked.

He started at her words. "What?"

"I only wondered what you could be thinking."

"I was wondering . . . tell me . . . What do you make of Reverend Trask?"

Angelique considered his question. Because of the countess's unceasing protestations that sorcery was at work in the household, a renowned witch-hunter had been summoned from Salem.

"I believe the witch should be found and destroyed," Angelique answered. "Reverend Trask is a devout clergyman, is he not?"

"I think he is a charlatan and a hypocrite."

"But if the governess is indeed a witch, won't he reveal it?" Phyllis Wick, Sarah's tutor, a new addition to the domestic staff, had impressed the family as a very odd person. She was high-strung and nervous, lacking in social charm. She rarely spoke to anyone and never smiled. Even Sarah was afraid of her. Angelique welcomed the suspicious feelings aimed at the governess, for it had taken all the attention away from her.

"Phyllis Wick is not capable of harming anyone," Barnabas said.

"How else can you explain the strange things happening in this house?"

"I am convinced that the governess had nothing to do with it."

Angelique saw the opportunity to argue a point, and she could not let it pass. "You must admit, Barnabas, you haven't always been the best judge of women."

"You're referring to Josette . . ." he said bitterly, taking the bait.

"Did you judge her well? You believed she loved you, but did she? She deceived you. With a member of your own family."

"Please, Angelique, don't . . ." He rose and walked away from her, and she felt her anger flare.

"Can't you bear to hear the truth?"

"I don't want to think about her."

"Why, because you still love her?"

"No."

"Do you hate her?"

"Yes."

"Say it. Say that you hate her!"

"I . . . despise her!"

His face was contorted, drawn with pain. When she saw his expression, she felt a wave of weakness flow through her, and she fought it, saying bitterly, "In time you will mean that."

"I mean it now."

He seemed sincere, or at least resolved. Unable to restrain herself, she went to him, hesitated, then moved into his arms, drawing him to her and feeling the warmth of his body against hers. His nearness gave her strength. "Barnabas . . . you loved me once. You could love me again. I love you with all my heart. I can make you forget all your griefs, all your disappointments. Won't you give me the chance to make you happy?"

He looked down at her, a quizzical expression in his eyes, and she could feel him trembling. The strain of the past few days had deepened the lines in his face, and a profound weariness seemed wrapped around his spirit. His voice was very soft, almost a whisper, when he said, "Yes, I will." And he crushed her to him and kissed her deeply.

Her heart flooded with joy. "Will you come to my room later tonight?"

He nodded, his breath warm on her neck.

"Do you promise?"

"Yes. Yes, I promise."

That night, however, Jeremiah breathed his last, and the house was shrouded in gloom. Various members of the family milled back and forth in the hallway, sometimes looking in on Josette as she sat mourning at his bedside, a dull expression on her face. It was Joshua who finally covered the figure with a sheet and ordered the body to be wrapped in a shroud. Jeremiah was to be buried in the Collins mausoleum. The family used the funeral as an excuse to finally vacate the old house and move to the new estate, Collinwood, which had recently been completed and was the finest mansion in the county.

One evening, as she had every evening, Angelique waited in her room in the new servants' quarters, but she knew Barnabas would not come to her. Now that he had finally responded to her, she was frantic to think that Josette was free once again. She sat on her bed and stared at the sack of herbs open on her lap.

Unable to resist, she pulled loose the wrinkled *ouanga* and untied the dried-up knot. The moonstone flashed as vibrant as ever, and, as she rolled it in her palm, she was suddenly wrenched by sobs of helplessness.

She felt as though slivers of hatred and jealousy were slicing her thoughts to ribbons. Josette had never given Barnabas reason to hope. Every moment since her marriage she had been a faithful and devoted wife to Jeremiah, as it was her nature to be virtuous and true. However, Barnabas did hope; deep in his heart, he longed to be reunited with Josette. Oh, why had Jeremiah died? It was the cruelest twist of fate, when the spell had worked so miraculously. But she could not control everything. The *Bokor* had been the prophet, and Jeremiah's death was the consequence.

"You will never know when your powers will fail you." The Devil had spoken these words. Perfectly aware that she was flirting with disaster, Angelique crept out of the house just before midnight. She took with her the loaded pistol that had inflicted the fatal wound, stolen from Barnabas's chamber. As she crossed the wide lawn on the way to the cemetery, her heart beat wildly and her throat clenched tight with dread. Could she remember the spell? She had not called up the dead since the *Bokor* had taught her the incantation in Martinique—a dangerous spell, difficult to execute, more difficult to control. But it was necessary that Jeremiah remain close to Josette, still claiming her as his own. Angelique would not think about the outcome.

The mausoleum gleamed white in the moonlight,

and she approached the door with renewed determination. She pulled at the iron ring, and the heavy vault sprang open. Jeremiah's marble tomb lay on the pedestal. The acacia leaves fell from her fingers on the sepulchre, and she stirred them into newly dug soil. She lit each of the four white candles and set them at the corners of the room. When she heard the distant thunder, her heart echoed the pounding. She drew herself up like a statue, but when she lifted the pistol, she saw that her hand was shaking. She fired the first shot, and the explosion rent her ears and ricocheted off the inner walls. In a wavering voice, drawn from a savage place within her that was deeper than any memory, she began the incantation.

"Spirit of Jeremiah, fading now, departing, I require you to return to the land of the living. Come to me now, and do my bidding." She stiffened, dreading the jolt she knew would come, fearing the pain in her gut; but there was none, only a deep vibration within the stones of the building. She took courage. "Do not vanish, Jeremiah, do not flee, for you are needed here once more. Join not your ancestors at this time, but rise, and walk among us, that we may know you and endure your presence."

The roof rumbled and the stones beneath her feet shifted, then shook with a violent heaving, as though an explosion had taken place deep in the earth. Again she lifted the pistol and fired. This time the sepulchre shuddered, and she stood aghast as, with a grinding sound, incredibly, the heavy marble covering inched sideways on its coffin and the dark opening loomed from within. There was a flickering movement, and a yellow hand reached out and groped for the air.

The Reverend Trask conducted intense interrogations of every member of the Collins household. He wasted little time with Angelique, who was able to convince him that she was a devout Catholic trained by nuns in Martinique. It was unfortunate, however, that Barnabas was forced to witness Trask's questioning of Josette. She was even more lovely than before, as her grief bestowed on her an ethereal resignation. Her black lace of mourning shadowed her face, revealing the exquisite delicacy of her features.

As Angelique watched Barnabas, she could see that he was moved. It was impossible to believe that he despised Josette as he had maintained, for his expression was one of utter remorse and total sympathy. Ironically, her suffering had given Josette's character greater depth. She had acquired a soulfulness unsullied by pride, and perceptiveness and sensitivity shone from her eyes. Her gentleness and humility impressed even the Reverend. When he discovered the mark of the pitchfork on Josette's hand, he cried out, "This is a sign! A sign of the Devil! The Devil destroys goodness and purity wherever he finds it!"

"Please . . . it's only a bruise . . ." Josette protested helplessly.

"It is the brand of the Devil!" he thundered ominously. "He places it on those he wishes to entice!" And then he made his most disturbing pronouncement. "You are possessed!"

Barnabas frowned, and a darkness fell over his countenance. He still failed to come to Angelique's room as he had promised, and when she questioned him one morning, he simply stared at her and said, "Angelique, I'm sorry. I cannot give you what you want."

"But, why?" She knew what he would say.

"Because . . . I love Josette. I love her still. I know it's difficult for you to understand. It's difficult for me as well. I-I still love her. In spite of everything, I worship her."

"Have you been with her?"

"Yes, but only to exchange a few words."

"What did she say to you?"

"She said nothing, except that Jeremiah was her husband and she will be faithful to his memory." Angelique secretly rejoiced, but at the same time, she was very nearly moved to tears. She ran to him and took his face in her hands.

"Look at me, Barnabas, please, think back. I could fill your life with happiness. That's all I want. Don't you know that? Let me love you, let me give you joy, I can—I will—"

But he placed his fingers over her mouth to stop her words, and said gently. "Don't. Don't torture yourself. Try to understand. I want Josette. I'll never stop wanting her. I'm not capable of loving anyone except Josette."

"But she deceived you, and betrayed you!"

He turned to the fire, a confused look on his face. "Perhaps . . . what happened . . . wasn't entirely her fault. Perhaps she is under some kind of . . . spell." He laughed weakly at his own ridiculous conjecture.

Angelique felt her heart harden, and she moved away from him. "So once again you are telling me that I am not good enough for you."

"Angelique, please . . . that isn't true."

"That you prefer to believe you love a scheming, conniving . . . *liar,* who has no feelings for you, over a devoted . . . attentive—"

"Angelique . . . you are a beautiful girl. I am alone now. It would be so easy for me to pretend that—that I care for you. I could effortlessly make love to you again. But it wouldn't be fair to you. Don't you see that? It would be cruel to deceive you."

But she could not see it. Once again he had allowed her to hope, set her bright dreams on the precipice of a new existence, then plunged them heartlessly, viciously, into the dark. A vile taste came to her mouth. "Your cruelty began in Martinique, Barnabas," she said. "That was when you deceived me. A long time ago."

Sarah's little cloth doll lay on Angelique's dresser with the long thin hatpins alongside. Angelique paced the room, covetous rancor filling her soul. She was beyond caring whether the Devil noticed her sorcery or even whether her need for vengeance destroyed an innocent child. She was amazed at her own coldness, her bitterness, and her overwhelming desire to make Barnabas suffer. A sea of troubles would not be enough to repay him for the heartache he had caused her.

Once she had been a child near Sarah's age. The desperate man who believed he was her father had imprisoned her and used her as a charm to manipulate others. How different was she? At last she understood his insidious design. Perhaps she did have his vile blood in her veins after all. She snatched up the doll and summoned the snake of flame as easily as if she had been taking a single breath.

Quivering with hatred, she said, "Sarah . . . your dear little sister . . . when you see her suffer, Barnabas, you will suffer as well." Then, grimacing, she added, "You are going to regret abandoning me, Barnabas. Someday you will wish you loved me still."

And, with vicious intent, she stabbed the pin into the soft blue cloth, another, and a third. In her mind's eye she saw Sarah cry out and fall to the floor, the governess's worried look, the family rushing to her, and Barnabas's anguished face.

When Angelique heard the knock at her door, she swiftly hid the doll beneath her pillow. Barnabas burst into the room, his face destroyed with worry.

"Have you seen Sarah's little doll," he cried. "The little blue doll with the white apron. She is crying for it, and we can't seem to find it anywhere."

"No. Why would it be in here?" she asked in an icy tone.

"I thought I saw you pick it up earlier."

"I put it with her toys. Please, leave my room, and don't bother me again."

He paced, casting about as though he was sure he could find it. "It's just that she's so very ill, and crying for it, and I've looked everywhere, I thought perhaps—"

"Sarah's ill?"

"Yes. It's unbelievable. She had terrible pains and collapsed suddenly."

"The poor child! Did you send for a doctor?"

"Yes, of course, but he said there's nothing he can do. My mother is hysterical. The whole family is completely overcome with grief. The doctor . . . said . . . she may not live through the day."

"Where are her pains?"

"Oh . . . I don't know . . . her shoulder and her stomach. She sobs hysterically, and then screams and doubles up as though she were being stabbed. Oh, God! It is more than I can bear. She is so young, and I love her so much. I don't think she's going to live!" He collapsed, sat on the bed, and buried his face in his hands.

Angelique moved to Barnabas and placed a hand on his shoulder. "Listen to me, Barnabas. There is the chance that I might be able to help her."

"You? How can you pretend to know more than the doctor?"

"I . . . had an illness very much like the one you describe when I was a child. I almost died from it. I would have if my mother hadn't known what to do. She brewed a tea for me of special herbs. After I drank it, I was well again. Shall I brew the tea for Sarah?"

"What possible good will a tea do?"

"It may have some restorative powers. It can't do her any harm."

"All right. I'm willing to try anything." He looked at her with vague interest. "You did tell me once that your mother was a healer, I remember. . . ."

She walked to her dresser, her manner deceptively calm although her pulse was racing, and she turned to him. "If I should cure Sarah, you'd be very grateful to me, would you not?"

"Of course. I would be indebted to you for the rest of my life."

"There is one way you could repay that debt."

"Angelique, I'll give you whatever you want, but I don't think herbs and potion—"

"There is one thing I want. More than anything."

"If you were to cure Sarah, I'd give it to you," he said wearily.

"I want you to make me your wife."

"My wife!"

"Is the price too high?"

"But Angelique . . ." He sighed, looking at her with total incredulity.

"If she lives . . . will you make me your wife?"

He hesitated, then sighed again deeply. "I would do anything, yes, yes, anything, naturally, if somehow you could save her."

After Sarah drank the tea, Angelique returned to her own room and removed the pins, slowly, one by one. The tight feeling in her own chest relaxed. She found that she was relieved that Sarah had not died. Pity for the child came over her, and hot tears sprang to her eyes. Was she ashamed? All she thought was that Barnabas would be so grateful to her, so overjoyed, that he would come to her room at any moment to thank her and embrace her. But he did not come.

The next morning she found him reading in the drawing room, and her heart flew out to him when she saw him.

"Barnabas. Good morning."

"Angelique."

"How is Sarah?"

"Much better. It's amazing, her illness disappeared as quickly as it had come."

Why did he say nothing? He had been willing to bargain last evening, but now he seemed oblivious. Surely he had not forgotten. She tried to quell her anxiety, but her eagerness was such that, since he had not mentioned his pledge to her, she felt she must broach the subject.

"Barnabas?"

He looked up.

"How soon will you tell your family?" She forced gaiety into her tone. "It will be quite a surprise to them that we are to be married."

"What? We never spoke of marriage."

"We did. Don't you remember? Once again you promised to marry me."

"But . . . I thought Sarah was going to die. I was desperate . . . forgive me, but you must know I would not make such a promise in any other situation . . . besides, I do not think your tea had anything to do with it. Herbal medicine is primitive and . . . it was a coincidence, that's all. Surely you understand."

Angelique turned away, her face burning.

"Don't say any more. I do understand. I understand perfectly. I love you, but you cannot love me, and you cannot accept me as your wife. I must concede that you find me unworthy. That you always have. Your duplicity knows no bounds. You betrayed me in Martinique, and you have betrayed me once again, heartlessly, without shame, making rash promises only to secure your own desires."

Barnabas rose and stared into the fire. "Let me ask you something, Angelique. Could you accept me, become my wife, could you endure that, knowing my feelings for Josette?"

"All I know is that I love you, more than anything . . . more than my life."

"Then . . . I won't break my promise."

She looked at him, not believing what he had just said. He continued. "If you will accept me—as I am—then I will marry you, Angelique, and try to make you happy."

For a moment she was stunned. Then he looked at her, and somehow she found the words to answer him. "I will be an obedient and devoted wife throughout our married life," she said, her heart soaring. "You are all my world, and I will love you and cherish you always."

As was expected, Barnabas's father exploded with fury. Nothing could have inspired his virulence more than for his son to marry beneath his rank. He felt certain that Angelique had taken advantage of Barnabas following his disappointment with Josette, and to him, the marriage was nothing more than "a devil's bargain." He insisted that she present herself to him.

As she waited outside the drawing room, Angelique overheard Joshua Collins expostulating with Naomi, Barnabas's mother. "Tact? Why do you insist on tact? Tact is not important when addressing a servant! Is this peasant girl your idea of a daughter-in-law?"

So he is to be difficult, she thought. She vowed to remain composed and respectful, and not be intimidated. Naomi hushed him as Angelique entered the room.

"Come here," Joshua ordered her. "No, you are not to sit. Stand while I am speaking to you!"

Angelique said nothing, waiting for him to continue.

"So you wish to marry my son."

"He wishes to marry me, sir."

"He did not phrase it in that manner. His voice was completely lacking in emotion."

"It is not so when he speaks to me, sir."

Joshua paused. "Why do you wish to marry him?"

"I love him."

He scoffed at this remark and turned his back on her. She could see that contempt for her had poisoned his heart.

"A reason," he said, "I find most incomprehensible." He turned to Naomi, and said, "Her love has sprung from nowhere! Perhaps I don't understand about love."

Naomi looked at Angelique, and she thought she saw some sympathy registered there.

Joshua continued, "I find it appalling to speak of love between two people who can't have spent more than an hour in each other's presence."

Angelique felt she must defend herself. "I have spent many hours with Barnabas—"

"You have taken gross advantage of him, in a time of personal grief."

"The circumstances are not important. We would have married anyway."

Joshua eyed her coldly. "Gentlemen are not in the habit of marrying servant girls."

His words stung, and she took a deep breath before responding. "I entered your house as a servant, sir. But I understand in this great democracy of yours it is no crime to rise above your station in life and change your circumstances."

Joshua continued to watch her carefully. "It is understandable that you would want to change your circumstances," he said. "I have an offer for you."

"I have the only offer I desire, sir."

"How much do you want?"

She was surprised. So that was his plan, to bribe her away.

"I only want your goodwill, sir, and your blessing."

Joshua assumed a proud stance, lifting his chin. "That . . . you will never have!" He paused and his gray eyes appraised her coolly. "Ten thousand," he said. "In gold. A small enough ransom to pay for my son's future. What do you say?"

She shook her head. "Surely you don't believe I would—"

"You want more?" He paused. "Twenty thousand and be done with it!"

Angelique spoke slowly. "Monsieur Collins, there is no sum great enough for me to abandon Barnabas. I love your son and—"

"Come, girl, think what you are doing. You could return to Martinique a wealthy woman. Open a shop, or buy a small plantation. You could be admired. A fine lady in your world. Whereas, if you insist on this . . . this connection, I will disown Barnabas and you will have secured both his dishonor and his penury."

So that was the way it was. Barnabas had still not been granted his inheritance. At one time, before she had been with Barnabas in Martinique, such a sum of money would given her all she could desire. But now there was nothing she could ever want save the love of the man she worshiped. Her mind was clear, and she had never been more confident.

"All I ask is that you try to accept me, Mr. Collins. I will always treat you with respect, but I do not love Barnabas for your fortune or his. I love him for his fine character, his generosity, and his noble spirit. I hope you will give me a chance. But if you do not, I fear your life will be all the lonelier."

Her eyes fell on Naomi, who looked up at her and smiled faintly.

Joshua was inflexible and refused to be placated. He raged at Barnabas.

"I cut you off without a penny! I have written you out of my will, and you are no longer a member of this family. You will both leave this house, by nightfall, and never return. I will never speak to you again. I am no longer your father, and you are no longer my son."

Tenderhearted Naomi, however, gave Barnabas the deed to the old house as a wedding present, and there Angelique and Barnabas were to reside. The ceremony was to be a small affair; the only attendants were to be Naomi, who refused to question or chastise her beloved son, and Ben, who was Angelique's sole acquaintance. Joshua refused to be present.

Naomi, however, graciously accepted Angelique as Barnabas's chosen bride, and she even found a simple white dress for Angelique to wear. Preparing for the ceremony in her room, Angelique looked at herself in the mirror. She was disappointed in the gown, but there was nothing she could do. She made some small adjustment with the sleeves and lifted the skirt to see if it would fall more gracefully, but it was stiff and of poor material. Wistfully, she remembered the watered taffeta in the shop in Martinique, when all her dreams had soared with love.

That seemed so long ago, and she now had her wish: She had won him over at last, if not by love, then by weariness, and Barnabas was waiting for her downstairs in the drawing room. Suddenly Angelique drew back in dismay, gasping at her reflection. It was impossible! How could that be? Her skirt was pure white, without blemish, but, to her horror, the dress in the mirror was streaked with blood!

"You look very pretty," Naomi said, obviously seeing nothing, as Angelique attempted to hide her shocked reaction. "My dear, what is it?"

Angelique felt the fear crawl across her neck, but she tried not to reveal it. "I-I so wanted to look like a bride. And you were generous to give me this dress, but it is so . . . plain." Naomi came up to her and pinned a small gold-and-ivory cameo to Angelique's bodice. "This was my mother's brooch," she said. "I want you to have it." And she kissed her gently.

Angelique felt her thoughts swim when she looked down at the pin, and her eyes filled with tears.

"Why, my dear, what is it?" Naomi said. "Why are you crying?"

"I'm crying from happiness," she answered, and it was partially true. "It has been so long since anyone was kind to me. I am so grateful to you. And I will never forget you." Naomi embraced her with pity and affection, almost as though she understood Angelique's distress somewhere in her own heart.

The ceremony proceeded without incident, although the bride was vague and distracted. Barnabas pronounced his vows stiffly, as though he were performing a recitation, but he maintained his composure valiantly, and even smiled at Angelique as she pledged her love. At last she heard the Reverend's final words, "By the powers invested in me, I pronounce you man and wife. What God has joined together, let no man put asunder." All Angelique could think was how joyless it all had been.

"We should have had flowers," she said sadly. "I

love flowers, and there are so many where I come from."

"We have champagne," said Barnabas with a determined effort at gaiety. "Ben, as the best man, you shall make the toast." Ben lumbered out and returned with the champagne and the glasses, and set them on the table, while Naomi and Angelique stood waiting in silence. When Barnabas took up the bottle to pour a glass for Angelique, she felt the same creeping shiver of fear.

Naomi gasped, and Barnabas drew back, his face a mask of disgust. To everyone's horror, the champagne in the glass was viscous and crimson.

"What is it?" Angelique whispered. "This isn't champagne. . . ."

"No!" Barnabas said, stupefied. "It—it's blood!"

She looked up and saw his face, contorted, not comprehending, and she dashed from the parlor and up to her room, where she looked wildly around at the walls, the windows.

"You have come back, haven't you? You never left me! Where are you now?" she cried. "Why must you torment me?"

There was no answer, only the clawing of branches against the windowpanes. She ran and threw open the casement, stared down at the dark trees. "Answer me! Why will you never leave me be?"

A cold blast of air struck her in the face, and she gasped and pulled back, slamming the casement, but the latch failed to catch and the window battered against the frame. All at once there was a shuffling sound outside her door. She whirled. "It's you, isn't it? Isn't it? Answer me!"

Incredibly, at that moment, she heard a tinkling sound, a musical chiming that she had never heard before. A music box, encrusted with jewels, stood open on the top of her bureau. Trembling, she walked toward it, wondering where it could have come from. It was exquisite, skillfully formed, with Baroque cupids in high relief and made of solid gold. Never had she seen anything more beautiful. Her heart soared as she realized that it must be a present from Barnabas, a wedding present, and she took it up tentatively. How could she have ever doubted him? He had bought her this beautiful gift. The delicate box played a charming tune, like rain on a silver drum, and she listened to it with her whole heart. She was about to go to him when the door flew open, and he was there.

His face was livid. "Where did you get that?" he cried sharply.

"It—it was here, on the dresser."

"Give it to me!" He snatched it away. Instantly she understood.

"It's hers, isn't it! It's Josette's!"

He answered her vaguely, "No, it's mine."

"But you bought it for her, didn't you?"

"Yes, yes . . ."

"Why is it here? Why is it in my room? I found it here."

"I don't know. I don't know how it came here. But it won't be for long!" He turned and strode from the chamber, as she screamed after him.

"You love her! You love her still!" The door was slammed in her face. Furious, she reached for the handle to follow him, and flung it open.

"You love her—" She gasped and pulled back, staring out at the appalling, unbelievable thing standing in the hallway, some man, but not a man, some creature whose face was wrapped in tattered rags, streaming with blood and pus. She smelled the odor of rotted flesh, and her eyes stung with the foul emanations of a walking corpse. Something about the figure was familiar, and beneath the filth of the attire she recognized the brocaded waistcoat that had belonged to Jeremiah.

"No-o-o-o-o!" she screamed, backing away. "Stay away from me!" But the apparition approached her, reaching out. As he drew closer, she could see that one eye had fallen from the socket and lay against his cheek.

"Why are you here? Who sent you?"

The frayed lips did not move, but the voice echoed from within the decaying body, a guttural monotone that bubbled with phlegm.

"You have disturbed my rest."

"No! No! I did not!"

"You must be punished for what you have done. You must learn what it is to live without peace in the land of the dead."

She stood her ground and threw up her hand to stop him, but he continued to approach, his bony fingers stretched out before him like a blind man. In the iciest voice she could muster, she intoned the Devil, searching for the force within her limp, terrified body. "I-I call on you, Dark Spirit . . . Beelzebub . . . to save me! Return this phantom to his grave!" But her incantation was feeble, and Jeremiah did not stop his slow shuffling. She screamed, "Go! Back to the earth of which you are a part! I command you to go!"

The voice whined, "You will not sleep until I sleep. You will have no rest until I have my eternal rest. "

"Who controls you? Whose power are you following?" she shouted, hysterical now, but he had her, and her screams were in vain. He lifted her in his oozing arms and pressed her to him, burying her face in his emaciated chest, and he flew with her, out the window and down among the trees. She fainted, and when she awoke, he was standing beside her, and she was lying in an open grave.

She could see the walls of newly excavated dirt surrounding her, and she could smell the putrid odor of the dead, as the fiend began to shovel the moldy soil over her face.

She screamed, "Ben! Ben! Help me!" But her lungs filled with dust, and blackness closed in on her. The weight of the earth was on her body, pressing down on her more as each shovelful fell, and there was no air—no air left—in her lonely tomb.

Unconsciousness had folded around her mind when she felt Ben's thick fingers in her mouth, digging for the dirt, and she heaved up with spasms of choking and coughing as he lifted her out of the hole.

"You've done it now, haven't you?" he said, not unkindly. "Something turned on you for a change." Roughly, he brushed the grime from her face and dress, then picked her up and carried her, still whimpering, back to the house.

She sobbed and babbled incoherently, her voice smothered in his neck. "He came for me! He tried to kill me! I'll never do anything again, Ben. I'll never cast another spell. I won't!"

He placed her in the empty bed, and she remembered, as he pulled the cover over her, that this was her wedding night, the night she had dreamed of and longed for through years of loneliness. She felt for the broach Naomi had given her and found it gone. "Ben," she said in a hoarse whisper, "please . . . go back. . . . I've lost the cameo, the gift from Barnabas's mother . . . find it, please . . . it's in . . . the grave. . . ."

chapter

30

Suspicion reigned in the Collins household. The many untoward occurrences were adding up to one thing—the presence of a witch. Even those who had eschewed superstition were swayed. Joshua seethed with contempt for the whole idea, but he was helpless to explain Barnabas's choking, Sarah's sudden illness and just as sudden recovery, Josette's reversal of affections, not to mention his own son's inexplicable marriage to a common servant girl. Even Ben had fallen prey to the sorcery, for he had been caught robbing graves late one night, and was now in the county jail.

The word *witch* was irrationally and irresponsibly bandied about among the members of the Collins family, but everyone in his or her own way was unable to explain what was referred to as "these strange goings-on." The time had come for Angelique to protect herself. Even Barnabas looked at her now with a cold expression in his eyes. She knew the signs would point in her direction if people began to investigate, and her only choice was to throw suspicion onto

Phyllis Wick. The hapless governess with her gloomy manner was the perfect culprit.

The family, so concerned about what the countess continued to refer to as "an evil force in this house," meaning the house where Barnabas now resided with Angelique, had summoned the Reverend Trask a second time, and he had agreed to perform an exorcism. Barnabas, taking pity on Phyllis, and believing her to be innocent, had given her shelter in an upstairs room, where she was hiding from the accusations of Trask, too terrified to face him. The stage, therefore, was set for Phyllis Wick to be exposed.

Angelique decided to build a house of cards— tarot cards. The countess, who possessed several decks, had left a set in the parlor. It seemed fitting that the countess, who had begun all the talk of witchcraft, should now supply the means for Angelique to make the spell of her own disguise.

Angelique retired to her old room in the servants' quarters, where she knew no one would find her. The window was close enough to the front door for her to hear the ravings of the charlatan, Reverend Trask, who was soon to begin his invocation. How impotent his powers were compared to hers! The so-called Reverend was a feeble quack, but he would be useful nevertheless, and his flaccid conjurations would serve their purpose.

Delicately, she erected the house of cards on the bare table, carefully balancing the beautifully painted symbols in leaning pairs, creating twice, a roof for the next level. The house of cards, which could have collapsed with one breath, held steady, and its lightness would give it wings. She spoke to it with her mind.

"You are the halls of the room where Phyllis Wick is hiding. You are the place where she is lying now. First the chilling wind, and then the fire. That room is here, completely within my power."

Angelique could hear the Reverend's nasal voice as he began. "I call the Powers of Light to come to do battle with the Powers of Darkness. Phyllis Wick, I give warning that the Powers of Light are at hand, and they are about to strike your very soul! Your destruction is at hand! Come forth! Surrender yourself!"

Angelique knew that he had drawn a sign of exorcism in the dirt outside the door, for he cried out, "Phyllis Wick, the dust now knows your name, and the earth shall proclaim it to the sky! Come forth, before the burning fires of Hell consume you forever!"

She could picture poor Phyllis huddled in the corner of her room, afraid to move or breathe, terrified of the Reverend's admonishments and his self-righteous commands. Angelique had a flickering vision of another time and place, where she had been that same cowering wretch, but the image faded as swiftly as it had come, and she returned to her task. The girl would never show herself, unless she was forced to do so. Angelique, shrugging off thoughts of the depravity she was uncovering, or of the malevolent being to whom she was speaking, began the incantation. She lit the taper and held the flame to the fragile dwelling that protected an innocent girl. She began to chant.

"I call upon the Heart of Fire that burns within

the Heart of Ice." She trembled. She fully realized what she was doing now. She had fallen so far that she would ask for the Devil's help. She could hear Trask calling as well, as though they were working in consort, creating a force of their blended wills.

"Evil! Show thyself! Come forth to this threshold! Cross from darkness into light! Before the burning fires of goodness drive you forth in terror and in fear!"

The house of cards flared and burst into flame, and Angelique felt her body engulfed by the heat. The charge flowed from her fingertips and streamed from her lips.

"Heart of Fire," she whispered, "that burns in the Heart of Ice. Fire that freezes and does not consume itself. I summon the Eye of Fire that burns within the Icy Eye and watches over all things evil. I call it to the room of my own choosing. Heart of Fire. Heart of Ice. Fiery eye of coldest Evil. I command you to come. Come, and burn! Burn! Burn! Burn!" Angelique knew the fire was beginning in Phyllis's room now, snaking across the floor, and the terrified girl was cringing in dread. "Eye of Fire. Heart of Ice. I summon you from the icy waters of the world beyond—"

There was a sound outside her door, footsteps, someone passing down the hall. They paused, and in that instant she thought she saw the knob turning from the pressure of an unseen hand. But at that same moment, Phyllis Wick screamed, "Fire! Help! Someone help me! Fire!" and the footsteps sped away.

Phyllis Wick rushed down the stairs and into the arms of the jubilant Reverend Trask. He caught her to him, and shouted maniacally, "The Powers of Darkness are conquered now! The Powers of Light are triumphant! Down on your knees, Sorceress! Down! Down! I have the witch! I have the witch!"

As the Reverend Trask led the helpless Phyllis away, Barnabas displayed the first tender emotions Angelique had seen in weeks. Instinctively he seemed to know that the governess was innocent, and to Angelique's increasing irritation, he assured Phyllis that he would do everything within his capacity to see that she was released.

Barnabas knew something; Angelique could feel it in his manner and see it in the coldness of his gaze. Had he been the phantom outside her door? But if he suspected her, he had no proof. Ben was the only person who knew the truth. Ben was in prison, and if Barnabas were to visit him and Ben uttered one word against her, he would grow mute.

Still, her husband's glacial manner and hostile responses to all her inquiries took their toll. He appeared to be suppressing a palpable rage, and it filled the air between them with a sour odor. Whenever she spoke to him, he answered with a few indifferent words; and whenever she moved to caress him, he drew away.

At other times, incredibly, he was almost kind to her, and all her hopes rekindled. If he were merely civil, she counted the politeness more than the coldness. When she felt his antipathy, she only hoped that one day he would realize that all she had done was for love of him. Her actions, which might appear so ruthless, were desperate attempts to regain his love by whatever means she could. It would all be worth it if he returned to her again.

One evening, to her complete surprise, he came back after a long day away from the house, and when she asked whether he had been to the shipyards, he answered her with unexpected friendliness. "I seem to have acquired a chill riding home from the village," he said. "I believe I'll have a glass of sherry. Will you join me?"

His invitation was so unusual that she was at a loss. He went to the cabinet and took out the goblets. After he had poured the sherry, he handed her the glass, and retired to the chair by the fire. Joyfully she joined him, sitting on the floor at his feet. For a fleeting moment she felt a surge of happiness. Although they had been married for several weeks, they had not yet slept in the same bed, and she was beginning to realize what he had meant when he had told her she must accept marriage to him in the full knowledge that he did not love her. Perhaps tonight things would be different.

"I have a proposal," she said brightly. "I would like to take a wedding trip. Get away from all this."

Barnabas's voice was flat. "I don't think it's possible to ever escape everything that has happened here."

She placed an arm across his knee, felt him flinch, but persevered. "I can make you forget," she said, smiling up at him.

"How would you do that?"

"By loving you."

He was watching her intently, and just as she was about to put the sherry to her lips, there was a knock at the door. Angelique rose to open it, and Naomi entered, looking concerned.

"Barnabas. I heard what happened. Are you all right?"

"Yes, perfectly fine."

"What do you mean?" Angelique inquired.

"Didn't he tell you? He went to visit Ben in the jail, and that desperate ruffian struck him on the head with a bottle and escaped!"

"You were visiting Ben?" Angelique asked, disturbed by this revelation. What had he discovered?

Barnabas continued to reassure his mother, his mood still affable. "Really, Mother, he did me no harm. In fact, he was actually able to knock some sense into my head."

Angelique remembered her duties as a hostess and offered Naomi a glass of sherry, which Naomi gratefully accepted, needing something to calm her nerves. Since she had drunk not a sip of her own sherry, Angelique handed her goblet to Naomi and crossed to get another for herself.

Unaccountably, Barnabas became violently agitated and insisted that he could see a chip on the rim of his mother's goblet. Naomi waved him off and raised the sherry to her mouth, whereas he lurched forward, clumsily knocking the glass from his mother's hand, spilling the wine on her gown.

"Oh, Mother, forgive me! Look what I've done! I've ruined your dress."

"Please, dear, it is nothing," she responded. Angelique went numb, as suspicion worried its way into her mind. She dabbed at the spilled wine with her napkin, picked up the empty glass, and walked back to the serving table. Running her finger along the edge of the crystal, she discovered no chip. She sniffed the empty goblet and detected the unmistakable odor of poison.

Through the blur in her brain she could hear Naomi telling Barnabas that she had brought with her a package that had just arrived from France. As she watched Barnabas move eagerly toward the parcel, she was amazed at how, even at that moment, she loved him. His movements were vigorous and powerful, and his magnificent face was carved by elegant shadows. *Oh, that deceit should dwell in such a gorgeous palace . . .*

He leaned over and unwrapped the package with one graceful tug of the paper, stepped back, and breathed a sigh. It was a portrait of Josette.

"There's a note," Naomi said, glancing guiltily at Angelique. "What does it say?"

Barnabas read in a strained tone. "When my father insisted this be his wedding present to you, I laughed, and said, 'Papa, why does Barnabas need a portrait?' His voice broke at the next words. 'He will have me.'"

Angelique watched as he crumpled the note in his hand, and his shoulders sagged with weariness.

"You still love her, don't you?" she said. She saw his sorrowful face. "I'm only jealous. It's painful for me to see you looking at the portrait, when I love you so much."

"Angelique," he said grimly, "what do you think love is?"

So he hated her. He wanted her dead. The realization struck her like a blow in the chest, and suddenly she was aware that her heart had turned to stone, as hard and dense as coldest alabaster. She was without feeling. Barnabas was growing insane out of misery, and she was in mortal danger. Grief and suspicion had warped his judgment until now he was her bitterest enemy. She must find a way to protect herself, some way to survive his anger, his plotting, until he had regained some measure of reason. She must be wary now of his every move.

That evening, after they had both retired for the night, she formed the shape of a sleeping body in her bed and hid behind the door of her boudoir. Dreading the worst, and praying that she would be mistaken, she waited in the cold darkness until her limbs were stiff and aching from fatigue. The faint glimmer of moonlight cast flickering shadows across the room and she could see her reflection in the mirror opposite. She was shocked to observe that her image was ghastly and cadaverous, hovering in the gloom, as though it were the true reflection of her soul. Just as she was about to abandon her ambush and sink with weariness, she heard a sound outside her door, and the knob turned slowly. Stealthy, Barnabas entered the chamber and crept toward the bed.

She wanted to weep when she saw the knife raised in his hand, catching the light as it hovered, then plummeted, driven by his rage. Viciously, he stabbed the soft coverings. Then he stopped, puzzled, put down the knife, and jerked the quilts aside to reveal the empty bed. Suddenly, certain she was there, he whirled to face her, his chest heaving, his face glowering with fury.

"Do you hate me so much," she asked, swallowing a sob.

His voice was venomous. "You are the witch!"

She shook her head helplessly. "I never wanted you to know."

"I listened, outside your door, when you made Phyllis Wick run from the fire. I heard your incantation. I know everything, now."

"That I love you? Do you know that? That I love you still? That I will always love you?"

"Love! You and I define that differently, my dear! Your love is like venom! Bizarre! Corrupt! That is not love! It's obsession—perverse, misguided obsession! You have made me despise myself! You have ruined my life!"

He lunged for her with the knife, but she flung up her hand and stopped him, bracing herself for the flash of fire that spurted through her. As he cried out in pain, she sucked it in before the knife turned in his hand. He hurled it from him and, with a furious growl, reached for her with his bare hands, clawing the air around her neck, struggling to choke her.

But she stood her ground. Her body arched backward as fire flew from her eyes, and she said in a harsh whisper, her cheeks hot with tears, "You cannot kill me. You cannot touch me. I have many powers, Barnabas. Once long ago I tried to warn you, but now I am sorry that you must know the truth. You cannot come near me unless I will it."

Still he forced his hands toward her, grappling the air, greedy for her flesh, and he said, "I will despise you until I end your life. And I will end it!"

"Put your arms down, Barnabas," she said. "If I told those same arms to embrace me, they would do so. But I would not be that cruel."

"Cruel? Have you ever been anything else?" Spittle flew from his mouth, and his lips curved in a snarl. "You turned the only woman I ever loved against me. Unleash all your powers!" he said. "I defy you to do so! Try as you will, you cannot stop me from loving Josette."

"I would not do that. I would never want you that way. I loved you because you were a man, not a marionette. I would not turn you into that now, even if it was the only way I could have you. When we met in Martinique, you saw me as a woman, not a witch. You desired me, pursued me, loved me. That woman stands before you now."

"All I see is the vile and rotting flesh beneath your glittering exterior. The witch is still in your heart! Think what you have done!"

"The night I first arrived and came to your room, I had done nothing yet. I had resisted and rejected all my sorcery for years. If you had loved me as you did in Martinique, none of this would have happened. Why did you reject me?"

"I love *Josette*! Can't you accept that? My God,

Angelique, I lay with you! A vestal virgin would not have made such a fuss. It's the world's oldest story, an officer and a peasant girl. I'm sure you roasted plenty of broomsticks before you met me!"

"Villain! How dare you! You are blind to the truth! That first night you made me so angry, I didn't want to love you anymore. I wanted you . . . yes, I wanted you dead!" She took a breath, trying to relieve the pain in her chest. "But, when I saw you suffering, I couldn't bear it. I took the spell away! Don't you see? I love you! I could never, would never harm you."

"And for this I should pity you? You . . . made . . . Sarah deathly ill, with her toy . . . her little doll and some pins . . . you tricked me into marrying you. . . ." She could see that the full realization of her evil was weakening him now, and he turned toward the door.

"Where are you going?"

He did not look at her. "I'm leaving this house. I'm going into Collinsport and turning you over to the authorities."

"No. You will not do anything of the kind."

He laughed bitterly. "You think we can go on playing as though we were happily married?"

"That is exactly what I think. And as the years go by, you will learn that we can have a good life together."

He turned and stared at her with a look of utter contempt, as though she were out of her mind. His eyes were bloodshot, and he swayed slightly as he listened to her bitter ultimatum.

"If you leave me," she said, her voice laden with scorn, "if you tell anyone about me, or say anything against me, if you act in any other way than as my attentive husband . . . then something will happen . . . to Josette."

She saw the blood drain from his face.

"Do you want me to conjure up for you a vision of Josette's death?"

"No . . ."

"I could do it so easily. It would not be real, but it could become real. For the sake of Josette, you will remain with me. Always."

Early the next morning, Angelique awoke to thunder that crossed the heavens like a thousand kettledrums struck at once. The wind came up from the earth, and for the whole day, a slow, cold rain fell out of a white sky. A fine drizzle coated the tree limbs with sleeves of ice, and each branch shone like crystal.

Angelique stood at the window and looked out. Everything—tree trunks, bushes, even the path—was coated with ice. The extra weight bowed down the branches of the trees in great arcs, and every tiny twig or bud glistened.

One by one, the branches of the greater trees began to break, snapping under the heavy weight and popping like gunshots. When a branch fell in the still, silent air, the crash was followed by a tinkle like shattered glass.

Slowly, methodically, she drew a pair of eyes on a piece of paper and lit it with a slow-burning flame. "Eyes of the night," she intoned, "there is a body you can become that can see in the darkness. You have the power to fly on invisible streams of air and hover in silence. Find him. Tell me where he goes. Watch him well." Shivering from the cold, she walked outside the house and looked up at the chimney glazed with ice. The bats had not ventured out in the storm, and she could hear their squeaking voices, twittering and chirping, as they fed their young and settled for sleep. She pressed the loose brick, and it cracked sideways, exposing the smoky interior. The dim light revealed the silken bodies huddled together, clinging upside down to the walls, their papery wings folded upward over their backs and their red eyes staring out at her.

Just as she had suspected, it was not long before Barnabas arranged an interview with Josette at the new house. The scene played across Angelique's tortured mind as she heard and watched it all. Josette was more beautiful than ever in her indigo-velvet dress and her mourning lace, a black mantilla veiling her lustrous hair.

"I know you never willingly deceived me," Barnabas was saying.

"My marriage, even then, seemed like a dream."

"I have made a terrifying discovery. None of this was your fault. There was a spell cast over you, by a witch!"

"A witch? You can't mean that? Who would hate me that much? And why?"

"Even now the witch is watching and plotting your death."

"What shall I do?"

"I will protect you. You must not be afraid."

Angelique watched as Barnabas gave Josette the jeweled music box that played the lilting melody, and Josette's eyes lit up with delight. "It's beautiful. . . ."

"It was to be my wedding present to you. Please keep it as a reminder of me. I will be with you again very soon."

"I'm so frightened."

"You must trust me. Tell the driver to stop at the inn just outside of Portsmouth. I will come to you there."

"But I have the feeling that you are the one in danger. That if I leave you now, I may never see you again."

"The next time you see me I will no longer be married to Angelique. I cannot say any more."

"Are you sure this is not good-bye?"

"Think of me and know that I love you. Very much."

Then Angelique saw him take Josette in his arms and kiss her tenderly, and her blood raged with fire.

When Barnabas returned he was implacable and refused to respond to Angelique's accusations. He ignored her smoldering anger and busied himself with a lacquered box which he kept inside his secretary, turning his back on her tirade.

"You have made a great mistake, Barnabas Collins. You have already betrayed me. You think if you send Josette away, she will be safe. Look behind you!"

Glancing up indifferently, he saw her pointing toward Josette's portrait. He could not help but recoil in horror as the fresh demure image of the dark-haired girl was transformed before his eyes to a withered hag, the skin raveled and rotted, the mouth a bloody toothless grin. Angelique saw him start, then compose himself, and he turned back to her with an imperturbable stare. "Spare me your pitiful tricks," he said coldly. "I will not be frightened."

"You have already been unfaithful to me!"

"I have not," he responded wearily.

"You have seen her alone. What treachery have the two of you devised?"

"None."

"I don't believe you! You are lying to me, just as you lied to me in Martinique, and you will go on lying to me." The more passive Barnabas remained, the more Angelique raged inside. She felt herself losing control, as though she were in a treacherous undertow and the sand was slipping beneath her feet. "You sent her away so that you could go to her as soon as you have killed me!"

Barnabas turned, and she saw that his expression was one of such complete loathing that she felt as though he had slapped her across the face. Her cheeks flared with the heat from the imagined blow, and her eyes filled with hot tears.

"You think by sending her away you can prevent me from keeping you here? Josette may be safe. But no one else is!" She flew for the stairs and raced to the landing. She had stopped breathing, and her chest was in a vise. Running to her room and turning out a drawer, she grabbed Sarah's doll, still hidden beneath her clothes. Black waves drowned her thinking.

The next thing she knew, she was standing before Barnabas, the doll and the hatpins in her fingers. "Sarah had a terrible pain, didn't she? Here!" She jabbed the cotton shoulder of the little effigy with the wicked lance. Out of the corner of her eye she saw Barnabas flinch. "And here!" She pierced the doll again, feeling it quiver in her hand.

Her eyes burned and her vision blurred, as she hissed in a snake's voice, "This pin is aimed at her heart. She will not die unless you deceive me again, but she will come close. Very close."

By then Barnabas was begging her. She could hear the supplicating tone, the anguish. "Stop it! Please, please stop. Remove the pins, I beg you! I will do anything you want. I will never leave you!"

But she could no longer hear him. The blood was rushing through her ears and pounding in her head. She heard herself say, "I don't believe you."

He fumbled with something in the box in his secretary and wheeled on her. She saw him raise the gun and aim it, and she looked into the eye of the muzzle. She saw a flash of light and heard a barking retort. She reeled with the blow. The bullet ruptured her shoulder, which spurted blood, and she felt her body turn to water as she slid slowly to the floor. In a vague stupor she saw Barnabas, his blackened form, his wide stance, warp and fade, as her vision misted and she tasted blood. His towering shape reached for the doll, and his shaking fingers removed the pins one by one. Then he stood and backed away from her unsteadily.

She knew she was dying. Blood oozed through

her fingers, and the wound was like a tentacled creature radiating pain though a body enveloped in a great
swelling cloud of hatred. She searched deep within
her for some curse, some irrevocable pronouncement
of doom, before the end came. The Cata fluttered,
arrhythmic, fading, but the huge Maman pumped
stronger than ever, and she knew in her violent stupor
that the Dark One had come to witness her prayer for
revenge. The floor beneath her dissolved, and she felt
as though she were floating upward into billowing
clouds of smoke. Pain swept through her body, and a
voluminous ball of fire exploded in her deepest core,
funneling through her and out her mouth.

Barnabas wavered at the blast of her breath as
though it were a wind of flame, and she could no
longer see his face. He was floating on dark undulating waves, and she could hear the water rushing,
rushing, as she strained to speak.

"You didn't do the job well enough, Barnabas!"
she gasped. "I am not dead yet! And while I can still
breathe, I will have my revenge! I set a curse on you,
Barnabas Collins! You wanted your Josette so much—
well, you shall have her. But not in the way you have
chosen. You will never rest. And you will never be able
to love anyone. For whoever loves you will die. That is
my curse! And you will live with it through all eternity!"

Somewhere in the dim recesses of the room, the
casement slowly opened, and out of the darkness the
bat fluttered, chattering, jerking, looping above Barnabas's head, reeling in a gyre, diving for his neck. He
saw the creature and lifted his hands in a feeble ges-

ture, his expression one of confusion, then horror, as the beady eyes glittered crimson, and the sharp teeth gleamed like tiny daggers. He waved it away, but it came on, ducking from his blows, striking again and again, until it landed, flapping against his neck, clinging there, and his eyes widened in terror as he felt the teeth ripping his flesh. He screamed a gasping, wrenching howl that was the final cry of doom.

When Angelique regained consciousness, she was lying on the floor where she had fallen, in a pool of her own blood. She dragged herself to her feet, her head reeling from the pain, one leaden thought pulsing in her brain. She was not going to die. She knew that now. The wound was deep, but it was not fatal, and something had happened, something hideous and irreversible, that was her own doing, that she must find some way to prevent. Clinging to the banister, she slowly, with great effort, pulled herself up the stairs.

Outside the door to Barnabas's room, she could hear Ben saying to him, "Anyone who's lost as much blood as she has would have to be dead." Somehow she managed to stagger into the room, clutching for the wall to keep from falling, and confront Ben's astonished expression.

Barnabas lay on the bed in a sweating fever, his hollow eyes clouded with delirium. Two deep gashes on his neck streamed a dark stain. "How is he?" she said to Ben; and when she spoke, she felt she would swoon.

"He's almost dead, thanks to you."

"No! I don't want him to die! If he does . . ."

Barnabas stirred at her voice, then stared at her, fiercely accusing, and rasped, "A curse . . . she put a curse on me . . . she made a bat appear . . ."

"He's been rambling on about being bitten by a bat," said Ben incredulously. "Did a bat do that to him?" He pointed to the fang marks, and she nodded slowly.

"What kind of a monster are you?" Ben asked, his face contorted with disbelief.

"You don't know how sorry I am," she said in a trembling voice. "I thought he had killed me—but I'm not going to die—and—I don't want the curse to over-power him. I must care for him, nurse him, find some way to cure him, because if he dies, there will be no way to remove the curse, and . . ."

"What? What will happen to him?"

"Something . . . irreversible. If he dies, he won't die completely . . . he will become . . . one of the living dead."

"What? Dead people don't come back to life!"

"Yes, they do, Ben. They return as monsters, and when they return, they are cursed with eternal life!"

Never had there been a potion she had made with such care. She created an antidote as powerful as death itself, with ancient powders brought from Martinique. Then she went to the chimney and removed the loose brick. Reaching into the cavern, she felt for a sleeping bat and closed her hand around the struggling body; she drew it out and, holding it to her breast, carried it back to her room. There, as it clawed at her hand, she pierced its heart and milked its blood into the tankard.

Sitting by Barnabas's bedside, she waited for him to wake. He was delirious, and mumbled, "Josette . . . wait for me . . . I am coming. . . ." Then his eyes fastened on Angelique, and in shuddering spasms, he cried out, "Get away from me! Witch! Murderess! Don't touch me!"

Her heart aching, Angelique knew she would do anything now to save him, even send for Josette. She was drained of all desire for revenge, and, finally, her love was stronger even than her jealousy. She leaned in to him. "Tell me where she is," she said, "and I will bring her to you."

But his eyes flared, and he gasped, "No! You will never find her! She is safe from you now!" Then he fell back, exhausted, murmuring, "Josette . . . I'll come to you . . . nothing will stop me. . . ." After a few moments of tortured breathing, he became limp, and whispered hoarsely, "Something terrible is happening to me, I can feel some horrible change. . . ."

Angelique spoke to him softly. "I am going to help you."

"Can you stop it? Can you stop this dreadful thing?"

"Yes," she said. "I won't let it happen. I will save you. I promise." She lifted the tankard to his lips. "Drink this. It will help you. I'll hold it while you drink. Drink slowly."

"Will it stop this . . . ripping . . . I feel though my body?"

"Yes. It must!" And as he drank, she said softly to herself, too softly for him to hear, "If only you had loved me, as you did once."

She stroked his brow, and said, "Close your eyes." She pressed her fingertips into his forehead and tried to lift the darkness into her hands. His skin was clammy, and the dark tendrils of hair were matted against his brow. She felt the strands of the curse beginning the metamorphosis, poisoning his blood, and she strained to draw them into herself. "Close your eyes," she said, "and open them only when I tell you."

"Let me sleep. If only I could sleep . . ." he murmured.

"Yes, sleep now. You are going to survive. Can you feel it now? The potion is working. Don't open your eyes until I tell you to."

"No, I don't want to open my eyes. . . ."

Tremulously, with faint hope and sinking dread, Angelique walked to the window. She reached for the heavy scarlet drape and, taking a quick breath, heaved it back. Sunlight streamed into the room, flashing on all the surfaces, flowing across the bed.

"Open your eyes, Barnabas, now!"

He writhed, jerking his head back and forth. "I don't want to open my eyes. . . ."

"Open them!"

He did, for only a moment, and when he saw the sunlight, he screamed in agony, the shriek of a creature in mortal pain, and covered his face with his hands.

"It's too late," she said, letting the curtain fall. "What's done cannot be undone."

chapter

31

Angelique stayed with Barnabas all the day and listened with a heavy heart as he raged maniacally—calling over and over for Josette. At times panic would seize him, and he would stare as though mad. Once he found her hand and clung to it, not knowing whose hand it was, and squeezed her fingers until she gasped. It was after midnight when he finally lapsed into a fitful swoon. She left him and walked out into the night.

There was no moon, and the stars were hidden in a shroud of mist. Fog swirled at her feet, but she was no longer afraid when the Dark Spirit appeared before her, his flickering shape more distinct now, the planes of his face shifting from ebony to ivory. His voice was the hum of the wind, but the sounds were almost human.

"A vampire! What an interesting choice, my dear. I must admit even I am intrigued."

"Don't let him die."

"But, Angelique, this is your doing. How many times have you said to me, 'My powers belong to me.

They come from me!'" He laughed a bitter barking laugh.

"I know that is not true. I could not have done it alone."

"And now you are sorry."

"I regret it with all my heart. I could not bear his anger and his contempt when I love him so deeply. I was not strong enough. If only I could take it back, begin again, I would let him have her and live with the heartbreak."

"Why have you summoned me?"

"Please . . . let him live."

"In human form he will always despise you."

"I know that now. I accept that."

"Will you go with me?"

"Yes . . ."

There was a long sigh, as if the trees all dipped their branches. "You forget, my darling, I am not the Lord of Creation. Death is my province. There is only one way he can remain alive now, and that is through your curse. He will then possess what I offer you: immortality."

"Life?"

"Yes. Eternal life."

She waited by Barnabas's bedside, still hoping for a miracle, and she depored her feeble powers. When he died that night, it was with Josette's name on his lips. "Wait for me, Josette . . . I will come back. . . ."

He never knew he breathed his last breath in Angelique's arms. She kissed his face, so still now, and the hollows of his eyes.

"I love you," she said. "I've loved you since the first time I saw you. And I will love you forever."

The Dark One was in the room.

"Forever . . ." he said.

"Always the same covenant, and the same lies," she said, her tears falling.

"Not the same. Come with me and serve me, and someday, centuries from now, I will release you."

"No. I will not."

She found the caretaker, sitting on his bench, deep in mourning. Ben's huge body heaved with sobs, but she felt that all his grief would fill only a small part of her own aching heart. She was like a sleepwalker, staring out with unseeing eyes, thinking only of what she must do.

"Ben. You must help me. Cut down a holly tree and fashion for me a small stake from the trunk, ten or twelve inches long, thick enough to be hit with a mallet. Make one end of it needle sharp."

"What do you want it for?"

"Do as I say, or we will all die when dusk falls."

Slowly, Angelique raised the lid of the coffin. The creaking of the hinges echoed in the secret room of the mausoleum, and the odor of bat guano rose to her nostrils. Barnabas lay there, even more beautiful in death, but there was a profound change in his countenance. There was a porcelain cast to his skin—translucent over the skull—and the sunken areas beneath the cheekbones and within the sockets of the eyes were darkly shadowed, as though he were the portrait of a god in a masterpiece. His soft locks curled at the hollowed temples, and the eyebrows were thicker now, and shaggy, as if the hair had grown in the grave. A reddish gleam lay along the insides of his lips, and his hands, the hands that had loved her, were folded over a waistcoat of crimson satin.

She was not afraid, but she trembled, for her breast flooded with pity as she placed the stake above his heart, aiming carefully. The mallet was heavy when she lifted it above her head, feeling her own heart pound, bracing herself for the final blow—the destruction of the vampire, the negation of negation, the end of all she loved.

She hesitated, feeling the mallet's weight, one moment, another. And then she knew—she could not do it. She could not snuff out the one light that remained.

At that instant, Barnabas woke. His eyes flew open, and he stared up at her with pure malevolence. A growling sound came from his lips, and his hand was on her throat, crushing the small bones of her neck. She wrenched away, the stake and mallet clattering to the floor; but he sprang up, lightly, and was on his feet, lunging for her. He caught her and crushed her shoulder in his grasp.

"What were you about to do?" he snarled, then looked around in astonishment. "Where are we?"

She answered in a tremulous voice. "In the Collins mausoleum."

"A coffin! Why was I in a coffin?" His bewilderment only added to his menace, as he flung her away and paced the room like a caged panther. She saw at once that his body was more vigorous—agile, loose, and powerful. Gone was any check to his fury, any civilized restraint. He was all passion, and even as she was frozen in panic, she was dazzled by his power.

"Why?" He stared at her, his eyes smoldering, rimmed in scarlet. "Oh yes, I remember now—the bat—a fever—lying in bed—I knew something horrible was happening to me—I was afraid I would die. . . ."

She slipped toward the door, but he saw her move and snatched her to him, savagely, holding her as though she were a weightless thing that he could break at any moment. "That's what happened, isn't it? I was in the coffin, because . . . I was dead!"

She tried to remain resolute, but her bones felt like reeds. "Yes," she said softly. "You are dead."

"I've returned . . . from the dead! How? Why?" He looked at her, baffled, incredulous.

"You will know soon enough."

Then his eyes narrowed. "You! You put a curse on me!" His voice was cold fury, ice scraping on ice.

"I tried to stop it!" she cried. "I tried to free you from it."

"And you failed, didn't you? That's why you are here. You wanted to prevent it—my returning—" He stared at her, his rimmed eyes narrowing, and she smelled his hot breath. "You're afraid, aren't you? What are you afraid of? Is it what I have become?"

She backed away from him, trying to place the

coffin between them, fear stabbing at her body like pieces of jagged glass.

"Are you afraid that you no longer have any powers over me? Damn you! Witch! Tell me what has happened to me!"

It took all her effort to answer him. "The curse . . . has made you . . . one of the living dead."

He made a moaning sound, reeling from her words as though struck.

"But you can only live at night," she whispered. "When the sun rises, you must return to this coffin, to sleep, to live in seclusion, or you will be destroyed."

"I remember the curse," he said raggedly. "'All who love you will die.' Didn't you say that? Well? Didn't you?"

"Yes . . ."

His eyes brimmed with fire. "And do you still love me, Angelique? Is that why you tried to stop me?" His torment was unbearable, even greater than his rage, as he descended upon her. "Did you know you would be the first?"

She shook her head, afraid to speak, and he lunged for her, viciously embraced her. She pushed against him feebly, helplessly, as he bent her back over the casket.

"Were you lying when you said you loved me?"

"No! I love you still. I will always love you!"

"Then according to the curse, you must die!" He crushed her to him. "Love me, Angelique! Cling to me! Kiss me, with the kiss of death! All your powers of witchcraft cannot save you now!"

He drew her lips into his, and she felt her heart rush out of her wounded mouth as his powerful hands closed about her throat. The pain was searing, excruciating, as her breath slowly, mercifully, was stopped, and she was in the dark water at last, deep down in the fathomless current where there was no air and no light, and the swirling blackness enveloped her forever. The last sound she heard was his tormented howl. "What have you done to me? Sorceress! I would rather be dead than go through eternity as I am! As what I have become!"

The Dark Spirit was waiting for her.

"You want me still?" she asked.

"More than anything."

"Why?" she asked, puzzled.

"I am the void. I am nothing without a presence— a mind to imagine me. What you see is only your dream of evil incarnate."

"But do you exist?"

"Come, Angelique."

He led her down even deeper into the dark, where there was a light from the coldest of all fires, and there he removed her clothes. He unfastened the taffeta skirt and the embroidered bodice. He pulled the pins from her hair and let it fall.

When she objected, he said, "The ways of the Underworld are my ways."

He pulled the jewels from her ears and she sighed to lose them. She had not had them long. He took the *ouanga* from her neck, and she wept to see it go. The moonstone fell in the slime. Next he undid the laces of her corset and the ties of her petticoats. He slipped her camisole over her head. She loved the delicate underthings, but he said, "Do not question me."

Then she stood before him naked and holy—like all women—the source of life and love, and for a moment she was resigned. Then he took her skin off her bones, and she was lost to him, and her soul merged with his.

Barnabas closed the journal and let it fall against his knees. He placed his hand on the cover of the diary and stroked the rough leather with his fingertips. Reading Angelique's story had brought her back so acutely, as though she had lived again, and his heart felt light and released from bitterness. He breathed a long sigh, and rose and walked to the window. So it was love that motivated her all along. She had never given up hope.

What would have happened, he wondered, if he had stayed with her—before she was destroyed by heartbreak, before the madness began. It was all so long ago. If he had taken her away, caressed her and held her, easing her pain. She had cursed him with his loathsome divinity, but she had left him with life—life as a monster—but life, nevertheless. And she had forfeited her own life for the chance to make his journey with him.

He had always maligned his vile existence, and had lived as a creature in torment, but now, look what had happened. Here he was today, prepared to begin again. It was 1971. He was free to live as an ordinary man, and he had so much to look forward to. Sunlight streamed across the lawn, and Barnabas realized that it was morning. There was a knock on his door.

"Come in."

Julia appeared, dressed for the day, brisk and smiling, her manner, as usual, tentative but hopeful. He was glad to see her, and he went to her and embraced her.

"Barnabas, Roger has asked that you meet him in the drawing room."

"Very well. Tell him I'll come down immediately, and . . . perhaps . . ."

He liked the shine on her auburn hair.

"Yes, Barnabas?"

"Perhaps we can go for a drive later in the day. Just the two of us. I would like so much to be with you."

Her eyes lit with unexpected happiness, and she smiled. "That would be lovely."

When Barnabas entered the drawing room, Roger was standing by the fireplace speaking to a visitor. He was amiable and jocular, rather energetic for this hour of the day, Barnabas thought.

"Barnabas, come in," he exclaimed the instant he saw him. "My dear boy, I have some extraordinary news."

"What is it, Roger?"

"Why, I'm absolutely delighted. We have had an

offer on the Old House! Well, that is to say, on the land. An individual who possesses both vision and means wishes to perform a complete restoration. Oh, I'm so sorry, please forgive me. May I introduce, with pleasure, Miss Antoinette Harpignies."

The tall, fair-haired woman looking out the window turned slowly as Roger spoke. She smiled and walked toward Barnabas with her hand outstretched.

"Mr. Collins," she said, "it is such a delight to meet you."

As he shook her hand, he was startled to see that he was looking into eyes of the brightest possible blue.

NOTE FROM THE AUTHOR

When Dan Curtis decided to resurrect *Dark Shadows* for prime time TV in 1991 one of the writers called me to ask whether I could remember how Angelique became a witch. I said no, there was never any mention of it on the daytime show. However I was intrigued and so began the imaginative wanderings which resulted in this book.

Since I played the role of Angelique on the soap opera, I chose to tell the story primarily from her point of view. This is Angelique's story told as she remembered it and as she believed it happened. I take full responsibility for any differences between this story and any character attributes or actual events of the television show. Even though I tried my best, I could not incorporate every detail, and in truth, Angelique herself might well have changed the account of her own childhood over 175 years earlier to suit her own purposes.

I have the deepest respect for the work of the writers and the actors on the show and great affection for the series, which was my inspiration. It was my sincere intention to remain true to the soul of *Dark Shadows* and I hope I have done that.

Lara Parker
August 28, 1998

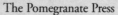